# COURTING TROUBLE

## by Elaine Drew

TAIKUN
ARTS

CALIFORNIA

PLEASANTON, CALIFORNIA

This is a work of fiction. All of the characters, stories, legends, myths, places and events in this novel were either created by the author's fevered imagination or are used fictitiously.

Taeran Arts, Pleasanton, CA 94566

COURTING TROUBLE.

ISBN 978-0-9833236-8-6

# DEDICATION

This book is dedicated to all those who are ready to escape the woes of contemporary life while they take a light-hearted journey through the woes of Dark Age England.

# ACKNOWLEDGMENTS

Until I wrote this book I didn't realize that preparing a book for publication takes a village. Without my husband Rob Drew rescuing the manuscript from its earliest incarnation in outdated word processing software and nagging me yearly to finish it, this book would not exist.

A special thank you to my editor, Carol Markos. In the pas de deux of writer and editor, she never missed a step and was always en pointe. Thank you to first readers Dori Pendergrass, Mary Angotti, Jenny Badger Sultan, Henry Sultan and Lisa Rigge for their invaluable suggestions, and to Barbara Jean, Ann Gomes and Carrie Kingman for their support and encouragement.

Thank you, Randall Crittenden and Scott Crittenden, for technical assistance with the intricacies of Old English.

Thank you to my friends in Easton and Itchen Abbas, and especially to my neighbor Jean Wheeler, for accompanying me to Southampton University on blustery winter evenings to study Anglo-Saxon history and archeology.

Thanks to the archaeologists who uncovered Saxon remains at my children's school in Itchen Abbas for piquing my curiosity about their era.

And finally, thank you to the Easton W.I. (Women's Institutes) and to our local church, St. Mary's, for introducing me to the flavor of village life.

# A NOTE TO READERS

Our story begins in the year 801 and is set in the kingdom of Wessex. Here we encounter a society on the cusp of Christianity and barbarism. Like a medieval tapestry, the story weaves together myth, legend and fairytale. I hope you'll have fun untangling the threads.

Most of the characters are Anglo-Saxon. I have simplified their names as much as I could while still keeping the flavor of the time. One of the trickier names belongs to our heroine:

CYNETHRITH (pronounced KIN A TRITH).

I include a complete **Character List** in the back of the book, as well as a **Glossary** for terms that are not used in contemporary English.

# Contents

*SCENE I* MEET CYNETHRITH

You've heard my story already. Or rather, you think you have. I've heard it myself a few times on visits to my grandchildren, bellowed out in the hall by some whelp too green to know a thing about it—and too dim to realize that the source of his fable is sitting right in front of him. I think that's why the old die in the end: we get so disgusted with young people.

Speaking of disgusting young people, did I tell you about the bishop's visit last week? Our reputation for medicinals has been spreading, and he wanted to know what we're up to. He came to the abbey trailing one of his sycophants—you may have seen him, the monk from Wealtham with one short leg who bobs up and down when he walks like a chicken after scratch. Despite the pain in my spine I felt I should show them around myself. That pleased the bishop.

"Good, good," he said. "There will be three of us. God loves the Trinity." I knew from experience that whenever the Trinity was mentioned the bishop would feel compelled to tell the story of St. Rumwold.

"Abbess, do you remember blessed St. Rumwold, the infant prodigy?"

"Yes," I said.

"Though he only lived on this earth three days, God gave him the gift of speech, and do you know what he preached about?"

"Yes," I said.

"He preached about the most blessed and heavenly Trinity."

"Yes," I said. "I often wish the young would hold their tongues." Because I'm old, I can get away with remarks like this. People think I didn't understand what they said.

"And to think this most reverend saint was a grandson of that servant of the devil—that pagan king of Mercia. God be blessed."

There was no need for the bishop to remind me of Mercian history. While I felt sure that God was blessed, I muttered "God be blessed" a couple of times to assure this tiresome ecclesiastic of my senility. With the aid of my cane I led them to our dispensary. We made a queer procession. First was the tall, emaciated bishop. His pate was bald. As if to make up for it the rest of his head sprouted a great bush of hair that joined his brambly beard without stopping: he reminded me of a male ruff at mating season. Next came the short, jerky monk, and then me, not as tall as I used to be. My spine has become as flexible as a stone cross. I had to move slowly and carefully—how my senescence mocks my youth.

The dispensary was busy when we got there. A local woman was sitting next to the table with a feverish child on her lap. She must have rushed him over. His leggings were not laced up. One of my nuns mixed him a potion while a second handed her ingredients. A third pulverized wormwood with a mortar and pestle. I showed the bishop and the monk baskets filled with the plants we had collected, labeled and stored. I pointed out a few of the plants and their uses.

"This is groundsel for poulticing," I said.

"Yes," said the bishop.

"Here we have buckthorn for purging, and sneezewort for toothache."

"Oh, yes," he said. Then I pointed out one of our most popular medicines. "This cures sword wounds. It's made from yarrow pounded with quail fat." Egbert had taught me about that one. The bishop tried to stifle a yawn. "How interesting," he said.

The three of us endured the tour. He wanted to see our new scriptorium, built to record the knowledge we were accumulating. As we walked there I felt the edge of blackthorn winter. We stayed near the garth's hedge to shelter from the gusts. I showed the bishop the budding oaks we had recently added to provide our calligraphers with a source of ink. Every now and then, when the April sun threw off its cloudy mantle, the box and holly gleamed like the king's silver. But the bishop didn't notice this. Actually he didn't notice much of anything. I soon realized what was on his mind. The bishop was preoccupied with his relic collection, as well he might be. Its growing fame was the reason he had been appointed bishop.

"Yesterday after Vespers I got a letter from one of our holy brothers whom God granted a pilgrimage to Rome. Do you remember?" He turned to Short Leg for agreement.

"Yes, indeed," chirped Short Leg, happy to have something to add to the conversation. "But I thought it was after Compline. Remember we sang of all the saints?"

The bishop sighed in a way that indicated impatience with a lesser intellect. "I was asking if you remember the pilgrimage, brother, not when I got the letter." Never one to let an issue slide, the bishop went on to address what had, in fact, been sung at yesterday's services. "And anyway, we did do the saints at Vespers. At Compline we did the seven psalms with the litanies."

"Oh, right, right," said the monk. "I must have got it mixed up because we usually do the seven psalms at Nones."

"Oh really?" I said, allowing an edge of confrontation to creep into my voice. I was hoping to derail the bishop from his relics, a topic I found as interesting as someone else's genealogy. "I never heard of that. We always do the seven psalms at Prime."

The bishop would not be thrown off course. "Never mind. As I was saying, the brother said that on the way to Rome he met a fellow from Sicily who may be able to get me something important." He gave me a look pregnant with meaning. "Do you remember the story of St. Agatha, Cynethrith?"

"Yes," I said.

"The virtuous virgin who would not give in to the despicable carnal passions of Quintianus?"

For once he was too excited to recount the grisly details of the virgin's martyrdom, a small but welcome blessing. His voice was fervent as he rushed on, "This fellow thinks he can get—it will be expensive of course but just think of it—the sword that was used to cut off Agatha's breast."

He practically hopped in his enthusiasm. "This is a wonderful addition. God is so good to me. Have you seen my collection lately?" He felt so good about himself that he threw a bone to Short Leg. "This monk has been such a great help to me with the cataloging."

"Yes," said Short Leg, "You can't imagine how difficult it is."

"I can, I can," I protested. It didn't help.

"It's really tricky because we like to cross reference them, first by saint's name, then type of relic—you know, body part: hand, arm, thigh bone, fingernail, hair, whatever. Or it could be a possession, like a piece of jewelry or a scourge, and then there are the ones that didn't belong to the saint at all but were the source of the saint's martyrdom, like a rack or—"

"Fascinating," I broke in. I put on a regretful face. "What a shame it's almost impossible for me to travel."

"I'll pray to God for your ease. You really must see it. I've only told a few people about this," the bishop lowered his voice, which quavered. "I've got a piece of the stole worn by the Virgin's mother during the immaculate conception—"

"Do you think she had to take it off?" I interrupted innocently. The bishop turned a little red but pretended not to hear.

"I'm getting the index finger of St. Denis, and I'm trying to persuade the priest from the minster church to give me a piece of the arm of St. Branwalader—he doesn't need the whole thing—in exchange for a piece of the arm of St. Samson. What do you think?"

"Absolutely fair," I said.

"But the best thing, the crowning glory so to speak, is there's an abbot in Germany who thinks he can get one of Christ's thorns for each of his favorite English monasteries."

"Do you think there are enough to go around?" I ventured.

"Cynethrith, my dear Cynethrith, where is your faith?" I wondered that from time to time myself, God forgive me. "Don't you remember the story of St. Teilo?"

"No," I said, trying a different tack. Maybe he'd tell me to go read it. "Tell me the story, Your Excellency."

"You don't remember the story? Cynethrith, you surprise me. You're an abbess, and you don't know the story about St. Teilo? I must say I'm disappointed. When St. Teilo died in our great grandfathers' time, three communities squabbled over his remains. God realized the brothers' faith and love were making them enemies, and so in his limitless mercy and wisdom he multiplied the body of the saint three times and gave one to each community."

I wondered (to myself this time) if the saint would have preferred to have had one of those new bodies while he was still alive. I know I would.

At last we made our way inside, into my hall. The nuns led me to a chair near the fire, tucked a blanket around me, and placed my feet on a footstool. They pulled up chairs for the bishop and the monk and went to warm some wine. Then for the first time that day, the bishop noticed something. He dismissed Short and Jerky with the suggestion that he inquire after a cure for headache. I assumed it was rampant among the priests he supervised.

He cleared his throat and swallowed a number of times. I watched with mild consternation as the cords on either side of his Adam's apple went in and out. Finally he was ready. He lowered his voice so the nuns wouldn't overhear.

"Don't you think, Abbess Cynethrith," he said, "that you set a bad example for the young ladies of your order when you dress in such ostentatious and unnecessary finery?"

I make it a point to dress well. Old women should never relinquish any symbol of power, and I'll be damned if I will. Vanity in a young woman is valor in an old one. In fact, when I'd heard this abstemious young prig was coming I chose my richest brocade. I was amazed he presumed to mention it. I couldn't decide if he were truly concerned about my soul or if he were trying to get me back for my crack about St. Anne's stole.

"Look to your spirit, madam. Focus your thoughts on less worldly concerns. Soon you will be judged by your Creator."

The subject aroused him. His face began to glow. Looking at it objectively, I have to admit it improved his appearance a little. He addressed me in the ridiculous diction priests usually reserve for the pulpit.

"God Almighty is not interested in the externals of one's adornment."

I stared at him for a long moment before I answered. Egbert always did that when somebody was making an ass of himself.

"Quite so, Your Excellency," I said.

This was followed by complete silence, which had been, after all, my objective. Then one of the nuns came back with the wine and announced that dinner would be served shortly. The worst was over. I could soon give my guests to Athelflad, my prioress, to entertain over dinner. The bishop and his trailing appendage left immediately after the meal. I trust to God's mercy that I won't see them again for a while.

But I digress. You know what my excuse will be, so I won't bother to make it. As I was saying, my story gets more distorted every time I hear it. It barely resembles what really happened anymore. So I intend, here and now, to set the record straight.


My story begins long ago in the year of our Lord 801. I was young and unfledged: full of energy and opinions like most young people. I lacked experience of the wider world. Since birth I had lived in the small village of Easton. It all began with the unexpected arrival of King Beorhtric and his party in Winchester. The rumor had been that the royal party would go to Cheddar this year. Once fighting season was over we knew they would go to one of his palaces, but the locals had not anticipated it would be the one in our nearest town. The royal presence meant those of us in the surrounding villages had a lot of extra mouths to feed, and that amounted to a tax we didn't want to pay. I was the first to hear the news.

For several years, my stepmother had sent me to a monastery along the road leading west to sell our extra eggs. I was a much better rider than my stepsisters, who could hardly manage a trot, so this job fell to me. It was one chore I didn't mind. I had become friendly with some of the brothers and could look forward to hearing whatever gossip travelers had passed along. As usual I entered the monastery near the granaries and milled about in the priory garth, biding my time until I could find someone who felt like a chat. Today everybody was too busy to be bothered. This was not normal. Then I noticed there was a guard posted outside the guest hall, so I knew something was up. About mid-morning I saw one of my friends, the bishop's cup filler, who offered to find the cellarer so I could deliver the eggs.

The cup filler fancied himself a ladies' man, but he enjoyed the chase rather than the kill. He had no unlawful carnal knowledge and was happy in his ignorance. If a lady misunderstood his overtures he hid behind his cowl and his orders until she went away. Long ago he had sized me up to see if I would be safe sport, and I was happy to indulge him with some harmless flirtation. But today I had another agenda. I figured I probably had a few moments to pump him before I got involved in the business transaction.

Since he served wine at the bishop's table, he must know something. I started with flattery, an easy weapon to use against most men and practically unfair against this one.

"It must be very difficult," I said, "filling the bishop's cup." My voice had trailed off a little at the end as I thought about how lame that sounded. He didn't seem to notice.

"It is difficult, very difficult," he said. "My position requires the utmost tact and sensitivity."

"Yes, I can imagine," I said. But of course I thought filling the bishop's, or anybody else's, cup must be the softest job on earth. "It must be even more . . ." I searched for a word and then fell back on our old stand-by, "difficult when other important people visit."

"It's a nightmare," he said, practically overcome by this reminder of the delicacy of his position.

Then he remembered he liked to flirt. He stopped walking and gazed helplessly into my eyes, a look I suspect he rehearsed when bored at vespers. With his fat cheeks and sloping forehead he looked like a water vole that was, for some unknown reason, in a state of rapture. He took my hand in his damp chubby one. "Yes, it's a nightmare," he was saying. He wanted to show that he could flatter, too: "Few women are capable of understanding it."

"I'd like to understand it," I said, picking up the cue and looking down with contrived modesty. "Tell me about it."

The monk fell back on what had always been one of his most effective gambits. "I'd rather talk about you," he said.

"Things are pretty dull in Easton these days, and of course my stepmother is a complete pain—"

"I love your smile," he said, "and your eyes are dreamy." He touched my mantle, near my ear.

"I've never met anyone like you," I said. "Who's the most important person you've ever poured for?"

"Oh, the king, I guess." His finger had moved to my cheekbone. "I may be a monk," he said, "but a man's still a man."

"And when was that?"

"I've always been a man," he said, offended.

"Of course you have," I said, catching my mistake. "You're so much a man I get flustered around you. I don't know what to say."

I touched his arm. "I'm not used to important people like you." I began to wonder how long this was going to take. "If I saw the king I would faint on the spot."

"I'll protect you," he said, pitching his voice lower. "I won't let him come near you." He pulled me into an alley between the infirmary and the latrines.

"Is he here?" I asked.

"No, he doesn't use the common latrine. You're so willowy," he said, running his hands from my underarms down to my hips.

"So he's at the priory?"

"Yes, but don't worry," He backed off a bit.

"How long is he staying?"

"If I didn't have to go to Mass right now," he blurted, "I'd make love to you. Don't tempt me too far, my angel. You know I can't—I mustn't—it's a mortal sin."

This seemed a little over the top, under the circumstances. "I would never let you fall away from your vows," I said. "I could never forgive myself."

The cup filler, his virginity intact, was not in such a hurry to get to mass anymore. I reminded him about the eggs and the cellarer. He marched about showing me off, calling attention to himself by asking every brother he saw if he had seen the cellarer recently. I could tell he was enjoying his secret prize.

When we found the cellarer he was only too happy to get some extra eggs, and I made sure I got a good price for them.

"I'll need extra eggs for the rest of the week, and next week through Wednesday. They're going on to Winchester at dawn on Thursday."

Once the business deal was struck, the three of us chatted like old friends. The monks were as eager to talk about the royal party as I was to hear about them. The cellarer said that the group included 30 warriors, many of them famous heroes like Unferth, Werwulf and Erpwald, whose reputations spread before them like road dust before horses' hooves. One of the priests traveling with the group had told him the latest story about Werwulf.

"He had a beautiful lady friend at their last encampment whom he treated very well. He gave her gold rings and a jeweled belt. He brought her to court—everyone knew her. The night before they were to leave Werwulf visited the lady in her bower and made love to her.

"'I must leave you, my lady,' he said. 'And how will you fare without me?'

"The lady wept. Then she said, as they must part and there was no help for it, she hoped she would find a younger lover. Werwulf took her in his arms, embraced her tenderly, and bit off her nose."

I was shocked, but the cup filler said he had already heard that story. It was making the rounds of the feast last night. The king was swallowing some wine when the story teller got to the line about the woman's nose, and Beorhtric burst out laughing so suddenly he practically choked to death. It was a frightening moment. "Luckily," he said, "the king was good-natured. Instead of being angry he asked for the story to be told again so he could enjoy it some more."

The cellarer asked the cup filler what he knew about the disheveled and dirty man who was riding in a cart half full of bones. He seemed an odd creature to be part of a royal entourage. My affectionate guide had been curious about that peculiar fellow himself, but had little to report. No one seemed to know why the bone man had the honor of traveling with the court.

The king, both monks agreed, loved his sport, and they had heard he rewarded his falconer and his huntsman as well as any king. The cup filler had been in a position to observe that His Majesty could drink more than any man in his hall, except perhaps for his friend Warr. In fact, the cellarer added, it seemed that Beorhtric drank so much and feasted so late that he never got out of bed until after noon. The cup filler had heard the warriors boast as impressively as warriors anywhere, and he said that the men fought with each other just for fun when they had no enemy to fight. They were a merry bunch.

I said nothing, but turned from speaker to speaker with an expression that showed the full extent of my absorption in the topic. The cup filler noticed my interest and wondered if there might be something he could do to prove his love. "Cynethrith," he asked, "would you like to see the king?"

You can imagine my response. It would be like attaining sainthood without having to endure martyrdom. It would be like watching my stepsisters do the laundry for a month. It would give me lots to talk about at the village well that evening, and I enjoyed being the center of attention as much as any girl. "Yes," I said. "Sure I'd like to see him."

"What do you think?" The cup filler asked the cellarer. "I bet he's still sleeping it off. What if I give her a habit, and we send her into his bower with a pitcher of water?"

"It might work," said the cellarer. "Sure. He didn't get up until vespers yesterday."

"I'll be right back," said my friend. He went to fetch the habit. The cellarer got a ewer from the kitchen. When the cup filler returned I put on the habit. Then he and I walked to the well in the middle of the garth. He briefed me as we went.

"I'll get you in past the guard. He'll recognize me. I'll tell him you're an acolyte."

I nodded. This would be magnificent.

"Just go straight in," he resumed, "and put the fresh pitcher and basin on the table. And don't forget to bring out the old ones. Simple, right?"

Of course it was simple. They drew some water to fill the ewer. It takes a lot to rattle me, but the idea of seeing the King up close was so exciting that my hand shook all the way up to my elbow. I spilled some water.

"Easy now. Get a grip on yourself," said my boyfriend.

We walked to the guest hall. The guard found us uninteresting and barely raised an eyebrow in the direction of the door to indicate that I could pass through. The cup filler waited near the door, chatting like an old lady to the unresponsive guard.

I entered the chamber. The light was dim and the first thing I noticed was the smell. The sour breath of the sleeping monarch hung in the air like the still fog of a summer morning. I set down the pitcher and turned to look at Beorhtric. He was lying on his back on the bed, his legs apart. His tunic had worked its way up above his waist, and his penis was practically lost in a great mass of gray and black pubic hair made even more eye-catching by the pale white of his skin. A linen sheet, intricately embroidered along one end with colorful interlocking beasts, covered only his chest and then trailed onto the floor. There was a pillow under his neck, and his head fell back, diminishing the effect of the great wattles of flesh beneath his chin. His mouth was open. He snored loudly and with great inventiveness.

I was interrupted in these observations by the sound of a woman's voice behind me.

"And what exactly are you doing here?" the voice said.

I jumped. I turned around and saw a woman who could have come from the stars. I didn't think it was possible to be so beautiful. On her head the woman was wearing the sheerest of veils. Rather than concealing it seemed to create an aura around the dark brown hair pulled back from her face and braided into labyrinthine patterns. She was about average height for a woman, but stood in so erect and commanding a posture that she seemed as tall as a man. Her head was small, and her features finely chiseled. Her gown was embroidered all over with gold thread that gleamed even in the dim light of the chamber.

I suddenly realized that I didn't dare talk, because my voice would give me away. On the other hand, I didn't dare not talk. How could I refuse to answer this magnificent creature? I opened my mouth, but no sound emerged. Just when I started thinking my life was over, the cup filler burst in and fell at the feet of the queen.

"Oh your most exalted and kind Royal Highness," he whined. "Please forgive this poor unfortunate's inability to speak. He is a new acolyte we have taken in and he has vowed himself before God and the bishop to eternal silence."

I relaxed a little. "He's brighter than he looks," I thought.

The queen said, "And why was he standing here gaping at my husband's private parts?"

"Forgive him, Your Royal Highness. I'm sure he didn't even notice our beloved monarch's—uh—monarch's—hmm—uh—state of— well—state. He is a simple country boy and was overwhelmed, I'm sure, at being in the proximity of one so noble."

I took the cup filler's lead and dropped onto my knees, nodding my head in agreement.

The corners of the queen's mouth turned down. There was a pause as she stared at the two of us. From the look in her eye I think she was trying to decide if it was worth the trouble to execute us. Finally she said, "If I see him again he's dog meat." She turned with a precision more military than majestic and left.

The cup filler and I scurried out behind her, looking for a safe place where we could relive the excitement of the adventure. We felt safe from the royal entourage behind the latrine, where we huddled together. Between visits from the brothers we whispered and laughed until we had told and retold the story dozens of times. When it was time to go home, he walked me to the granary. I looked at him warmly and smiled. "Thank you, thank you, my dearest. I'll never forget today."

His eyes got misty. We hugged each other, and I left.

## SCENE 2 WESSEX GETS A PUPPET KING

It was true that I had been excited about getting to see the king close up, but not because I admired him. I loathed him. We all did. My mother had been an elite archer who fought for Wulf, the last king in the Wessex bloodline. She had died at his side fighting the Mercians when I was a very small child. Our current king, Beorhtric, was a disaster as far as I was concerned, and I was far from the only one who felt that way. To understand the depth of my feelings about this monarch, let me take you by the hand and lead you through the labyrinth of our recent history. The trouble started when my father was a child. At that time our royal house, the house of Wessex, fallen from past glories and ignorant of future ones, emitted not even a dim glow to hint at its future brilliance. If it radiated any light at all, it was the flicker of the fire by which it tried to consume itself.

It began, I guess you could say, because there were too many athelings. In those days not only the king's sons but his brothers and their sons were all considered athelings, princes of the royal blood, equally eligible for the throne. When a king died the Witan chose his successor from among them. Unless the council chose the toughest, trickiest man at the outset, we were in for trouble. When the previous king died they missed, choosing as king a devout, otherworldly man and leaving a more able contender, Wulf, very disgruntled.

Not a man to take defeat in stride, Wulf gathered a faction around himself and started a smear campaign against the priestly king. That, combined with the king's ineptitude in the field and a few well-placed bribes, convinced the Witan to depose their original choice, and within a year he was dead. The stories about his death had this in common with toadstools: what you could see on the surface was an insignificant fraction of what was going on underneath. Nevertheless, with his rival out of the way Wulf became King Wulf, and the memory of his sins shriveled and disappeared like a weed in autumn. Sanctified by royal office Wulf became an effective ruler, rewarded his followers sufficiently to increase their number, and most important beat the hell out of the Welsh.

However, just as the dead weed leaves its seeds, Wulf's sins left a bitterness that would sprout into disaster. The priestly king's family had been trained and were duty-bound, as are all men, to avenge a murder committed against a family member. They felt that no blood price—had one been paid which of course it hadn't—would have been sufficient to compensate for the loss of a son, a cousin, an uncle, a king, a direct link to the house of Wessex. But their moral outrage was tinged with hypocrisy. The deposed king's brother Cynric had in fact been toying with the idea of usurping the throne himself when Wulf beat him to it. Instead, he became the focal point for the family's disaffection. Cynric spent the greater part of each day thinking about how to regain the kingdom for himself under the attractive guise of punishing a murderer. The new king, meanwhile, spent most of his time in the north fighting the Mercians or in the south fighting the Jutes—when he wasn't in the west fighting the Welsh. To him Cynric and his cousins were irrelevant.

Twenty-nine years went by, and nothing happened. The people thought it had all fizzled out. The insult to the deposed king's family would go, it seemed, unanswered. Cynric did nothing but drink and talk—and pursue his peculiar interest in pigeons. Unfortunately, even after all these years, his favorite topic was still how he was going to kill Wulf.

Late one autumn the king's retinue returned to town to rest after a summer of difficult border wars with the king of Mercia. A child then, I learned that one harrowing engagement had cost my beloved mother her life. Among King Wulf's retinue there was a troublemaker who sought to make himself look important by passing on a detailed account of Cynric's ravings. King Wulf, understandably in a very bad mood, was fed up. It became known all over Hampshire that the king had decided the time had come to get rid of this exasperating challenger. When Cynric found out about the king's intentions, he had to think seriously—perhaps for the first time—about how to kill Wulf before the king killed him.

These days the stories you'll hear told in my son's court about the events at Merantun Hall glorify this episode of power lust and blood lust, when in fact what happened there almost destroyed the house of Wessex. Over time details of this tawdry episode have come to light. Servants are observant, and they like to talk. People tend not to notice them, and rarely censor their behavior just because a scullery maid or a house cleaner is within earshot. I learned what really happened during my forays into the palace—but more about that later. Even if all the gossip isn't true, enough is to get the idea of what took place.

Cynric was informed that the king was at Merantun Hall visiting a mistress. People never figured out how the king chose his mistresses, but the servants knew. There was no common color of hair or shape of figure. It didn't appear he cared about big hips or small breasts or blue eyes or a pretty face or even age, except that he never chose very young women. Overall, he liked older women: there was that element of gratitude. It was known that he never slept with a virgin, and people chose to believe this was because he was a religious man with a certain delicacy of feeling. Wulf's real reason was that a virgin was just too much work. Seduction did not interest him at all.

If the court, like the servants, had enjoyed a window on the king's private moments, they would have discovered that there was one quality the women did have in common. It was enthusiasm. The king never pushed himself on a woman, not out of gallantry, but because it didn't please him to do so. What determined whether or not he returned to a particular woman who had made herself available to him was, simply, how much noise she made. The mistress of this particular day was effusive by nature. The first time she and the king were together, she noticed the effect of her vocalizations, and she intensified what didn't need much enhancement. She quickly became one of the king's regulars, and he visited her more frequently than most.

You might see the woman's behavior as a crime against her husband, as indeed we have been taught. But she was not false to her husband—quite the contrary. The two of them had discussed the subject once or twice. They agreed that if she weren't the king's mistress someone else would be, and she could wangle boons more effectively if she were the king's mistress than if she weren't. In the two years that the king had been favoring her with his visits, her husband had been promoted from no court job to wardrobe thane. He had been given a gold arm band, a sword forged by Weyland and inscribed with runes ensuring victory, and two horses with tooled leather saddles and stirrups. His land holdings had increased substantially. The king had been generous. Her husband felt it was a small price to pay.

So if the husband were at home when the king arrived, he was happy to entertain the king's guard in his hall while his wife entertained the king in her bower. On this particular day the king's guard was comprised of ten warriors. It was well known that the king never took a large guard when he was feeling romantic. His men, happily plottzed on mead, were singing some favorite songs. As they were giving full voice to *Only Valor Wins Valhalla*, the woman was making a different kind of music. The king had arrived with an exquisitely worked garnet cloisonné necklace that inspired his lover to arpeggios of ecstasy.

Trouble, meanwhile, was approaching. When Cynric and his men entered the area they saw horses tethered near the hall and heard the singing. He sent twenty-five henchmen to surround the building. Cynric and the remaining forty searched for the king. It wasn't long before the woman's singing led them to him. The naked mistress was on her hands and knees on the bed facing the door when the men stormed into the room. The king, who had entered her from the rear, was standing on the floor behind her on tiptoe so he could reach her. She broke away and ran screaming out of the room. The king got almost as far as the bench where he'd left his sword before Cynric and his men stabbed him to death. King Wulf's men in the hall were alerted to the danger by the woman's screams, and rushed to arm themselves and protect the king. As they emerged from the hall, they were slaughtered. Cynric held Merantun.

The woman and her husband assured the insurgent that he had their full co-operation. "Yes," she said to him, tears in her eyes, "As you can see we have been victimized and abused by that king in unmentionable ways." Her liaison with the king had given her unwarranted confidence in her seductiveness. She put her arm around the victor's shoulder and whispered in his ear, "I know we can trust you not to expose our shame."

"Lock her up," said Cynric.

When word of the day's events reached town, the rest of King Wulf's men rode to Merantun to rout the murderers. They surrounded the building. The subversive Cynric figured he was in a good bargaining position.

"Come over to my side," he hollered to his opposition. "Support me as king and your past allegiances will be forgotten."

But Wulf's men had fought beside him for thirty years, and they were not going to forget his slaughter so easily. Cynric tried the blood-kin gambit.

"A lot of the men here with me are your cousins," he said. "They'll be in the front line if you storm me." King Wulf's men said that they would grant their kin safe passage. Contrary to the heroic version of the story, quite a few of Cynric's men were ready to accept the offer. He wouldn't let them go. In the end, the king's men stormed, and the fight was too well matched. Everybody managed to kill everybody else. The only survivors, other than the servants, were the mistress because she had been locked up in the granary and her husband who was hiding in the pigsty.

After the servants told the townspeople the story, the woman was turned over to the priests who did their best to save her soul before burning her to death for adultery. The servants didn't mention the king's boons—they probably found other aspects of the story more interesting—so her husband got to keep them. I came across the records of the land grants years later when I was searching the court register for something about my mother. The husband remarried a very young girl and watched her like a hawk.

Why is this tale important to my story? The upshot of the incident was that all the adult contenders for the throne were dead. The house of Wessex became carrion for foreign crows to feast on. Chief among them was Offa, the king of our ancient enemy Mercia.

Wulf and Offa had been at war for twenty-five years. The depletion of the house of Wessex enabled Offa to have a hand in the appointment of our new king, the same Beorhtric I had observed sprawled out half naked in the priory bed chamber. Our Witan, realizing we had no military leader and too few trained fighters, bought peace from Mercia by agreeing to accept Offa's choice. Suddenly we found ourselves a vassal state.

Once Beorhtric became king, Offa helped him banish the only remaining atheling, a boy who might someday have presented a rival claim to the throne. The exile fled to the continent for safety. Some said he went to Charlemagne. We heard nothing from him or about him, and most assumed he was dead.

To make matters worse, Beorhtric's first wife died unexpectedly during a state visit from Offa and his daughter Odburh. This sparked the rumors you might imagine: that either Offa or Odburh dabbled in the black arts or one of them was a poisoner. It certainly didn't look like coincidence, especially when Offa offered Beorhtric his daughter's hand as a token of their friendship. The people who remembered when Wessex was a free kingdom had one more thing to disgust them. In addition to a puppet king, we now had the daughter of our enemy for our queen. Odburh, of course, is the very same queen you just met: the one who was ready to kill the bishop's cup filler and me for gazing at her husband.

So Offa, long dead, had left us this legacy: King Beorhtric and his foreign wife. We had endured them both for fifteen years at the time of their imminent visit to Winchester. Still, people can accommodate themselves to most things, and after all this time we had learned how to accommodate ourselves to Beorhtric. Some clung to the fantasy that the banished atheling was alive and would return to set us free, but to most that seemed a fairytale. The current king didn't affect our lives that much. We made sure of that. In fact, making sure was what created the intense activity that followed the news that King Beorhtric was coming to Winchester.

*SCENE* 3 MEET THE VILLAGERS

When I got home from my egg selling mission at the monastery, I went to the well and spilled the beans about the king's location and his expected arrival in the nearby town of Winchester. Our village, named Easton in the relentlessly practical way of our ancestors, was a short walk from the east side of town. Here the Itchen River runs through the bishop's pasture, passes slightly to the north of the houses of both freemen and peasants, and then collects at the base of the slope behind St. Mary's before turning southwest toward town.

The next evening my stepmother sent me to vespers alone. She had more important things to do. I think she was making an embroidery for the cathedral. As we villagers were leaving church, Osbert, the bishop's reeve, stopped us. He wanted to discuss what we should do about the king's visit. Osbert was tall and handsome and I, like everyone else in the village, enjoyed hearing him talk. He had a tiny little wife that he doted on; I was never sure why. I didn't dislike her, but sometimes I used to imagine all the different ways she might die and how I would console Osbert.

The villagers had assembled under the yew trees, and the royals were the hot topic. One of the women had apparently heard a good one about the queen. The village gossip Tidburg, quick to sniff out a story, slithered into the group right next to the speaker, a person who was often discounted. She looked like a middle-aged cherub and had the personality to match, but her last statement had attracted considerable attention. She glanced around as if to make sure the queen wasn't nearby.

"Go on," urged Tidburg.

"She said that when Beorhtric and Odburh were at Cheddar—"

"Which time?" inquired Tidburg.

"On this last trip, last month," said The Cherub. "There was this abbot traveling to see the king."

"Which abbot?" probed Tidburg, who pulled information like a badger pulls worms.

"I don't know." The woman was getting annoyed. Tidburg usually had that effect on people.

The Cherub went on, "The abbot stopped and went behind a bush to relieve himself. And while he was hidden there, he saw the queen change herself into a horse." By now most of us had grouped ourselves around The Cherub and Tidburg.

"Did she ever change herself back?" This interruption, accompanied by a chortle, came from the woodward. Tidburg, whose eyes had been fixed on The Cherub like a dog's on his master when that master has food in his hand, shifted her attention long enough to give the woodward a grumpy look.

"Then, wait a minute." The woman, who still hadn't gotten to the good part, tried to focus the group's attention. "Then in this disguise she well, she. . ." The Cherub didn't know quite how to say it. "She had relations with that group of young warriors, you know, those favorites she keeps around her."

"While she was a horse?" asked a white-haired thane's widow who was the picture of what regal ought to be. She had a slave whose sole job was to do her hair and care for her wardrobe. She was deliberate in her speech. I was deliberate in nothing in those days.

"Were the warriors horses as well?" I asked. "Or was she a horse while they were still men?" I was trying to imagine the scene.

"I don't know. I don't know," said The Cherub. This was getting too complicated. "All I heard was that nothing was enough to satisfy her."

"Nothing wouldn't satisfy me, I can tell you," interjected Tidburg. She thought this was so clever that she repeated it three more times.

The Cherub bravely soldiered on. "And the abbot, who couldn't leave . . ."

"So who was stopping him?" asked Tidburg.

The Cherub ignored her. ". . . and was forced to watch the whole thing, felt that this showed it was true what he had always thought."

"And what was that?" asked Osbert. He wanted to get on with his meeting.

"Well, that she is a witch. That she practices the black arts."

Quite a few heads nodded in agreement. If the queen were a witch it certainly wouldn't have surprised anyone. "It's like I've been saying for years," said the thane's widow, shaking her head with certitude, "we need to plant some elfthone in this churchyard."

Edith, who knew more about herbs than anyone, corrected her. "Elfthone protects against elves. It's rowan for witches."

"I use herb bennet," muttered one wife to another. "My sister told me it's the most powerful."

"No, I still think rowan would be best in this case," said Edith, glancing at the speaker. "You have to remember the witch—I mean the queen—is going to be close by for a while."

"I haven't finished," said The Cherub.

"Stop interrupting," interrupted Red, the village storyteller. Perhaps he was looking for some new material.

"The abbot was so rattled by this experience that he ran most of the way to Cheddar, and in his excitement stumbled so often that his hands and face were full of scratches when he arrived at the castle," The Cherub went on. "He struggled with his conscience about whether to tell the king or not."

Everyone was listening once again. "What did he decide?" asked the smith.

"He decided that for the sake of the queen's soul he'd better tell him."

There was that sound audiences make when everybody inhales abruptly at the same moment. Then it was dead quiet. Not even Tidburg spoke.

Osbert broke the silence. "How did the king take it?"

"I don't know how he took it, but the queen took it better than expected. At least that's what everybody thought. Odburh told the abbot that he was mistaken, that an evil spirit must have taken her form, but she thanked him for his concern. She sat next to him at dinner. They chatted amiably. After dinner Odburh very graciously gave the abbot a huge bouquet of flowers to take to his room and told him to be sure to put them in water and enjoy their fragrance."

"Maybe she's not so bad," said the shoemaker's wife.

"Don't be naive," said Tidburg. "She was just trying to shut him up."

"Well somebody shut him up," said The Cherub, "because the next day he was dead."

"Dead?" asked Tidburg.

"Yes, dead."

"So what did he die of?" said Tidburg, for once asking an interesting question.

"That's what's so spooky. No one could tell," said The Cherub. "His room was locked from the inside. Nothing had been disturbed."

"So he died in the night?" asked one of the women.

"Yes, some time in the night," said The Cherub.

A woman nodded as if this represented an important clue. We all looked at her. "Could be witchcraft," she said. "Very likely."

"Yes," agreed The Cherub, "there were lots of people there who whispered, and I believe this part, that the queen was only pretending not to be angry, and that she killed him with a hex."

Edith looked thoughtful. "You said the queen gave him flowers?"

"That's right."

"I wonder if the queen had wrapped a cloth around the flowers so that she didn't have to touch them?"

No one knew. But we wanted to know why it mattered.

"There are flowering plants that are lethal if touched, especially if the skin is broken. Monkshood, for example."

This story did nothing to reassure us villagers about our monarch and his wife, which was convenient for Osbert, who, while we were still muttering over The Cherub's story, quickly took over.

"I'd like to thank you for bringing this story to our attention," said Osbert to The Cherub. "I think you all know the sort of people we're dealing with here. I'm sure you'll agree we have to take some steps to protect ourselves."

There was no disagreement on that point, although after that story most of our fears were on the macabre aspect of the threat, and Osbert had a more practical concern.

"As you know, we're going to be stuck with feeding the royal court for a while, which is bad enough in itself. But in addition to that, there's a good possibility Beorhtric's going to be looking for more revenue."

To say to the villagers of Easton, or any other villagers for that matter, that the king was going to be looking for more revenue was like saying that the sun was hot. We all knew about the bounty Beorhtric paid Mercia, his generosity to his warriors, the feasts he hosted, the lavish jewels his wife wore. Some of the children wandered down to the river to throw stones at mallards. Osbert threw some bait to the crowd.

"We've been lucky in this village. Thanks to a lot of good advice from men like Arkil and Cole," he nodded to each of them, "and some good weather, we've had five years of good crops. Edith, with all she knows about herbs and medicine—" Edith averted her eyes. "—has kept us and our children healthy."

Nods of agreement and a little applause. Osbert spotted the priest near the edge of the crowd. "Daniel's done a good job blessing the crops. We've prospered. A lot of us have had extra produce we've sold in town. I know a lot of you women have been selling poultry, butter, eggs."

"That's right."

"Yes, we've done better than some."

"Can't complain."

Everyone was enjoying this bout of self-congratulation so much that nobody seemed to wonder where it was leading. Osbert wiggled the bait. "So, our production's improved. The market's been good. Some of you have even been sending grain down to Southampton to be shipped abroad."

It was true. We were doing well.

Osbert reeled us in. "What do you think the king will do if he comes here and finds a prosperous looking village?"

Everybody waited for somebody else to say something. Osbert waited too.

"I guess he'll try to find a way to get some more out of us," said a young freeman, who had moved closer to the front when Osbert started talking.

"You bet your sweet life he will," said Osbert. "Anybody here want an increase in their food rents?"

The king's creativity in interpreting the traditional taxes was well established. It occurred to the villagers that their newly gained prosperity could be eroded. "Of course not," said one of the men.

"Then my question to you is," said Osbert, "how are we going to prevent it?"

"We'll just tell the king to shove it," said the freeman, with all the confidence and forethought of youth.

"How big do you think his security force is?" asked Osbert. One man thought it probably numbered in the thousands. The priest said he had seen the king and his guards when the southern provinces had met with the papal legates, and he was sure the guard was only about three hundred.

"I think we're outnumbered," said Osbert. "He could shove harder than we could. Anybody else got an idea?"

The Cherub said, "Why don't we just go to the king and explain that we feel we are paying enough taxes already?" Osbert didn't say anything. The Cherub began to get uncomfortable. "I don't know. That's my idea, anyway."

"Thank you," said Osbert. "Anybody else?"

"It might not hurt to look a little less prosperous," Cole ventured. Osbert looked interested. "Go on," he said.

"How much time do we have?" Cole asked. Arkil estimated the

trip from the monastery, with stops along the way, would take the royal party about a week. "That might be enough time to build some sheep hurdles and dig some dikes for the cattle," said Cole.

He was way ahead of everybody, and it took him a little time to explain what he had in mind.

"How about this:" said Cole, "if we can hide some of our livestock from the king's men it will look like we don't have any extra to hand over."

That seemed logical to the villagers. "But hide them where?" asked Edith.

"How about one of the scrubby areas of Hampage Wood?" suggested Arkil. The wood began just to the south of the small manor chapel at Avington, only about a mile from Easton.

"Never work," said the smith. "What about thieves? Wolves? Foxes?"

"No question about it," said Arkil. "We'd have to take it in shifts to protect the animals day and night."

"So," said Osbert, "the idea is we'll build the pens in an area away from the village where the king's men are not likely to meander?"

"Right," said Cole.

"What they can't see they can't tax," said Osbert. He turned to the villagers, "What do you say?"

After serious discussion over the pros and cons, the consensus was that the plan was doable. The more we talked, the more we liked it. After a while, in fact, everyone was a little exhilarated at the idea of pulling one over on the king.

"Wait a minute," said Edith, "if we can hide cattle, why can't we hide other things?"

"Like what?" said the thane's widow.

"Like grain, like looms."

"Like gold and silver," said the widow, forgetting that I was the only other person whose family had any.

"Like your embroidered tapestries," I said quickly.

"Like your best drinking horns," said one of the men.

"Or your finest linens," said a woman.

Hiding as much as possible from the prying eyes of the king's tax assessors became the order of the day. For a while we all competed to see who could think of the next thing to hide, then we were left to grapple with the practicalities. First we needed a look-out. We picked out the four fastest runners from among the children and told them to go to Winchester every morning, climb the city wall, and watch for the arrival of the king's messenger. We knew the messenger would arrive a day or two before the king since it was his job to make sure that the local palace had been adequately prepared.

Then with much communal merriment and free ale for all unknowingly donated by my stepmother, the men built sheep folds and cow dikes in the scrub near the forest. The rest of us built pathetic-looking shacks on one of the downs to camouflage some of our grain stores. We had the slaves build kitchens near them, and we hung some ragged clothes on nearby bushes to create a lived-in look. We hid half the women's looms in the storage areas under their weaving huts. Many of the villagers buried their valuables, some in the rubbish pits behind their houses. The thane's widow told me that she put her gold and silver jewelry in her grandmother's tomb. I smeared a silver goblet my mother had left me with mud and placed it in the bower where it sat looking like a clay vessel. I left the jewelry and gowns Mother had bequeathed to me where they were. I had hidden them underneath the floor long ago to keep them safe from my stepmother and her daughters.

## SCENE 4 MEET CYNETHRITH'S FAMILY

Although no one in Easton was exceptionally wealthy or influential, my family had been granted four hides of land, 16 acres of meadow, and rights over twelve peasants as a reward for my mother's military service. We were the leading family in the village. Osbert himself made it a point to tell my stepmother what was going on with the cattle and the grain. I was relieved. I was sure he could do a better job of getting her backing than I could. But he wanted me to persuade her to hide our good tapestries and silver.

"See if you can get your stepmother to play down how well off she is," Osbert had said to me.

"Right," I had said. I put it off as long as I could. The afternoon we finished the shacks I went into our hall to talk to her. She was sitting behind an embroidery frame, working gold thread onto a fabric strip for the bishop's vestment. Her two daughters were with her. Hilda was standing near my stepmother reciting, with more feeling than required, a poem about the crumbling remains of a once magnificent city that had been built by giants.

Her other daughter, Wulfwaru, was sitting by herself near the door. She sat very erect on a bench, her lower back pressed in and her rear end pressed out. Her head was tilted to one side, her nose in the air, and her eyes were half-closed. Her mouth was pursed in a little pout.

As I passed I stopped and peered at her. "Did you eat something sour, Wulfwaru? Your mouth is all scrunched up."

Wulfwaru started out of her reverie and scowled at me. I smiled at her sweetly.

"Hello, Mother," I called to the other end of the hall. Hilda stopped reciting. Waldberg peered at me over her embroidery.

"You're a mess," she said. "Get that hair out of your face."

"Yes, Mother," I said. I went over to inspect her embroidery. The overall design on the linen strip was a series of roundels, their backgrounds covered with red, blue, and green silk. She was working the foreground, contouring a creature that resembled a deer.

"It's beautiful," I said.

"Hmmm," she said. She was working with two needles. One sewed a gold thread on the surface of the work, very close to the previous gold thread she had laid down. With the second needle she sewed tiny silk stitches across the gold to anchor it to the cloth. She had explained to me once that this technique was used so that the expensive gold thread was not wasted on the wrong side.

She stopped working and looked at the embroidery. She sighed. She was trying to decide if she thought it was beautiful. "It's fantastic," I said. And it was a wonderful bit of work, but I was more interested in softening her up than anything else.

"Hmmm," said Waldberg again. She wasn't completely satisfied. She never was. "I'm afraid the bird's head got a little too big in this section," she said, pointing to a roundel near the top. But she didn't wait for my opinion. She wasn't interested in other people's opinions. She suspected people who praised her didn't know what they were talking about, and people who criticized her didn't understand what she was trying to do.

"Did you feed Offa and Edgefrith today?" she asked. She was referring to our dogs. I had named them after the previous two Mercian kings.

"Right after supper," I promised.

She frowned. "Don't make me remind you," she said.

"No, Mother," I said. "I guess you've heard about the king's visit—"

"Right. That Osbert is getting too big for his britches. I don't know why he wants us to look like a bunch of paupers. That won't do much for our social standing, now will it?"

"Well, no, Mother," I agreed, "but you might be a little richer at the end of the day."

"And if no one knows I'm rich how will it help me get husbands for my daughters?" I looked at Wulfwaru and Hilda. "I understand your concern, Mother," I said.

"Thank you very much," said Hilda, whose eyeballs and front teeth competed to see which could protrude more. Her chin had conceded defeat and was trying to leave the field.

"But of course this pretense is only temporary," I continued.

"And I suppose you're going to tell me next that I should hide my linens and my embroideries and live like one of our peasants?" said Waldberg. It seems she had heard about the frenzied hiding of household goods that was taking place all over the village.

I tried to approach it from her point of view. "You mentioned marriage, Mother."

"With three of you of an age to be married it's a subject I often think of," she said.

I knew perfectly well that she was planning to ship me off to a convent as soon as she could without causing a lot of talk. In any event, I certainly wasn't going to sit around and wait for her to arrange a match for me. As the ancient wisdom of our people advises:

*Girls, steal secretly to your sweethearts*
*So no one says*
*That you were bought with booty.*

But for the time being I went along with her pretense.

"That's just the point, Mother," I said. "Everyone in the village is taking part in this. And they've all got friends in the neighboring villages. If you don't go along with it, we will be ostracized. No one will marry any of us."

She looked upset. "These walls, these barren walls, cold, drafty—sitting here staring at wattle and daub—how can you expect me to live like that?" Waldberg's flare for the dramatic surfaced around the oddest things. "What are we to put on our beds? Can it possibly matter? Surely you don't expect the king's men in your bedroom? Or do you?" She looked at me suspiciously.

Wulfwaru twittered. I was irritated. "For heaven's sake, Mother," I said.

Wulfwaru, seeing I was losing ground, left her perch near the door and floated over. I noticed her brown hair was getting red. She must have been tinting it with calendula. She picked a subject dear to her heart. "And as for clothes, are we to wear rags?"

"Of course not rags," I said. "Second best will do."

"Go to court, be presented at court, in second best?" shrieked Waldberg. It was unfortunate for my case that this topic had come up. She'd waited for three years for a royal visit and seemed to think she was going to be invited to court. Waldberg stood up from behind her embroidery frame. I was always surprised by how short she was: she only came up to my shoulder. She sat down upon her stool again, her shoulders slumped, and circled her fingers around her closed eyes. "It's a nightmare. Tell me I'm dreaming."

Two servants entered to prepare the hall for supper. Wulfwaru called to the younger one.

"Does cook understand that I will eat nothing but goosegrass soup?"

"Yes, miss. I told her, miss."

"Are you still trying to lose weight?" I asked.

"You must eat a balanced diet, Wulfwaru," lectured Waldberg. "The way you starve yourself is absurd. You'll get sick."

"I know what I'm doing, Mother," said Wulfwaru. "All the thanes' wives in town use goosegrass."

"It wouldn't hurt her to lose a few pounds," I said. I don't think she appreciated the way I jumped to her defense.

"This doesn't concern you, Cynethrith," said Waldberg.

And I'm afraid we continued in this manner until supper, when the whole focus of the meal was on what and how much Wulfwaru would eat. I tried to console Waldberg by pointing out that it didn't matter how little Wulfwaru ate at supper: her serious eating always took place about an hour afterwards. I was so busy trying to mediate this family dispute that I completely forgot the purpose of our earlier discussion.

A few days later, having learned that I had been unsuccessful in persuading Waldberg to abandon the trappings of her status, the thane's widow, The Cherub, and Edith took it in turn to visit her. Waldberg told them she didn't think she could bear to live without beautiful things around her. They pointed out she was more likely to have them a year from now if the king didn't get his hands on them. It was all to no avail. Waldberg would not be swayed. The next morning I heard Tidburg outside the hall.

"Waldberrrrrrrg!" She stood at the door croaking—her weapon, like the adder's, in her mouth.

To Waldberg, who had just started a painting, Tidburg must have been as welcome as a mouse in the larder. "You're up early this morning," she greeted the woman. Once inside the hall Tidburg stood stock still, nose in the air, observant as a weasel on its haunches.

"You got a lot of nice things," said Tidburg finally.

"Thank you," said Waldberg.

"More than most people."

"We're very fortunate," said Waldberg. Yes, I thought, no thanks to you.

"Some in this village can't afford to lose everything," said Tidburg, who aped poverty the way others aped riches. Only after she died was it discovered she had squirreled away considerable wealth.

"Are you implying that I can?" asked Waldberg. I could tell she was getting annoyed, but then, it didn't take much to annoy Waldberg.

"You should know," said Tidburg. "Most of us are willing to hide what we got, to keep it."

"This is ridiculous," snapped Waldberg. "Do the people in this village seriously believe the king is going to look under their beds to try to find more money? I'm sure he has quite enough without that."

"You're in your own little world, Waldberg," said Tidburg. This may be the only thing the woman ever said that I agreed with.

"You got three daughters," said Tidburg. Two daughters, I mentally corrected. One innocent victim.

"What's that got to do with anything?" asked Waldberg.

"So far, they got good reputations."

"What are you driving at?"

"Nothing, just it would be a shame if there was bad things said about them." Waldberg looked at Tidburg uncomprehendingly.

"Some girls never get married, once their reputations are lost."

"You're not serious."

"I'd really hate to pay any more taxes, Waldberg. I'd really, really be unhappy about that. And there's no reason to, if everybody cooperates."

"Are you trying to blackmail me?" gasped Waldberg.

"I'm not trying, Waldberg."

In the end, Waldberg was persuaded. While I was amazed at just how low Tidburg was willing to stoop, I had to admit her methods were effective. The idea of being unable to marry off the step-ghouls must have been a terrifying one for Waldberg.

She removed the tapestries from the hall and hid her silver goblets, one of her weaving frames, and half her jewelry. She put up a good fight, backed by Wulfwaru, on the clothes issue. In the end she very grudgingly agreed not to wear her best gown if she were invited to court. She refused to budge on the bed linens, but that didn't bother anyone because nobody seriously expected the tax assessors to go so far as to inspect bedrooms.

As for me, I soared around the village like a whirlwind, not quite knowing what to do with all my excitement. The king's coming, and all our preparations for his arrival, had whetted my appetite for adventure. As our group deception neared completion, I began to play with the idea of planning an exploit of my own.

*SCENE* 5 A VISIT TO THE ABBEY

I decided to do what I always did in those days when I had something exciting on my mind: go to St. Wihtburh's Abbey and talk to my best friend Athelflad. Early one afternoon my stepmother saw me heading toward the stable and called after me to find out what I was up to.

"You're not involved in that cattle hiding business, are you?" she said.

"I'm going to St. Wihtburh's," I said, avoiding her question.

She never objected when I went to visit Athelflad. She liked me to spend time at the abbey. She said the same thing she always said. "Good. You should support the abbey your mother founded. Take a gift."

That's what she said, but I knew what she meant. The real reason she liked me to go there was so I'd get used to it. When the time came to give me the old heave-ho into the nunnery she hoped I wouldn't cause any trouble. "Wait a minute," she said, running in the direction of the pantry. She came back with two flasks of elderberry wine. "Here, give this to the prioress," she said. "Now I want you to stay far away from that business of Osbert's. I don't like it, and there's no father to pull you out of scrapes. Do you understand me?"

"Thank you, Mother," I said without enthusiasm, starting on my way again.

"Take the dogs," she hollered after me.

I rode along the Avington road toward Itchen. Edgefrith and Offa ran in circles around me. Every now and then Edgefrith would run alongside me with what I suppose was the dog version of a smile. He would look up at me with his mouth open, his upper lip curled back, and his tongue hanging out. I would smile back half-heartedly, and he would run ahead again.

It was one of those changeable days in late September when the sun is as unpredictable as a veil in a magician's hand. At times I felt hot and was sorry I had brought my cloak. Then the sun would disappear, the breeze pick up, and I'd shiver. I stopped near the river to admire a beautiful swan parade: mother, father, and eight cygnets, almost as large as their parents but still plumed in gray, gliding single file down a narrow fork. What wonderful creatures they are, I thought, their temperaments so at war with their form. Another family swam toward them, a mother swan with her brood of three. As if to demonstrate what I had been thinking, the first family's father hissed and chased them, leaving the fatherless brood no alternative but retreat.

The orphaned cygnets had my sympathy. On that autumn day my own father had been dead for four years, and my mother for many more. She had been one of King Wulf's best archers, but that hadn't saved her. I knew of her mainly through the nunnery she had founded, a monument to her virtue as well as her taste and refinement.

When I said earlier that no one in Easton was exceptionally wealthy or influential, it was both true and not true, because although I had no control over my money I was, or should have been, very wealthy indeed. My mother's father was a successful merchant. He had been made thane for crossing the sea three times in his own ship. My father told me he traded regularly with the Normans in Rouen and the Frisians in Dorestad. He had ventured as far north as Denmark. Grandfather didn't die in a shipwreck as everyone expected, but in a completely avoidable accident. He was visiting my mother one spring and had gone out for a stroll. He stopped in the middle of the road near a bend, his attention diverted for an instant by an early swallow swooping close to the river for a drink. A boy coming around the curve on a cart swerved to miss a pothole and toppled his cart on top of my grandfather.

My mother, his only heir, inherited a large estate and established the abbey that she endowed with a beautiful church, twelve hides of land, 32 oxen, 18 slaves, a mill, and 30 acres of meadow. When she died what remained of her estate, still a fortune by most people's standards, went to me. However—and this was the root of my problem—I was not to have control of it. My mother, anxious to prevent a rash youngster from squandering a fortune, had made out her will so that my father would manage my wealth (except for books, gowns and jewelry, which passed to me unencumbered) until I was an established member of adult society—in other words, a married woman.

I was too young when she died to fathom my loss. Instead I grew up with the awareness that through enormous good luck I was set for life. I was hardly out of infancy when my father remarried a widow with two daughters of her own. How he ever got Waldberg to think about something other than one of her projects long enough to agree to marriage is a mystery to me—she must have needed money badly—but all in all she didn't bother me. I found the level of abstraction in which she lived her life had certain advantages: I never suffered overly from supervision.

It wasn't until much later that I discovered the threat this marriage embodied. Shortly after he married Waldberg my father rewrote his will, passing control over my estate to her if he should die before I married. I can't believe he was a fool, so I guess he was too good a man to see the possibility of cupidity in someone he loved. As I got older he never thought to change his will, and I didn't even know about it. When he died one disaster led to another. Waldberg became my guardian. After my father's death she was more nervous and preoccupied than ever. She must have realized that my estate formed the bulk of the living for the family. My father's personal estate, which she had inherited, was far smaller than mine. She began to sell her embroideries and her paintings, and often complained about competition from the monasteries. The more she worried over money the more I began to fear she'd try to find some way to keep control of mine.

One day, shortly before we heard that the king was coming, my suspicions were confirmed. I came upon Waldberg and her brother in the garden whispering about an orphan who was shipped off to a convent so her relatives could get her inheritance. The relatives, her brother said, gave a nice dowry to the convent and nobody asked any questions. It happened all the time, he said. They got real quiet when they noticed me.

I had a lot of sleepless nights mulling over this conversation. My ideas raced all over the place. I thought of disguising myself as a boy and sneaking onto a merchant ship. I toyed with apprenticing myself to a thane so I could train to be a warrior. These escapades didn't seem too far fetched to me, I was as tall as any lad, and strong—I had beaten up most of the boys in the village at one time or another. Sometimes I thought I might be able to go along with my step-mother's scheme: I tried to reconcile myself to the concept of the religious life, but couldn't for long. At that age the closest I could get to a religious idea was to imagine how beautiful I would look beneath my veil, and what unexpected longing the local priest would experience as he watched me pray.

Anticipation of the king's visit and the activity it generated in Easton blocked out all other concerns for a while. I almost forgot about the trap Waldberg was laying. Then one night, too excited to sleep, the knowledge that the court was coming formed the backbone of a solution so simple that it seemed inevitable. I knew there were members of the old guard among the councilors and thanes, even during the current regime. I began to think, or rather, to be convinced, that if I could find a way to get into the palace I might, somehow, make a powerful friend or two who could help me hang on to my inheritance. There must be someone who remembered my mother. I would do this despite the current king, a despicable man if ever there was one.

These were my thoughts as I came to the Itchen road and turned off into the abbey. Within its gates, in contrast to my unsettled state, all was quiet. Figuring the sisters must be at Nones, I stabled my horse and went to the church, entering as inconspicuously as possible. I stood at the back of the tall timber building, dark as a tomb, my eye drawn to the distant altar candles sparkling on gold treasure. After I became accustomed to the dim interior I noticed the painted north wall undulate in the flickering light. I thought I saw Adam and Eve, trying to disentangle themselves from the foliage of paradise, exchange a look fired with earthly desire. I blinked my eyes. When I looked again the painting was flat and motionless.

Soon my thoughts came around, as they always did when I visited the abbey church, to my mother. Here she was tangible. The altar, covered with a gold-embroidered frontal, held a silver and gold chalice she had commissioned in East Anglia: around its rim fantastic birds interlaced so cleverly that you could hardly tell where one began and the other ended. Her father had bought the imposing altar cross of gold and precious stones from a Byzantine trader. In its center a tiny vial contained a drop of St. Etheldreda's blood. My eye came back to the chancel arch—its grappling angels and demons carved by a sculptor my mother had brought in from Kent—then was pulled to the center of the choir where, in darkness beneath the floor, lay my mother.

Inexplicably I found myself close to tears. I closed my eyes and inhaled the incense. One of the nuns was playing a lyre. She led the sisters in singing psalms. I opened my eyes and watched them. In the choir two groups of nuns faced each other, novices in front, the others on a step behind them. There were about thirty members of the order then, and all but one were at Nones that day. Their white faces gleamed in the candlelight. They seemed transported. They radiated a purity I found both admirable and totally alien.

I spotted Athelflad. She was second in from the altar. I found her voice reedy, but she loved to sing and was completely enthralled by the music. I shut my eyes again and prayed that an atheling would fall in love with me, preferably one who wouldn't have any connection to King Beorhtric. When the service was over I waited for Athelflad outside the church. Her dark hazel eyes sparkled when she saw me.

"I have to find the prioress and give her one of these bottles. We can share the other one," I said.

Athelflad looked tempted. "Where did you get them?" she asked.

"They're from the troll."

"You're too hard on your stepmother," reproved Athelflad. She thought everybody ought to love everybody else. This was probably because she had never been subjected to a family. Her father had proudly presented her to the convent at age three, because, he said, when she was given a selection of toys to choose from she had chosen a shiny gold chalice rather than a carved ivory horse or a straw doll.

"You don't have to live with her," I said.

We found the prioress in her hall, where she greeted me warmly. As soon as our interview was over, I turned to Athelflad.

"Where can we go to talk?" Normally we would have talked in the room beneath the dormitory, but today I didn't want to risk being overheard.

"How about the guest hall garden?" she suggested. "It's empty."

On the way over to the guest hall I reminded her to pick up a couple of glasses. I figured things would go down better if Athelflad had a couple of drinks first. Then I filled her in on the king's visit and swore her to secrecy over our ruse in Easton. As we chatted in the garden I began to flesh out the details of my own plan. The court coming to Winchester presented me with an opportunity. If I could make a friend there I would have an influential ally to help me wrest possession of my inheritance from Waldberg's greedy hands.

"I've been trying to think of how I can get into the palace," I said.

"What for?" said Athelflad.

"I'm curious." I knew I was being oblique. I didn't want to mention my suspicions about Waldberg. Athelflad would have told me I was nuts.

"About what?"

"I want to watch court life first hand. I want to see the warriors, the women, the king, the queen, the feasts, that sort of thing—"

"Oh, you do?" She thought for a minute. "I bet I can help. The prioress's brother-in-law is pretty important. I'll talk to him about wangling an invitation."

I wasn't ready to make an official visit to the palace. First I planned to do some careful reconnoitering. I needed to learn about life at court before being presented and making a fool out of myself. "I was thinking more along the lines of sneaking in," I explained.

Athelflad laughed in surprise. "Sneaking? You're joking."

"No," I said.

"I understand these places are guarded by men with no sense of humor," she said.

"So I've heard."

"And you're going to sneak past them?"

"Yes, but not in the way you think."

"This isn't another one of your hare-brained schemes, is it?"

"I've planned it down to the gnat's eyelash. Let me ask you something. What's always involved in moving house?" I asked.

"Sorting, packing, transporting, unpacking, putting away—shall I go on?"

"And the concomitant to those things is?"

"Fatigue?"

"Besides that?"

"Things lost, misplaced, broken; people tired, crabby—"

"Confusion, my dear, is the word I'm looking for. And it's just that confusion that's going to get me into the palace."

"You've confused me, for starters," she said.

"See? It's working already. Never mind, here's the plan. The palace steward will have to take on new servants with the king's party coming, am I right?"

"Yes."

"The king's party, I know from an eye witness account, has a number of its own servants and slaves. With me so far?"

"Do you think I'm a cretin?"

"Don't get snippy. When the two groups meet, nobody will know who anybody is. Therefore, on the day the king's party comes to town I, your humble friend Cynethrith, will trail in with the royal procession. I'll be just one more new face. Nobody will notice me."

"I don't know," she said. "It couldn't be that simple, could it?"

"Sure it could," I said.

"What will you do once you get there? Have a good look and then sneak out again?"

"No, not right away. The king and queen might not have a major feast the first day."

"You don't mean you're planning on staying there?" she said.

"Yes," I said.

"Don't you think they'll notice an idle woman wandering around after a while?"

"I won't be idle," I answered. "I'll pretend I'm a servant."

"You're not serious."

"Yeah, that's the idea. Don't you think I'd make a great servant?"

"No."

"What do you mean 'no'?" I was offended. I tended to assume I was good at everything.

"For heaven's sake, Cynethrith, you've never had to work a day in your life."

"I beg to differ," I said. "I work like a slave. Who feeds the dogs? Who has to fetch embroidery floss and gather dyes endlessly for the troll, and run messages to the servants until I could drop? And I'm immensely strong, you know. I ride and practice sword play and archery every day—well, almost."

"And that's the sort of thing you think servants do?" she asked.

"They do as little as possible," I said. "At least that's what ours do. Of course Waldberg never pays any attention to them so they get away with murder."

Athelflad looked at me and smirked a little, an uncharacteristic expression for her. "Maybe it's not such a bad idea," she said. "How long are you planning on staying there?"

"Long enough to see what it's like. Haven't you ever wondered about royal life? About money and majesty? Gold, gowns, jewels, men . . ."

"Not really," said Athelflad.

"Athelflad," I said. "If everything goes well, really well, maybe I can get you out of here."

"I like it here," she said. "But let's get back to this so-called plan of yours. You're going to sneak into the palace as a servant, and nobody there is going to recognize you, and nobody at home is going to wonder where you are?"

"Right," I said. I had worked out a great excuse for leaving home, but it had never occurred to me that I might need a disguise. Now that Athelflad mentioned it I realized it was possible that some of the local people might come to the law court, or a thane or two I had met some-where might remember me. I had an inspiration. "I'm going to disguise myself as an old woman. What about that?"

"Terrific, you'll probably be able to pull it off in about thirty years. And where is your mother going to think you are? Selling eggs under the butter cross?"

"She's going to think I'm here, with you."

"You're going to convince the prioress of that, are you?" she asked, for the moment concerned only about the part that involved her.

"No, you are. Oh come on, Athelflad, that's all you have to do. One little thing. If I can convince an entire royal court that I'm a servant you can certainly convince one measly little prioress that I'm here. How hard could it be?"

"You want me to lie to the prioress? You're only asking me to jeop-ardize my soul, you know. Besides, the woman's not blind. And what about the abbess—if she got wind of it—"

"Don't worry. I'll set it up. I'll tell the prioress I want to stay in the guest hall undisturbed and contemplate on St. Wihtburh. I'll tell her I had a vision of my mother, saying I should sequester myself for the good of mankind."

"Not altogether unreasonable," muttered Athelflad.

"All you have to do is cover for me in little ways, if needed."

"I don't like it."

"There's nothing to worry about, really."

"Are you eating, which means I somehow have to consume six meals a day, or do you plan to fast for the duration?"

"I'll fast, and when I show up at the end of a fortnight with all my flesh intact I'll probably be proclaimed a saint." I thought this was immensely funny.

"You're wicked, Cynethrith. Have you ever wondered why I like you? I wonder sometimes," said Athelflad.

"You like me because I'm exciting," I said. "I'll tell the troll that I'll be here, and all you have to do is go along with it if anybody from home comes nosing around, which they won't. And you don't have to lie. You can just say I said such and such, which is true."

"Tell me about this disguise of yours," she said.

"It's terrific," I said, thinking fast. "Do you know about gipsywort? The beggars use it to turn their skin brown. There's clumps of it along the Itchen. I'll darken my skin so I look Welsh like most of the riffraff.

No offense." Athelflad's mother had been Welsh, which accounted for her shiny black hair. She got her fair skin from her Anglo-Saxon father. "And of course there's chalk all over the ground, I'll grind some up to whiten my hair, not that much of it will show under the mantle. I'll cover a few teeth with seed pods, and there you have it, an old woman. Watch this."

I mimicked the arthritic posture of an old woman. Starting at the waist I rounded my back and hunched my shoulders forward. I let my knees bend slightly and relaxed my stomach muscles. I stuck out my chin. I pitched my voice to the back of my throat, and let some of the sound slide out through my nose. "Oh, pray for me, sister. I'll be with God before you will," I said, trying out the voice. It sounded raspy and a little more high-pitched than I would have wished.

"What do you think?" I asked.

Athelflad laughed and laughed. "You're going to keep that up day and night?"

"Yes," I said. "Absolutely."

"Why an old woman?" she asked.

"People don't notice them," I said.

"What about clothes? Don't you think yours are a little grand for a servant?" She looked at my fine wool cloak and my linen dress with the pretty woven trim near its hem.

"You know where I've hidden my mother's gowns, and jewels, and all her other stuff?" I asked.

"You've told me about it," she said.

"I also kept an old dress and mantle that belonged to my nurse. The dress is coarse enough, and brown, and the mantle's made out of nettle stems."

"Sounds all right," said Athelflad. "You seem determined, anyway." She warmed up a little. It might have been the wine, but I was going to hold her to it. "I guess I'll be hearing some great stories," she said.

"You bet."

"All right. When is all this going to happen?" asked Athelflad.

"I'll tell the prioress before I leave about my plans to come here for a while. Tomorrow morning I'll tell my stepmother that I had a dream about my mother and all that. I'll tell her I must soon go to the abbey to meditate. She'll love it. Then I'll get everything ready and wait for the kids to come back from Winchester with the news that the king's messenger has arrived."

"Okay."

"When the kids come back I'll take my leave of my stepmother and come here, make sure the prioress sees me, and settle into the guest hall. From there I can get into my disguise and leave for Winchester. Even if somebody sees me leave they won't know who I am."

"And if anybody mentions seeing an old lady I can say I've seen a beggar looking for alms," said Athelflad, slightly dubiously. We both knew she could say that with a clear conscience. There were enough of them about.

"Then I go to Winchester, stand near the palace gate, and wait for the king's procession. As it goes through I slip into the party and enter with the rest of the servants."

"This ought to be good," said Athelflad.

"It'll be great," I said.

SCENE 6 DECEPTION AND DISGUISE

The next morning I sought out my stepmother. She was sitting near her desk in the hall, painting a border for one of the bishop's manuscripts. She bent over her work closely; she was short-sighted. The piece was on a large wooden frame that held the painting upright. As I approached I took in her elaborate design. Two narrow gold borders were set around the page, one inside the other. Red, blue, and green leaves straddled the space between them. Sometimes Waldberg's understanding of form was a little wobbly, but I was always surprised at how sensitive her drawings were. It didn't seem to fit with the rest of her personality.

Her brushes were arranged in a box on her desk. Her pigments were set to one side, each in its own oyster shell. She mixed the colors with egg yolk on a small piece of wood that she held in one hand.

"Mother," I said. She was staring at the painting. It could be difficult to get Waldberg's attention sometimes. "Mother," I tried again.

She jumped. Then she frowned. "What?" she said sharply. "Must you interrupt right now? I'm under a lot of pressure here." I would have been sympathetic if some people had said that, but Waldberg couldn't spin wool and chat without feeling pressured.

I persisted. "Mother, I am going to have to spend some time at the abbey."

"And why is that?"

"I had a dream, last night, about my mother."

"And?"

"And she told me I should contemplate on St. Wihtburh." It sounded a little silly to me now that I was actually saying it. I hoped it didn't sound silly to Waldberg.

"And did she say why?"

"Only that a truth would be revealed to me."

"Cynethrith," she asked, "are you planning on entering the convent?"

If this was her idea of planting a seed it fell on infertile ground. "No, Mother, not really," I said.

"You will let me know if you are, won't you?"

"Yes, of course, Mother," I said.

"It's not such a bad life," she said.

Forget it, Waldberg, I thought.

"Peaceful, really peaceful." She sighed. Just then Wulfwaru entered.

"What's the matter with your face?" I said. It was covered with a thick white poultice.

"I had a blemish," she said in that peculiar high voice of hers. I was sure it was an affectation, and I often wondered why she chose it. Whenever I talked to her I found myself pitching my own voice lower, as if to show her how ridiculous she sounded. She went on, "I pounded ivory and mixed it with honey. It works wonders." She looked at my skin as if she had never seen it before. "You should try it."

"Cynethrith is going to be spending some time at the abbey," said Waldberg.

"Oh that will be a loss," said Wulfwaru.

"When will you be leaving?" asked Waldberg.

"In a day or two," I said, folding my hands and trying to look as otherworldly as possible. "I'm waiting for a sign."

"What kind of a sign?" asked Wulfwaru.

"I'll know when I see it," I said. "Then I might have to leave in great haste."

"Isn't she mysterious?" said Wulfwaru.

"Her mother told her she should contemplate St. Wihtburh," Waldberg explained to Wulfwaru.

"That's preferable to what she usually contemplates, I suppose," said Wulfwaru.

Waldberg looked tired. "I have to get this painting finished by tomorrow. Do you think I could have a little peace and quiet around here?"

"Yes, Mother," I said.

"Be sure to speak to me before you leave, no matter what your sign says, all right?"

"Yes, Mother."

I left them and went to the stream to gather gipsywort. In a secluded clearing, I extracted the dye and stored it in a leather drinking pouch. Then I filled a basket with chalk. When I got home I went to the bower to get my nurse's clothes from under the floor. It was the middle of the day, so I didn't expect anyone to be there. I was wrong.

When I peeked in the room I saw my stepsister Hilda standing at one end flailing her arms about. Both hands went over her heart and she dropped gracelessly unto her knees.

I entered quickly. "Are you sick?" I asked. I had a sinking feeling. If she were, I might not be able to get her out of the room before the king's messenger came to Winchester.

"Listen," she said, practically gasping for air. "Listen to this."

She began to recite an overwrought poem about a woman who had allowed herself to be seduced by a warrior who, after impregnating her, was nowhere to be found. Hilda had the most extraordinary memory. In fact, she was very smart, just not about anything useful. She paused at the end.

"Wasn't it beautiful?" she said in a whisper. Her blue eyes misted over.

"It was remarkable," I said. The poem had left me befuddled. The woman was deserted, no doubt about that, but otherwise I was lost. "Tell me something," I asked. "Are Eric and Edward the same person or two different people?"

"You didn't understand it at all, did you?" she said. "You have all the higher qualities of a pygmy shrew." I hadn't meant to hurt her feelings, and I was offended at her crack about the shrew, but miraculously she was so mad at what she saw as my obtuseness that she stormed out of the room. It couldn't have gone better if I'd planned it.

I pushed aside my bed and removed one of the floor boards. Beneath were the old clothes my nurse had once worn, resting on top of the box where I'd hidden my mother's finery. The servant's clothing was wrapped around a small gold-framed looking glass that had been one of my mother's prized possessions. I added the clothes and the mirror to the things I'd gathered that day, wrapped everything into a bundle, and waited for the lookouts to come running into Easton.

*SCENE 7* A STRANGE ENCAMPMENT IN THE FOREST

A day later word came that the king's messenger had been spotted. He had entered Winchester through the West Gate, as we had expected, and gone directly to the palace to make sure all was ready for the king's arrival. The king was expected in two days, and the town was in an uproar. I told my stepmother that I would be leaving for the convent the next day. Earlier that afternoon the bishop himself had come to collect the painting and the embroidery she had been working on. He had been pleased. Waldberg was unusually relaxed. She reminded me, as usual, to take a gift. A large gift, she said, if I were planning on spending any amount of time there.

Then it seemed a thought occurred to her.

"You're not in any sort of trouble, are you?" The woman actually looked at my abdomen.

"Of course not, Mother," I said. She was offensive sometimes.

"All right," she said, relieved. "What time are you leaving tomorrow?"

"First thing," I said.

She said she would see me off, if she were up.

The next morning, as luck would have it, she was up. She looked at my little bundle suspiciously. "What's in there?" she asked. "Is that all you're taking?"

"Mother," I said in the sanctimonious tone I took with Waldberg when referring to my real mother, "told me I should bring only rough clothes to wear to help me get closer to the saint."

"I never knew your mother to be so talkative in the past," said Waldberg. I gave her what I hoped was a saintly smile.

"I must go," I said.

"Take Offa and Edgefrith with you," she said.

"What?" I said. I couldn't believe what I was hearing.

"Take the dogs," she said again. "I don't like you walking around in the woods by yourself." She meant that she didn't want to have to take care of them.

"But Mother," I almost whined, "Who's going to look after them once I get there? I'll be contemplating St. Wihtburh. I'll be fasting. I don't intend to leave the guest house."

"Well, get Athelflad to look after them for you. There's a good girl.

On your way now." And she went back into the hall.

Athelflad had already heard the news about the king's messenger and was waiting for me near the abbey gate. Offa, Edgefrith, and I greeted her.

"Don't jump! don't jump!" I screamed as the dogs lunged for Athelflad. The dogs had terrible manners and as far as I could tell were not trainable. "Sorry they're so effusive," I said. "The troll made me bring them."

"Stop calling your stepmother *the troll*," she said. I think she was more annoyed at me than at the dogs. She said she didn't mind taking care of them; one of her children could do it. She was in charge of a group of about six orphans who had been left at the convent.

She led me to the guest hall and said she would tell the prioress I had arrived. I spent the day by myself, contemplating, I'm afraid, a brilliant marriage and future wealth rather than St. Wihtburh. I had told Athelflad that I would spend the night and then sneak away the next day when the coast was clear. This gave me the opportunity to dine with the prioress that evening, and over dinner I enhanced my alibi. When I returned to my quarters I set to work on my disguise.

I took off all my clothes and the knife I always wear strapped to my thigh. I poured some of the gipsywort infusion into the wash basin and mixed it with water so the color wouldn't be too intense. I rubbed the stain over my face, neck, arms and my legs up to the crotch, figuring it was best to play safe. I didn't want anyone to spot a white thigh in the latrine. Then I crushed the chalk into a fine powder and worked it into my hair. I pressed a few seed pods over some teeth to make them look rotten.

I gave the gipsywort time to dry and the powder time to settle, then I strapped on my knife and dressed in my old nurse's clothes. I looked into my mother's looking glass. Not bad, I thought. I danced around the room. Not bad at all.

A little while later I heard a tap on the door. Athelflad had come around to see how I was doing. We both laughed over my imitation of an old lady. We said our good-byes. I slept in my clothes, figuring it could only improve the costume.

The next day as the nuns prepared for the Feast of the Guardian Angel, I set out. The winds had been high during the night, but once the early mist cleared the day was beautiful, the sky bright with only a few puffy white clouds to intensify its blue. Along the road the dogwood leaves had turned purple. Bright orange berries covered the rowan. I entered the forest, breathing in the slightly murky smell of damp earth and rotting leaves. I saw a huge guelder rose with leaves as red as its berries. The hazels still had most of their leaves, and so did the fecund ash, its branches now flaunting masses of seeds. Suddenly my enjoyment of the walk was interrupted by a loud rustling in the vegetation. I flattened my body against a tree and reached under my skirt for my knife. Out from behind a bush charged Edgefrith, his lead trailing behind him. He jumped on me, tail wagging vigorously.

"Oh, no," I said. "What are you doing here? Did you escape your keeper?" I turned around to take him back to the abbey. "Come on, Edgefrith, let's go." He darted into a clump of hawthorn.

"Edgefrith," I pleaded. "Come. Come." But he wouldn't come; he couldn't. His lead had caught in the thorny bushes, but I cursed him just the same. I crawled in after him. A long spine punctured my scalp—the thicket was far too dense for me to penetrate. I crawled out again, and walked around to the other side of the bush.

By the time I got there, Edgefrith had gnawed through his lead and worked himself free. He greeted me joyously, and then bounded off into the wood. "Edgefrith," I called desperately. "Come here. Come. Come." I was tempted to leave him to his fate, but I was afraid that if he decided to go home to Waldberg she might come to the convent to investigate. I followed him.

After a while I realized I had no idea where the animal had gone, and I was not on a trail anymore. I waded across a small stream and couldn't see beyond where I was standing: a stand of elders obscured my view. Nearby was a large ash, so I climbed it hoping I might catch sight of Edgefrith. Instead I caught sight of something a lot more interesting.

The woodland opened into a small meadow. In its center sat what looked like a small royal encampment. Something near the top of my ribcage took a dive down to my lower abdomen.

There was a large white tent, and near it a circular table covered with a cloth and laid with knives, trenchers and bowls. Servants bustled about preparing dinner. Two cooks attended a cauldron of soup cooking over a brazier, and another watched a portable stove. A butcher stood at an impromptu table made out of a warrior's shield. He cut meat and fowl into chunks, skewered the chunks onto spits, and then handed the spits to another man to grill. No wonder Edgefrith had wandered off in this direction.

But was it the royal camp? It didn't make sense. The royals were coming from the west, and this camp was to the east of town. Anyway, it was much too small for that. There was only one tent and so far no people other than servants. I spotted some horses tethered to a tree. Their manes were odd: they weren't hogged in the usual fashion but were long and flowing.

While I was puzzling over all this the tent flap opened, and a tall warrior stepped out. I don't know what it was about him, but I think I stopped breathing. The servants went about their tasks with increased diligence. There was nothing soft about the man. His muscular frame was covered from shoulder to waist by a shirt made of shiny metal rings. Below that you could see the points of the leather shirt he wore beneath. He wore no helmet. The angles of his cheekbones seemed to provide their own protection. Were his eyes narrow, or was he squinting in the sun? The light glinted off the gold hilt of his sword, and I sensed danger in a primordial way, like a hare smelling a fox. I wondered how many women he had ravished, how many men he had killed. The ash tree still had most of its leaves, but even so I wasn't sure it would conceal me. I was glad for my dull costume. My heart was banging in my chest. My scalp tingled. I prepared myself in case he noticed me. I tried to think of a story that would explain my presence in the tree. Would he believe I was looking for my dog? Did he speak English, or had he come from across the sea to rape and pillage? If he saw me and came over to the tree could I jump him and slit his throat before he got me? I held on to the tree with one hand and reached for my knife with the other. I had to pull on it three times to get it out. I bruised my other thigh with the handle as I finally yanked the knife from its case.

Something made the warrior look up, and I felt my spirit leave my body: it flew up to the top of the tree and looked down at me. I pressed against the trunk of the tree, trying to disappear. The man's gaze scanned the trees. Did his eyes stop for a fraction of a second when they found me? I thought they did. I forced my spirit back and steeled myself for the confrontation. "If he gets near me I'll kill him," I said to myself.

I watched him closely, and his expression didn't change. By some miracle, he had looked at me without seeing me. The brown of my outfit and my brown face must have melded me to the tree. He turned away and walked over to the servant who was grilling the meat and watched for a moment. "How much longer?" he said.

While he was distracted with the cooking, I scrambled down from the tree. I didn't even feel the large scratches the bark made on the undersides of my arms. Edgefrith, looking very proud of himself, was sitting next to the trunk, tongue hanging out and panting, waiting for me. He could tell from my look that something serious was going on, and, loyal beast that he was, began to bark. My knees were shaking, and I felt as if my bowels were about to empty.

"Oh, shut up, for God's sake," I could hardly speak. He shut up. I heard someone in the camp say, "What's that?"

"Nothing," said the warrior. "A stray dog."

I thanked God the man, in addition to being blind, lacked curiosity. As I ran for my life I asked God to forgive me for my little joke about St. Wihtburh.

*SCENE* 8 THE ROYAL PROCESSION

By the time I got Edgefrith back to the convent and myself to Winchester the weather had changed. The white clouds had billowed until they filled the entire sky, then gradually darkened. It looked like rain. The streets of the town were teeming with people. Word was that King Beorhtric had just passed through King's Gate. I noticed a group from Easton, and I loitered near them, testing my disguise. Osbert, Cole and Arkil were so pleased with themselves for suppressing the true nature of their wealth that they had no trouble appearing jubilant at the king's approach. They had brought a keg of beer with them and were having a wonderful time. Two other villagers were taking bets on how many warriors the king would have with him. A few people, most notably Waldberg and Wulfwaru, looked glum. I was sure they were put out that the villagers had prevented them from putting on the dog for the king's arrival.

The wind picked up as the royal procession wound through the streets, turning left then right. They were now on the road that lead to the palace. The rain began to fall, only a little at first. I ran to the grounds near the west door of the minster so I would be well positioned to follow the party into the palace grounds. There were a lot of people there before me, but as tall as I am I had a good view.

First came the king's crier, on foot, proclaiming the procession and separating the crowd. He was followed by the standard-bearer, on horseback, carrying the colors of the house of Wessex: a golden dragon on a deep red background. Suddenly the rain began to pour down, and the wind slapped the standard into the face of the king's falconer, who was riding behind. The king's huntsman was next. He would ride ahead a few steps and then fall back a bit. His horse was balking. There were several hawkers, each with a hooded bird on his heavily gloved arm. Then came the priests and the important court officials: the members of the Witan and a large group of thanes. Finally came the stewards. They looked grim. It was probably the weather. The crowd was smaller now. Some people had run for shelter.

A middle-aged woman who was standing next to me with her two children looked at me with concern. "You'll catch your death standing out here," she said. For a moment I wondered why she thought I would catch my death but she wouldn't catch hers. Then I remembered what I looked like.

"It's all right, dear," I said, trying out my new voice. "If I see the king before I die I'll be happy." But I pulled my mantle further down over my forehead. I'd be in a pickle if my gipsywort started streaking.

Our attention was diverted by the arrival of about forty armed warriors. They were a fearsome looking bunch. Most carried spears that were taller than a man, and all had swords a yard long encased in scabbards at their sides. Some wore the scramasax, the dagger that gave us our name, around their necks. They used to smear these with poison in the old days but they're not used so much anymore. The warriors were clad in steel like the man I had seen in the forest. A few wore helmets—these ingenious devices extended down over their foreheads in front and ended with built-in eyebrows and nose guards. I spotted one man with a complete face mask: only his eyes were uncovered.

The men carried broad round wooden shields with decorated iron bosses in the middle. I noticed one huge warrior whose front teeth were missing. His shield was covered with deerskin and had an iron bar across it. The dome of his boss came to a cruel looking point and had probably poked out more than one man's eye.

In the midst of the warriors I saw a strange man, and when I saw him I realized he must be the fellow I had heard about the day I went to the monastery. He was young and very dirty and riding in a cart pulled by a donkey. He was surrounded by piles of bones, and he didn't look out at the town, the people, or anything. He seemed oblivious to the rain pelting down on him. He just sat there rearranging his bones.

After the warriors came King Beorhtric riding a horse with a braided mane. He wasn't armed, and he seemed merry. Gripping the bow of his saddle with one hand and the cantle with the other he pivoted his plump torso from side to side to wave at what remained of the crowd. He was the only person in the procession who didn't seem affected by the squall. On one side of the king rode a very fat brown-haired man, and every now and then he and the king would exchange a few words. On the king's other side was the queen, sitting very tall in her saddle, looking neither to one side nor the other. She had pulled her mantle forward against the rain, and I could hardly see her face.

Behind them rode a young man as beautiful as an ancient god. He had curly dark blond hair and an impressive straight nose. His upper lip was short, his mouth full. I had seen a face like his once on a coin I found in the woods. Edith told me the coin was left over from the days when the giants inhabited Winchester, before Christ drove them out. From the young man's regal bearing and his position in the procession,

I thought he must be the king's son, but it seemed hard to believe that someone who looked so refined could be this king's offspring. I asked the woman next to me who he was.

"That's Athelstan, the king's son, but not by this queen, by his first marriage," she said. So he was an atheling. I watched him until he turned into the palace gate, and his behavior fell somewhere in between that of the king and queen. He waved to the people like his father, but with reserve, like his stepmother.

After the prince came the high-ranking ladies who attended the queen. They huddled in their mantles against the rain and didn't put on much of a show. Next came a rowdy group of lads on foot, scuffling, joking, and slapping each other on the back. They were sons of thanes who had not yet been tried in war but were in training.

And finally, after these lads, came the servants. There were about 120 servants, I guess, and while their ranks and protocol were as clearly defined and well-known to them as that of the king and the court to the high-born, it was all a mystery to me. Luckily, the rain had caused considerable confusion. Most of the women were holding their mantles over their faces, and most of the men had put their cloaks up over their heads. I edged my way toward the street, obscuring my face with my mantle, and slipped into the group as it prepared to enter the palace grounds.

As we approached the palace hall my excitement became tinged with fear. I shivered. Perhaps it was my wet clothes. As I looked through the rain at the grandeur of that seemingly endless building, I wondered at my own boldness.

SCENE 9 THE PALACE

In spite of having lived in the area all my life, this trip inside the courtyard was the first time I had ever had an unobstructed view of the palace. Above the roof were golden turrets with boars and wolves snarling from their corners. Their gilded surfaces caught and intensified whatever dim light the turbulent skies were willing to cast down. The upper wall was shingled with carved wooden squares: light blue on the inside, bordered with crimson and edged with gold. At the center of each square was a small golden boss with an aggressive point. Intercepting these elaborate squares was an arching dark blue trim with sculpted griffins glowering from its interstices. Beneath the trim the wall was undecorated for a while, its plainness broken at intervals by two gilded strips. The bottom half of the wall repeated the same elaborate squares set on the diagonal to form diamonds.

Wide steps led to the hall's main entrance, its massive double doors reinforced with iron bands. The warriors and the thanes' sons entered there, then the doors were shut and barred. Two armed warriors stood on the top step to make sure they stayed that way. Another warrior restrained three ferocious-looking dogs, waiting until everyone was inside so he could release them to guard the courtyard.

As the procession broke up, the king's officials scurried off in different directions. The priests congregated together for a while and then walked to the minster that serves as the palace chapel. The servants stayed together until we reached the far end of the palace, where we split into groups. I wanted to work in the hall where I could observe the court, so I followed the group heading for a cobbled porch along its narrow end. The rest of the servants headed for the outbuildings.

We passed through a small pantry area, set off from the rest of the hall by a pillared cross passage. When we entered the main area I couldn't see much: the room was dim, the torches unlit, and what little light there was on this dull afternoon had to bend through the hall's high windows. I noticed the smell, a combination of damp wool and warriors' bodies mingled with the stale smoke of yesterday's fire.

I could see enough to make out that the hall was immense, a large rectangle with carved pillars separating some of the space into aisles. There seemed to be people everywhere. Not the royal family, though. They must have headed directly for their bowers. The warriors and the lads, who would normally have been playing games in the courtyard or creating disturbances in town, lounged about the hall because of the bad weather. The servants were immediately busy, weaving in and out among the warriors, beginning to prepare the hall for the evening feast. The strange man who had been in the cart with the bones was setting himself up in a corner. He had moved his bones into the hall, and I watched him arrange them in a circle around himself.

"You!" I heard a male voice bark. I looked around. The voice came from the center of the room, but all I could see was an enormous cauldron hanging from a rafter. Then I noticed that a very short man was standing next to it glaring in my direction. I wasn't sure he was talking to me.

"Who do you think I mean, your most illustrious Royal Highness?" said the little man, bowing deeply. His red face got even redder, making an interesting contrast, I thought, to his heavy black brows. He was holding a big stick in his right hand.

He stayed in the bow, but looked up. "If you could possibly spare a moment?" he said, frowning and jerking his head in the direction of some servants who were setting up trestle tables. I was pleased at how readily I was assumed to be a servant. I imagined gloating over it to Athelflad. I was so pleased, in fact, that I smiled at him. He slowly straightened up and stared at me.

"Is our beloved eminence all there?" he said. He tapped his head.

I ran over and grabbed one side of a table top. Each table was big enough for eight or ten people to eat around. They were heavy, much heavier than I expected, and we worked fast. We set up about fourteen tables.

"Now the head tables, children. Please, take your time. We have weeks and weeks," yelled the peculiar little man, leaning against a pillar and scratching his crotch. A bare-headed girl—probably a slave—with wide hips and a pock-marked face passed his command post on her way to get a table. He tip-toed behind her for few moments, pulling faces and silently panting. We placed three tables next to each other on the platform where the king and his party would sit.

"Benches! Benches, my handy helpers of the hall! Oh I do hope they aren't too heavy for you," said our boss at the top of his voice. "Are you having trouble with that, my dear boy?" He walked over to where one of the young servants was struggling to lift a heavy carved bench.

"Here, let me help, my sweet," he said. He followed behind the boy, singing a little song and striking him on the rear end with his stick in time to the music. The boy, bench and all, finally managed to get out of the little weasel's reach. The man went back to the center of the hall. "Anyone else need any help?" he called, contorting his nasty little face into a parody of benevolence.

A middle-aged woman placed a gold-embossed bench next to a table. As she passed him on her way back to the aisle to get another one he put out his stick and tripped her.

"Oh my poor dear," he said, as she got up. "You are clumsy, aren't you?" I was about to have a word with him when I saw that a few of the warriors had noticed what was going on. They wouldn't tolerate such behavior.

"Chairs!" he commanded. "Far aisle on your right." I passed him on my way to get one. He walked alongside me, putting one arm around my shoulders. "Are you happy here?" he asked, looking at me solicitously. "This isn't too much for you, is it?"

"It's all right so far," I said, trying out my new voice.

"Oh that is good news. Do let me know if there's anything I can do to help," he said, smiling at me pleasantly as he stomped his heel on my toe.

"You could get off my foot," I said.

"Was that you? Oh, I am sorry." I gave him a disgusted look. I was pleased to see that three or four of the warriors had stopped what they were doing and were staring at us. Surveillance by men of this rank would no doubt improve the despicable little man's conduct. He pointed across the hall to an elaborately carved claw-footed chair and, waving his hand in the direction of the head tables, said to me, "It goes there."

I strode over to the chair. Its high straight sides were covered by the carved torso of a beast—there was no place I could get a grip on it. My arms were not quite long enough to encircle it, and, strong as I was, I could barely lift it. I half-carried, half-dragged the heavy chair across the room. "Don't drag, it! Don't drag it, you idiot!" screamed the fellow when he noticed. "So stupid she drags the king's chair," he said to no one in particular.

With great difficulty I carried the chair the rest of the way and placed it where I remembered his pointing. "Not there—*there*!" he hollered.

I tried again. "There, there, *there*!" he thundered. "Is this your first time, sweetheart? I mean, in a king's hall?"

The watching warriors chuckled. The man looked at them. "Why me?" he said. "Why do they give me all the ones that are clumsy, half-dead, stupid, or all of the above?"

"TABLECLOOOTHS!" bellowed our boss. We laid the cloths. I incurred his disfavor again for not knowing that the head tables got two.

When one of the young girls bent over to straighten a cloth on one of the low tables I saw the little man come up behind her and, standing about a foot away, make thrusting movements with his hips. The warriors laughed.

"That Wermhere's a stitch." I heard one of them say, "Get over here, Erpwald, you'll miss it."

"Yeah," said another. "Never a dull moment. What did we used to do for fun before he came along?"

"Throw bones at Helmstan," said an enormous black haired warrior. They all laughed.

Wermhere sent some of us to the kitchen to get bowls and trenchers. I made a big effort to give him a wide berth, and so did everybody else. When I returned with a stack of bowls he danced over to me and grabbed a couple. He whipped a tablecloth off one of the low tables and put it over his head like a mantle, stuffing the bowls into his tunic and holding them in place with one hand. He sidled up to a boy who was placing trenchers on the tables and recited this bit of doggerel:

> The hawthorn is blooming
> My zeal is zooming
> Oh aren't you happy it's spring?
> Here's handy a hole
> Put in your Maypole
> And I'll dance around while you sing.

And so the afternoon progressed. Wermhere, egged on by the brutish warriors, never tired of his own jokes. But at last some higher ranking servants came in to set out knives and spoons, and the little dictator's behavior altered. He was subdued and deferential as the dish thane supervised the placing of silver goblets and the gold salt cellar. The warriors figured the fun was over and went back to their board games.

Two women servants left the hall and came back with firewood and aromatics. They set about preparing the fire on the hearth in the center of the room. Other servants filled the cauldron with chunks of pork and beef, chopped onions and leeks, spices and strong red wine. Several women stayed in the hall to attend to the cauldron and the warriors, while the rest of us were sent out to the kitchen.

Although we were not, strictly speaking, kitchen staff, in lulls between our hall duties we were expected to lend a hand to the cooks or the baker. When we got to the kitchen a cook was piercing a hole in the roof of a whooper swan's mouth. When she was finished she said, "Mince these," and pushed a pile of recently eviscerated entrails toward Wermhere. The cook went back to the swan, hanging it upside down to bleed, catching the drips in a pan.

"Cut the gut, you frank and friendly fairy," said Wermhere, pushing the entrails toward a shy thin-faced youngster. "Over here. Pound this beef," said another cook, taking a mallet off the wall.

"Beat the meat, you dim and dowdy dowager," said Wermhere to a self-effacing old woman named Mildred. She looked as if she were terrified she was going to be kicked, so of course he kicked her.

Another cook, who had been rubbing dried peas in a cloth, handed his job over to the pock-marked slave girl, and a boy was recruited to turn a spit. I began to wish I had once or twice entered the kitchen at home.

"Baker needs flour," a passing youngster shouted.

"You, my quaint queen of queers," said Wermhere. I looked behind me. He laughed. "You're a lot of fun, air head. What's your name, anyway?"

"What does it matter?" I said. "I've never heard you call anybody by their name."

The mallets, cleavers, and knives stopped. Wermhere looked at me for a second, and then decided to think this was the funniest thing he had ever heard. He laughed until he cried. He banged his little fists against the wall and repeated what I had said over and over. He gasped for air.

"Oh, that was a good one," he said, wiping his eyes. A few of the servants ventured tentative smiles. Wermhere took in a deep breath and whistled it out. He blew his nose loudly. He turned to me and was quiet for a moment. Then he said, "And if you ever sass me again I'll beat the shit out of you."

You and who else? I thought. I told him my name was Cynethrith. The name was common enough. There was no need to change it.

"But I say, Cynethrith, seriously, I'm sorry if we've given you the wrong impression. My dear Cynethrith, would you be so kind as to go to the storage cellar and take the baker four bags of flour, if you please?" said Wermhere.

Well, I thought, that's better. Some people just need to be stood up to. "Yes, of course," I said, wondering to myself where the cellar might be. As I passed Wermhere on my way out of the kitchen he gave me a sharp whack across the upper back with his stick.

"I meant what I said, tar-tooth."

I found the cellar and dragged the heavy sacks of flour to the baker. Then Wermhere told a tall skinny girl and me to gather strewing herbs and something decorative to put on the tables. The girl, who had a foreign accent, asked Wermhere how to avoid the dogs in the courtyard.

"Oh, right," said Wermhere, "the dogs. Maybe one of the cooks knows. Some of them have been here before. If not, throw them Cynethrith and run for it."

The girl questioned the cooks until she found a scullion who knew a back way out that by-passed the courtyard. Since both of us were new to the palace grounds we had to wander around in the drizzle for a while before we found a large patch of mint and enough sweet vernal grass to cover the floor. My companion, whose name was Tecla, was so shy that it almost seemed an affectation. Her skin was incredibly pale and her hair so blond it was practically white, even though she was young. After a while her curiosity got the better of her shyness, and she asked me how I came to be working at the palace. It was my first opportunity to try out my story.

"We were peasants," I said. "My sons died, and then my husband. I couldn't work the farm on my own, and the thane took it back."

"I'm sorry," she said. "What did they die of?"

"The fever," I said.

"All of them?" she said.

"Well, no. My youngest son got the fever, and my husband caught it from him. Then my older son broke his neck when he fell off a horse."

"Oh," she said. "I mean . . . it's just that I thought you said the sons died first."

"Well, they did," I said. "The son who fell off the horse was on his way to get the doctor for my husband." Bother!

There was a long pause before she said, "That's awful. But at least you're not a slave."

"How did you come to be here?" I asked. She said her family had lived far away, in a mountainous country across the sea, and pirates had sacked her village, killing her father and all her uncles. She and her mother and young brothers were sold into slavery.

We wandered around until we found some still flowering scabious and dried teasel heads for the table arrangements. We gathered fruiting hawthorn and sloe for filler.

"How long have you been with the king?" I asked.

"Two years," she said. Suddenly she seemed uneasy. "We'd better get back to the hall. Wermhere knows exactly how long any job should take, and heaven help you if you get on his bad side."

We went back into the hall, and I was relieved to notice that Wermhere and the warriors were elsewhere. I set to work spreading the herbs over the floor. When I looked up I noticed the guy in the corner with the bones looking at Tecla. Later I saw her exchanging a few words with him as she worked near his den. She came over to my side of the room. It had been a long day, and I was getting hungry, so I asked her when we would eat. She said the servants were always fed after the food was cleared from the hall. Then I thought of something. "Tecla," I asked, "what do you know about the weird guy with the bones?"

"He's not weird," she said, obviously upset. "And his name is Helmstan."

Oh God, I thought.

"I'm sorry, but haven't you been picked on enough in your life to know what it can do to a person?" She had tears in her eyes. "It isn't fair. It isn't right." The tears had spilled out onto her cheeks. "It was bad luck in my case, but King Beorhtric swore to Helmstan's father as a condition of the treaty that he would take care of his son. You see what his idea of care is."

"I'm sorry," I said. I put my arm around her. "I didn't realize," I wasn't sure what it was I didn't realize, but I knew enough to shut up.

Wermhere came in and hollered to us from the servants' entrance, "God's blood, are you still here? In the kitchen before I notice you."

Wermhere belted each of us as we passed him on our way to the kitchen. We ran. He followed, brandishing his stick. The kitchen was in a tizzy. I later found out later this was typical before the nightly meal. Wermhere lined up his servants in readiness to transport dishes of food to the hall. I was right behind the pock-marked girl. She had a platter of venison steaks, and I a platter of beef. I was glad there was someone in front of me that I could follow.

We stood there for what seemed like forever holding these heavy platters. It smelled wonderful. I felt weak from hunger. Wermhere stood beside the girl in front of me, caressing her neck. "Hmmm." he whispered, looking at her, "Good enough to eat." Then, getting his cue from heaven knows where, he said, "Now, you captivating kittens, out you go." He accompanied his command with a pat on my buttocks. I followed the girl in front of me over to the hall. We went into the servants' area and stood beneath the pillared passageway that created a visual, rather than a physical dividing line between aristocrat and servant. Torches had been lighted and set in their gold fittings around the walls. The fire blazed beneath the cauldron. It didn't look like the same room I had been in earlier.

High on the walls the light sparkled off antique gold shields and swords that had belonged to the early heroes. Above the shields, between the high shuttered windows, massive antlers of savage beasts glowed white against the wall. My eye was drawn back down by shimmering wall hangings, worked in gold and encrusted with jewels and pearls. They told stories of ancient champions. I could see one behind the king's dais that showed how Tyr tricked Fenrir the wolf into his fetters and another that showed Christ leading his warriors against the giants.

A gold embroidered bolster had been placed on the king's chair, and elaborately worked cushions adorned the benches of the head table. Silver bowls held arrangements of the flowers and fruits Tecla and I had picked. Goblets and knives gleamed on the table. Everywhere I looked I saw sparkle, shine, shimmer.

The warriors slowly began to come in. Their armor had been left to the sides of the hall in the aisles, and they were dressed as any group of rich thanes might be, in costly tunics dyed brilliant shades of red, blue, or green and trimmed with burnished metallic braids. I spotted one of the warriors who had enjoyed Wermhere's antics: he was a big, black-haired lout. He had trimmed his beard, and his cloak was fastened with a gold brooch large enough to feed the village of Easton for a year.

The room filled with thanes. Some beautifully dressed ladies appeared as well. I spotted some of the nobles coming in, and a few priests. I began to wonder if I were going to have to stand and hold this platter for the rest of the night. The thanes and ladies all milled around until a smartly dressed man came in and blew on a large horn. All was silent. It was the royal party.

*SCENE* 10 A NIGHT AT COURT

First came the king, all jovial, waving and smiling as he entered the hall with the queen, who trailed a magnificent dark red mantle embroidered in gold around its edges. She stood so straight and moved so smoothly that she looked like a carved goddess being wheeled in. Walking behind the plump king was the even fatter man he'd been chatting with as they rode in the procession—I found out later his name was Warr. On the other side of Warr I glimpsed the handsome atheling. The king stopped to chat with the warrior wearing the large brooch, who, along with a couple of his crass friends, had positioned himself near the king's entrance to the hall.

"Good evening, Your Majesty," the warrior said, bowing to Beorhtric. He turned to the queen. "Your Royal Highness," he bowed from the waist, but his eyes remained on Odburh's face. She looked right through him.

"Good evening, Badanoth," said the king, laughing and shaking his head. "Good looking brooch you got there."

"Thank you, sire. It was a gift from a lover," said Badanoth. He smiled, leered almost. Did I imagine it, or did the queen, stiff to begin with, stiffen a bit more?

"Great, great," said Beorhtric. "I'm all in favor of lovers." The king turned to one of Badanoth's friends, "Hunting's supposed to be good around here, Thingfrith," he said, and then he clapped the third member of the group on the back. "Hope you won't bag all the boars before I get a crack at one, Unferth."

Something distracted Beorhtric. He turned from the warriors and left the queen on her own, where she stood looking stranded. The king walked between the rows of tables to greet a handsome young thane who was flirting with a lady. Badanoth turned toward Odburh, but Athelstan, the atheling, quickly moved between them.

Now that the people were used to the king's presence their voices were no longer hushed, and I couldn't hear what Athelstan was saying to the queen. I watched him put an arm around her in greeting and then stand back with a smile as if to appraise her appearance. Beneath her mantle she wore a floor-length gown of white silk and a shorter pale blue tunic, trimmed down the front and around the hem with gold, garnets and pearls. He lifted the cloak forward on her shoulders a little and adjusted the wide gold cord that held it in place. He rearranged the drape of her veil. Its fine white silk covered her forehead down to her eyebrows and draped in soft folds next to her cheeks. Under her chin it formed a small cowl. Odburh seemed to lose some of her iciness in the warmth of Athelstan's attention. He had a wide smile and beautiful even white teeth.

Meanwhile, Beorhtric and the lad he was talking to had been joined by Warr, who was so fat he had to turn sideways to walk between the tables. The king must have told a joke because he punched the boy's arm in a friendly manner, and he and Warr laughed loudly. The girl and the lad blushed and smiled.

The king made the rounds of the tables, followed by Warr who lumbered along scraping the backs of the seated people with his belly. Beorhtric greeted individual guests with great enthusiasm, and then he returned to the queen.

"My love," he said as he picked up Odburh's hand and placed it on his arm again. He looked at Athelstan gratefully. The king led the queen to the head table where he took his place at its center, with Odburh on his left. As soon as they sat, two thanes with embroidered linen cloths draped over their shoulders approached, each carrying a gold ewer and basin. One basin was placed in front of the king, and one in front of the queen. Each thane poured a little water from his pitcher into a cup and tasted it before pouring the rest into the basin. While the royal couple washed their hands, the rest of the court cued for the ewery along the side wall.

The most important members of the court washed first and took their places at the head table. Warr sat next to the king. Athelstan next to the queen. The Bishop sat on the other side of Warr, and the rest of the seats were filled with Odburh's attendants and Beorhtric's champions. Unferth had pride of place next to the Bishop, followed by Badanoth, Erpwald, Thingfrith, and Werwulf.

When everyone else had washed and was seated, the bishop said a prayer and gave a speech welcoming the royal party to Winchester. He prattled on long enough to irritate the hungry court, but the king's smile never wavered. When the bishop was finally finished Beorhtric thanked him profusely and said he had been moved beyond belief.

At a signal from one of the higher ranking servants two boys passed the spot where the pock-marked girl and I were waiting with our platters and handed over a roe deer suspended from a pole. It was ceremoniously carved in front of the guests at the high table. Next Tecla brought in the swan we had seen the cook working on. The bird had been roasted and redressed in its feathers and was accompanied by a special sauce. This was presented to the king. At last some well-dressed servants came and wordlessly took the plates of meat. After the king and the head table were served these were placed on one of the lower tables.

It soon became apparent to me that during feasts the servants who worked for Wermhere were not allowed out of the servants' area. Later I learned that once the king left the hall we would be sent in to help with the clearing up, but for the time being we were kept busy ferrying vast amounts of food between the kitchen and the hall.

Each diner ate according to his station, with the best dishes and the greatest amount reserved for the head table. The hall servants dished out stew from the cauldron and placed one bowl between each foursome at the low tables. I carried in a large dish of two dozen young pigeons for a mid-ranking table, the birds culled before they learned to fly so their flesh was fat and succulent. There was roasted quail for the high table—a great favorite with the obese Warr who, I noticed, ate several all by himself. A middle table was given rolls of beef stuffed with parsley, egg yolk and suet, in a sauce of vinegar and verjuice. After a while I couldn't keep track of who got what. I saw chicken eggs and duck eggs and birds of all sorts: crane, curlew, plover, lapwing, greenfinch. Dish followed dish of vegetables: salads of fennel, borage, and garlic dressed in oil and vinegar, buttered parsnips, boiled burdock, shredded cabbage, charlock and legumes, boiled leaves of bladder campion. Condiments weren't lacking: there were dittander and pennyroyal, pickled black mustard, sliced leeks and onions, watercress. We carried stacks and stacks of wheat cakes cooked in honey. Later we were sent in with elderberry tarts, sweet cheese flan, hazel nuts, dried plums and spiced apples. Wine and mead flowed.

After the food was brought in we stood by to take the empty dishes back to the kitchen. I began to understand why it was called waiting on table. In between courses there was music: horns, trumpets, pipes, and rebecs, and jugglers as well. One of them was thrilling to watch—every now and then he would throw one of his spinning sticks so high into the rafters that I thought it would never come down again. I wondered what would happen if he missed his catch, but he never did. I saw the queen get up from the head table and summon the cup filler. He brought her a gold flagon, and she served wine, first to the king and then to the guests.

She smiled in a dignified way as she poured, quite proper for a queen, but once I saw her put her arm around the shoulders of a handsome young warrior. When she got to Badanoth he grabbed her wrist in a playful manner, and she gave him an indulgent smile. She must have run out of wine just then—at least that was what I thought at the time—because she summoned the cup filler for a new flagon before she filled his cup.

As the evening wore on and more wine and mead were consumed, the talking and the laughter got louder. Suddenly, apparently from out of nowhere, a Fool appeared. He was very little—smaller even than Wermhere. He had short arms and a very big head and was dressed in a tiny warrior's costume. He held a shield and a spear with a blown up pig's bladder tied to one end.

He darted around the room helter skelter like a bumble bee in a hut, only stopping to pop unwary people with the bladder. "Who's fool enough to think a contest with me would be fooling around?" he shouted in his high, squeaky voice. The warriors found this a good joke, and the older ones egged the younger ones on.

"Here's your chance to prove your manhood. How about it, Oswulf?"

Oswulf's friends began to push him toward the dwarf. Oswulf fought them off and gripped the bench with his arms and legs so he couldn't be lifted.

"Oooh, he's no fool, he's scared to fight me," taunted the Fool. He went over to the head table and bowed deeply to the king.

"Your Majesty, are you a fool?"

"No," laughed the king, "you're the fool."

"How can you tell?" said the fool.

"You're small like a fool, you boast like a fool, and you've got a fool's balloon."

"And by these reasonings, sire, you think I am a fool?"

"Yes."

"With all due respect, you, sire, are the fool."

"How is this, my little man?"

"A man who reasons with a fool must be a fool."

The king laughed and laughed, turning to Warr to share the joke. Warr laughed as well and grabbed the Fool's bladder and hit him with it. The king laughed even harder and made a gesture to his cup filler to refill their cups.

Meanwhile Badanoth was trying to find a champion to set against the Fool. "Forget Oswulf," he shouted. "How about Athelwulf?" Athelwulf leapt up and bolted out of the room through the servant's entrance before anyone could touch him.

The dwarf jumped onto one of the tables and walked along it until he came to an attractive woman, the daughter of a thane. "When I get rid of all you guys I'll have this beautiful lady," he said, jumping down and putting his little arms around her neck. "Want to fool around, sweetheart?"

"No, thanks," said the woman, "I've had enough fools already."

"Athelwulf's obviously terrified," said Unferth. "I know, how about Helmstan?"

"Yeah, Helmstan can fight him," said Badanoth.

All the champions seemed to think pitting the bone man against the fool was a good idea. The chant went up: "Helmstan. Helmstan."

The king nodded and laughed. "Show us what you can do, Helmstan," he said.

Helmstan had sunk beneath his wall of bones. I couldn't even see him. When his name was mentioned Tecla had come up next to me to get a better view, and now I felt her hand grip my arm.

Thingfrith and Unferth walked over to Helmstan's bone fortress. Each grabbed one of Helmstan's arms, and they lifted him out. Helmstan looked wild-eyed, even deranged.

"Is this my challenger?" said the dwarf, looking at Helmstan, who was so dirty that his fair skin looked black. Thingfrith and Unferth held the terrified Helmstan up on either side. The Fool jumped up upon a bench and made a low bow. "Your Majesty, Your Royal Highness, Bishop, ladies and thanes, warriors of the kingdom, this contest will settle a question that's been plaguing mankind since the beginning of time: Who's a bigger menace, a fool or a madman?"

"I'll put my money on the Fool," said Badanoth. A few moments passed while the men wagered on the outcome of the fight.

"Now," the Fool said to Thingfrith and Unferth, "you must release the warrior so he can fight." The Fool threw Helmstan a sword. "I may be mad, as well as a fool, but you may strike the first blow."

Helmstan struck at the Fool, and the Fool jumped neatly out of the way and made a face. The Fool began a game of chase. He darted around the hall, almost quicker than the eye could see. Helmstan seemed confused, but he pursued the Fool nevertheless. "Are you a fool?" the fool called to Helmstan.

"No," said Helmstan.

"Are you after a fool?" shouted the fool.

"Yes," yelled Helmstan.

"Then you're less than a fool," said the dwarf.

When he had managed to get two tables between himself and Helmstan, the Fool stopped for a moment and stood between two seated warriors, sticking his head between their shoulders. "Pass me the horn," he said, and when they did he drained it. "It's been a lovely evening," he said, "but only a fool drinks more than he can hold." He looked from one to the other of the warriors he was between. "Maybe you should leave now."

The Fool darted under a table, and the guests sitting around it peered under the cloth to see where he had gone. He had disappeared. A search began, with all the thanes and ladies milling about, looking under the tables and behind the tapestries. Unferth even looked inside the cauldron. They were about to give up and attribute it to witchcraft when Werwulf, one of the warriors, pointed to a fat woman's bulging backside.

"She's looking more voluptuous than ever," hollered Warr, noticing where Werwulf was pointing. The bulge seemed to get bigger and bigger, and more and more of the people were laughing and pointing.

"What are you laughing at?" the woman asked no one in particular, her face red. She tried to look behind her, which made the guests laugh all the more. As she turned in her awkward way, each time more quickly, the bulge turned with her. Her mantle flared out in back, and she looked like a top tottering near the end of its spin. Between spins the little rogue would stick his head out from under her skirt and make a face at the crowd.

When everyone had laughed as hard and as long as they could, the little fellow popped out and bowed to the astonished woman, "I salute women's legs," he said. "You come into this world between woman's legs, and you go out of this world between woman's legs." Then he spotted Helmstan, and said to the woman, "Dear madam, I love your butt, I mean, I love you but, alas, we can go around together no longer. I must fight, for I am a fool." Helmstan and he resumed their comic dance, Helmstan striking and the Fool jumping this way and that, hiding behind a lady or leaping onto a table or bench. Finally Helmstan got close and thrust his sword at the Fool, and the Fool raised his shield to catch the blow. By some trick of the Fool's, when Helmstan's weapon touched the shield his sword bent in half. The warriors practically collapsed laughing.

"And now I bet you're really mad," said the Fool to Helmstan. "Bad luck." The dwarf tossed Helmstan another sword. "Have a go with this one."

Helmstan struck at the Fool again. This time the sword stuck in the Fool's shield and wouldn't come out. I heard a loud guffaw from the king and looked over at the head table. The queen was smiling, but she looked as if she were thinking about something else. Helmstan pulled and pulled, finally wresting the sword and its attached shield out of the Fool's hands. "Madder than ever," screamed the Fool.

Helmstan had had enough. He held the shield over his head and started back to his bone fortress. A single bone, a remnant from dinner, came sailing through the air and bounced off the shield with a loud bing. Another bone soon followed, and Helmstan began to walk faster. Soon the entire hall seemed to be filled with flying bones. Some of the ladies ducked under the tables for cover, and the servants who were attending the tables retired to the sides of the hall. I wondered what the king would do. I looked over at him, and he was sitting at the head table, chatting with Warr as if nothing had happened. The queen still looked as if her thoughts were elsewhere. Athelstan, a grim look on his face, got up and left.

Helmstan ran back to what he seemed to feel was his island of safety and hid behind his bone walls, and that was the last I saw of the night's activities in the hall because one of the servants came in and told us we could go to the kitchen and eat now. I was so hungry that as we filed out of the hall I forgot all about the drama going on there.

When we got to the kitchen I looked for our food, but there was nothing—only refuse from the feast.

"Where's our food?" I asked Tecla.

She looked at me in surprise, and she didn't say anything. I watched as each servant went in turn over to a pile of soggy trenchers and took a couple. They found a place to sit on the ground near the kitchen and began to eat.

"That's it?" I said. I couldn't quite grasp that our meal consisted of the gravy soaked bread that had served as the guests' plates.

"That's it," said Tecla.

I briefly wondered what our servants at home were given to eat, then I thought about my own dilemma. I was starving, and I was also repulsed at the idea of eating what was on offer. I searched through the stack trying to find a good one.

"Is the cuisine not to Her Royal Highness' liking?" I heard Wermhere snort.

When I found a trencher that looked reasonably untouched I sat by myself in a corner, biting off small bits and chewing until my jaws ached to soften it. I discovered that a trencher that hadn't been soaked in someone else's gravy was as palatable as a wooden saddle. I could feel the seeds in my mouth becoming dislodged.

Tecla came and sat next to me. "You'll get used to it in a day or two," she whispered.

I averted my head when I answered her so she wouldn't notice my bad teeth had rearranged themselves. "It's not so bad," I lied.

It wasn't the only thing I had to get used to. After we ate, we helped wash up in the kitchen while we waited for the king to leave the hall, and then we were sent to prepare it for the night. The warriors were drunker than ever and singing by this time, but at least Wermhere didn't seem to have the energy for his earlier antics. We stripped off the tablecloths and disassembled all the tables. Tecla and I worked together, and she was even quieter than usual. I thought perhaps she was as tired as I was, but then I noticed her eye kept returning to the bone hovel where Helmstan lived. After we moved a table back to the side aisle near his fortress Tecla, furtively keeping an eye on Wermhere, made a small detour to look in on Helmstan. I don't know what they said to each other—it couldn't have been much because the whole transaction took place in the twinkling of an eye—but she looked relieved and was smiling as we started to haul the heavy benches.

"He's alive," she said to me. "He didn't get hit too badly, thank God."

We swept up the rushes and litter. After an area was cleared we had to drag in sleeping pallets for the warriors, most of whom slept in the hall. By this time I was completely exhausted. Fog seemed to fill my brain. I felt as if I were moving through a haze dense enough to feel. My legs and my lower back hurt from standing for so long. My upper back hurt from where Wermhere had whacked me. My arms hurt from holding heavy platters, and my shoulders hurt from lifting tables and benches. But at last we were finished. I couldn't wait to sink into my bed.

"Where do we sleep?" I asked Tecla, as we stood in the servants area.

"Right here," she said. I didn't see any beds.

"Where?" I asked.

"Wherever you like," she answered. She lay down on the floor, pulling her mantle around her.

"Good night," she said, yawning. "It won't seem so bad in a week or so. The first day's the worst."

"Tecla," I said, trying to get comfortable on the floor, "doesn't it worry you sleeping so close to the warriors?" I was glad I had a knife strapped to my thigh.

"Not when they've had this much to drink," she said. "Get some rest."

"All right," I said. "Good night."

As tired as I was, I didn't sleep well that night. The floor was hard and cold. My mantle made a coarse sheet. I felt a little nauseated from the memory of what I'd eaten for dinner, and the feeling wasn't helped by the air, heavy with the smells of cooked food, smoke, wine, and the drunken breath of snoring warriors. When I slept, fitfully, I dreamt I was attending a concert in hell. I awakened once thinking I'd heard a scream. I thought about leaving, of course, but a vision of the rest of my life confined in a convent loomed before me. Without that, I would have taken my chances with the dogs in the courtyard and run for it.

*SCENE* II BADANOTH'S FUNERAL FEAST

The next morning the palace was in an uproar. Badanoth had died in the night. His massive body was stiff and contorted, each limb locked in a position at odds with the next. His beefy face was all askew. The warriors were uneasy. They thought only an evil spirit could have been strong enough to overcome Badanoth, and they were sure he must have been bewitched not to shout for help. He was laid out in the hall so he could enjoy the funeral feast that was to be held that night.

There was a lot of gossip swirling around as the servants prepared for the feast. As I stood at my station that night I remembered what the villagers had said about the queen the evening we hatched the plan to hide our wealth, and then there was her reaction to Badanoth the night before—and seeing her switch pitchers when she served him. I wished I had noticed whether or not she had switched them again before she served the next person. I couldn't be sure, of course, but I began to wonder if Her Highness had something to do with this mysterious death.

After food had been placed on the tables and most of the serious eating was over, the men took it in turn to stand up and drink to the dead man, starting with the king, who greatly lamented the loss of one of his fiercest warriors.

"Badanoth," said the king, extending his arm in the direction of the corpse, "this loyal man. This brave warrior." He paused for a long moment. "He fought by my side for twelve years. I had no better friend. No one punished the enemy more severely than he. I'm sure all would agree that he earned his place in the mead hall."

The men shook their heads in agreement. There was no disagreement about Badanoth's ferocity on the field.

"He was my greatest fighter, a good companion. His name will live on as long as men fight and kings have halls. This man had so many outstanding qualities—I don't know where to begin to praise him. He fought like a champion. He drank like a champion. He played like a champion. When things got tough, he kept our spirits up with his jokes and pranks."

The warriors—at least the ones in Beorhtric's inner circle—nodded their agreement.

The king looked at them. "There were so many over the years, weren't there?"

"Remember the Isle of Wight?" said Werwulf.

"Who could forget it?" said the king. "For those of you who weren't with us, this goes back a ways, this was the campaign on Wight—how many years ago was it? Ten? Eleven? Ten? Ten. We had just creamed a large tribe of Jutes—"

"Just destroyed them," put in Unferth.

"—and captured their chief," said the king. "You had a hand in that, didn't you, Werwulf?"

Werwulf nodded, "And Thingfrith."

"And Badanoth," said Werwulf and Thingfrith together.

"Of course, let's not forget Badanoth," said the king, looking at the dead man who seemed to leer back. "As I was saying, we captured this chief. He just couldn't believe we caught him. The guy had this ancient scramasax around his neck. I've still got it somewhere. You know where it is, Odburh?"

Odburh shook her head. She looked bored. "So he thought nobody could take him because this weapon was so great, with all these bronze and silver whatzits, and the whole runic alphabet on the back." The king smirked. "So when we surrounded him his eyes kind of popped out like he ate too many onions." The king imitated the bug-eyed chief. "Well, we got this chief back to the camp—he was too stunned to give us any trouble—and settled him down for the night. Then Badanoth sneaks over to the cook—he didn't say a word to me about it—and tells him he's got a special seasoning for the guy's food."

Thingfrith started to laugh in anticipation. "So," said the king, "so, he put—" the king had to stop because he was laughing so hard, "—so he put I don't know how much flax seed in the guy's food—and it was the night before he and I were supposed to negotiate."

Werwulf and Unferth were laughing their heads off. Athelstan looked disgusted. "You should have seen that chief squirm during our talks," said the king. "I didn't know what the problem was. Every now and then Badanoth would look at him in all seriousness and ask him if he was all right. After a while I could see Badanoth was trying not to break up, and I started to lose it. So I started clearing my throat. Uhrher, uhrher, uhrhrhrhrh. After I cleared my throat about twelve times Badanoth just couldn't hold it in anymore—"

"Neither could the chief," interjected Werwulf.

"Badanoth started laughing so hard he doubled over and had to crawl out of the meeting."

It was hard to hear this last bit over the guffaws of the king's champions. When it quieted down the king took a deep breath and said. "I probably don't have to tell you who came out on top in those negotiations."

The king gave the court a moment to appreciate the story. Some laughed, but none as hard as those at the head table. Some smiled politely. A few looked disgusted. Then he went on. "He had a lot of other good qualities, besides his sense of humor. He was a generous man, always giving things away. When he got a new sword he always gave his old one to one of the boys—even if it was only a little rusted. Not everybody knew this, but he had a wealthy lover—yes, Badanoth. He had his softer side."

"The stories that man could tell!" said Werwulf. "The broad must have been hotter than a plowshare before an ordeal."

Unferth and Thingfrith poked each other. They must have heard the stories too.

"What about the gifts she gave him?" said Unferth.

"You wouldn't believe them," said the king, "Jewelled brooches and gold. He was too much the gentleman to tell us who she was, but at least we know she appreciated him. But the man was a true Christian. He never kept these treasures for himself. He gave them out to the poor slave girls in the hall."

The queen, who had been nibbling on the last of her meal, choked on something. Several of her maidens rushed to attend her.

"Are you all right, my love?" said the king.

The queen, still coughing a little, rose from her seat. "Please excuse me, Your Majesty," she said, making a beautiful curtsy to the king. "This sad occasion has weakened my constitution." She left the hall. Two ladies supported her, one on either side. A third walked behind.

"Yes," summed up the king, "no one knows how great a man he was better than I. It's impossible that an evil spirit killed him." There was some muttering. I don't think the men agreed with him on this.

The king persisted. "If it had been an evil spirit, he would have overthrown it." More noise in the hall. The men seemed to be debating among themselves whether or not this was so.

"No," said the king, emphatically. "Only my friend could have vanquished my friend, and if you think about it for a while you'll realize I'm right. He was great in all things: in war, in jest, in love, and even, alas, in appetite. He liked his food and drink too well. My physician assures me this paragon of our court died of indigestion. Let us drink to his memory."

After the horn was passed round, the oldest councilor of the court had the honor to toast next. He rose unsteadily to his feet. He couldn't stand erect, and his wine cup shook in his hand.

"It is sad," he said in a flat voice, "so sad to lose a warrior in the prime of his life. A young man and a good Christian. To lose one so pious and devoted to the Christian faith is a great loss indeed."

I began to wonder if the man knew who Badanoth was.

"I love Christ as much as any man," he went on. "We have Him to thank that the giants were vanquished, and I know it as well as you do, but the way we plant warriors in the ground like cabbages is an insult to their manhood. Who here remembers the old way?"

A few heads nodded among the older warriors. Some listened respectfully. Unferth yawned and summoned the cup filler.

The old man went on, "Up north when I was a boy a man was sent to paradise like a man, on a great pyre of burning wood—"

"That's right," piped up a wizened little fellow, apparently awakening from a little after dinner snooze.

"—with the smoke going up first to announce he was coming," said the councilor, "When our chief died in battle we worked for days cutting birch and made a frame as high as a cathedral, and we stacked wood all around it—"

"Then they'd go and get his ship," said the wizened one. The right side of his face didn't move when he talked, so all his words had to come out of half of his mouth, garbling his speech.

"Not yet—I haven't got to that part. The people brought food for a great feast, which we ate right next to where he was laid out—at least that hasn't changed—"

"—they'd lay them out in the middle of the camp, under silk awnings, so they could hear the toasts," added the other.

The councilor frowned at the wizened little man. "Stop interrupting, will you? I'm losing my train of thought. Where was I?"

"The feast," prompted Oswulf, one of the more civilized warriors.

"Right. The dead man bought the drink and there was plenty of it: it cost him a third of all he owned."

"And the men got on horses and rode around the corpse," put in the one who kept interrupting.

"Nobody rode around anybody. What are you talking about?" asked the councilor. The cup in his hand was shaking so much that the wine splashed over its brim. "He's not as old as me, and he's getting senile." He directed his next comment to his opponent "After the feasting and the speeches, when we were ready to burn him, then we got the ship." The councilor returned his attention to the assembly. "Next we gave him to the Angel of Death to dress."

"They were usually black by this time," put in the wizened one.

The councilor decided to ignore him. "She dressed him in beautiful clothes. She had made him silk breeches and a shirt and a brocaded tunic with buttons of gold. His cape had a hood lined with sable. She covered a bench on the ship with silk rugs and cushions and laid him on it. We covered him with gold and silver and steel."

"They put steel on them if they were conquerors, and gold and silver for the riches they brought to their people," added the other.

The councilor tried to talk faster. "We gave him liquor. We gave him food: bread and fruit, meat and leeks and a cauldron to cook them in. We put in his standard and his weapons: his shield, his sword, his belt. We placed his armor next to him. We dragged the ship onto the frame. His brother lit the fire. His wife died of grief so we put her on as well." Unfortunately, he had to pause for breath.

"It was usually a slave." said the other one. "They usually got some girl to volunteer while the guy was still alive, so she'd get an easier life." The councilor was shaking his head in disagreement. His legs, almost as palsied as his arms, joined in the dance. Wine splashed as high as his face.

The wizened one kept talking, "Then when the man died, they treated her real good and told her she would be in Paradise sooner than anybody."

"Not so. I never heard of anything like that," said the councilor. He was so stooped and shaking so much that he looked as if he were about to topple forward. Oswulf came up behind him to support him.

The wizened man talked louder. "It was so." He stood up. His right eye, imprisoned on the immobile side of his face, was watering. A drop rolled down to the middle of his sunken cheekbone. He used his useless right arm like a duster, grabbing its elbow with his good hand and swiping at the seepage on his face. "When they were ready to burn the man the Angel of Death would gather the six most important men in a tent and take the girl there. The other men stood around the tent and beat on their shields to drown out the screams."

The councilor elbowed Oswulf, who had grabbed him under the

armpits to keep him erect. "It took six men to kill one defenseless girl? What heroism!"

"No, you backward son of a retard," explained the other. "The six men weren't there to kill her. They were there to make love to her."

The councilor, clenching his shaking fists, shuffled as quickly as he could in the direction of his nemesis. Athelwulf stood up and intervened, laying a restraining hand on the old man's arm.

"Wait just a minute here, you cast off skin of a lizard," fumed the old councilor. "Your filthy imagination's getting the better of you. How could anybody—even from your part of the country—be low enough to make love to a girl who's about to be murdered?"

"It was a sacred duty," answered the wizened one, injecting as much dignity as he could into his skewed delivery, "and I'll thank you not to call names, especially when you don't know what you're talking about." The eye on the plastic side of his face spewed fire. The other eye looked strangely uninvolved. "They did it—"

"Didn't, if they were men," snapped the councilor.

"They did it to show their love to the dead man. The girl was completely unimportant, you stupid sod. It had nothing to do with her. Each man said to her, 'Tell your master I did this out of love for him.'"

"I've heard of people talking out of both sides of their mouth, but you can't even tell the truth talking out of one. The women never would have allowed such a thing," the councilor insisted.

"I know what I saw, you dottering old pansy," said his antagonist. "It wasn't one of their own. It was a foreign slave. Why should they care? And the slave volunteered, if you're capable of remembering what I said earlier. She got a pretty cushy life until the old boy stopped a sword."

"What happened next?" hollered Werwulf. The story was gruesome enough to hold his attention.

"The Angel wrapped a cord around the girl's neck and gave each end to a man. While they strangled her the Angel of Death slipped a knife in and out between the girl's ribs. Then they burned her with the man."

"That's sickening," said the councilor "I never saw anything like that. There was nothing like that when we burned our chief. His wife was already dead when she went with him. She wasn't blackmailed into it. There was nothing disgusting about it, and it was a lot better than rotting in the ground, God forgive me." He crossed himself.

The other man, lost in memories, wasn't angry anymore. "Remember how the village used to stink for a week afterwards?" he asked.

The councilor wasn't yet ready to be pacified. "It didn't stink. The fire was so hot it burned up the smell. Everything was purified." He, too, began to reminisce. "When the flames reached the chief he twisted around and heaved up. I thought he had come back to life. Then the blood spurted out of his wounds like water out of a whale. Soon there was nothing but ashes and dust, and our lord was in Paradise."

"That's the way to send off a warrior," agreed the other.

At a nudge from Warr the king quickly got to his feet, thanked the councilor for his speech, and passed the horn. The old man shuffled over to sit next to the man he had been arguing with and they drank, talked and disagreed for the rest of the night.

The speeches went on and on. Unferth, and Thingfrith were the next to talk. Unferth praised Badanoth's craftiness. He told about the time Badanoth bet a rival champion a gold-plated drinking horn he could kill a pig without its making a sound. When the rival challenged Badanoth to show how, Badanoth cut out the pig's squealer and then killed it. Thingfrith recalled the night Badanoth had gotten the hilarious idea of throwing bones at Helmstan. He dragged Helmstan up to say a few words, and when he refused, made him walk back to his bone fortress with a trencher on his head while the champions threw bones at him. If Helmstan dropped the trencher Unferth would make him start over from the king's dais.

Werwulf, who was very drunk, told about Badanoth's clever way of getting rid of lovers he was tired of. He chewed garlic before visiting them. "He used to tell me it saved a lot of talking," he said.

The later speakers, none of whom sat at the head table, confined themselves to praising Badanoth's prowess in war. The drinking and toasting went on until nearly daybreak. Anything that could have been said about Badanoth was, at least twice. The king, who was so drunk he slurred his words, summed it up at the end. "We loved that guy," he said. He shook his head. His eyes watered, and he blew his nose on the tablecloth.

In due course Badanoth was buried. After a few days things settled down.

SCENE 12 THE MYSTERIOUS STRANGER COMES TO COURT

I was learning the palace routine. In the mornings after Mass we helped the kitchen prepare supplies for the day. Most days, if the weather was fair, or if it was cloudy but not raining, the men of the court, accompanied by the more athletic women, went out to hunt. The king went with them unless he'd had too much to drink the night before. Once the hunters were taken care of we were sent to clean the hall. First we swept, dusted, and polished. On alternate days the floor had to be scrubbed.

On one scrubbing day Wermhere sent us off to get buckets and brushes and when we reassembled assigned us sections of the floor. Except for me: he forgot to give me one. I stood on the sidelines and watched as everyone else got down on their hands and knees and started scrubbing. Wermhere took up a position over the pock-marked girl, his short legs straddling her wide hips as she crawled along the floor. Finally he noticed me standing motionless. He clamped his legs around her so she couldn't creep away.

"What's the matter with you?" he asked.

"You forgot to give me a section," I said.

"I forgot to give you a section," he said. "How is it possible I could forget such a vision of womanly perfection? All right, take the part behind the tapestries. Just don't go to sleep back there." He went back to standing astride the girl, reciting as he walked.

> There was a young lady from Bath
> Whose purse tumbled onto my path
> I snatched it up quick
> And then used my stick
> On the lovely young lady from Bath.

I could still hear Wermhere reciting his doggerel while I worked behind one of the tapestries, concealed from view. Since I could tell from his voice that he was nowhere near me it occurred to me that I could take a break. I got up off my knees, straightened out my body, leaned against the wall and shut my eyes. I put my arms over my head and stretched. I stepped away from the wall and rolled my shoulders and my head around. Then I leaned back again and exhaled. I took heart from this little rest. I reminded myself why I had come to the palace, and I steeled myself to put up with my abysmal life until I accomplished two things.

First, I needed to figure out who might be a possible ally against my stepmother—in the assembled royal court of Wessex there had to be somebody who had heard of my mother and would be willing to fight for the daughter of one of Wulf's archers, especially when there was lots of money involved. I had to admit there were far more boors at the court than I had anticipated, but there were quieter thanes—Athelwulf, Oswulf, and some of the others who sat at the second highest table, for example—who seemed decent enough.

Second, because of the backward upbringing I had received from my stepmother, I needed to stay until I learned enough about court protocol to be able to approach this person in the proper way.

In spite of everything, it was worth a try. I went back to scrubbing in a happier frame of mind.

Later that afternoon I was sent outside to polish the doors to the main entrance. It was a dry day, but overcast and dull. Erpwald and Thingfrith had been posted on guard duty and were right in front of me. Erpwald was buffing the metal rim on his shield with a chamois while Thingfrith leaned against the stone stairs and stared across the courtyard. As much as I disliked Beorhtric's feral warriors, I realized that these two were the only barrier between me and the dogs, and I was glad they were there.

When I was almost finished and about to go inside, Thingfrith stood up and looked in the direction of the gates. I glanced to see what had caught his attention and saw a warrior coming through on horseback. Erpwald stopped polishing his shield.

The stranger riding toward us was tall and armed to the teeth. His head and face were covered with a boar-crested gold helmet, his torso sheathed in mail. He carried a large shield and a spear, and I could see a sword and an ax suspended from his belt as well. The sun suddenly broke out from behind the clouds for a moment, and the brilliance reflected from all that metal dazzled my eyes. When the sun went back in and I could see again I recognized the horse by its unusual mane. It was one of the horses I had seen at that inexplicable camp in the woods. I got goose bumps on my right leg from the knee down as I realized who must be hidden under that helmet. Had he seen me after all? Had he tracked me here? I imagined him by-passing the guards and grabbing me by the front of my dress.

*"This woman spied on my camp,"* he would say.

*"Is that all you want?"* the guard would say. *"Take her."*

*"No, no," I would yell as the man dragged me off. "My grandfather was a thane. You don't understand. I'm wealthy. I will be wealthy someday, anyway, if things go my way. I'll give you gold. My mother fought for King Wulf. I didn't mean to spy on your camp. I was only looking for my dog, Edgefrith. I named him after the last king of Mercia, don't you think that's funny? He's a rotten dog, and Edgefrith was a rotten king—"*

Stop being ridiculous, I told myself. In the first place, the guy never saw you, and in the second place, these guards don't seem completely thrilled by his arrival. Nor did the dogs. At the first sign of the intruder the dogs had rallied round, chasing his horse and barking their heads off. The guards stared at the man, but made no attempt to draw their weapons. Their arms were folded across their chests.

"Let's see how proud he looks when the dogs are eating him for supper," said Thingfrith.

"Remember the last two guys who tried to get past them?" said Erpwald

"Yeah, it was outstanding."

The stranger rode up until his horse stood nearly at the foot of the stairs. The dogs kept pace with him. One of them snarled and leapt up to bite his ankle. The stranger kicked it in the face. He looked at Erpwald and Thingfrith.

"Call off your dogs," he said to them.

"Sic him, boys!" shouted Erpwald

The dogs circled the horse in a frenzy, spotting the man with their wild eyes. They couldn't wait to tear into him. The stranger reached into a pouch and pulled out a piece of meat. He threw it just past the dogs, who scrambled after it, now more interested in edging each other out than in attacking him. The man dismounted, and while the dogs' heads were bent to devour the meat he pulled out his ax and chopped through the backs of their necks.

Erpwald and Thingfrith drew their swords. The man walked up to them, pushing aside their swords with his hand. "Put those away," he said. "I've come to see the king."

Thingfrith wavered. "The king allows no armed men in his hall," he said.

The stranger set down his shield and his ax. He removed his helmet. There was no doubt about it: this was the man I had seen in the woods. He unsheathed his sword and gave it to Erpwald to hold while he unbuckled his sword belt. He took off his mail. "Have someone look after my horse," he said. He put his weapons and armor on his shield and carried it up the steps. I pressed my back into the side of the arched entrance, trying to disappear as he passed me, and perhaps I succeeded because he didn't even glance at me as he walked into the hall.

When he was at a safe distance I followed him. The tables, benches, and tablecloths had been put in place for the evening meal, and there was some extra time. Wermhere had put everyone to work polishing the hall's metal fixtures for the second time that day. I picked up a rag and started polishing the brass-trimmed fire poker near the cauldron. The stranger placed his arms-laden shield under one of the side arches and propped his spear against a wall. Then he strode over to investigate Helmstan's bone fortress.

I don't know what he must have thought when he looked inside and saw that shadow of a human being crouched behind the bones, but to everyone's amazement he reached in with one hand and pulled out a cowering Helmstan.

"Leave me alone, for God's sake," begged Helmstan. The man dragged Helmstan over to a bench. I figured the warrior didn't know too much about protocol because he chose the bench right across from the king's table where the top warrior, after the champions, usually sits. Helmstan was shaking so violently that it looked like he had the ague. Tecla hovered nearby.

"Get me some water," the man said to her.

Tecla came back with a bowl of water. She glared at the man, and for a minute I thought she might throw the water at him. I grabbed the fire poker and sidled closer in case she did. The man stripped off Helmstan's filthy clothes. He summoned one of the young male servants.

"Burn these," he said. "And get some clean clothes out of my saddle bag. The guards outside will tell you where it is."

The stranger ripped a piece of linen off the end of one of the tablecloths. Wermhere gasped, and I realized we hadn't heard a word from him since the stranger had entered the hall. He dipped the cloth into the water Tecla had brought and scrubbed Helmstan, starting with his head. When the water got dirty he summoned whoever was nearby to get some more. After a while Helmstan was clean, and his skin was as white as swan's down except for some old bruises and a few spots where the skin had been broken by sharp bones the other night.

The man spotted me this time. "Fetch some woundwort and some knapweed root," he said.

I found his supercilious manner offensive. The real Cynethrith would have told him to go get it himself, but I had a part to play, so I did what everyone else did. I ran out of the hall to look for the herbs.

When I came back he tied the woundwort leaves around Helmstan's injuries with strips from the tablecloth. He sent the knapweed to the kitchen to be grated into some wine. Then he handed Helmstan the clothes the servant had brought in.

"Get dressed," he said.

When the knapweed decoction came back from the kitchen the stranger told Helmstan to drink it. Helmstan looked skeptical.

"It's good for bruises," said the man.

By now a few warriors were straggling into the hall. They were the first ones back from the hunt. They had already heard about the stranger from Erpwald and Thingfrith. They looked at the warrior, then at Helmstan, and shook their heads. Helmstan tried to slink off to his cave, but the man grabbed his arm and forced him to sit next to him.

"Why are you set on killing me?" asked Helmstan.

"Stay where you are," said the man.

As more and more men returned from the hunt there was an undercurrent of muttering around the room. The warriors stood in groups of four or five and openly glared at the stranger who had dared to set Helmstan—and himself—in a place of honor in the king's hall. The man seemed completely oblivious to them, and I wondered how anyone as dense as he seemed to be had lived to reach manhood. Anyway, I supposed I wouldn't have him to worry about much longer.

It was time for us to clear out of the hall and get ready for our nightly job of standing in the servants' section holding plates until better dressed servants came and took them. Even that totally mindless job didn't seem boring tonight, there was so much excitement in the air. Everyone was waiting to see when and how the warriors were going to kill the newcomer. Tecla was in a state over Helmstan and couldn't stop cursing the warrior.

"I don't care if they kill that man. I hope they do," she said about a hundred times. "I just don't want Helmie in the middle of it."

Poor old Helmie. When I looked over at him I didn't know whether to laugh or cry. He was sparkling clean—as white as a sheet, in fact—and dressed in beautiful new clothes that hung on his lanky, emaciated frame. He sat all slumped over. He was still shaking, and anybody could tell he wasn't there by choice.

The horn sounded as it did every night, and after a few minutes the royals entered. The stranger condescended to glance at the king and the queen. I thought he spent half a moment longer on the queen than on the king, and I couldn't say I blamed him. She was very beautiful. She looked in his direction. I thought she noticed him. She had a way of raising her upper lip that formed an expression somewhere between a sneer and a smile. For some reason I thought of a story, almost forgotten, that I had learned in my childhood.

It was about a Frankish woman, a relative of Charlemagne, who was very beautiful, but only on the outside. The woman committed an act of unpardonable vileness—no one would ever tell me what, no matter how much I begged—and was condemned to death, but because she was Charlemagne's kinswoman, it was determined that out of respect for him she should not be burned or hung. So she was put into a boat and pushed out to sea. After a time the wind rose into a gale and she was swept to the shore of Anglia. There she was found by some peasants who took her to the king: the same Offa, enemy of the kingdom of Wessex, that I told you about earlier. The woman told the king that she had been terribly mistreated by people who envied her and that she had been plotted against and condemned to die an unjust death, but God had intervened, and angels had pushed her to safety. The king found it easy to believe such a beautiful woman and gave her to his mother to look after. In time his mother began to suspect that this woman was a sorceress. The king, sensing his mother's disapproval but determined to satiate his passion, secretly married the woman. By the time his mother revealed her suspicions it was too late: the woman was pregnant. She had a daughter and named her Odburh.

But then the story went right out of my head as Athelstan entered the hall, a trifle late tonight. He was as handsome as ever. His tunic, trimmed with gold braid around the hem, was deep forest green. The color brought out the green in his hazel eyes. Over this he wore a rich crimson cloak, lined with pale sea green silk and clasped on his right shoulder with a magnificent gold brooch. His leather shoes were embroidered in beautiful shades of red, blue, and green. The ties on his garters were tipped in gold. He was more regal than the king. It was almost impossible to believe that such a noble, exquisite man had sprung from the loins of a man like Beorhtric. There was a young woman with Athelstan. She was short and had no bosom, but he was very attentive.

The king seemed uncomfortable with the mood in the room and

didn't mix with the guests. He led the queen directly to her seat, and he sat down as well. Unferth came over to the king while he was washing his hands and whispered to him, looking in the direction of the unwelcome guest. The king looked unhappy. The evening progressed in much the same way as the other nights. Some dancers with swords entertained the people between courses, and a man with a very high voice sang a few songs. The men seemed to enjoy the first act in a grim sort of a way, but the singer darkened the warriors' moods even more. The queen offered wine around as she usually did. She even gave some to the newcomer. The court fool made no appearance, and as much as the warriors drank there was no laughter.

When the queen returned to her seat, I saw Unferth throw a small bone in the direction of Helmstan and the stranger. The bone hit the man on the arm, but he was occupied picking an unsuitable particle out of his still uneaten curd flan. He ignored the bone. As far as I could tell he never felt it. Helmstan started to get up, but the man grabbed him by the tunic and forced him to sit down again. More bones began to fly, and soon the hall was filled with them, just like the first night. Bones hit the man on his back, his arms, and his chest. Helmstan started and whimpered with each new hit, but the man did nothing. The bones started to get bigger, and one of them grazed the man across his cheekbone.

"Are you insane?" said Helmstan. "It's okay with me if you want to die, but for my part I'd like to take cover."

"Be still," said the man.

Then I saw Unferth reach over and take something off Werwulf's plate. It was an ox's knuckle with the leg bone still attached. He stood up and took aim. The man's attention seemed riveted on the tapestry behind the king's table. He was so outnumbered and so pitifully unaware that I almost screamed a warning. From where I was standing I would have sworn that he never saw Unferth hurl the bone. But suddenly the stranger, on his feet, caught the bone before it struck him. He flung it back at Unferth's head with such force that the king's strongest champion fell down dead.

For a moment there was silence in the hall. Helmstan dived beneath the table. Some of the warriors grabbed the closest hard object, a goblet or the largest bone within reach, and stood, ready to pounce. The warrior on the stranger's right hauled back his fist. Just before the blow could land, the stranger swerved. With nothing to stop him, the attacker sprawled forward, his face in the remains of Helmstan's dinner. The hall descended into chaos. Another guy jumped up on the table. He lunged for the stranger who grabbed the guy around the knees, lifting his feet. I heard his jaw crack on the edge of the table. Two guys tried to jump the man at the same time: one from the front, the other from behind. The stranger stepped to the side and they smacked into each other, hard. This made them so mad that they started swinging at each other. The low rumble in the hall swelled to a roar. As more men approached the table I was surprised to see Helmstan's hand emerge from beneath it, bashing their shins with a large bone he must have picked up from the floor. I saw the stranger whack a couple of heads together and throw one man onto his back on the table.

The king stood, palms facing outward. "Enough!" he hollered. There was silence.

The man turned to face the king. Neither spoke. Finally the king, looking as stern as his pudgy face allowed, said, "Who are you?"

"Egbert," said the man.

"You have deprived me of my greatest champion, Egbert," said the king. "He's the second I've lost this week." I wouldn't have thought it possible for Beorhtric to look so solemn. "Give me one good reason to spare your life."

"If your men attack me, you will lose more men."

The king, perhaps startled by Egbert's confidence, remained silent. Or maybe the man's point had struck home.

Egbert broke the silence: "You have lost two men. Helmstan and I will take their places."

The king looked astonished. His eyes surveyed the room, then the warriors to his right and left. They wouldn't be thrilled to have this gatecrasher in their ranks, and as for Helmstan! That was unthinkable. On the other hand, this Egbert promised to be a fierce warrior, and Beorhtric was a pragmatist.

"You may have a place in my hall," said the king. "And as for this fellow, I don't begrudge him food, but I cannot allow him to sit with my warriors."

"He sits next to me," said Egbert. This, I thought, was pushing it.

"Father," said Athelstan. He pointed to Helmstan. "This man has been terribly abused in our hall. I've spoken to you many times about the despicable behavior of your champions."

The king stared into space for a moment or two. Finally he looked at his son. "I'll give him a chance because you plead for him, Athelstan," he said. Then to Egbert, "You better be worth two warriors to make up for him."

Egbert, pulling Helmstan behind him, walked over to the king's table. He stepped over Unferth's body and said, "Your majesty, I won't give you two warriors—I'll give you two champions." He sat down in what had been Unferth's place of honor. He pushed the men apart on either side of him to make room on the bench for Helmstan, who looked as if he would rather crawl under the table than sit at it.

The king addressed the court: "Whoever wishes to challenge any of my champions must follow court rules. Stealth will not be tolerated."

I'm guessing that's the only reason Egbert and Helmstan survived the night.


"Wasn't he a hero?" I said to Tecla as we curled up to sleep later that night.

"You're not calling that detestable, meddling brute a hero now, are you?" said Tecla.

"He's hardly a brute," I said, confused. "Weren't you pleased at the way he stood up for Helmstan?"

"He dragged him out of a safe place. He had to know the warriors would attack him. Do you call that standing up for the man?" she said.

"Shut up, you two," said a girl nearby. "I need some sleep."

I whispered. "The way he stood up to his father, and dressed him down for the rotten behavior of the warriors..."

"Father? What father? Who are you talking about?" yawned Tecla, too tired to care any more.

"Athelstan," I said. "Who did you think?"

She never answered.

## SCENE 13 EGBERT AND HELMSTAN SAVE THE KING

The day after Unferth's burial the warriors went out to hunt. The king went along this time, and so did Egbert and Helmstan. We servants fell into our usual routine of cleaning the hall. About mid-morning, in the middle of dusting, sweeping and polishing, we all stopped to gape as Athelstan led the queen into our midst. Wermhere quickly extricated himself from under a ladder where he had been standing so he could look up Mildred's skirt as she polished a lamp.

Athelstan stopped and stared at one of the walls. "I think if the tones got lighter as they went up, say the same hue but different values and intensities, starting with maybe a dark inky green here closest to the floor—" He raised his eyes to the antique swords and shields, "—then we could have a medium rich green to set off all that gold, and a paler shade near the ceiling behind the antlers."

He darted over to one of the columns that set off the aisles from the main part of the hall. The queen followed him. "We'll need some spots of color and some gold interlace in between the sections and around the columns: There's a fellow in town who's very good."

He walked to the center of the room near the cauldron. "This is fabulous, don't you think?" he said, indicating the impressive chain that supported the pot. Then something displeased him. "Who's in charge here?"

Wermhere came forward, looking humbler than I would have thought possible.

"When was the last time you polished this?" asked Athelstan.

Wermhere broke into a sweat. Somehow the chain on the cauldron had escaped his attention. He looked around for somebody to nail, and his eyes fell on a young boy.

"Get over here," he shouted. When the boy came close Wermhere grabbed him by the front of his shirt and kicked his knee. "How many times did I tell you to polish that chain? Do you think we feed you here just so you can produce fertilizer?"

Wermhere didn't wait for an answer. "Get on a ladder and have that glowing brighter than the cover of the holy Bible before dinner or I'll have you whipped till you bleed. Son of a bitch."

Athelstan had moved on. He looked disgusted and I heard him mutter "these people" as he led the queen as far away from Wermhere and the boy as possible. From his new vantage point across the room he looked up. "Should we decorate the rafters? No, just plain, I think.

What do you think? Or do you?"

"Yes," said Odburh.

"I mean there's a lot of wonderful stuff here but no concept. I don't mind barbaric splendor but we need some restraint. No?" asked Athelstan. "Your gold gowns will look wonderful in here once we're done."

"Do you think so?" said Odburh. He had gotten her interest at last. She went on: "Yes, they would, wouldn't they? I think you should go ahead. I'll get Beorhtric to pop for it. Getting his attention is the only hard part."

"He's worse since those big jerks got planted, isn't he? Never mind. We can convince him. At least he can look like a king."

Athelstan pointed across the room to the space that held the artifacts of our previous kings. "We'll rearrange the swords and shields in this section. Some of them need to be more important, especially Cerdic's and Cynric's."

He took the queen by the hand and started over to one of the tapestries. He tripped over the remains of Helmstan's bone fortress, which in the few days since he'd stopped living in it had begun to creep around the room. He hollered over to Wermhere, "Why is this crap still here?"

Wermhere's mouth began to move. "Never mind," said Athelstan, intelligent enough not to be interested in anything Wermhere might have to say. "Just get rid of it."

He continued on to the tapestry. It looked dreary in the daytime when there was no fire to play on its gold threads. "We really must have this cleaned. It's beautiful."

I looked at the tapestry he was referring to and tried to see something beautiful about it. The colors were dull, but that might have been from years of accumulated grime. The tapestry showed St. Dympna turning away in distress from her father's perverted passion. Snakes and mythical beasts with remarkable fangs, their writhing bodies elongated and twisted around each other, surrounded the figures. On the outer border were naked men with greatly enlarged penises. It was dramatic, and I guess you could say it was artistically done. Perhaps that was why Athelstan liked it.

The atheling and the queen walked over to one of the columned aisles. He said, "I think we need to section off this area with some new hangings. They keep the table tops here in the daytime. There must be someplace else they could put them but Haedde says no—"

"Who's Haedde?" asked the queen.

"The stupid dish thane—and a lot of the warriors throw their gear here. People are such slobs. We need to find a way to make the room look cleaner, you know?"

"Yes," said Odburh.

He led her out of the room in the direction of the servants' quarters. On their way out I heard him say. "This floor is wonderful. Very Roman, don't you think?" I looked down. I'd never noticed the floor before. I'd only seen it as one more thing that had to be cleaned. It was made out of tiny colored stones. The stones were arranged into circles bordered with different kinds of braid, and inside each circle was a picture. One of the pictures, repeated every so often, was of a remarkable creature with the wings of a bird, the body of a serpent, and the tail of a fish. Another depicted a beast that started off as a lion and ended like a horse. Still another showed a winged man riding a giant fish.

Athelstan was still talking. "Maybe we could get them to stop throwing weeds on top of it every night. But come with me, I've been going through the old linens in the cupboard. Your women could copy some of these."

For the rest of the day, each time someone came into the room I looked to see if Athelstan had returned, but he never did. I was almost glad when the warriors began to straggle back from the hunt, offering a distraction.

Excitement was in the air, and I saw why when Erpwald and Werwulf entered carrying Thingfrith on a makeshift stretcher. Helmstan came over to Tecla with a bundle of elder leaves and instructions from Egbert on what to do with them. He said to sprinkle them over water that had boiled for the length of time it takes to walk 30 paces. Then leave the mixture off the heat, covered, for the duration of ten Our Fathers, stirring occasionally, before straining. When Tecla brought in the prepared infusion Egbert used it to clean Thingfrith's wound, a nasty cut to the leg, then covered the gash with selfheal, holding the herb in place with strips of linen.

All we wanted to know was how it happened, and that was all the warriors wanted to talk about, but it took a while before I could piece together the sequence of the story from their disjointed comments. Here's what I got: In the morning Helmstan and Egbert had ridden off together on Egbert's horse (since the warriors had sold Helmstan's long ago). The huntsmen had set up some snares, and the warriors and dogs were chasing a stag toward them while the king waited near the nets so he could be the one to make the kill. Thingfrith, on horseback, had stayed near the king, and so, apparently, had Egbert and Helmstan, although no one was aware of it at the time.

All at once, out of nowhere, an aurochs charged the king. The king, who had dismounted in anticipation of spearing the deer, threw his weapon at the attacking beast. The animal veered out of the spear's path and went for Thingfrith. The warrior, stupefied into inaction, sat on his horse clutching his spear while the aurochs gored his horse. Thingfrith was still on the animal when it fell. He was trapped beneath his horse, his leg badly cut by a piece of flint. The aurochs turned around to charge the king and would have killed him except that Egbert threw his ax and split the animal's skull. The aurochs was stunned, but not yet dead. Egbert handed his spear to Helmstan.

"Back me up," he said, a bit unrealistically I thought when I heard it. Then he went over to the animal and hacked off its head with his sword. He pulled the horse off Thingfrith and stanched the warrior's bleeding leg, sending Helmstan to gather some selfheal.

This latest incident did nothing to improve Egbert's popularity, except perhaps with the king. The men resented his deed at least as much as they admired it.

That night after the banquet the queen, whose golden veil brought out the gold in her eyes, smiled warmly at Egbert as she poured his wine. She chatted with him for a long time. She must have been grateful to him for saving her husband's life. Or was it something else? Once she had served the rest of the important people, the warriors told stories and boasted, and the king gave out gold.

Erpwald told about his first battle, undertaken while he was still a lad, in which he killed twenty-four seasoned warriors before he left the field. He told about the time he strangled a giant with his bare hands and how one summer he tamed a winged serpent that he used to ride across the sea and back in the space of an afternoon, so fast did it fly. He swore that if he ever left his lord on the field before the foe was vanquished he would clean the floor of the hall with his tongue, give his armor to Wermhere, then walk on his knees to the end of the earth and jump off. The drinking horn was passed around, and the king gave him two armlets worth 50 mancuses of gold.

Athelwulf said that he had followed the king ever since his father had apprenticed him to the court as a lad, and he had earned his place on the mead bench by fighting with good valor in the king's wars. He had never deserted his lord on the field, and he hoped the sweet drink of the king's hall would poison him if the Valkyries summoned his lord and he, Athelwulf, was not ready to go with him. Mead was passed, and wine, and the king gave Athelwulf a gold-adorned horn cup.

Thingfrith, the same Thingfrith who earlier that day had done nothing when faced with an attacking aurochs, told about the time he had chased a half-human monster into the fen and then jumped into a murky pool to follow it for three days under water, not knowing which direction was up or which was down, the water was so dark. When he tried to kill the monster in its underwater cave he found his sword had rusted into its scabbard, and he couldn't get it out, so he had to kill the vile creature by biting it on its neck. On the return swim he was chased by seven sea snakes and a fish whose teeth were as big around as a horse's hooves and as sharp as a blade of grass. But he said he would go back to the very cave where he slew the monster and bare his chest to the monster's mother, who still lived there, if he even thought about leaving the battlefield before the enemy was routed, or he, Thingfrith, was dead.

He was one of the king's favorites, and Beorhtric gave him a sword with a pattern-welded blade. The hilt alone was worth 120 mancuses of gold, and there were four pounds of silver on its sheath. The evening wore on in this manner, with each warrior telling of his greatest deeds and swearing his fealty to the king, the talks interspersed with the passing of drink and gift giving.

## SCENE 14 EGBERT TELLS A TALE

It was Egbert's turn to speak. The men shifted about in their seats, and you could almost hear them groan, as they anticipated how he would outdo them. Egbert stood and looked around the room. He began to speak softly, and in spite of themselves, the warriors quieted down so they could hear him.

"When I was a young lad I sought the hall of a famous chieftain who lives across the sea, and I fought beside him until I became skillful at combat. Although he rewarded me well and I grew rich, when none of his enemies and no man at his court could out-fight me, I left to test my strength.

"I traveled for several months through many countries engaging challengers, and no one defeated me. One day I came to a crossroads in a land far from the usual dwellings of men. A sightless old crone sat by the side of the road pulling carved runes from a bag.

"'What do you seek?' she asked, hearing my approach.

"'I seek to know if I can vanquish the world,' I said.

"'Ah,' she said. She turned over a rune and felt it with her fingers. I could see it was hail.

"'Do you expect bad weather?' I asked.

"'Not I,' she said. She turned toward me. She had no teeth to support the lower half of her face. It caved in beneath her cheekbones. Her mouth was drawn in, too. It was as if some inner whirlpool were sucking in her outer aspect. 'Can you be dissuaded from your quest?' she asked.

"'Not I,' I said.

"'Then,' she said, 'you must follow the yellow road until you come to a garden that is only visible by the light of the full moon.'

"I gave the woman a silk scarf for her trouble, and then rode on a little and made camp. I meant to get a good rest that night since no full moon was due for a week, but within an hour I saw one rise in the sky. So I broke camp and rode along the yellow road as fast as my horse could carry me. Just before the moon went down I spotted a garden and pulled my horse to a quick stop.

"Near the entrance to the garden were two lads with golden curls, dressed in yellow satin and armed with bows made of ivory and strung with whale gut. I could see the sparkling tips of their arrows arcing like shooting stars as they aimed at the retreating moon.

"'That will teach her to come on the wrong night,' said one.

"When their quivers were empty they bickered over whose turn it was to fetch the spent arrows. They didn't resist my passage. As far as I could tell they didn't even notice me.

"I entered a garden that was unlike any garden I had ever seen. Its herbs produced leaves big enough to hide a man and giant flowers that glowed white in the dark. They were as fragrant as honeysuckle on a summer's night. In the distance I saw the largest and grandest palace I have ever seen. It gleamed golden in the black night as if its walls were on fire.

"When I knocked at the door it was opened by a beautiful maiden, and when I went inside I saw nineteen more. These maidens were so beautiful that the plainest of them was even more beautiful than our lovely Queen Odburh."

The queen had been staring, rapt, at Egbert as he told his tale. We all were. I glanced at her when he mentioned her name and saw her look down.

Egbert went on: "The maidens led me to a hall where I was seated next to a large bald-headed man whose yellow brocade gown pulled a little across his stomach: he was no warrior. The man was friendly and talkative in an easy-going way. Big as he was he had a way of giggling as he talked that made everything a joke. I soon felt I had known him all my life. In his hall I ate and drank as well as I have eaten or drunk anywhere, or better. He invited me to stay for as long as I liked.

"I was tempted to accept his offer, and for an hour or so, surrounded by so much conviviality, I almost forgot why I had come. Then the man asked me what had brought me to his palace, and I was forced to remember my quest, which I explained to him.

"'Oh, that's too bad,' said the man.

"'Why is that?' I asked.

For the first time that evening the man looked serious. He stared into space and began to chew one of his fingernails.

"'Hmmm . . . Uh . . . I know what you could do,' he said slowly, 'but no, better not to.'

"'But I want to,' I said, becoming, like most youths, determined in the face of opposition.

"'I don't like to be responsible,' he said. I pressed him for a while, and finally he relented.

"He said, 'You must awaken just before dawn and follow the path until you come to a man dressed in black with one arm, one leg, and one eye in the middle of his forehead. This man will direct you to a deep well. When you find the well you must dive into it. On the bottom is a stone as heavy as three men that you must carry up to the surface. Once you get the stone onto dry earth you must cleave it in half with one blow from your sword.'

"That didn't sound too difficult, at any rate, not impossible. I knew that objects weighed less in water. Then the little man sent me off to my chamber with one of the beautiful maidens, saying it was the custom among his people, and I must not insult the girl by refusing her. The girl was beautiful, as they all were there, and I wouldn't have insulted her for a king's ransom. She had one trait, however, that became more disconcerting as the night wore on: she never stopped laughing.

"Soon it was almost dawn, and the maiden, still laughing, kissed me and reminded me of my venture. I poured several pitchers of cold water over my head, put on my armor, and left.

"As I rode along the terrain became less and less hospitable. The hills became craggier. Wild beasts growled in the distance and sometimes sounded as close as my shoulder. My horse balked, and I had to get off and lead him. The trees were enormous, gnarled and ominous. Their restless canopies whistled and moaned as if some torment had become too much to bear. I ran out of food on the third day out. On the fifth day a pack of aurochs chased me miles in the wrong direction. On the sixth I was charged by a wild boar.

"Finally, after a week, I spotted the one-legged man dressed in black peering at me with his one eye. He flagged me down with his one arm.

"'I heard you were coming,' he said. His cheek twitched up and down near where one of his eyes should have been. 'Let's see . . . you're after the goose.'

"'Goose?' I said.

"'You know, goose, egg, gold, all that.'

"'Never heard of it,' I said, 'I'm—'

"'Wait a minute, hold on, hold on,' he compressed his mouth and looked away briefly. 'The grail, am I right?' he asked.

"'No,' I said. 'Nothing to do with birds. I want—'

"'I said *grail*, as in Holy Grail, not quail, you wally,' said the man.

"'Well I don't want any grail either, holy or otherwise,' I said. 'What I'm looking for is—'

"'Stop. I've got it,' he said, 'It's the fleece.'

"'Wrong again,' I said.

"'Sleeping princess? You kiss her, get the kingdom?' he asked.

"'No.'

"'This has to be it—you want the shoe that only fits your true love!'

"'How about you let me tell you?' I suggested.

"The man looked petulant. 'Well, all right then. I give up. What do you want?'

"'The location of a well,' I said.

"'Oh that. Ha. Good. Serves you right.'

"'Go on,' I said.

"'One furlong straight ahead, left to the pollards, left again at the pear tree, follow the hedge, right at the ivied alder, cross the hazel coppice, 16 paces straight, cross a meadow in the direction of the swollen foot oak, left, left again at the red-leaved beech, right at the bramble-thorns, quick left when you see an apple and maple growing together, climb an embankment, through a wood, come to a stream, follow it, you'll find the well. Got it?'

"'Yes.'

"'Oh.' He sounded disappointed.

"I followed his directions. The well I found wasn't the kind that men dig into the earth, but rather the source of the stream I had been following. It wasn't deep enough to dive into. If I had I would have broken my neck, so I waded in and looked for the stone my host had described. I found a large stone, but it was nowhere near the weight of three men. It weighed about half what I do. I began to think I was wasting my time. Nevertheless, I lugged out the stone, set it onto the ground, and prepared to hack it in two with my sword Uruz, pretty sure that all I would get for my effort was a dull weapon.

"But when I struck the blow, the sky, which a moment before had been clear, turned as black as a moonless night. The wind roared. The earth heaved as if it were a boat tossed at sea. I was thrown off balance and fell to the ground. The rain swirled about in currents, and hail the size of birds' eggs pelted down. I quickly ran to my horse and protected both our heads beneath my shield.

"After a while the wind, rain, and hail stopped. The sun shone as brightly as before. I looked about and saw that hardly a tree was left in the wood. Most lay this way and that, uprooted and thrown down by the storm. The few trees that remained had no leaves. Birds lay dead everywhere. There was no sound. Not a creature had survived except me and my horse.

"Then the sky turned black again. But instead of another storm I heard a voice bellow till the earth shook, 'Who challenges me?' I stepped boldly out from under my shield, ready to confront what I had been seeking.

"'I do,' I said.

"We faced each other, this opponent and I, swords and shields at the ready. The creature made a sound even more terrible than his bellowing. He charged at me, and I raised my shield. The blow from his sword shattered my shield into fragments smaller than dust.

"Seeing him ready to charge again I clasped my sword in both hands to fend him off. When his sword hit mine the sparks made new stars. I staggered back from the impact. When I got my footing I aimed at his neck, but was a little low. He dodged, but not enough, and I nicked his shoulder. He got angry and struck my sword with such force that it flew out of my hand and into the flank of my horse, killing him.

"I reached for my ax to throw at him, and as it left my hand he stepped out of its path and threw his at my helmet, which split in two. My skull was cut to the bone.

"I fell. Now I had no shield, no sword, no ax, no helmet, and no horse. When I wiped the blood out of my eyes, I saw my enemy leaving the field. He didn't bother to kill me or take my weapons.

"When I could get up I went back to the golden palace. The boys with the golden curls were lounging against the garden wall, their bows by their sides. I passed them and collapsed at the door of the hall. Twenty beautiful maidens hastened to attend me, removing my blood-soaked armor and clothes. They bandaged me and put me in a room to rest, without, I thanked God, any company.

"Soon I was well enough to attend a dinner with my host. Neither he, nor anyone else at the palace, ever asked me about my adventure."

There was a stunned silence in the room for a moment or two when Egbert had finished. No one had ever heard a man tell a tale more to his discredit. Then, all of a sudden, there was a funny sound as Athelwulf tried to stifle a laugh. Everyone looked at him in horror, fulling expecting Egbert to dispatch him with a wine goblet. Instead, Egbert put back his head and began to roar with laughter himself, and before long every warrior in the room was laughing and telling the guy next to him his own story about a time a fight had not gone exactly to plan. Drinks were passed round, and the men seemed to feel that Egbert wasn't so bad after all.

The king gave a signal to one of his thanes who went to the door of the hall and led in a beautiful white horse, with a gold-plated harness and a saddle ornamented with precious stones. The king thanked Egbert for joining his court and gave him the horse. Also on that night, Egbert was given a private bower.

## Scene 15 Egbert Confronts Cynethrith

The days that followed were busy ones. In three days it would be All Hallows Eve, and when we weren't cleaning or serving we were expected to help stitch the fanciful creations the court ladies were planning to wear. Meanwhile, Athelstan's renovations had started.

We saw quite a lot of him in the hall. I watched him day after day as he painted sample colors on the wall. He'd paint a stripe, stand back, squint at it, walk around the room to view it from different vantages, and then return to paint another. Occasionally he would escort one lady or another into the hall to explain the plans to her. He kept quite a few of the women busy embroidering tablecloths or restoring old tapestries. Craftsmen were in and out for supervision. He was demanding of them. If he was pleased he was very pleased indeed. When he wasn't, he could be dramatic. He broke the prototype for the new pillars in half in front of the fellow who delivered it. Its shape lacked refinement.

While we saw more of Athelstan we saw less of the king. On some evenings, as soon as the queen rose to pour wine for their guests, he would retire to his bower, taking Warr and his cup filler with him. I sometimes noticed a dangerous look in the deserted wife's eye as she watched them leave, but she covered her feelings as best she could, sitting and laughing with the warriors. She often sat between Egbert and Helmstan and appeared as if she hadn't a care in the world.

Helmstan was as uncomfortable as ever. He sat at the table with the champions looking as awkward as a swan on land. All the warriors ignored him, and Egbert ignored his discomfiture. You could see in Tecla's eyes how she pitied him. She snatched a word with him whenever she could.

There was less drinking in the hall on the nights that the king kept to himself, and that had a down side for us servants. The warriors were no longer too drunk to have any interest in fornication. One night I opened my eyes and saw a man standing in the frame that separated the servants' quarters from the rest of the hall. I reached under my skirt for my knife but he seemed to know who he was looking for, and it wasn't me. I saw the warrior drop down next to somebody, and I was ready to respond to a cry for help, but it never came. Other warriors came later, and I didn't sleep for the rest of the night, listening to their noises, wondering if I would be next; wondering if all, or any, of the participants were willing, and most of all wondering if I should intervene. I asked Tecla about it the next day. She got very red, smiled, and told me to mind my own business.

The next day I didn't feel the effects of my sleepless night while it was still light but by dusk I was tired. That night there was the usual endless waiting with food at the edge of the hall and nothing interesting to watch. The queen and Athelstan were elsewhere, and there was no entertainment or dancing. When at last the members of the court had eaten their fill we servants scuttled back to the kitchen with empty dishes and used trenchers and ate our allotment of leftovers. The king left the hall, and Wermhere sent us back in to do some further clearing up. Some of the warriors and ladies were milling about. Others sat at their tables and talked. I heard Werwulf, Ercenwald, and Athelwulf arguing the merits of their weapons, debating whether it was better to finish a pattern-welded blade with oil or water. They were getting quite hot about it. I waited for Wermhere to turn his back for a moment, and then I stole behind one of the tapestries for a break.

I had barely gotten behind the curtain when someone clasped my wrists, jerked me around, and pinned me against the wall. It was Egbert. I was so astonished I couldn't speak.

He pulled my arms over my head and held them there with one hand. His other hand went up my skirt. I found my voice.

"Rape," I screamed. Or tried to scream. Before I got the word out he let my arms go and pressed his hand against my mouth, holding me in place against the wall with his body. He said in a low but convincing voice, "You scream rape again and you'll get raped."

I punched him in the face. I was too close to him to get any kind of leverage, and I think it hurt me more than it hurt him, but that didn't stop me: I was mad. I bit his hand as hard as I could. I tried to wiggle my right foot in between his legs so I could knee him in the balls. He pressed his legs against mine more tightly. I couldn't move.

The hand under my skirt found what it was looking for. He removed my knife from its holster and threw it into the wall, above my reach. Then he used both his hands to restrain me while he stood back enough to look me in the face.

"Who are you working for?"

I was speechless. Could he care so much if a servant sneaked off for a few minutes?

"Who are you working for?" he said again. I could tell by his tone that he wasn't kidding, but it still seemed unbelievable.

"Wermhere," I said.

"Wermhere." he said. He seemed to mull that over. "What's his interest in this?"

"I never stopped to ask myself that," I said.

"Who's Wermhere working for?" he said.

"Haedde, I guess." I said.

"And Haedde?"

"What about him?"

"Don't play stupid with me."

"What was it you wanted to know?"

"Who gives Haedde orders?"

There seemed to be no end to the man's curiosity about the palace's domestic arrangements. "Why ask me?" I said. I was getting tired of being bullied. "I'm sure there are plenty of others who know the pecking order better than I do."

"Why are you here?" he asked.

"God, I often wonder," I said. "You start something. Sometimes you don't know when to stop." I sighed. "I guess I'm here because I have nothing else."

He was silent for a while. His grip had relaxed ever so slightly. I thought he was softening so I asked him if I could have my knife back. "You must think I'm three kinds of an idiot," he said. Naturally I thought he meant for attacking me, so I made a joke about it so he'd think there were no hard feelings. "Oh," I said, "one or two kinds, maybe. Certainly not three. My knife, please."

"You don't understand," he said. "When somebody lurks behind my table with a knife I take it personally."

"I wasn't paying any attention to who was sitting where, for Christ's sake. I just wanted a rest," I groused. Noticing I was still alive I got braver. "If you and your over-sexed buddies stayed on your side of the hall at night I might not be so tired. And, anyway, as you may have noticed, the knife wasn't out."

"I beg your pardon. I guess I should have waited. And excuse me for not walking under that tree in the forest so you could jump me."

So he had seen me. "I can explain that," I said, although I had no idea how.

"I've got all night," he said.

"But I don't," I said. "If that little weasel catches me back here there'll be hell to pay."

"You said you were working for him."

"I am, and he can't stand to see anyone idle."

Egbert was incredulous. "Tell him the attempt took longer than expected."

"The attempt?" I said.

"To kill me," he said. He looked grim and pinned me tighter for emphasis. "Stop playing games."

He had pressed the air out of my lungs. "I wasn't trying to kill you," I gasped. What an exasperating man.

He backed off a little so I could breathe. "I suppose you've got a good reason for sneaking up behind me with a fire poker the day I arrived?"

"You noticed that," I said.

"I'm alive because I notice things," he said. He regarded me closely for a while and then backed off a little. "Because you are," he paused, "an old woman, I won't kill you. This time. You've got three days to find out who Haedde's working for." He looked out from behind the tapestry and then back at me. "And don't try to run away because I'll find you. Now get out of here."

I left the curtain feeling that my brain was floating above my head. The servants were breaking down the trestle tables. I joined in, helping Tecla. I hadn't realized I was frightened until I noticed that my hands were shaking so much that the table top we were carrying was wobbling.

"What's the matter with you?" asked Tecla.

Suddenly I was so relieved to have gotten away from Egbert that I felt like crying. I couldn't wait to tell her what had happened, but of course I had to. Wermhere noticed me and came over to us.

"And where has my favorite goddess of loveliness spent the greater part of the evening," he said, "while the rest of us have been doing an honest day's work? Making love to one of the warriors behind the curtain, were you?" I wondered if he knew where I was or if it was a lucky guess.

"I would have thought Egbert would have chosen someone a little more attractive to plank," he said, answering my question, "but then there's no accounting for taste." He looked at me hard. "Of course," he said, "maybe he knows something I don't know."

He moved next to me, so close his hip was touching my thigh, and put one of his small arms around my back. It was all I could do not to kick him. "Do you have some interesting talents?" he said. "Tell papa all about it."

"Get your hands off me," I snapped.

"I can see you're not in the mood right now," said Wermhere. "Did macho-man tire you out?" He turned his prurient gaze on me, waiting for an answer.

"I guess you could say that," I said.

"Never mind," he said. "We can talk about it some other time, my dumpling." He licked his lips. "In the meantime," he got an ugly look on his face, "get back to work."

I saw him lift his stick but was too mentally exhausted to move. It crashed down across my back, and I fell to the floor. I wondered if Egbert had seen what happened, and if he had, if he thought it was my punishment for not succeeding in the "attempt," as he called it. As I lay there on the floor, I felt as if I was sinking into a quagmire. With the force of a revelation I suddenly realized how childish, stupid and impractical my idea of finding a savior had been. Like the lady whose husband's been unfaithful, I wondered why it had taken me so long to figure it out. It was time to face reality: there was no one here I could ever turn to for help, and I'd been an idiot for putting up with this nonsense as long as I had. I supposed I had Egbert to thank for my new clarity of thought. It was time to give up this stunt and get out, before it was too late.

One thing I didn't give any thought to was why Egbert had made the assumptions he had. Later, when I was out of the situation and could look at it more objectively, I did begin to wonder why he seemed to believe there was some sort of plot to kill him. But that night I focused on my own situation. I had spent more time in this demeaning guise than I had intended. To be sure I had learned a lot (perhaps too much). I knew names and the ranks that went with those names. I had observed court life and etiquette: I had learned how to act. I knew the hand-washing protocol and the polite way to share food. I knew when to stand, when to curtsy, when to sit. I had studied the intricate movements of the court dances. Ironically, now that I could pass for an educated lady, I had no reason to.

## SCENE 16 DAY BEFORE ALL HALLOWS EVE

My new objective became to figure out the most propitious time to disappear. All Hallows Eve seemed a heaven-sent opportunity for just that. On the plus side, townspeople and villagers from all around were coming to the festivities. There would be lots of people in costume and lots of coming and going. It would be an easy night to slip away. On the minus side, it pushed me right up against Egbert's three-day deadline. On balance, I decided the advantages out-weighed the one disadvantage, considerable as that was. To be on the safe side, I determined to find out if the dish thane had to report to anyone. Egbert could have very easily discovered that on his own, but there was no point in trying to understand why the man was making such a melodrama out of it. Two days later I still didn't have the answer. Tecla and Mildred thought Haedde took orders from the bower thane, but the others thought he reported to the butler. Judith, a slave who had been well-borne, said they were all crazy and Haedde only answered to the royals. As much as I hated the idea, it looked like I was going to have to find out from Wermhere. A direct question would be a mistake, that was obvious. I decided to try a trick I'd seen a reeve from Easton pull when he wanted to find out how many sheep an unfriendly farmer had sold at market.

I whispered to Tecla, when Wermhere was close enough to over-hear, "It's too bad for Haedde that he has to report to the stable thane."

Wermhere couldn't resist correcting me. "What makes you think he reports to the stable thane, you perplexing profusion of putrefaction?" he asked.

"What makes you think he doesn't?" I said.

"What makes me think he doesn't, my vile and venerable vixen, is that he doesn't," he said.

"You may think you know a lot about the palace, Wermhere," I said, "but I have it on very good authority that Haedde does exactly what the stable thane tells him."

"Your information's lower in the gutter than you are," said Wermhere. He grabbed the arm of the nearest warrior, who happened to be Ercenwald. "Will you tell this exuding effluent who Haedde's superior is?"

"Are you referring to this elderly servant?" asked Ercenwald extricating his arm.

"Yeah, tell the old broad," said Wermhere.

Yeah, I thought. Tell me.

"Wermhere," said Ercenwald, "your attitude toward the staff is despicable."

"I'm sorry, sir," said Wermhere. "It won't happen again."

"Good," said Ercenwald, starting to walk away.

"Wait!" I fairly shrieked.

"Yes, Woman?" asked Ercenwald. He looked a little irritated.

"Who," I croaked, "does Haedde work for?"

"The butler."

I felt brilliant, but not for long.

As soon as Ercenwald was out of earshot Wermhere said, "See, miss uppity puss? Was I right, or what? A warrior planks them and they think they got an infusion of brains or something. Which reminds me," he put his arm around my shoulders and led me away from Tecla. "You and I have a few things to talk about."

"You and I don't have a thing to talk about, Wermhere."

"You were wrong about Haedde and you're wrong about this." He was leading me over to an empty part of the hall where the trestle tables were stashed in the daytime. Great, I thought, lots of barricades to fornicate behind. I stopped where I was. "You know," he went on, "you don't look like much, but I want to find out what a guy who could have anybody in the entire palace, up to and including the queen, found so appealing." His face got red, and his eyes glittered. "Do to me what you did to him."

*Punch you in the face?* I thought. I smiled. I didn't want to cause a scene when I was so nearly out of there. "It's not what you think," I said. "It was a business deal."

"Who paid, you or him? I'll do it for nothing, baby." His face was about an inch from mine. One of his hands made large, nervous circles on my back.

"Forget it, Wermhere."

"Broad like you couldn't get too many offers." He tried to push one of his legs between mine.

"I'm not in the mood, Wermhere," I said.

He grabbed the back of my neck with his two little hands and I saw his open mouth reaching up toward mine. This was the limit. I stepped back, bent my fingers so the knuckles protruded, and socked him in the windpipe. My father had trained me well: I didn't pull the punch but aimed to go through his throat to the back of his neck. When he lurched back gasping I punched him in the stomach. He doubled over forward, and I pounded him near the top of his spine with the side of both fists. He fell face down on the floor.

"Well done," I heard someone say. I looked up and was dismayed to see Egbert, sitting not five feet away on top of a stack of table tops. "You must have been hell on wheels when you were young. Get a bucket of water."

I came back with the water, which he threw on Wermhere's head. He stirred.

"I would certainly hate to hear," Egbert said to no one in particular, "that a member of the palace staff mistreated a servant because he held a grudge."

I opened my mouth to tell him I had found out about Haedde, but he was gone.

*SCENE 17* WERMHERE IS KING FOR THE NIGHT

As much as I hated to admit defeat, I felt good about my decision to leave. I'd been away from home for as long as I could get away with it. Wermhere wanted to kill me, and Egbert's behavior was so irrational I was afraid he might.

It was late afternoon on All Hallow's Eve, and there was plenty of activity in the hall. We were put to work carving out the insides of various roots. As we finished, Athelstan and some of his friends cut ghoulish faces into them and placed candles inside.

"Wait till you see how creepy these are going to look at night," Athelstan was saying.

"It should be a super party," said one of the ladies. "Even the straw gnawers are fun on a night like this. Who's doing the story?"

"A local named Red," said Athelstan. "He auditioned for me a couple of weeks ago—he was terrific."

I wondered if by any chance it could be the same Red who entertained us straw gnawers in Easton.

"Any of the dust dudes coming to the next party?" asked Elfwinne.

"All of England's coming to that one," said Athelstan.

"When is it?" asked Elfwinne. "Because my parents are threatening to make me visit my boring old grandmother in London after Christmas, if you can believe it."

"It's . . . just a minute," Athelstan turned to me. "Do you think you could go get a few more of these out of the garden?" He pointed to a mangelwurzel.

"Yes, Your Royal Highness," I said. I didn't move. In spite of myself I was curious about the next party.

"I need them right away," he said.

I got up and made a show of organizing what I had been doing.

"What was I saying?" he said. "Oh, the date. It's set for the middle of January, St. Fursey's Day."

Just before dark torches were lit on either side of the long path that led from the palace gates to the hall, and guests began arriving soon after. First to appear were the villagers from Littleton. The ladies, in mantles of woven straw and with straw braided into their hair, carried little straw dolls representing the spirit of the harvest. The men had straw sticking out from under their hats. It was much too early for the court to assemble, but apparently none of them knew. They wandered around the empty hall looking as out-of-place as they must have felt.

Athelstan ignored them when he came in to put a few finishing touches on the decorations. He checked that the hall fire was completely out and had new logs and lots of tinder laid upon the hearth. He and two helpers began placing the carved roots around the room. Athelstan was particular about where they went. Two young men lit the candles, and the army of root faces leered and frowned and flickered all over the hall and looked as much like evil spirits as anything I ever hope to see.

About an hour later the warriors started wandering in. Athelwulf wore stilts and looked like a troll. Oswulf was a monk, and another a ghost. Thingfrith had dressed himself as an ancient witch with great wobbling breasts. People from the town came next. One corpse was cleverly engineered with cords that looked like worms dangling from its exposed gut. Some men wore elaborately carved beast heads. One enterprising woman had made herself a crown of teasels and covered her entire robe with seeds. Then I spotted the group from Easton.

Red, the storyteller, had no costume, but was dressed only in black. So was Edith, who stood next to him. The Cherub looked like an adorable middle-aged fairy. Arkil was the devil, tail and all, and the burly toothless smith a maid. Osbert wore antlers and a very large nose, but I could hardly waste time looking at him when I saw my stepmother wearing a churn, and Wulfwaru and Hilda dressed as milkmaids. Even in this get-up Wulfwaru had managed to tie a sash tightly around her waist to emphasize her bosom and her hips.

By now we servants were at our stations. When the hall was so crowded that it looked as though not another body could fit in, the horn sounded, and the royal party entered. The king was dressed as a fool and carried an inflated bladder. The queen was breathtaking. She was an angel. Her white gown, made out of layer after layer of sheerest white silk, floated over her body. It was restrained at her waist by a narrow gold belt, studded with jewels, its pointed ends joined in a decorative knot that rested about mid-thigh. There was gold, too, in the simple band around her temple that decorated her hair without confining it: her loose tresses fell to her waist. She wore large wings of kestrel feathers, so cleverly assembled I wouldn't have been surprised to see her fly away. Athelstan was dressed as a magician.

When the meal was over and plenty of ale had been served, the king stood to begin the ceremony. "Good evening to you all. It is always a pleasure to see so many of our dear, dear friends, and Odburh and I are delighted that you could all be with us this evening. I'm sure every one of you knows how important you are to us. So without further ado, let's begin the evening's festivities. As you know, we have a couple of posts to fill for the ceremony this evening." There was a tittering of anticipation from the crowd. "First of all, we have to choose the King of All Hallows."

There was a lot of whispering and nudging as the people consulted with each other about whom they wished to elect. "Now you can nominate anyone you please, as long as he's a servant or a slave. Do I hear any nominations?"

There was a babble of suggestions. "One at a time, please. Yes? What was that?"

A serving woman from my mother's monastery in Itchen Abbas nominated her husband. Several of the townspeople nominated their servants. Werwulf nominated a young slave, and Warr nominated Wermhere.

"We've had a few nominations," said the king. "Will all the candidates come up here, please?"

Several men filed up to the front. "Is that everybody?" said the king. "No? Who's missing? Who's hiding back there?"

"It's Edwulf," shouted one of the men from Littleton.

"Come on up here, Edwulf. Don't be shy. We're all waiting for you," said the king.

The reluctant man came forward. "Now we've got everybody," said the king. "This is a fine looking group this year, the best we've ever had. Aren't they a fine looking group?" he asked the guests.

Cheers, whistles, and clapping ensued. The king turned to his wife. "Odburh, pass around some wine, these nominations can take a while, and we don't want anybody getting thirsty."

The queen extricated herself from behind the head table and summoned the cup filler. The king asked each of the nominees his name and where he came from. There were great bursts of enthusiasm from the villagers for the contestant they knew, even if they had never liked the fellow. "Now I'm going to ask each one of you to tell the people what you will do for them if you're elected king," said the king. "We'll start with Stewart." The king had memorized all their names already. He was remarkable that way.

Stewart rocked back and forth from foot to foot, looking both pleased and embarrassed to find himself in the limelight. "Free booze," he said, delighted with himself for thinking of it. The next few, perhaps having their wits taken away by the necessity of speaking publicly for the first time in their lives, couldn't think of anything to add to that. Finally one of them said, "Free meat and booze."

"Free meat, booze, and a marcus of gold," said Edwulf. They were catching on now, and perhaps it was just Wermhere's good luck that his turn came at the end. "Free meat, booze, a marcus of gold, and *broads!*" he yelled, shaking his little fist in the air.

The warriors at the king's table liked that, except for Egbert, who seemed indifferent, and Helmstan, who had never relaxed at the king's table and always did whatever Egbert did. The rest of the champions shouted, "Wermhere, Wermhere, Wermhere." Egbert looked across the room at Athelwulf and rolled his eyes. Athelstan got up and walked over to his father.

"Well," said the king, not bothering to consult the rest of the hall, "I can see how you all feel about this." Athelstan started to whisper something to him, but the king held up his hand to stop him. "I am happy to give to you your new King of All Hallows, King Wermhere." The king turned to where Athelstan had been, but he had returned to his seat.

An attendant came forward with a robe, and another with a crown. They placed these on Wermhere, who looked as elated as a man who has seen the face of God. The king bowed to him, "Your Majesty," he said, "it is my duty to remind you of your rights and obligations as King of All Hallows. You are to preside over tonight's festivities, and all will obey you. First you must pick, from among the servants, your Queen of All Hallows."

My heart sank. I hoped the beating I had given him had cooled his recent ardor. Wermhere looked around the room. I was relieved that when his glance fell on me he only gave me a dirty look. He chose a brazen looking young girl whose front teeth overlapped slightly. She came to the front of the hall, blushing and smiling broadly. In between her smiles her mouth worked as if she were chewing something.

"An outstanding choice, Your Majesty," said the king. "My dear, let me be the first to congratulate you." He kissed the girl on the cheek. "Curtsy to your lord, sweetheart. What's your name?"

The girl looked down coyly and mumbled her name. "What was

that? Fannie? Frida? Frida! I now pronounce you Queen of All Hallows."

The attendants robed and crowned the girl, who towered over Wermhere by one and a half heads.

The king addressed Wermhere again. "Sit on my throne, and your lovely queen can sit on Odburh's. You will need to direct the procession and light the hearth fire." More softly he said, "Don't worry, this gentleman will walk you through it." The king indicated the butler, a personage much too high ranking to speak to Wermhere under normal circumstances. "Your final duties," concluded the king, "are to introduce our storyteller and start off the dance. You will be king until midnight."

The king left the front of the room, went to Odburh who was once again sitting at the head table, and escorted her to another part of the hall. Attendants led the new king and queen to their places of honor at the head table. Wermhere tripped over his robe several times on the way. It it was much too long for him. The hall servants abandoned their places, and so did my group. We all dispersed into the crowd. On this night chaos reigned. The pock-marked girl, who I think was miffed that Wermhere hadn't chosen her for his queen, had a costume ready. She had darkened her face with soot from the fire and pronounced herself a gypsy sorceress.

Wermhere sat in the king's seat, waving a goblet in the direction of the champions and grinning like a lunatic. Several of Odburh's women hovered over him, feeding him and handing him drinks, all the while giggling behind their hands. "Isn't he adorable?" I heard one say. Athelstan tried to engage the new queen in conversation, but it appeared to be rough going. Wermhere stood up. The room quieted and everyone looked at him in happy expectation.

"On your knees, you tawdry trembling toadies," shouted Wermhere. The entire hall fell to its knees. It was as quiet as a moonless night. Wermhere stood there for a moment, surveying the prostrate crowd. For probably the first time in his life he couldn't think of anything more to say. "Aw, go on," he said. "You can get up now." He turned to Frida and said, "Go pour out some wine. That fellow over there will give it to you." He meant the king's cup filler.

"Hey, my man," he yelled to the cup filler, "take care of the queen, will you? Good lad." When his queen had gone he looked at one of Odburh's women, a fair young woman with curly brown hair. "It's hard work being a king," he said.

"But you do it so well," she said.

"Do you really think so?" he asked. "Come sit here." He indicated his lap. The lady sat on his lap and he put his little arms around her and whispered to her. She laughed and laughed.

After a while the butler came over to Wermhere and, bowing low, reminded him that it was time for the ceremony to begin.

Everyone, except for the thanes in charge of seeing that every light was extinguished, had to leave the hall. This would have been a good time for me to disappear, but I didn't want to miss Red's story. I figured I could just as easily slip away when the dancing started.

As we filed outside, boys and girls wearing braided sashes handed rowan branches to the women and torches to the men. Two boys dressed in orange carried a large brass bucket with a fire inside and bowed low before Wermhere. Then Wermhere, followed by the boys, led us in a procession around the building three times. The women waved their branches and we all shouted, "Evil spirits keep away, go to hell and join the fray."

After the third trip around the hall, Wermhere and the boys with the fire went to the far end of the courtyard and waited while the rest of us reentered the dark hall. Once we had reassembled, the butler gave a signal and the men put out their torches. We stood expectantly in the pitch black.

The two boys carrying the hearth fire entered, then Wermhere. The three of them walked to the center of the room near the cauldron. The butler stood right behind Wermhere.

A priest bowed to Wermhere and then asked God's blessing on the hall. Thingfrith, the champion who had served the king longest, and Egbert, the most recent arrival, were expected to say some stirring words. Thingfrith said he hoped the sweet mead would flow in Beorhtric's hall as long as the river Itchen drained the valley. Egbert said he hoped the House of Wessex would live forever in the minds of men as the royal house that produced the greatest king in all England. I thought it highly unlikely. Beorhtric beamed.

Then another priest asked God's blessing on the hearth fire. The butler gave a signal to one of the thanes who handed Wermhere a taper. The two boys moved closer to the cauldron. The butler whispered to Wermhere, who placed his taper into the bucket until it caught fire and then put it under the logs.

It was a tense moment. If the fire sputtered and took a long time to catch, it meant a hard year. If it went out altogether it meant disaster. If it caught quickly and burned brightly, as it did this time, it meant a brilliant year for Wessex. The people cheered. Warriors passed Wermhere drinks. The ladies grabbed him and kissed him. Wermhere took the hand of the nearest and didn't let go. King Beorhtric came over and clapped Wermhere on the back. The wall tapers were lighted, and the re-lit root faces gleamed as wickedly as before. The hearth fire blazed. The brilliance seemed magical.

Wermhere, slightly drunk by now, raised his arms over his head to get everyone's attention. "It's gonna be," he shouted, "a really good year. Huh? Did I do it, or what?"

He turned to the lady whose hand he was holding. "Take me home," he said, under the roar of the cheering. The butler caught Wermhere's eye and signaled him to start the next event.

Wermhere said to him, "You know, you're one hell of a kill-joy."

He raised his little arm again for silence. "Now if you could all settle down. Shut up! Find yourselves a seat somewhere and take a load off. Come on, come on, don't take all night about it." He tapped a foot impatiently while the people found seats or settled themselves on the floor.

"Now we're gonna have our story. I don't know this guy myself. He might be a complete jerk for all I know, but they tell me he'll keep you awake till the music starts." A few drunk people laughed at Wermhere's wisecrack. The sober ones were appalled by his bad manners. The butler whispered again.

Wermhere went on. "All right. All right. Never mind, people, it's just whining. The butler's busting my butt. The guy's as much fun as a nun during Holy Week."

Everyone was quiet except for a fat red-faced man dressed as a beggar, leg sores and all, who spat out an uncomfortable laugh. "So where was I?" said Wermhere to no one in particular. "Where are my sibilant sycophants when I need them? Does Beorhtric have this problem?" He grabbed the nearest woman, a lady from Avington, the sister of a priest, and pulled her next to him. "You'll have to fill in, you seductive scamp. What was I talking about before that butler got me muddled?"

"The story, Your Majesty," said the woman.

"Oh, right. She's good. I could go for a girl like you. Or any other girl, for that matter. Even a boy, in a pinch."

The woman smiled lamely and started to pull away from Wermhere. He shot out his foot, and she stumbled over it. The butler caught her and apologized profusely.

Wermhere smiled broadly at them both. "Anyway, as I was saying before I was so rudely interrupted, I'd like you to welcome my man from elegant Easton, where the dead fish wear nose clips so they don't have to smell the people. Welcome Red the Wretched. Just kidding folks. Come up here, Retch. We're lucky we got him tonight, he usually only comes out when there's a full moon."

I saw the butler whispering to two of the queen's ladies, who quickly made their way over to Wermhere and began to cajole him in the direction of his seat on the king's dais. On the way Wermhere stopped and called over his shoulder. "Keep the crowd happy, Retch, or else." He passed his index finger across his throat.

*SCENE* 18 RED TELLS A TALE

Red moved away from the cauldron and stood at the corner of the king's dais. There was less light on him there. His black clothing was swallowed up by the shadows. All you could see of him were his face and hands.

"We've been trying for years to keep it quiet about the fish," he said. This got a few chuckles. People were relieved he wasn't offended. Red looked around the room and waited until everyone's eyes were on him.

"Long ago," he said, "in an ancient kingdom, lived a wealthy thane. He had a beautiful daughter, and he doted on this girl.

"The maiden was very accomplished: she could spin and embroider, write and paint, and out-ride any man. The problem, as far as her father was concerned, was that while she could out-ride any man she didn't often choose to. She had an amorous eye and a lusty disposition.

"Her father was trying to arrange a match for her, and he was sure that a girl as beautiful and talented as she would marry brilliantly unless, of course, she ruined her reputation by making love with one too many warriors. He decided that for the time being, until his negotiations were finished, seclusion was the best policy. He built her a bower near his hall with a high spiked fence all around and posted a guard at the gate. He also posted an old woman at the gate to watch the guard.

"Naturally the maiden was angry at being confined, and she sulked and stormed. When her father came to talk to her she threw the leftovers from her table out the window at him. He hollered up that it was all for her own good.

"'I wouldn't do this if I didn't love you,' said the thane, dodging a mildewed trencher. 'This bower is costing your mother and me a lot, you know.'

"The maiden threw some yellow liquid out the window in her father's direction. Some of it splattered on his clothes, and he didn't want to know what it was. 'If you didn't go around planking everything in cross-gartered hose,' he yelled, 'this wouldn't be necessary.'

"She refused to talk to him or even to see him. On those occasions when her father managed to get across her small courtyard, she barred the door and wouldn't let him in. The thane, like most fathers, was a soft touch for his daughter. At home he brooded over her hostility. 'I know, Mother,' he said, 'let's send her some gifts to cheer her up.'

"'Send her whatever you like,' said her mother, who tended to have less patience with the maiden's little foibles than her father. 'As for me I'll send her a switch so she can beat herself.'

"'Now, Mother,' said the King, 'you were young once yourself.'

"'That was different,' said the mother, but she had to smile.

"The thane began to send gifts to his daughter, one every other day. He sent her a tiny golden apple, a carved box made out of ash, and an unusual snake with the most beautiful pattern in its back, which he had bought from a gypsy who said it had magic powers to bring its owner good luck. And I suppose it did, but it took a while.

"When the maiden got the apple she threw it across the room. When she got the box she put it near the window so she could throw it at her father the next time he came near her bower. But when she got the snake she thought it was adorable, and she couldn't help playing with it and feeding it little scraps of food.

"The little snake crawled around her bower, exploring its new domain like a kitten. When it found the gold apple, it curled up around it and went to sleep. The next morning, it seemed to the girl that the apple was larger, but she thought she must be mistaken.

"The little snake crawled over to the window and curled up inside the ash box. The maiden thought the snake looked so sweet in there that instead of throwing the box at her father she kept it as a house for her snake. She noticed how much the snake liked curling around the golden apple, so she put the apple in the ash box with the snake.

"Each day it grew larger. The snake was growing and so was the golden apple it curled around. There was no doubt about it, the girl realized. The snake had outgrown his ash box, and within two weeks it had outgrown the bower. She hated to let her companion leave, but she realized she must.

"The snake loved the maiden as much as she loved him, so while he agreed to go outside, he refused to leave the bower compound. He took up his post, his body encircling the girl's home.

"Soon the snake began to change. He sprouted fin-like wings from his back and grew four legs with long-clawed paws. When he was hungry, as he often was, he roared, and fire came out of his mouth. He was no longer a snake. He was a dragon.

"The thane was beside himself. He had arranged the maiden's match but he couldn't deliver the maiden. No one dared approach the bower—even the outer fence was scorched by the dragon's frequent complaints about tardy mealtimes. The young warrior who had promised to marry the girl broke off the match. He said he couldn't wait forever, you know. The father tried to interest the local men in helping him free his daughter, but they all said that while she was lovely, and one heck of a good time, they really had to be leaving to campaign against those blood-thirsty Peckies, or to squash the marauding Wigesta, or something equally pressing.

"One day the golden apple, which had been growing larger each day just like the dragon, became so heavy that it rolled along the floor of the bower and broke through its wall. So now, in addition to the dragon, the maiden's courtyard contained an enormous apple of pure gold. This was the first that the father knew about the apple, and when he saw it he felt it offered the best hope of a solution to his problem.

"The father let it be known that any man who could kill the dragon that encircled his daughter's bower would be privileged to have both her hand and the golden apple.

"A year went by, and nobody responded to his generous offer. At least the girl would talk to her father now when he came to the edge of her courtyard and hollered up to her.

"'My life is ruined,' she would say, 'and it's all your fault.'

"Meanwhile, in a distant kingdom, there lived an old king. He had spent his entire fortune fighting his rotten and covetous neighbors. If he didn't find some source of revenue to fund the lavish gifts necessary to buy fighting men, his kingdom would soon become a satellite of this hateful tribe. This king had a son who was known for valor. The youth was as merciless to the enemy as he was generous to his friends. And he was good-looking, too. The king called this son to him and explained the situation.

"'Father,' said the prince, 'do not expect to see me again until I come to you with enough gold to pay all our warriors and buy all those of our enemies.' With those brave words, he gathered a troop of twelve loyal companions and left the country.

"He traveled for several months, raiding the hamlets of nearby kingdoms and just about making enough to live on. One day he came to a village, intent on pillage, when an old woman boldly approached his horse and flagged him down. The old woman had recently heard the story of the thane's offer. So while the men of her village ran around arming themselves with scythes and pick-axes, she sallied forth to divert their attackers.

"'Spare us,' she said, 'and I will tell you how to get more gold than you can ever use.'

"The prince, not an unreasonable lad, was all ears. The old woman told him about the thane, the maiden, the dragon and the golden apple. Being very analytical, the old woman had figured out that either the kid would be killed by the dragon, which was okay with her, or would kill the dragon, get the gold, and go back where he came from, which was also okay with her.

"To entice the prince further, the old woman told him how he could protect himself against the dragon's fiery breath. She said that if he and his friends would mind their manners she would sew him a long tunic made of leather and lined with heavy fleece.

"The lad conferred with his friends, and they decided that this was a venture worth undertaking. They stayed with the old woman for three days. And they weren't allowed to wear their boots in her house or put their elbows on the table, either. When it was time for them to leave, she gave the prince the most confusing directions she could think of, just in case the story about the dragon wasn't true. She didn't want him to be able to find his way back to her village.

"The men proceeded on their way with the typical sort of mishaps and grumbling and dissension that you might imagine. But as they got closer, it became apparent that something strange was going on. The dragon was the talk of all the neighboring kingdoms.

"Everyone knew the way to the maiden's bower. Unfortunately, not everyone knew the same way, so our warriors got lost a couple more times before they found themselves, quite unexpectedly, staring at a scorched wooden wall against whose inside edges pressed a large and vicious dragon. How it roared when it heard them!

"The prince thought it best to leave the fight for nighttime. He hoped that the creature, if cold blooded like most reptiles, would have less energy by night.

"After dark he donned the costume the old woman had made for him. He left his companions near the scorched wall and sneaked inside the gate. As soon as he went through the gate he tripped over the dragon, who awakened and roared a fierce roar with its hot breath. The prince could feel the heat on his face, but his body was protected by his bulky leather garment. The dragon tried to lash at the lad with its tail, and claw him with its claws, and bite him with its razor-sharp eye-teeth, but actually, it was wedged between the bower and the fence so tightly that it couldn't move.

"The girl was awakened by the commotion and looked out the window. What a jumble of emotions she was. She wanted to be released from her prison, but she didn't want to see her dear friend the dragon killed. She wanted a man, but she wanted to have some choice in the matter. She would have enjoyed spending that huge lump of gold herself, but now it would go to her deliverer.

"'Get the hell out of here, you interfering S. O. B.,' she screamed at the prince. He didn't look particularly handsome in his baggy leather fleece.

"The prince lifted his spear and drove it into the dragon's spine. The dragon wrenched its body around. Its back was on the ground, its soft belly exposed. The lad drove his spear into its loins and twisted it. The spear head came off inside the dragon.

"'You vile disgusting creature,' screamed the maiden.

"The prince thought she meant the dragon.

"'It's all right now,' he said. 'Its dead.'

"'Murderer!' screamed the maiden, over and over again.

"'Oh, shut up, you miserable bitch,' the prince yelled back at her.

"The prince went back to his friends. 'The dragon is dead,' he said. 'Let's go in and see if we can drag out the gold before the bitch's old man shows up and I have to marry her.'

"It took seven men to lift the dragon's body and the other six to roll the golden apple out from under it. They managed to roll the apple out of the courtyard and down to the bottom of a hill. They covered themselves and the apple with leaves, while the people rejoiced over the freeing of the maiden and wondered who the lucky lad might be who had won both her hand and the golden apple.

"Night after night the warriors traveled, rolling the golden apple before them. It took them a year to get home. When they got back, they found the prince's father being held for ransom and their people enslaved by their ancient enemy. The returning men used the gold to buy warriors and free the king and their people.

"The thane, meanwhile, was a man of his word, so he was determined that his daughter should be saved for the man who had freed her. When the dragon was cut up for dragon stew, he found the prince's spearhead wedged between two of its lumbar vertebrae, and said that whoever owned the spear shaft that fit into this spearhead should have his daughter, and none other. He offered a reward for information leading to the whereabouts of the spear and its owner. The first year several adventurers presented shafts to the father in hopes of claiming the maiden and her dowry. None of these, however, fit the spearhead. After the first year no one tried.

"Five years went by. A monk on pilgrimage stopped at the thane's hall for the night. The maiden was still handsome, but by now middle-aged and resigned to spinsterhood. As usual when they had a guest, the story of the miraculous dragon was told. The monk immediately recognized the story as the same one he had heard in the king's hall, give or take a few details. For example, the maiden's beauty and accomplishment were not mentioned in the version he had heard.

"He told the thane that he knew the identity of the maiden's rescuer. The very next morning, the thane, spearhead in hand and maiden in tow, headed for the far off kingdom. The maiden didn't give her father any trouble. She had learned by now to humor him.

"When the visitors arrived at the distant court they were very kindly and enthusiastically received by the frail old king, who believed they were, at least in part, responsible for his deliverance from the hands of his enemy. Every night the old king remembered these unknown friends in his prayers.

"The prince, old enough now to be charming even to a woman he wasn't particularly fond of, greeted the maiden and her father graciously. The maiden couldn't help noticing that even though he was older he looked a lot better now that he wasn't wearing a baggy leather-covered fleece.

"After dinner that night they told the story of the dragon once again, and the maiden and the prince talked about that extraordinary evening. 'You should have seen yourself,' said the maiden, 'trying to keep your footing on the dragon's back—'

"'It wasn't easy, I can tell you,' said the prince.

"'You were as white as death,' said the maiden, 'and you kept hollering to your men that you had everything under control.'

"'Just trying to convince myself,' said the prince.

"'I can still see you thrashing about. You looked like an old woman beating a rug. What were you wearing, anyway?'

"The prince laughed. 'Never mind,' he said.

"'As a hero I'm afraid you weren't quite what I had pictured,' said the maiden.

"'And I'm afraid what I did that night was somewhat more heroic than what I'd been doing,' the prince said.

"'But to be fair,' said the maiden, 'I guess I looked a little ridiculous myself.'

"'Not a bit,' he said, 'you looked quite fetching standing at the window with your hair sticking out in all directions screeching like a barred owl.'

"The maiden laughed. 'Hard to believe I was so stupid. But believe it or not I felt sorry for the dragon.'

"'We were so young,' they both said.

"The prince looked at the maiden. He liked the shape of her mouth. 'You were sweet,' he said, 'to care so much about a reptile.'

"The maiden looked at the prince. His cheekbones were cut at just the right angle. 'And you were the only man brave enough to rescue me,' she said.

"They gazed into each other's eyes. They fell in love.

"'Stop everything,' said the maiden's father.

"'Now what?' said the maiden.

"'We have to check the spearhead.'

"The prince called to a servant to fetch his spear. He removed its head. The one the father handed him was a perfect fit.

"The maiden and the prince were married, and as old as they were God blessed them with six healthy sons and two daughters."

Red paused for a few moments before continuing: "You might think the story ends here, and for the maiden and the prince it does, but for you perhaps it doesn't. There was another part to the charm of the dragon that the gypsy didn't tell the father."

For the first time since his tale had begun I looked away from Red. I glanced up and noticed the shadows cast by the antlers ringing the hall. They bent around the corner where the wall meets the ceiling, hovering over us like ghouls with outstretched arms.

Red continued, "This dragon has two lives. After the prince killed it the monster abandoned its carcass like a lizard discards its skin, and it turned once again into a tiny snake. Men say this snake has been traveling the countryside in search of its lost gold ever since. There are reports the Hwicce have seen it, and I know it's roamed the Andredeswald for many years. It is said that one day the snake will see the gold dipped roof of a king's hall and think it has found its missing treasure. Then the snake will turn into a dragon again, ten times fiercer than before."

The tapers had burned down. The light in the hall was dim. Red, his head and hands seemingly unattached to anything corporeal, looked like a wraith.

"The dragon will harass this hall," he said, "and give no peace until it has stolen all the king's treasures and taken them to its nest."

The light from the hearth lit Red's thin face from below: he looked demonic. His voice got louder and louder. "The dragon will come back night after night. It will kill everyone. It will rip apart your flesh with icy claws sharper than iron nails. It will bite off your heads and hands. Its eye teeth are like daggers. The dragon will crunch your bones into powder with its molars and slurp down small children whole."

He stopped a moment. "Your blood is like wine to this beast."

The root faces we had carved earlier that day, collapsing from the heat, shriveled like death's heads. Red's voice was very loud now. "After the dragon has all the treasure its lair can hold, it will burn this hall to the ground. No man will escape. No man can kill it."

He paused. We were speechless. Then he spoke quietly. "The first night it comes it will stand outside in the cold and breathe fire against the hall door until it opens."

Suddenly, the hall door sprang open. You could see a flame shooting across the outside of the doorway. People cried out in fear and grabbed the nearest person for comfort.

"It's looking for the maiden. It feels betrayed. But it doesn't remember exactly what she looks like. Any beautiful maiden will do."

All at once a woman screamed. The piercing sound penetrated every corner of the hall. No one moved. Outside the door you could hear a clatter of running feet and see the dragon's fiery breath retreating into the distance.

"No point in following it. You'll never catch it," said Red. And that was the end of his story.

*SCENE* 19 EGBERT AND ODBURH

I had been planning to leave the hall as soon as Red's story was over, but with a dragon outside I had second thoughts. I decided to wait until the Easton contingent were ready to go and trail behind them. I was still working out the details when I was approached by no less a personage than the dish thane.

"I say, Woman," said Haedde, "don't you work here?"

For a moment I was tempted to deny it, but I didn't think I could get away with it. I admitted that I did.

"Come along with me, will you?"

He took me aside. "Look," he said, pointing out the queen. "This is a disaster. No one is attending the queen. I want you to stand next to her in case she needs anything until I can find someone more suitable."

Most of the tables had been broken down for the dance. The queen sat at one of the few remaining, which had been pushed back close to the pillars. There wasn't a servant in sight, nor was she attended by any of her usual entourage. Her ladies were playing with Wermhere, and Athelstan was standing near the cleared area waiting for the dancing to begin. As for the king, he was at the far end of the hall rolling dice and drinking with Warr and Thingfrith. In fact, the only people sitting around Odburh were several of the nicer warriors—the kind of fellows who were too polite to abandon a lady. Haedde led me over to a spot right behind the queen's elbow.

"Don't move from here," he said to me, "until I send someone over to take your place." The thane then had a brief word with the queen, during which he looked apologetic and glanced in my direction.

The dancing started. Normally the first dance would have been lead by the king and queen, but tonight it was Wermhere's job. He was drunk by now and needed two of the queen's ladies as well as his own brassy queen to get him onto the dance floor. The four of them lumbered around together confusing the other couples, their movements an obscure parody of the dance's complicated formations. Athelstan looked annoyed. The ever watchful butler summoned a replacement couple and then motioned to the ladies supporting Wermhere to get the weaving catastrophe off the floor.

Egbert came over to have a word with Ercenwald, who was sitting at the end of the table. As he was leaving, the queen raised her arm.

"Your Royal Highness," said Egbert.

"Sit down," said the queen. The gold ringlet at her temple couldn't contain her hair: an escaped lock tumbled down over one eye. The warrior who had been sitting next to the queen excused himself and left. The queen looked at Egbert and then glanced at the empty seat. He sat down.

The queen looked around the table. "Why don't you all get lost?" she said. I wondered if that included me.

She held up a finger. "Wine," she said. I assumed that request was directed at me. I went off to look for some. It took a little while because I had to find Haedde and get him to give the okay before the wine steward would hand over a pitcher of wine and two goblets on a silver tray. When I came back, Egbert and the queen, alone at the table, were turned toward each other with their knees touching. I put down the goblets and poured the wine. They didn't seem to notice. I went back to my post behind the queen.

Odburh's jeweled hand was on Egbert's forearm. "That story tonight . . ." she said, making a little shudder like a cat shaking its fur.

"It was only a story, Odburh," he said.

"No. I could see the beast's eyes. I saw its teeth."

The woman has remarkable vision, I thought.

"I don't feel safe," she said. She was looking down, pouting ever so slightly. Her hair, falling forward, obscured her face like a partially drawn curtain. She lifted her chin and shook her hair back. It was an amazingly provocative little toss. She turned her golden eyes on him full force. Her fingers stroked his arm. "I feel better when you're with me, Egbert," she said.

He gave her a glance that could have saved a blacksmith the expense of a fire. I looked away, but I couldn't avoid hearing. "I'd like to be with you," he said. His voice was as intimate as a touch. I wondered if Egbert knew her reputation. This man who claimed to notice things! I hadn't expected him to be so gullible.

"The king has had a lot to drink tonight," said the queen. She sounded as if she were running out of breath.

"Yes," said Egbert. His hand was on her thigh. I looked around the room to see if Haedde and my replacement were anywhere in sight. I felt a little sick to my stomach.

The queen smiled. Her tone lightened up. "How do you like my outfit?" she said.

"Perfect," said Egbert. He was looking at her mouth.

"I'm sure the king won't come to my bower tonight," said the queen. She sounded serious again.

"He's a fool," said Egbert. For once I agreed with the man.

"I'll be waiting for you," said the queen. She started to get up. Egbert grabbed her hand.

"You don't mind, then?" he said.

She looked at him uncomprehendingly. "Mind what?" she said.

"Oh," he said. He looked upset. "You don't know. That's it."

"Don't know what?" said the queen.

Egbert couldn't talk for a moment. "You don't know what could happen."

"What?" said the queen.

"I don't know why I always think everyone knows about it." he said. His anguished look might have caused a less calculating woman to throw caution to the wind. "It was stupid of me." Then his voice was very quiet. "I hoped it wouldn't matter, Odburh."

The queen didn't say anything.

"The other night," said Egbert, "when I talked about that quest"—

"That pathetic story—" said the queen.

"I'm afraid it wasn't the whole story," said Egbert.

"What was?" asked the queen.

"Things got worse," said Egbert. He stopped for a moment. "The old woman with the runes—" he said.

"Yes?" said the queen.

"I met her again when I was leaving."

"And?"

"You remember what she looked like?"

"A walking corpse?"

"Close enough. When I saw her again, at the same crossroads as before, she flagged me down. She asked me to come with her. I thought she needed help. We went to an old hovel by the side of the road—it was small, like a work shed, with a dug-out dirt floor.

"She took me inside. Death and decay hung in the air. I tripped over something. When my eyes got used to the dark I realized it was a rusted sword splattered with gore. There was garbage everywhere—stacks of rotting leftovers—instead of burying these outside the old lady had pushed them back against the walls and left them.

"'Come on, come on, don't dawdle,' the woman said.

"I took another step into the room and put my foot into some sticky ooze. I saw what needed to be done and started to sort out the mess. It was obviously too much for the blind old woman. She sat down on the floor and took off her clothes.

"'Do you want me to wash those?' I said.

"She laughed. It was a harsh sound. 'You are a tidy boy, aren't you?' she said. Or something like that. Anyway, she held out her knobby old hand to me. Three of the fingernails were half white and lifting from their bases. I took her hand. I thought she wanted to get up. Instead she pulled my arm sharply and caught me off-balance. I fell down next to her. She smelled vaguely putrid, like the flower of a cuckoo-pint."

"'Make love to me,' she said.

"'What?' I said.

"'Something wrong with your ears?' she said.

"'But madam,' I said, 'I can't do that.'

"'Something wrong with your pecker?' she said.

"'Yes,' I said, trying to get out of it without offending her.

"'You're lying,' she shrieked. 'I could have forgiven a simple refusal, but I cannot forgive what you have done: You have transposed your prepositions and confused your past participles.'

"'You've lost me, madam,' I said.

"'You lied to me, when you should have lain with me,' she said. She stopped dead still for a minute, and I thought she might be having a fit. I wrapped some large rags around her. She stirred, and I asked her if she were all right.

"'Leave me alone,' she snapped. 'I'm just sorting out your curse.' She sat up and massaged her brow with her hand. 'Got it,' she said. 'Listen up. I curse you with a curse that will lay upon your head until you lie in your grave. From this time forward, you who would not lie with an old woman will only be able to lay old women.'"

The pitcher I was holding slid off its silver tray and bounced twice on the floor. The wine that didn't splatter the queen's angel wings sat in a puddle precariously close to her feet. I wedged myself under her bench and used my skirt to clean up what I could. My head stuck out near the queen's knees. I glanced up and saw her and Egbert looking down. "Excuse me, Your Royal Highness," I said.

"Stupid hag," the queen said fiercely. Then she returned her attention to Egbert.

"Does this mean," she said to him with a dangerous edge in her tone, "that you don't want me? Am I wasting my time here?" *This is finally getting interesting*, I thought.

"No," he said, sounding surprised. One of his knees was between hers. His calf muscle rubbed against hers. I had a good view of that from where I was. "No, that's just the point," he said. "Be patient. It's a long story, and I have to tell you everything—or it wouldn't be fair. Where was I?"

"You can only do it with crones," said Odburh.

"Right. The perverted old bat looked proud of herself. 'Not too bad, huh?' she asked me of all people. I just looked at her, wondering if it would affect the curse one way or the other if I bashed her brains out. She must have seen the blood in my eye, because I got the feeling she was trying to pacify me when she said, 'If you fall in love with an ugly old woman the curse will be lifted.'"

"'In that case why bother?' I snapped.

"'Because,' she said, 'when you fall in love with an old hag she will become as young and beautiful as she was old and ugly.'"

Sometimes things just flash into your mind whether you want them to or not, and this was one of those times. I imagined Egbert, thinking I was an old woman, telling me he was in love with me. I imagined myself telling Egbert that he couldn't be in love with me because I was really a young woman. Then Egbert would tell me I had only turned young because he loved me. For an instant I could feel his body pressing against mine as it had that night behind the curtain. I wished I had taken my chances with the dragon and left when I could.

"That curse will never be lifted," the queen was saying. The dangerous moment had passed, and now she was almost sympathetic. "No man could possibly fall in love with an ugly old woman. How could you?"

Egbert sighed and looked desolate. "And that's not all. After the hag made the curse she seemed to mull it over. I had had enough of her. I turned to leave.

"She laughed. 'Relax, sonny. You can't go until I'm done with you. I like it,' she said, 'but it needs something.'

"When she was ready to speak again the witch turned her face in my direction. Her foggy eyes gazed past my right temple. 'I know what I almost forgot,' she said. 'Just in case you meet a young woman so powerful that she threatens to defeat my spell—'"

Here Egbert interrupted his narrative to study the queen's eyes and say, with all the incredulity of a man who has just seen the heavens open and heard angels sing, "And that's what you've done, Odburh."

He whispered the next bit: "I used to think it was hopeless." I could have killed Haedde for making me watch this. I craned my neck to look for him.

The queen looked at Egbert with more tenderness than I would have thought she possessed. Egbert moved his mouth close to hers, and for a moment I thought he was going to kiss her, right in front of everybody. But then he seemed to remember where he was, and he wrenched himself away from Odburh and went back to his story.

He became very solemn. "I wish I didn't have to tell you this part, Odburh. You mustn't let it frighten you." He looked at her.

The queen's eyes were dreamy. "I don't frighten easily, Egbert," she said. Egbert waited another moment before going on, then he spoke as if he were determined to get it over with.

"The woman said to me, 'Remember what I am going to say. Should some bewitching young woman manage to make you want her, and you dare make love to her, that woman will become as old and ugly as she was young and beautiful.'"

The queen turned pale, but Egbert didn't seem to notice. He unwisely elaborated on what he had said.

"'Where her hair was thick and stranded with gold it will become white and so skimpy her scalp will show through. If her eyes were glistening they will become clouded. If her skin was white and flawless it will become the home of warts and boils. Her joints will swell. Her teeth will loosen. Infections will ooze from her gums. No glorious gowns will conceal her misshapen form, and all the incense in Christendom will not be able to improve her smell.'"

Egbert looked at the queen. There was a greenish tinge around her mouth. He put his arm around her shoulders, and she went rigid. "Don't look so bleak, Odburh. It's going to get better. Stay with me. As you can imagine I was furious. I put my hands around the old crone's neck and choked her until she gagged. She flailed her bony arms around uselessly. When I saw I had made my point I let up the pressure.

"'You take back that curse,' I said, 'or you have breathed your last.'

"'Wait a minute,' she gasped. 'I can't take it back.' I throttled her again.

"She sputtered something. 'What was that?' I said.

"'Wait, wait.' She was desperate. 'I can't take it back but I can modify it.'

"'Get busy,' I said.

"'Not until you promise to keep your filthy hands off me,' she said.

"I agreed. She made me swear on my sword. Listen, Odburh. She said, 'The beautiful young woman won't always turn into a monstrous old hag.'"

Egbert looked at the queen anxiously. "You see it isn't hopeless, Odburh," he said.

He went on, "The witch reached up as if she were pulling something out of the air. Then she said, 'Only two out of three will.'"

The queen was staring straight ahead, looking as amorous as the village scold at vespers. Egbert looked at her intently. His voice was low. "We can defeat her, Odburh," he said. "We've got one chance in three."

The queen said nothing.

"Will you?" he said.

She squeaked, "Will I what?"

"Will you take a chance?" asked Egbert.

"You're not serious?" said the queen. She was shaking. She started to get up. Egbert looked hurt.

"I understand," he said. His tone was cold, though.

"I'm sorry," said the queen. "I really am." She extricated herself from behind the bench and looked at the door.

"It's all right," said Egbert sadly. He didn't sound angry anymore. He stood up and took Odburh's hand. I thought she cringed a little.

"Thank you for . . . breaking through her curse," Egbert was saying. "And if you ever change your mind—"

"I have to go," she said. Egbert shook his head slightly in agreement.

"You know where to find me," he said. He pressed her hand. She pulled it away and ran out of the hall.

Once the queen was out of the hall, Egbert slumped down on the bench and leaned back against a pillar. He shut his eyes and breathed out a great breath. It seemed like a good moment to slink away. Just as I was backing off, he opened his eyes and looked at me. I stumbled over a shield some thoughtless warrior had left in the aisle.

He sat up. "Cynethrith," he said. I stopped in my tracks. *He knows my name.* For a moment he looked as if there were something he wanted to say to me but he couldn't quite remember what it was. Would he murder me or try to make love to me, I wondered. I couldn't decide which prospect was scarier.

"I know who Haedde works for," I blurted out.

"Let me guess," said Egbert. He grinned at me. "I bet you're going to tell me that Haedde works for Wihtred."

I was so incensed I completely forgot my place. "God damn you, Egbert," I said. "If you knew all along, why the hell did you attack me?"

He got serious. "I've been meaning to apologize for that," he said. "I hope I didn't hurt you."

I glared at him. He hadn't hurt me, exactly. It was the principle of the thing.

"I can't explain it," he said, "but I was wrong, and I'm sorry. I'll do what I can to make it up to you."

He reached into his belt. I felt my face getting red. "Here's your knife," he said.

I took the knife, warm from his body. He leaned back against the pillar again, his arms folded across his chest. He smiled at me disarmingly.

"Can I watch you put it away?" he said.

"*May* I," I coldly corrected.

"Please do," he said.

Just then Athelwulf came over and sat down next to him, saying, "You got rid of her?"

"Yeah," Egbert said, with what seemed like a sigh of relief. Then he chuckled.

Dear God, I thought, how callous can you get? He must have murdered some other woman instead of me. And he's laughing about it. With the insensitivity typical of fighting men their conversation moved with no transition from the murder to the food in the hall, which could be bad this time of year. Athelwulf said, "If I were you I'd watch what I eat for the next few days." The two of them didn't notice me walk away. I was glad to know I was seeing the last of Egbert. If I'd known about his peculiar predilection earlier I would have left long ago.

SCENE 20 CYNETHRITH FLEES

It was just about midnight. I watched a stupefied Wermhere carried from the king's throne and deposited on the floor of the servant's alley. It was lucky that I got away from Egbert when I did because I noticed the group from Easton edging toward the door. There were two things I had to do, and fast. First I found Tecla.

"Tecla," I said. "I'm getting out of here. Tonight's the best opportunity I'll have."

"Yes," she said. "Godspeed." She hugged me. There were tears in her eyes.

"I'll get you out of here somehow, Tecla," I said.

"I'll be all right," she said. "I have to stay and look after Helmie."

I was going to tell her to warn Mildred about Egbert, but just then the old woman passed by.

"Mildred," I said, stopping her.

"What is it Cynethrith?" she asked.

"Has Egbert ever—" I paused, but this was no time to pussy-foot around. "Mildred," I said, "watch out for Egbert. He can only have sex with old women."

"Really?" she said.

"Yes, I thought I'd better warn you."

"Egbert?" she said. "The good-looking one?"

"The one that killed Unferth. Look, I have to go. Just watch out, okay?"

"Yes, all right," she said. She didn't look a bit concerned. In fact, she walked away smiling. Maybe she didn't believe it.

Having done not much (but the best I could) by my fellow servants, I wormed my way into the midst of the anxious guests standing near the door and trying to get up the nerve to go outside. I pushed past them and escaped the hall unnoticed, catching up with the Eastoners on the far side of the courtyard. They didn't seem a bit nervous. In fact, once we left the palace grounds they all began laughing as if their sides would split. People congratulated Red over and over again and told him how brilliant he had been. I had to admit he told a good story, and parts of it were slightly humorous, but overall I didn't see anything particularly funny about it, especially not the last part. To my surprise nobody seemed a bit worried about the dragon. I figured they must have had a lot to drink.

As we got farther from the palace, and I felt the probability of encountering the beast had lessened, I edged my way toward the back of the group. Then I stepped into a hedge and let them get ahead of me. The first thing I did was to spit out the seeds I had kept wedged in my mouth for all those weeks. I ran my tongue over my gums—they felt sore. I was afraid they were infected.

The moon was high, luckily it was a clear night, and except for frequent muddy pits along the path the going was not too difficult. It was not yet dawn when I reached the abbey and found the key to the guest hall tied to the post where I had left it. I went inside, took off my clothes, threw them in a heap, and collapsed. No eastern luxury could have felt better than the clean sheets and mattress of this abbey bed. The next thing I knew Athelflad was standing over me saying, "Thank God."

"Go away," I said. "I'll tell you all about it tomorrow."

"Did you get my message?" she asked.

"What message?" I asked.

"I guess you didn't," she said. "I asked one of the servants who was going to the party to tell you to come back."

"Did you tell her who I was?"

"No, of course not. I told her to ask the old women servants if they knew a nun from Itchen Abbas named Athelflad, and if one said yes just to say, 'Return immediately.' I figured you were the only one who would know what it meant. Anyway, it was the best I could do in a pinch."

"She may have tried," I said. "Last night was complete chaos. What was so urgent?"

"Your stepmother has been camped out in the prioress' quarters for the last three days demanding to see you."

"Oh, God," I said.

"I don't think I could have put her off much longer."

"What got her so interested?"

"She heard you weren't eating. She was afraid you were going to die."

"You mean she hoped I would," I said.

Athelflad snapped, "I don't mean anything of the sort. The woman's been worried sick."

There was no point in trying to explain Waldberg to Athelflad.

"Anyway, you look awful." She examined my scalp. "You're totally infested," she said. "We've got to clean you up before Waldberg comes storming over here."

"See if you've got anything for infected gums," I said.

Athelflad was back in the twinkling of an eye. Besides soap and water she brought chamomile milk to whiten my skin and a decoction of privet leaves for my tender mouth. She sectioned my hair and soaked each segment with an infusion of juniper berries and vinegar, then combed it carefully with a fine-toothed comb. "Do this at two-week intervals, three times. And in future, make sure you wear your veil at all times," she lectured.

She picked up the clothes I'd left on the floor, holding them at arms-length from her body. "I'll burn these filthy rags for you," she said.

"Oh, no you don't," I said. "I may need them again some day."

"They're full of fleas, and they stink," said Athelflad.

"Hide them outside somewhere. I'll wash them later," I said.

When Athelflad came back to inspect my appearance I was dressed in my own clothes again and ready.

"You look all right," she said. "A little thin, but other than that you're okay. I'm going to get Waldberg now, and you better have a good story to tell."

A few minutes later Athelflad returned with my stepmother and the prioress. Waldberg looked at me, and when she saw I was still alive she was so disappointed she burst into tears. The prioress put her arms around Waldberg, who broke away to berate me.

"How could you put me through this, you selfish, unfeeling, ungrateful child?"

I stared at her coldly. "As much as I love you, Mother," I said, "I must put the love of God before you." Athelflad gave me a dirty look.

"My work here is complete, for now," I said. "St. Wihtburh has released me back into the world for a while. I will go with you whenever you wish."

"You look thin," said Waldberg. "You better stay here for another week and rest before you travel." It was obvious to me the woman didn't want me back in her house, or my house, I should say.

Waldberg looked at the prioress. "Make sure she eats. Use a funnel if you have to."

That was brilliant. The prioress nodded in sympathy. Waldberg had them all eating out of her hand. If she told them one morning I had died in the night, no one would suspect a thing.

"I'm going home now," said Waldberg. She looked at me. "You can use the next week to try to create an apology that I will find acceptable." She swept from the room. It was amazing that such a little person could stir up such volatile air currents.

Athelflad stayed with me once the prioress had gone. "You were awfully cold to your stepmother," she said. Dear innocent Athelflad. She really was unbearable sometimes.

"I'll try to do better," I said. That seemed the quickest way to get her off the subject. "Are you ready for some stories?"

Athelflad was such an enthusiastic listener that I forgave her for being an insufferable do-gooder. We hashed and re-hashed the events of the last month. I told her each story several times, and each time it was as if we lived through the incidents together. We both laughed over a lot of things that hadn't seemed funny at the time, but even so, she seemed to think my encounters with Egbert were a lot funnier than I did. She was appalled, however, to hear that he was prepared to commit adultery with the queen. She thought that the curse the witch put on him was a blessing in disguise which would, in the end, save him from perdition.

As usual, she was determined to see the good side. "There must be something good about a man who risked his life to rescue another from a hall full of tormentors," she said when I told her how Egbert had pulled Helmstan out of his bone castle. I tried to explain to her that was just Egbert's way of asserting himself and winning a place at court, and it had nothing to do with good or bad. Besides, risk is a way of life to a man like that. But reality was something Athelflad preferred to ignore.

Even she, however, was hard pressed to find something good in Wermhere. "Are you sure you're not exaggerating?" she said. "You do have this way of seeing the worst in people." I told her she could borrow my servant's costume and see for herself. She said she would be content to pray that I would be more charitable to my fellow man and that this particular fellow man would be uplifted by God's love. Of course Tecla's story touched her very much, and I fervently hoped that most of her prayers would be on that poor girl's behalf.

I lounged in bed for a week at the abbey, playing the invalid. It was wonderful. My prognostication that I would be hailed as a saint was not far off the mark. The sisters brought me food and watched discreetly to make sure I ate it. To be honest I could hardly stop eating it, and it was hard to be as restrained as my quasi-saintly status required. The nuns combed my hair, treated my gums, and bathed my skin with lavender water. Several of them could read, and they read to me by the hour. They treated me like a living relic. They still do. I never could shake the effects of this girlish prank. At the time I found it amusing and said as little as possible, assuming this was the safest way to maintain my aura.

SCENE 21 BACK IN EASTON

Finally the dogs and I walked back to Easton. I had equipped myself with a set of words that I hoped would make it possible for Waldberg and me to coexist until I could formulate a new escape. She looked angry and upset when she saw me walk into the hall. I went over to her, ensconced as usual behind her embroidery frame.

"Hello, Mother," I said.

"Cynethrith," she said. I had decided the best thing was to go along with the little fiction she had created about being concerned for me.

"I'm am terribly sorry, Mother," I said, "if you were worried over my health."

"I should hope you would be," she said. Her face got scrunched up, and for a moment I thought she was going to cry again. Even after a week she still hadn't gotten over the disappointment of finding me alive. I couldn't help rubbing it in a little. "As you can see I'm as lively as a lyre."

"It's a miracle," she said. Then she sighed. "I'm sorry I was so upset. Perhaps you are following the will of God. I will try to allow you to be guided by your own soul." That threw me for a moment, then I marveled at the subtlety of the woman. Now that there was no prioress to overhear she was slyly egging me on to do it again. She no doubt thought I couldn't possibly live through it twice.

"Yes, Mother," I said. "I'm so glad you understand."

I was relieved when this interview with Waldberg was curtailed by the door banging open. My dark-haired stepsister rushed in, eyes sparkling, cheeks pink. I realized at once this could mean only one thing.

"Sorry I'm late, Mother," she gushed. "Werwulf had something special he wanted to show me."

"I'll bet he did," I mumbled.

"You're back," Wulfwaru said flatly. "I would have thought all those weeks contemplating a virgin saint would have lifted your little pea brain out of the gutter."

"Welcome home," grinned Hilda, sitting up and stretching like a cat. She had been lying unobtrusively on a bench against the wall ever since I'd entered.

Waldberg bent over her embroidery. Her mouth had a determined set to it.

"So many marvelous things happened while you were gone," said Wulfwaru, inspecting her fingernails. "Just last week there was a fabulous party. At the palace. What a shame you had to miss it. Wasn't it wonderful, Hilda? There probably won't be another party like that for years and years."

"It was a good time," smiled Hilda, her face all teeth.

"It was spectacular," said Wulfwaru. She had changed her hair color again: this time it looked almost striped. "The hall was beautiful. The food was out of this world. The men were fantastic, but I guess you don't care about things like that."

"What party was that?" I asked innocently.

"All Hallows," she said. "The king opened his hall and invited all the villagers. Don't you remember it from other years?"

"We were too young to go other years," I said.

"Right," said Wulfwaru, "but not this year. Too bad you missed it. The king and queen were there. The queen is perfect. I don't know why some people tell stories about her."

"I understand she's loose," I said. I couldn't stop myself.

"They just say that because she's gorgeous," mewed Wulfwaru. She tilted her chin. "A lot of beautiful women have the same problem, but of course it's not something you need to worry about."

"The king's a lot of fun, a nice guy," said Hilda. "I rolled a few dice with him."

Where was I, I wondered, while Hilda was rolling dice with the king?

"And his son—what a doll," said Wulfwaru. "I danced with him."

I had missed that, too. All this must have taken place while I was imprisoned behind the queen and Egbert. I felt like saying, *Oh yeah? Well you'll never guess what I did. I crawled on my hands and knees under a bench sopping up wine with my skirt while the queen and the king's strongest warrior sat above me drooling over each other.* Why is it the best stories can never be told?

"To be honest a lot of the riffraff were there, too," Wulfwaru went on, "but the warriors I met could tell the difference."

"Is that what they told you?" I smirked.

"You're revolting," Wulfwaru assured me.

"Wasn't that little man something who got to be king for the night?" said Hilda.

"He was cute," said Wulfwaru, "so tiny, like a little toy."

"Adorable," said Hilda.

They were talking to each other now, as if I weren't there. I was used to it. They had done it since we were children.

"He ought to be a poet," said Hilda, "Did you notice his alliteration? And funny! I almost split a gut when he introduced Red. Everybody calls him Retch now."

"He was hilarious," said Wulfwaru, "but you didn't dare laugh. I loved it when he picked on that sourpuss crone from Avington."

Wulfwaru had to address her next comment to me, since she was itching to talk about it, and I was the only one who hadn't heard . . . and heard. "I met a man, one of the king's champions. He's in love with me."

I put two and two together, and I didn't like what I came up with. "That's not the Werwulf you were just talking about, is it?" I asked.

"Yes." She was as pleased as a fox with a bird in its mouth. "It is."

"But he—" I said, then I stopped. How could I tell her that her dreamboat was famous for biting off a woman's nose?

"Oh, you envy me! You're positively green," gloated Wulfwaru.

"I—uh," I didn't know what to say.

"I'd like you a little better if you'd admit it for once in your life."

"Just be careful," I said. "Okay?"

"I don't believe it," she said. It was amazing how much disgust she managed to convey with those four words. "You're such an old maid."

"Don't do anything to make him jealous," I said.

"Oh for God's sake," said Wulfwaru.

"Don't curse, for heaven's sake," interjected Waldberg. "Especially not in front of Cynethrith."

"Oh, right," said Wulfwaru, "she's gone all holy on us, but that doesn't stop her giving advice on romance."

"Don't ridicule what you don't understand," said Waldberg.

"You should have heard Retch's story," said Hilda, changing the subject. The two girls burst into laughter. There it was again.

Without thinking I said, "Why does everyone in Easton think that story is so bloody funny?"

"Who have you talked to?" asked Hilda.

"They told me his story at the abbey," I said, passing over her question. "And it didn't sound particularly funny."

"It's not the story that's so funny," said Waldberg, grimly.

"It's Osbert," said Hilda.

"Osbert?" I asked.

"Yes, it's phase two."

"Phase two?" I must have been gone too long.

"You remember before you left we pulled one over on the tax as-sessors?"

"Of course," I said.

"Well, that worked, as far as it went. But the problem, as the men see it, is that the king is still here. He seems to have settled into Win-chester quite comfortably—"

"And," said Wulfwaru, "there doesn't seem to be any chance he will pull out before spring."

"And," said Hilda, "guess who's feeding him and all those hungry Werwulfs at court?"

"Oh," I said, "okay. We are, no doubt, coming up with most of the food—except for the odd deer or boar the thanes catch."

"But what really got the guys wound up," said Wulfwaru, "was when they heard about the other party they're planning at the palace. Well, of course, you wouldn't have heard about it, but the best people from all over England are supposed to be coming. It's going to go on for a fortnight or more. All the guys are convinced it's going to cost us a fortune." She looked off into space. "Maybe I'll get an invitation . . . ."

"I hope you're not thinking about mentioning this plan to your precious Werwulf," threatened Hilda. "If I get the idea that you might I will see to it that the two of you are never alone."

"This is serious business, Wulfwaru," said Waldberg. Every now and then she surprised me by paying attention to what was going on. "I think you know how I feel about it. I was against these deceptions from the start. But your sister's right—everybody in Easton could get executed if this gets out."

"And that includes you, for Christ's sake," Hilda pointed out to Wulfwaru.

"Watch your language," said Waldberg.

"I'm certainly not going to tell him, you idiot," said Wulfwaru to her sister. "I don't have to tell him, Mother. Werwulf is so fearless—you should hear some of the stories he tells. I don't have to tell him a thing. When he sees that dragon he'll go out and chase it, and our guys will have to run for their lives before he gets close enough to see it's a fake."

"He'll have to get pretty damn close before he could spot this one as a fake. Have you seen it?" said Hilda.

"So what's all this got to do with Red's story?" I asked, although I was beginning to see the outlines of the ruse fairly clearly.

"I keep forgetting you weren't there, poor girl," said Wulfwaru.

"What it has to do with it is that Retch's story was carefully designed to make the court nervous."

"I think it did that," I said.

"How would you know?" said Hilda.

"I mean it sounds like it did," I said.

"That's what we all thought," said Wulfwaru. "On the night of the party they used a flame held by a couple of guys to fake the dragon. They figured they could get away with something simple because it would be so unexpected."

"And I mean to tell you it worked," said Hilda. "You should have heard some of the descriptions of the dragon that were floating around that hall right afterwards. I heard its scales described, its wings, its claws, its fangs. The human imagination is a wonderful thing."

I remembered what the queen had said about seeing the dragon's eyes. She wasn't the only one.

"And guess what's being built in Arkil's barn at this very moment?" asked Wulfwaru.

"A new plow?" I said.

"Very funny, as usual," said Hilda. "Go take a look. It'll make a believer out of you."

It wasn't often that I followed advice handed out by a member of my family, but I decided that I would go take a look at whatever was being built in Arkil's barn. One of the farmers, who appeared to be casually weeding couch grass in a field near the barn, was serving his spell as lookout. As I approached he stood up, yawned, and stretched both his hands over his head. Arkil immediately came out of the barn and walked over to me. I could see in these details the hallmark of one of Osbert's operations.

"Cynethrith," he said. "Your stepmother was afraid you were dead."

"I am dead," I said.

"Very funny. What brings you here?"

"I heard I missed out on all the fun."

Arkil laughed. "You should have been there. We're still laughing."

"Do you really think you're going to be able to pass off this thing you're making?" I asked.

"Piece of cake. Last week we fooled the entire court with two guys and a torch. Did you hear about it?"

"It's the talk of the village," I said. Arkil looked pleased.

"May I see it?" I asked.

"Better than that. You can work on it," he said. "We could use an extra pair of hands."

He led me into the barn where I was surprised to see one quarter of Easton's able-bodied population occupied at large tables set up around the perimeter. In the center, suspended from the ceiling, was a creature of immense size. The front part of the beast, carved out of wood, consisted of a large head attached to a long neck that slid with no discernible break into an upper torso with front legs. The dragon's mouth, arranged in a growl, displayed spectacularly toothy jaws. It's forelegs appeared to walk: one clawed paw crept low and forward; the other, stalking behind, was raised.

"Notice how the mouth is open?" Arkil asked.

"Very intimidating," I said.

"Listen to this." He led me over to a worktable where the smith was hammering on a configuration of tubes and funnels. "How about a demo?" Arkil asked him.

The man blew into the contraption, and it hissed loudly. I jumped.

Arkil and the smith laughed. "Good, huh?" Arkil said.

"Terrific," I said. "Who's riding inside to blow it?"

"Don't have to," Arkil said, "which is just as well in case we have to scuttle Cerdic," as they called the beast. The man showed me how the tube was constructed. "When the wind blows it will automatically hiss," he explained.

"Brilliant," I had to admit.

"And wait till he finishes this," said Arkil, pointing to a metal torch. "It goes in his mouth as well, and it'll look like he's breathing fire."

At the next table a basket weaver was bending young hazel twigs into hoops. "She's figured out how we can get some movement into the body," said Arkil.

"These," the woman said, pointing to the wall where a line of hoops started large and got incrementally smaller, "are his ribs. As you can see he'll get smaller and smaller until he ends in a tail."

"Are you planning on covering them?" I wondered.

"That's what all that sacking's for," Arkil said, pointing to a pile on the other side of the barn.

"You said he would move?" I prompted.

"His tail's not stabilized by any struts so when the wind blows—"

"—it lashes around," finished the woman.

Arkil led me over to a sewing table. A slave was getting instructions from Edith, who was showing her how to put together pieces of sacking cut in tapered sections, scalloped at the wide end.

Edith looked up as we approached. "Hello, Cynethrith, I'm glad you're all right," she said, "Somehow I couldn't believe you'd let yourself starve to death in the abbey guest house. You sure had your mother worried, though." This was getting embarrassing. I wondered if there was anybody in Easton Waldberg hadn't blabbed to. Probably not. The woman was so obvious.

Edith turned her attention to the slave. "Stitch this edge, and make a small casing here, right along the seam, about three-eighths of an inch. Leave it open at this end for the boning."

"You asked about the covering," Arkil explained, "This particular bit is for his wings, but the body covering will be the same. Of course it will look totally different once its dyed and starched."

We were standing near the refreshment table, where Cole was taking a break. "Would you like a drink?" Arkil asked me.

"Thanks," I said. He poured ale into wooden cups.

Cole had a question for Arkil. "Did you find anyone?"

Arkil nodded. "Edith's cousin works at the palace."

"What did you tell her?"

"Missing stock: six sheep and two oxen. The numbers will be bigger when the story gets there."

"Good," said Cole, walking off. "That'll keep them edgy."

"What color is he going to be?" I asked.

"Mostly greenish yellow, with a little purple thrown in here and there," said Arkil.

"Saw-wort and marjoram?" I asked.

"Exactly," he said. "All we need now is starch. Lots of starch."

"Cuckoo pint?" I suggested.

"You know where you can get some?" he asked.

"Yes, I think so," I admitted. "There were a lot in the linden wood last summer."

"Good. How would you like to dig up about a hundred and fifty?"

"Sounds highly entertaining," I said.

"We knew we could count on you," said Arkil.

"Just a minute," I said. I decided to negotiate for the pleasure of seeing the king's hoodlums scared out of their wits by a fake dragon. "Does this mean I get to come to the party?"

"No," said Arkil.

"How badly do you want the 150 cuckoo pints?" I asked.

"It's dangerous," said Arkil.

"I'm the fastest runner in the village," I reminded him.

"Let's say you trip," said Arkil. "You'll be tortured."

"Here's my final offer," I said, "No party, no cuckoo pint."

"If there's trouble you're on your own," he said.

"You got a deal," I said.

SCENE 22 THE DRAGON VISITS THE PALACE

I worked like a slave for two days digging up the floor of the wood where I remembered having seen cuckoo pints the previous summer. I dragged sacks full of the roots to Arkil's barn, where we shredded them into large vats, added water and boiled the mixture until it was as thick as porridge. We dipped the pre-cut and dyed sack cloth into the vats, wrung it, and squeezed the excess moisture out between old blankets. While the cloth was still damp, and therefore pliable, we stretched it around the rib hoops and stitched it into place. Once it dried it was as stiff and leathery as any reptile's skin.

Cerdic looked wonderful. I got excited about the operation. After mass on St. Willibrord's day it was time for Cerdic's field test. Our first discovery, made as soon as we tried to lift Cerdic off the floor of the barn, was that he needed hand grips. The wood carver was elected to design some. Our second problem, apparent when we got outside, was that when Cerdic's whistle was activated by a blast of wind he hissed much louder than anticipated. We were still cheering this when the butcher pointed out that we might not want him trumpeting our presence as we sneaked him through the streets of Winchester. Making the hiss optional was assigned to the smith.

And there were a few other hiccups. When we dragged him into the field and observed him in action we realized he had to be slightly off the ground for his body to writhe properly. That meant that we couldn't leave him and run. We would have to suspend him from a tree in the palace courtyard. We also noted that when there was enough wind to activate his hiss and wiggle his tail, there was too much wind for his torch, which blew out. Cole devised a wind screen that covered the length of the torch. When the wind gusted the fire would retreat behind the screen. When it was still, the fire spewed forth. These variations added another dimension to Cerdic. It looked as if he were choosing when to send forth bursts of flame.

We set the date for our expedition: the first dry windy night of the following week, when a full moon was expected. I was a little worried about how I was going to get out of the house. I didn't want to use the abbey as an excuse for a one-night excursion, so I practiced sneaking out of the bower after Waldberg and the step-ghouls were asleep. They didn't stir. It seemed they slept like the dead, but the problem was they didn't go to bed early enough. So on the first dry evening of the next week, St. Brice's day, I slipped a little poppy syrup into their wine. They retired earlier than usual, and after a short while I poked my head into the bower to make sure they were asleep. Then I dressed in my darkest clothes and put on a cloak with a hood, as instructed, and ran over to Arkil's.

Most of the men, not having to sneak away, had arrived long before I. If it hadn't taken longer than they had expected to secure Cerdic onto the cart they would have left without me. "Oh, shit," enthused Osbert when he noticed me. "What are you doing here?"

"You'll be glad I'm along," I assured him. "I know that palace courtyard like the back of my hand." This was something of an exaggeration. I had ventured into the palace courtyard twice: once on my way in and once on my way out.

"Arkil!" he hollered.

"Sorry, boss," said Arkil. "She kind of put me over a barrel." I smiled sweetly.

"You would be a much greater help," Osbert said, "if you stayed here in case any of Beorhtric's men come snooping around."

I laughed. "Nice try, Osbert," I said. "I'm coming . . . that is, unless you want to give me back 150 cuckoo pint roots."

He compressed his mouth and snorted a little. "So that was the deal. All right. Watch your step, young lady. I hope you realize none of us will be in a position to rescue you should a problem arise." I had never realized Osbert had this boring parental streak.

"Understood," I said.

We transported Cerdic on the cart as far as town. I wondered how we would breach the wall. Of course we couldn't use any of the gates. They were guarded, after a fashion, day and night. I should have known the route had been carefully planned in advance. In fact, Osbert, not a man who liked to waste his—or anybody else's—time, had studied every aspect of the scheme before he had presented the idea to the village. Early in the planning stages he had sent Cole to reconnoiter a route. Besides inspecting the wall for vulnerable spots, his collaborator had tried different approaches through the town in the dark.

So, according to plan, we crossed the Itchen near Durn Gate and followed the town wall along its outside about a quarter of the way in the direction of North Gate. Then Cole stopped us at the spot he had chosen for our encroachment. He had picked this particular spot because, although the wall had crumbled further in other places, this one was the most secluded, giving us the best opportunity to hoist Cerdic over without alarms going off. In addition, the marsh and brambles on the outside of the wall afforded reasonable concealment for our cart, which we had to abandon at this point—its wheels would have made too much noise going down the street. On the down side, it hadn't been particularly pleasant walking through bramble pulling a large dragon along a muddy track. As I lifted myself over I discovered, in the most unpleasant way possible, quite a few sharp stones sticking out from the partially collapsed wall.

When we were all on the other side Father Daniel passed out bread for us to throw when the dogs barked. We avoided the streets as much as possible and walked across town through a maze of alleys that Cole had charted. I think there was one thing he overlooked. Some were barely wide enough for Cerdic, so we had to balance him over our heads as we walked.

When we neared the palace courtyard we could hear music and laughter. Light blazed from the hall's high windows. Osbert and Arkil climbed the palace wall, an antique conglomeration of stone that, like the town walls, must have been left over from the days of the giants. Those of us remaining outside handed Cerdic over. All of us except the smith, who waited to pass over the light for Cerdic's torch, climbed a large ash with limbs overhanging the courtyard. By the light of the moon we strained to watch Osbert and Arkil, in their black clothing barely visible even at twenty paces, as they hung Cerdic from the lower boughs of a giant oak. As soon as they had him in position Osbert, running low, came back to the wall for the light. When he returned to the dragon Osbert lit the torch, and Arkil removed the hiss inhibitor. The two men dropped to the ground and crawled behind the nearest bush.

A high-pitched, unearthly screech rose from the dragon. His tail lashed convincingly. The music inside the palace stopped abruptly, and the screaming began. We could barely stop ourselves from applauding. I watched the palace door, expecting momentarily to see armed warriors emerge. The door never opened. After a while Osbert and Arkil got bolder. They surfaced from their hiding place and, staying behind the glare of his torch, untied Cerdic, using the ropes to tow him around the courtyard, slowly getting closer—but not too close—to the palace. The screams from within intensified. Quite bold now, and not wanting to give the court time to get too accustomed to the beast, Arkil and Osbert lugged Cerdic in the direction of the gate. Before they got anywhere near it the guards ran for their lives, wailing. We laughed so hard that the baker lost his balance and fell out of the tree into the court-yard. Arkil opened the gate. Osbert removed the dragon's torch for a moment and singed the latch so it would look as if Cerdic had burned his way out. The man was always thinking. The rest of us rushed down from our tree and ran over to meet them. In jubilation we decided to tow Cerdic back through the streets of the town. We pulled our black hoods down over our faces and walked close to the buildings. I don't think anyone in the entire town noticed us. Quite a few people, how-ever, awakened from their nighttime slumber and saw a huge, writhing, whistling, fire-breathing dragon stalking the streets of Winchester.

In the brilliant blossoming of our plan was sown the dark seed of our ultimate failure. There is no doubt in my mind that had we left matters as they stood, Beorhtric and his court would have been out of town by the end of the week. But we, the people of Easton, had this wonderful dragon that had taken a month of hard work to create. To disassemble him was unthinkable; to use him again irresistible. It was a temptation not even the practical Osbert could forgo.

### SCENE 23 HELMSTAN DEFEATS THE DRAGON

It was decided to take Cerdic into town again before the moon waned, if the weather were favorable. The very next night I again drugged my family, a little more heavily this time so they would fall asleep that much earlier, and raced over to Arkil's barn. No one objected to my presence this time.

Although Osbert had allowed himself to be slightly carried away by victory, he was prudent enough to prevail against our inclination toward over-confidence. We followed the same route to the palace this time as last, and moved just as discreetly. He and Arkil carefully repeated their routine of the previous night, suspending Cerdic from the same oak tree and retreating just as quickly behind the bush once they had activated his hiss and his whistle. The rest of us, trembling with happy expectation, climbed silently onto the branches of the now familiar ash.

The wind was stronger than it had been the night before. The dragon hissed and spewed fire even more dramatically. His tail whipped and lashed to and fro with fearsome abandon. On this night there were no sounds of music or gaiety coming from within the hall as there had been the night before. The screams when they came, frenzied and dreadful, rent only silence.

To our surprise, shock I might even say, the double doors of the palace were thrown open, and a man emerged, dragging another man behind him. There was some frantic whispering in the tree as we tried to understand what we were seeing. In their desperation to expiate the beast had the court decided to try human sacrifice?

As the two men struggled forward, I became more and more convinced that the weaker would be thrown to Cerdic. Had Osbert considered this possibility? What would we do with the guy? Perhaps leave his hat and left shoe in the courtyard and spirit the victim back to Easton, hiding him in a weaving shed until the king left town? I left off conjecturing as I watched the warrior pick up the other man, limp with fear, and throw him across his shoulders. That there was, in actuality, no danger didn't lessen the inhumanity of the act. As the two approached the center of the courtyard their faces were illuminated by Cerdic's torch. I wasn't surprised, but I was sickened, to see Egbert dump Helmstan onto the ground, where he retracted into a quaking ball, his head tucked between his arms and his knees.

"Stay here and don't move," Egbert said to him—as unnecessary a command as I think I've ever heard—before beginning to walk in the direction of the beast. We should have run for it, but this unexpected turn of events riveted us in place. Although it was a cool night I could feel the sweat trickling down my body. How close would Egbert dare to come? What would we do if he discovered the hoax?

He walked directly over to Cerdic and stood about ten feet away from him. The beast was hissing and bellowing fire and smoke for all he was worth. Egbert drew his sword and lunged. He jumped and leapt, striking first from one side, then ducking below the beast's fire to strike from the other. I could hear the clatter of his sword whacking Cerdic's wooden neck, and the warrior's battle cries and grunts of exertion were nothing short of remarkable. After quite a few minutes of this Egbert recoiled and cursed, as if hurt. He doubled over, clutching his stomach, and staggered behind Cerdic's wing. When he got out of the glare of the torch I could just about make him out, standing motionless next to the beast.

"Helmstan! Help, help," he hollered. This was interesting: the fearless Egbert, screaming in terror as he stood next to a wooden dragon. I liked it. Helmstan tentatively moved one of his elbows below an eye to peer in Cerdic's direction.

"It's got its tail around my waist, Helmstan." No doubt about it, Egbert was scared. He had started to imagine things. I'd heard stories of things like that happening to sailors lost at sea.

"Helmstan, I'm trapped," he yelled. From the desperation in his voice I would have believed it myself if I hadn't known it was impossible. More screams. It was awful. Helmstan sat up and looked across the courtyard in consternation. I began to wonder if Egbert had somehow entangled himself in Cerdic's ropes.

"It's got my sword. Sweet Jesus." I almost felt sorry for the man. "It's got my arm. Helmstan, quick, bring your knife, or I'm dead, for God's sake." Helmstan, his urge to help at war with his fear, stood up.

"Hurry, God damn it," shouted Egbert. I was stifling an irrational urge to rescue the man myself when I noticed the torchlight glinting off his sword, which was extended between Cerdic's head and the oak bough. It seemed that Egbert, despite the frenzy he appeared to be in, was cutting the dragon's rope supports. Helmstan, his wavering knife poised—more or less—for the kill, ran to him.

"Stab him, Helmstan, right down the throat," hollered Egbert.

Helmstan stabbed. Egbert wrenched the beast around by its middle and pressed its face into the dirt. Cerdic's flame went out.

"Thank God," said Egbert. "You've killed him. You saved my life." Helmstan collapsed onto the ground in relief.

"Wait a minute," said Egbert, "I've got a flagon here. I'm going to catch some of his blood." He pulled something out from under his tunic and held it next to the side of Cerdic's mouth. Poor Cerdic, snout in the ground, really did look dead somehow. After a few moments Egbert handed the flagon to the prostrate Helmstan. "Drink this," he said, "You will never feel fear again."

Helmstan took the flagon with shaking hands and drank. When he was done Egbert pulled him to his feet and put an arm around his shoulders. "You've saved the entire court from certain death and destruction," he said. Members of the court, beginning to realize the danger was over, were rushing into the courtyard.

"Stay back, stay back," yelled Egbert. "Sometimes they get a second wind. This one may be okay, but it won't be entirely safe until we hack it to pieces and bury it. I'll do it. Helmstan's done enough for one night. Give the man a drink," he said, pushing Helmstan in the direction of the palace.

A dazed Helmstan approached the cheering members of the court who hoisted him onto their shoulders. As they marched up the steps to begin their celebration, Helmstan, whose features had been contorted somewhere between shock and delight, smiled and clasped his hands over his head in victory. Egbert, who was supposed to be hacking up Cerdic, walked over to the bush where Osbert and Arkil were hiding.

"Do you want to come out?" he said, "Or do you want me to come in and get you?" Very subdued, but not cowed, Osbert and Arkil materialized.

"A remarkable job," said Egbert.

"Thanks," said Osbert.

"Why did you do it?"

"It's a long story," said Osbert.

"I'd like to hear it," said Egbert, "but not tonight. I'll come to your village tomorrow."

Osbert, while he must have been relieved to have escaped execution, couldn't have been thrilled at the idea of one of the king's men snooping around Easton. Nevertheless, they arranged a meeting. Egbert nodded in the direction of Cerdic. "Now get him the hell out of here."

Instead of going back into the hall, Egbert jumped the wall not ten feet from the tree we were hiding in. He whistled. A horse appeared. He mounted, waved in our direction without looking back, and set off for heaven knows where.

## SCENE 24 EGBERT VISITS EASTON

It seemed the excitement was over, at least for a while. The morning after our near-disastrous foray I was going out the door on my way to Arkil's barn to help disassemble Cerdic when I encountered Waldberg, more irritable than usual.

"Are you the young lady responsible for the mud that's covering the entire floor of the bower?" she demanded.

It was possible. We had dragged Cerdic across some dismal tracks. Under the circumstances, sneaking into the bower in the middle of the night, I had neglected to check my boots. "I might be," I said.

"Do you, or do you not," she asked, "have any control over where you put your feet?" I didn't answer. I felt like putting my hands over my ears. "This is the second morning in a row I've found the floor caked in mud. Do you think I want to spend the rest of my life following you around with a bucket and a rag?"

"Of course not, Mother," I said. I was going to be late if she kept this up. "I'll tell the servants to scrub the floor."

"Scrub it yourself," said Waldberg. "Maybe it will teach you to be more careful."

When I entered the bower carrying a scrub brush and pail I found Wulfwaru lying on one of the beds, her hair tied back from her face, wearing only a large towel and rubbing a green viscous substance over her face and chest.

"You look wonderful," I said.

"So do you," said Wulfwaru. "A pail and brush really suit you."

I started to scrub at the far end of the room, near the ewery. Wulfwaru said, "I'm awfully glad you're cleaning up that mess. I practically ruined one of my shoes walking through it this morning."

After scouring a small section with the brush I mopped up the dirty water with a rag, wrung it out into the pail, and got up to slosh some more water onto the floor. I noticed Wulfwaru peering at me as I dropped back down to my hands and knees. She lovingly patted the green ooze into her skin.

"Of course," she said, "I couldn't help noticing the mud wasn't on the floor when we went to bed last night."

I worked energetically, observing with a certain satisfaction how black the water in the pail was becoming.

"I wonder if Mother has put two and two together," Wulfwaru went on.

"Excuse me," I said, "I have to change this water."

"I have the sneaking suspicion," Wulfwaru persisted, "that a certain party did not sleep in the bower last night."

I walked to her bed and stood over her, tipping the pail in her direction. "What was that?" I said.

"Nothing," she said.

"That's what I thought," I said.

It must have been my lucky day. As soon as I got outside I saw loping toward me a woman I could have recognized by her gait alone as the village gossip. "Ooh, hiya, Lady Cynethrith," Tidburg called, waving a hand attached to an empty sack. She bounded over and stared at my head. "You forgot your veil."

"So I have," I agreed.

"Your mother home?" she asked, "I need flour."

"Yes, go right in," I suggested.

For a moment she cocked her head back on her neck like a weasel sniffing for a succulent morsel. "Raw day for messing with water, Lady Cynethrith."

"Isn't it though?" I answered, trying to arrange my features into a reasonable facsimile of a pleasant countenance. "Waldberg will be so pleased to see you."

"Your servants ill or something?" she offered.

"They are quite well, thank you," I said. "You mustn't linger out here and catch cold."

"Such filth," she said, watching me dump the water.

"That it is," I answered. "Well, I must get on." I turned in the direction of the bower.

"Looks like it was used to clean," she hollered after me. I smiled and waved good-bye.

Back at the bower, Wulfwaru's toilette had progressed. She was standing at the ewery splashing herself. Watery green goop slid down her body. It made me shiver. I guess it made her shiver, too, but she thought it was the November air that came in with me as I entered.

"Hurry up and shut that door, you inconsiderate weevil," she hollered.

I dawdled as long as possible. She splashed more vigorously: soon there was more water on the floor than in the basin. Stepping over the puddles she had made, she carefully dried herself before putting on her most beautifully embroidered undergarment (I made a mental note of that) and nicest dress. She sat on her bed and tweezed some hairs from under her chin, then worked on her nails for a while.

When she thought I wasn't looking she retrieved a red-marbled glass jar from under her mattress. She turned her back to me for a moment. When she turned around there were spots of red glop on her cheeks. She dropped her jaw, making a round mouth like a fish while she rubbed them in.

She leaned her head over to brush her thick, lately reddish, hair. As she brushed she lifted her eyes to watch me wipe up the water and green slime she had spilled onto the part of the floor I had already cleaned. I began to hope Werwulf would bite off her nose, or some other part of her anatomy. I tried to imagine how she would look with no upper lip.

"Oh you poor dear," she said, intruding upon these pleasant thoughts, "it's still such a mess in here. I'm awfully glad I don't have to do that. It must be terribly boring for you."

"Not at all," I smiled. "I have a very rich inner life." It was time to change the water again.

For the second time that morning I was near the road pouring out dirty water. Hearing a rider rein in his horse I glanced up and was so startled to see Egbert smiling down at me that I lurched the bucket and soaked my right foot.

"Good morning," he said. Does he often address young ladies he doesn't know, I wondered?

"Hello," I said, not looking at him. I was really annoyed about the water. My foot was getting colder by the minute.

"Beautiful day, isn't it?"

The November weather had set in, cloudy, cool, slightly turbulent. "Not particularly," I said.

"I wonder if you could point me in the direction of Arkil's barn?"

This was awkward. I was going there myself in a minute. If I pointed and then came trailing afterwards, he'd think it very peculiar that I hadn't offered to show him the way. On the other hand, if I suggested I'd take him there he'd pull me up onto his horse, and I'd have to sit with him. Our bodies would be close enough to touch. Inevitably, they would touch. I'd probably be safe because of the witch's curse, but the man was so irrational and unpredictable—what if the curse became ineffective, as it had with Odburh? *In a flash I could see it: he would turn his horse and ride off with me into the wood. At a secluded place he'd stop*

*abruptly, pull me off the horse and look at me the way he had looked at her.*
*Without a word he'd throw me on the ground. Then he'd be on top of me,*
*pining me down, kissing me. Struggle as I might the outcome was clear: I'd*
*be ravished then and there.*

So horrified was I by the inescapable consequence of showing Egbert the way to Arkil's barn that I'd almost forgotten he was there. Then I heard him say, "Never mind." I looked up and he winked at me. "I see you're struck dumb by my charm and good looks. It happens to a lot of girls. I'll find the way." And he started to ride off. "Be sure to dry off that foot," he called over his shoulder.

The morning had not gotten off to a good start. By the time I got to the barn, Osbert and Egbert were deep in conversation, with the villagers who had been dismantling Cerdic grouped around them. I unobtrusively joined the gathering.

"We were pretty sure nobody from the palace would come out and actually take a look at him, close-up," Osbert was saying.

"Not unreasonable," said Egbert.

"But you did. Anybody besides you willing?" Osbert asked.

"You're forgetting Helmstan. He's the one who killed him."

"He didn't appear to be entirely willing."

"That's true, but I had an advantage. I knew it was fake."

Osbert looked crestfallen. "How could you tell?"

"I wasn't there the first night." (And where, I wondered, had he been?) "The next morning the hall was in an uproar. There was a lot of conflicting information floating around, but one thing everybody agreed on: the entire court and half the people in Winchester saw the dragon leaving, but nobody could remember seeing it arrive. That was my first clue."

"How so?"

"A real dragon wouldn't have to be subtle about its arrival. A fake one would."

"So you concluded he was fake?"

"Not that fast. I snooped around outside and found a few things that confirmed it."

"Such as?"

"There were burn marks on the inside of the gate showing how he left. Logically, he would have entered the same way, but of course he didn't. There were no burn marks on the outside of the gate: that proved it. So I concentrated on figuring out how he got in."

"And did you?"

"I went over every inch of the wall and finally found a spot where there were broken pellitory stems on both sides and shallow scratches across the top."

"So? Couldn't a slithering dragon have done that?"

"Possibly, but the slithering dragon probably wouldn't have been accompanied by as many as seven or eight adult humans, including one woman."

We looked at each other in astonishment. "How did you know that?"

"Boots leave distinctive prints in soft clay," said Egbert. I guess I should have known that. Mine had certainly left distinctive prints all over the floor of the bower.

"Then there was the burnt taper you discarded. An actual dragon wouldn't need a light."

"All right, but how did you know which bush Arkil and I were behind?"

"The knee and elbow marks you made in the grass led right to it. Plus your clothing left tufts of fabric on a few thorns. Of course if you'd changed bushes the second night I would have looked pretty silly."

"We kind of wondered how it was you came right to us," put in Arkil. "It sounds awfully simple now that you explain it."

"It always does."

"Was I imagining things or did you wave to the folks in the tree when you rode off?" asked Osbert.

Egbert laughed. "When I examined that tree, which I did because it was so close to the dragon's entry point, I found a piece of fringe from a scarf caught on the bark and quite a few recently broken twigs. And I knew the other five or six people had to be somewhere. By the way—oh, never mind."

We all looked at him quizzically. "I was just wondering if somebody fell out of the tree," he said. I could have sworn he looked at me.

"No," I said, surprising everyone by answering. "Nobody did." He didn't have to know everything.

Osbert looked very serious. "Have you told the king Cerdic was a ruse?" he asked.

"No, and I won't if you won't," said Egbert.

"Don't get me wrong. I'm glad to hear it, but why not?" Osbert asked.

"Perhaps we could talk privately," Egbert suggested. He and Osbert left the barn, and we all stood near the door and watched them walking to and fro in the nearby field for three-quarters of an hour. Egbert didn't come back into the barn, and when Osbert did he spoke only to Arkil and Cole.

SCENE 25 THE INVITATION

Things were quiet for a time, and, try as I might, I couldn't come up with a new plan. But it did occur to me that in the meantime it wouldn't hurt to capitalize upon the tinge of sanctity still gilding me after my prank. If nothing else it would give me flexibility: whenever I wanted to get away all I would have to say was that I needed to go to the abbey to meditate. So I perfected my new persona: Cynethrith the holy.

I felt to be most effective the metamorphosis should be public. Anything Waldberg heard from the neighbors would count double compared to anything she observed at home. Although I couldn't read at the time, I carried about a worn prayer book that I extracted from its cover and leafed through whenever I saw Tidburg or any of the other gossips. I soon discovered an unexpected benefit—Waldberg never gave me a chore when I had my book out. I studied it until my eyes went bleary. I went to church several times a day. I didn't mind. I spent the time praying for success. I learned from that that you have to be careful what you pray for. Success—if that's the right word—arrived in such an unexpected way that I couldn't for a moment doubt God's involvement.

The hardest part, of course, was to forgo sniping at my sisters, but even that proved possible. For example, one day before Christmas when Waldberg made Wulfwaru and me take food to the poor families I used the excursion as an opportunity to practice humility: whenever we passed someone we knew I lowered my eyes modestly and retracted my head beneath my mantle.

"Don't mind her," said Wulfwaru the third time she caught me at it. "She thinks she's a turtle." Instead of making a smart answer or elbowing her in the ribs, actions one would have expected of the old Cynethrith, I forced myself to contemplate how devastated she was going to be once I got control of my money, and I smiled serenely.

Then one day late in December a ruffled servant ran into the hall to announce a royal messenger.

"Show him in, for heaven's sake," twittered Waldberg, putting a last few hurried stitches into her embroidery while awaiting the emissary's appearance.

"I knew Werwulf would come through," squealed Wulfwaru, dancing around the room. "I just knew it."

When the door opened Wulfwaru stopped dead still and arranged herself in an impressively haughty posture.

"Wulfwaru—" he started.

"That is I," intoned my step-sister.

"—her mother and sisters," continued the messenger, ignoring her, "by kind invitation of the king, are invited to a feast to be held at the royal palace on St. Fursey's day." He turned on his heel and left without another word.

Bedlam erupted. Wulfwaru started planning her wedding. Waldberg determined that Osbert or no Osbert, new gowns were required. Hilda hoped the adorable little guy who was king on All Hallows would be there.

"But he's a servant," I heard myself say, in the most disapproving tone imaginable.

"And you're an insufferable snob, and what's worse, a total Philistine," she assured me. "You don't have enough going on upstairs to recognize a poet if you tripped over one."

"A poet!" I scoffed, "You're calling that sadistic, over-sexed little pig a poet?"

"And when, may I ask," she snorted, "did you meet him?"

"Don't let her get your goat," said Wulfwaru, who hadn't the slightest idea what we were arguing about. "She's always thought she was too good for us. If she doesn't shape up soon—and I really think she's incapable of it—we can ignore her when we're living in the palace."

Waldberg planned to take us all to Winchester on a shopping expedition as soon as possible. When the day came I put on my most sanctimonious look and assured her that one of my old frocks would do. The truth was, I wouldn't have shown my face in Easton with those three harpies, and I certainly wasn't going to go to a feast in the palace with them: the humiliation of being presented in such company would have been unendurable.

"You aren't going to embarrass me by appearing at court looking like an orphan," scolded Waldberg. I knelt down, stared into space, and started muttering.

She ignored me for about forty minutes then stopped as she was passing and nudged me. "It's almost time to go, Cynethrith. How about getting dressed?"

I pretended not to hear. She went about her business for a while, then came over and put her face close to mine. "The wagon is going to be ready in ten minutes. You can pray on the way if you want."

"Oh, really, Mother," said Wulfwaru. "Don't encourage it."

Hilda, who had been perching on a bench, arms folded, watching me from across the room, came closer and crouched next to me.

"If you don't get your clothes on right now, we're going to have to leave without you," called Waldberg, who, like a magpie, was darting about snatching up shiny bits of embroidery floss. Wulfwaru glided behind like a harrier.

"Do you like my hair this way?" she asked. She had spent all yesterday afternoon braiding it into countless plaits. "Or better the way I had it time before last?"

"Who moved that roundel I was working on?" bellowed Waldberg.

Hilda, still squatting, studied me so fixedly she didn't blink. Without this intermittent restraint from her lids I feared her bulging eyes might leave their sockets. *I saw her eyes, one following the other, bubble out of her face and spiral upward like the song flight of a wood lark.* As I swayed my head around to follow their loops Hilda moved her face in tandem. "This is really intense," she said.

Wulfwaru, tired of pursuing her mother, had flown out of the hall. She now fluttered in flapping two mantles. "Which one shall I wear?" she cried. "Just a minute, I'll try them on."

"If I can't find a sample of that floss this entire trip is for nothing," fumed Waldberg, scavenging through the considerable detritus that flowed in the wake of her artistic endeavors. I pondered how someone with such a highly developed aesthetic sense could live in such clutter.

Hilda knelt next to me. Weary of watching her eyes fly, I was addressing the problem of the pain in my kneecaps by transporting myself elsewhere. *I had been abducted by a prince, broodingly handsome and dressed all in black, except for his flashing gold sword and intricately wrought cloisonné shoulder clasps. I had these precious moments to pray before he carried me over to the silk-brocaded bed and forced me to acquiesce to his unspeakable, luxurious desires.* My muttering took on a certain passion. "I think she's really getting in touch with something," Hilda said.

Wulfwaru wrapped herself in one of the mantles, draping one end rakishly over her shoulder. She strutted across the floor, chin held high. "What do you think, with this dress?" she asked.

Waldberg stopped foraging to look at Hilda. "Are you ready?" she demanded.

"Yes, yes I am. Be quiet I want to hear what she's saying." She put her ear close to my lips. I was afraid I was going to run out of nonsense syllables. I concentrated on keeping the rhythm going.

"I don't know what to do," whined Wulfwaru, settling onto a bench between the two mantles.

Waldberg finally looked at her. "Wear the blue one," she said. "You're ready, right?" You can be sure if a trip to the trimmer was on the agenda, Wulfwaru would be ready. "I'm going to leave you here, Cynethrith," Waldberg threatened. Leave me, leave me, I silently begged.

"I never thought I'd hear myself say this," said Wulfwaru, "but I think I liked her better the other way, awful as that was."

Hilda held up a hand for silence. "Listen. She's speaking in tongues. Can you hear her?" She aped my position, upper torso lifted, arms extended from the body with elbows bent, palms touching, eyes firmly fixed on one of the rafters. "This is wonderful," she said breathlessly. "Wonderful. Can you see her aura? I can feel it."

"Great," said Wulfwaru, "Now both of them have gone bird."

"Maybe I'll stay with her," said Hilda, "and watch her and study at her feet." I started praying in earnest.

"You'll do nothing of the kind," said Waldberg. "You're the one who doesn't like the local shoemaker. We're leaving, Cynethrith," she said.

She was practically out the door when she turned to me to deliver, at the top of her voice, her parting shot: "If I hear one word of complaint when I get back I'll beat you with a stick."

The door closed with a bang. I was more than ready to relinquish my uncomfortable position, but I was forced to maintain it yet a while. Gossip Tidburg must have been hovering near the door: as the women exited I could hear her prattling on to Waldberg about why she hadn't been able to return something or other.

Once they were out of the house and I could think, I thought I might take advantage of the invitation after all, and go—on my own. Going to Beorhtric's normal court was completely uninteresting, but I remembered overhearing Athelstan and his friends saying that on this occasion thanes from all the other English kingdoms—Anglia, Northumbria, Mercia, and so on—would be there. I liked dancing and parties as much as the next girl. And who knows, I thought, maybe I'll meet somebody. As for dresses, my mother had left me a trunk load of the grandest gowns imaginable. I'd hidden them under the floor of the bower for safekeeping after my father died.

I went to the bower to consult my oracle. I'll pull something from my secret cache, I decided: if it's the perfect dress to wear to the feast, it's a sign I should go. I appealed to my mother in heaven for help, then crawled under my bed, removed the loose floorboard, prised open the lid of the elmwood chest, and selected an outfit—by touch.

The first garment I pulled out was a knee-length tunic of iridescent sea-green silk brocade, trimmed with a pattern wrought in gold, pearls and garnets. Pinned to the tunic was a separate, heavily jeweled circular collar. It was a promising start. These would look lovely over my best gown, floor-length pale violet with a narrow gold band at the hem. Invoking my mother again I felt for sheer fabrics until she placed in my hands a shimmering gold veil. When I saw it I felt convinced Mother wanted me to go to the party.

"But my dear," I could almost hear my angel-mother say, "you'll need a cloak." I rummaged around in the box until I touched fur: I pulled out an ermine mantle. That should do it, I thought. I tried everything on together and moved Mother's little hand mirror around to see how I looked. Wonderful, I thought. Surprisingly beautiful. Then I noticed my feet.

Back to the box I went, groping for suitable shoes. Mother selected a pair embroidered in gold, violet, green, red and blue. They couldn't have been better, and the fact that they were ever so slightly big could be easily remedied by a strap across the instep.

I placed these treasures in a sack and took them over to the abbey. The clothes needed attention, and the secluded convent guest house seemed the safest place to work on them. When I got there no one was around. I knew where the key was hidden, so I settled in, steaming the grand old silk into shape and re-stitching loose jewels. After several hours of work the pieces looked as magnificent as the day they were made. I arranged the clothes, carefully stuffed with muslin, about the room and went to find Athelflad to ask her to keep the other members of the convent out of the guest hall for a few days.

"Now what are you up to?" she wanted to know.

"I restored a dress of my mother's. I'm going to wear it to a party at the palace—"

"You're not sneaking in again?"

"Not at all—it's all on the up and up." Well, almost. "A royal messenger arrived on the doorstep with an invitation for the entire family." I couldn't bring myself to tell her we were invited because of Wulfwaru.

"So why do you need the guest hall?"

"Oh. I wanted to leave the dress I'm restoring here until the party," I explained.

"What's the matter with your house?" she asked.

"Not enough room," I said. She gave me a funny look. I needed to distract her, so I changed the subject.

"Where, by the way, did you bury my servant's costume?"

This worked like a charm: it took me a quite a while to persuade Athelflad to tell me where the flea-infested thing was, and in the meantime she forgot all about my flimsy excuse for using the abbey. After relenting and pointing out the spot, she stood over me making disgusted noises as I dug. I have to admit the costume looked wonderfully pathetic—not quite good enough for a beggar.

When I returned home there was no one about, and I had nothing to do, so I carried a tub to the well, immersed the tattered garments and started to scrub out a month's worth of grime. My thoughts wandered, as they so often do, even now, when I perform a mindless job. Soon I was passing the time with a romantic little fantasy.

*A handsome thane from Anglia and I were dancing on a sunny day in a woodland covered, as far as the eye could see, with lilies of the valley. A delicate breeze chimed the flowers' enticing fragrance into the air. Onto this lovely stage marched some ruthless warrior, an Egbert-type, who challenged the handsome thane to fight for me. I collapsed at his feet and begged him not to. Egbert pushed me aside.*

*When handsome thane slumped down in defeat, his red blood flowing over the white lilies, saying that each moment with me had been worth a thousand deaths, I leapt to his side and swore that the man who had deprived me of my love (probably, knowing Egbert, by some rotten trick) would never have me. Lifting high the sword still glistening with handsome thane's blood, I plunged it into my own breast, leaving a surprised, no, a grief-stricken, chastened Egbert to grapple with the evil he had done.*

*How beautiful we looked, handsome thane and I, lying together, a perfect matched set: the same height, the same gold-tinted skin, the same curly blond hair—once I lightened mine a little—tumbling over the flowers. What dark despair the guilty Egbert felt as he renounced all comfort, all cheer, all women. The skies opened and choirs of weeping angels rushed down to transport us as we died, paling into ivory carvings,* when who should appear as unexpectedly as a stoat from a hedge but Tidburg, a large sack in her arms.

"You got a long face on," she said.

"I'm fine," I said, wiping a tear from my cheek.

"I thought you were out. I got this for your mother. I owe her," she said, nodding at the sack. "The miller finally came around."

She had a way of holding her arms in front of her body that reminded me of a small carnivore on alert. She was shaking her head. "I told your mother this morning that man's got a problem." She cornered me between herself and the well. I wiped my hands on my dress and took the flour. She looked at me.

"You ought to keep your hands out of water. They'll get chapped, putting them in water in this weather," she sniffed.

I reminded myself of my new persona. "How kind you are, Tidburg, to be concerned for my sake." This may have been a mistake. She edged closer.

"Is your mother home?" she asked.

"No," I said.

"Your sisters?"

"They've gone to Winchester for the day," I said.

"So why didn't you go?" she asked. I didn't say anything.

"You mean they left you here on your own?"

I tried to look as if I regretted missing out on all the fun in town. "I'm afraid so," I said, smiling wistfully.

"You poor thing," she said. She squinted into the wash tub, trying to make out what was swimming in the filthy water. "What's that you're washing?"

"It's nothing," I said, "just some rags."

She was distracted by two women from the village walking along the road. "I must be off, darling," she said, hurrying in pursuit.

## SCENE 26 CYNETHRITH MEETS THE ATHELING

The night before the feast I crushed some chalk and put it under my pillow. The next morning I rubbed the powder into my face and lay in bed. When I didn't go to the hall for breakfast Waldberg sent Wulfwaru out to check on me.

"You look worse than usual," she commiserated. "Maybe you won't be able to go to the dance tonight."

"I'll go," I said, "if it kills me."

"I might not mind your going if it actually did," she called on her way out the door.

I made a servant bring a decoction of tormentil rhizome, which I drank to make me sweat. Later Wulfwaru came back with Waldberg.

"She looks sick," said Wulfwaru in her high-pitched nasal little voice, "I don't think she'll be able to go tonight."

"What seems to be the matter?" asked Waldberg.

"I'm okay," I quavered.

"You look terrible," bleated Wulfwaru. "It would be totally embarrassing to show up with a sick person, Mother."

"Really," I rasped, "I'm fine."

"It looks like ague," said Waldberg.

"Ague?" wailed Wulfwaru. "What would Werwulf think if we brought somebody with ague? It's mortifying. She did this on purpose."

"Really," I said, "there's nothing wrong with me." I writhed on the bed.

"Oh my God," bawled Wulfwaru, "look at her. Do you think I'll get it, Mother?"

I imagined the two of us, lying in bed glaring across the bower at one another while Waldberg and Hilda danced at the palace, an idea too terrible to think about.

"It must be a punishment from God," said Wulfwaru, so anxious she squeaked. "He's tired of listening to her babble all the time."

"Perhaps you're right," I agreed, jerking my head as I talked. "But I'm sure you won't get it: God only punishes those He cares about. Yes," I said, my voice trailing off, "it's a kind of spiritual malaise."

"And you're a kind of spiritual disease."

"Don't worry about me," I said. I put my hands over my mouth, jerked myself out of bed and lurched over to the wash bowl, executing such magnificent dry heaves that I thought for a moment I really might barf. I went too far.

"We can't leave her alone like this," said Waldberg. Oh right, I thought dismally. What would the neighbors say?

I got back under the covers. "I feel much better now," I said. "I'm practically well. A little rest should do the trick."

"We'll keep a close eye on her," said Waldberg.

And they did check on me, constantly it seemed. Whenever I was thinking about something particularly pleasant, like Wulfwaru finding Werwulf with another girl or Hilda married to Wermhere, in they'd march. I took care to appear to be getting better after Waldberg's threat to stay with me. I ate about half the food they brought me.

By early evening when Waldberg, Wulfwaru and Hilda came in for the last time, I was sitting up in bed and said I had recovered completely. I knew Waldberg well enough to gamble that no matter what I said she would latch on to the excuse of my recent illness to insist I stay home. As far as she knew I didn't have a suitable dress, and I was pretty sure I could rely on her overly acute social sensitivity to ground me. I knew I was right when I caught sight of Wulfwaru's sly smile.

"I'm afraid, Cynethrith," said Waldberg, "that you must stay home tonight."

"Poor thing," said Wulfwaru.

"And miss the opportunity of a lifetime? Oh, come on, Mother," I pleaded. "I feel fine. It must have been something I ate."

"I won't take a chance with your health. You're young. There'll be other parties."

"Yes, Mother," I said. "Of course you're right."

"Such a shame," said Wulfwaru. "I feel so sorry for her."

I watched them dress. No silks and jewels could transform Hilda's dumpy figure, but she, not realizing it, piled ornament upon ornament: their competition mimicked the unending war for ascendancy between her nose and her teeth. Wulfwaru, while she looked good, had chosen colors far too flashy to be elegant. The bright blue of her mantle grappled with the red of her hair. Waldberg, on the other hand, in shades of rich brown set off by some simple gold jewelry, probably looked as good as possible for a woman her age.

"Have a good time," I said, smiling weakly as they left.

Almost before their carriage cleared the driveway I was outside, ready to head for the abbey. Tidburg appeared.

"Isn't tonight the big night?" she said.

"What?" I said. I had a lot on my mind. I wasn't prepared to fend off her nose.

"Aren't you going to the palace? What day is this?" she asked.

"Well, uh—" I said.

"I'm sure your mother told me it was tonight."

"Perhaps it was," I said vaguely. "I've not been well."

"Oh? What's wrong?"

I couldn't think of any disease that I particularly wanted everyone in the village to think I had. "I guess I've just been working too hard," I said.

"Where's your mother?" she demanded.

"She's gone," I said.

"Not to the palace?" she barked.

"I think perhaps so," I said faintly. "Well, uh, sorry, I have to go. Sick or well, I have to exercise the horse, you know." I mounted and rode away.

I rode to the abbey to dress for the feast, then made for the palace without delay. As I dismounted in the torch-lit courtyard, littered with brilliantly saddled horses and grand carriages, a beautifully dressed attendant came over and bowed smartly—I looked behind me. Determined not to make another gaffe, I gave him my horse, assumed my most regal posture and mounted the stone stairs that lead to the hall. Smiling as I passed through the doors I used to polish, I noticed the room was, as I had hoped, crowded. I didn't see my family, and even if I had, I didn't think they'd recognize me dressed so differently from my usual style. It was hot inside. I handed my ermine mantle to a servant collecting wraps near the door as if I had done it a thousand times.

I was a little late. The royal party had already entered and were sitting at their table. I queued with the others waiting to be introduced. When it was my turn the thane handling introductions asked my name. I knew exactly what was coming. He escorted me the few steps to the king's dais and presented me.

"Lady Cynethrith," he said. I executed a perfect curtsy, with an attitude carefully poised between deference and arrogance. The king acknowledged me with a lift of his goblet, a gesture I knew to be reserved for not terribly important people. The queen eyed me coldly. I was astonished to see Athelstan smile engagingly.

"Byzantine silk," he said, looking at my tunic. "It's beautiful."

"Thank you, Your Highness," I said.

I moved along, as protocol demanded, and mingled with the

crowd. I felt eyes watching me. Swathed in luxury I was a star. I noticed one person who wasn't watching me, however—it was Egbert. He was preoccupied chatting with a very glamorous woman, slightly older. Was she old enough, I wondered, to be able to excite his passion? I wouldn't have thought so.

I watched the dancers. One fellow, attractive and athletic, cavorted with unbounded energy. It took me a few moments to recognize Helmstan, so changed was he. His hair and skin were as fair as ever, but his body was as muscular and robust as it had once been scrawny and shrinking. He seemed popular enough with the ladies, and I suddenly wondered about Tecla. I glanced at the servants' quarter, but dinner service over, no one was in sight.

I wandered around for a while, taking it all in. No one asked me to dance. I began to feel a little self-conscious. I was looking about for a likely person to strike up a conversation with when I became aware of someone at my elbow.

"Cynethrith," I heard a male voice say. "Would you like to dance?" I turned and saw Athelstan.

This was too good to be true. "Yes, sir," I said, curtsying.

He smiled at me. He had a brilliant smile. It made me feel, oddly, as if he knew me, liked me. Then he took my hand in the friendliest way imaginable and led me to the dance floor. As we walked I racked my brain for something to talk about. Then I remembered overhearing him describe his redecorating project to Odburh when I worked in the hall.

"The hall is beautiful," I said, quickly looking around for whatever changes he had made since I left. "Barbaric splendor is okay in its own way, but this hall seems to have a unifying concept."

"Do you think so?" he asked eagerly. "We've been working very hard on it."

"And this magnificent floor—" I said, "isn't it roaming?"

"Roman? Yes, I'm sure it is. Where are you from?"

"Not far," I said.

Soon we were dancing and there was no further need for conversation. Athelstan was a wonderful dancer, rhythmic and stylish without falling into any mannerisms. I had a talent for movement and did pretty well, even though a little uncertain of the steps. We danced for a long time. Finally I felt light-headed from so much activity when I'd hardly eaten all day.

Noticing, Athelstan asked if I'd like a rest. "Yes, sir, please," I said.

"You don't have to be quite so formal," he said, putting his arm around me.

When we left the dance floor we were joined by some of the court youths. A petite curly-headed young lady dropped the hand of her attractive but scrawny companion and hugged and kissed Athelstan.

"Where have you been?" she asked. "We thought we might do some riddles."

"Elfwinne," said Athelstan, "I'd like to you meet my friend Cynethrith," he said.

"This is my friend Elfwinne," he said.

"Nice to meet you," I said, smiling warmly.

"You have the greatest smile," said Athelstan. The young man accompanying Elfwinne grimaced.

"And this," said Athelstan, indicating the youth, "is my best friend Yurmin."

"Hello, Yurmin," I said. He seemed to be far away.

"I just heard this one today," said Elfwinne. "'Outside I'm ornamented. Inside I'm dark. A lady takes care of me and, when her lord is feeling valiant, takes me to him. He upends me and puts a hairy thing in me. It's a tight fit. Soon he'll be thrusting. What am I?'"

We all looked at each other and giggled.

"An embroidered shirt?" said Athelstan.

"No,' said Elfwinne.

"I bet it's a carved chest, with a lock on the bottom," said Yurmin.

"Keys aren't hairy," said Elfwinne.

"Cynethrith?" said Athelstan.

"I guess . . . it's a helmet," I said.

"You've heard it," pouted Elfwinne.

"No, she's just brilliant," said Athelstan. He turned to me, "Want to dance?"

"Okay," I said.

We danced and danced. I had the time of my life. When the musicians took a break I noticed people were leaving. "Good heavens," I said, "is it late?"

"Only about midnight," said Athelstan.

I looked at the door and caught sight of Wulfwaru's flashy blue mantle exiting. Suddenly all I could think about was that I had to be in bed before the others got home.

"I have to go," I said.

"So soon?" said Athelstan.

"Yes, I'm sorry, it's been wonderful, but I must," I said, heading for the door. Athelstan followed me. As if by magic he summoned a servant who appeared with my cloak. At the door there was a back-up while people waited for the servants to sort out their horses and carriages. I headed straight for the stables.

"Where are you going?" asked Athelstan, grabbing my arm.

"I have to get my horse," I said. "I can't wait."

"You don't have to." Athelstan stopped one of the boys. "Get this lady her horse," he said. "Be quick about it."

When I saw my horse coming out of the stable I started to run in its direction. What little composure I still had was undone when I observed Hilda, hand in hand with Wermhere, emerge from between two out-buildings.

"I'll come see you," called Athelstan, "where do you live?" I didn't answer him. I didn't even realize I'd lost a shoe until I was riding away and saw Athelstan waving it in his hand.

I rode like hell. When I got home I awakened the stable boy and told him to take care of my sweating horse. "You haven't seen me tonight," I said, giving him a silver coin.

"Certainly haven't," he said.

I ran to the bower and disrobed, stuffing my clothes under the bed. I jumped beneath the covers and blew out the candle just as Waldberg opened the door.

"Are you awake, Cynethrith?" asked Waldberg. "I noticed the light on as we were walking over."

"Yes," I said. "I was sick again. I feel a little better now, though."

"Well, it's a good thing you stayed home then," said Waldberg.

"Yes," I said, "you were right. Did you have a good time?"

"It was the greatest night of my life," said Wulfwaru.

"Mine, too," said Hilda.

And mine, I thought.

"It was all right," said Waldberg. "I think I'm too old for this sort of thing."

"I'm sure Werwulf is going to ask me to marry him," said Wulfwaru.

"I've found a kindred spirit," said Hilda. "So brilliant, so sensual. I wouldn't have thought it was possible."

"Isn't love wonderful?" I said.

## SCENE 27 CYNETHRITH RETURNS TO THE PALACE

The next day I realized I had to do something about getting back my shoe. Obviously the only thing to do was go to the palace and ask for it, embarrassing as that was. I wanted to go immediately and get it over with, but Waldberg wouldn't allow me out of the house. She wanted me to believe she really had thought I was too sick to go to the feast the previous night, so she made me stay in bed for three days. Finally, after breakfast on the fourth, I dressed as nicely as I could without engendering suspicion and rode off.

It was a brilliant day, but one of the few cold days we had that winter. The ground, the shrubs, everything you could see, was covered in thick white hoarfrost. The ice, sparkling in the sun, made the world look like a fairyland. When I got to the palace the guard at the gate waved me through without asking my name. The party, as the Eastoners had feared, would probably go on for weeks. An unknown lady was no novelty.

In the hall the servants were cleaning and polishing. I felt a pang as I noticed Tecla. She was as pale as ever, but I was glad to see she seemed to have put on a few pounds. Something had changed about Wermhere, and for a while I couldn't figure out what it was. Then it struck me that I hadn't heard a word out of him. He stood leaning against one of the pillars, his stick in his hand, paying no attention whatsoever to the workers, but staring abstractedly into space with a silly-looking smile on his face.

I spotted Elfwinne across the hall. I waved. She pretended not to see me. I walked over to her. She had suddenly become very intent on carving marks into a small wax tablet with a silver stylus, and she didn't look up.

"Hello, Elfwinne," I said.

She looked bothered by the interruption.

"If you're looking for Athelstan I don't know where he is," she said.

"Actually," I said, "I'm looking for my shoe."

"Oh," she said, "so it's your shoe."

"I'm sorry?"

"Athelstan's been terribly boring carrying this shoe around and telling us over and over again how beautiful it is."

"Well, if I could get it back," I suggested, "he wouldn't be able to do that anymore."

"I'll see if I can find it," she said.

Elfwinne soon reappeared followed by Yurmin and the atheling, who was carrying my shoe. Athelstan beamed when he saw me.

"I was hoping you'd come back for it," he said.

I held out my hand for the shoe. "Thanks very much," I said.

"I'll carry it for you," he said, guiding me away from the others. We walked to the center of the hall. "What do you think of the color?" he asked, indicating the newly green walls.

I thought it looked a little stark, but I knew what he was trying to achieve. "It's very effective," I said. "I like the way that medium shade sets off the gold, and the arrangement's very clever: you can immediately tell which shields are important. Those two belonged to Cerdic and Cynric, didn't they?"

"Yes, I'm glad that comes across."

I turned and looked at the cauldron as if I had never seen it before. "That chain!" I enthused. "It's beautiful."

"Isn't it?" he said. "You won't believe this, but it wasn't even polished when we got here."

I shook my head in disbelief. "Cynethrith," he said, his beautiful hazel eyes glowing, "why don't you come to the palace for the rest of the party? I'll arrange everything. We can put an extra bed in Elfwinne's bower."

"I'd like to—" I said.

"There's going to be some great entertainment in the evenings, and you can help with this project. I can see you've got a terrific eye."

"I will come," I said, "but not immediately. I have some things at home I have to get in order."

"Wonderful," he said. "When can we expect you?"


On my way home I stopped off at the abbey to visit Athelflad.

"It won't be a bit like last time, Athelflad. This time I've had a chance to lay the ground work. Waldberg is firmly convinced of my heavenly calling."

"I worry about the way you mock God," she said.

"I'm not mocking God. I spend a lot of time in church and, believe me, He's fully aware of what I'm up to."

"Tell me again why it is you want to go back there?"

"You're going to think this is crazy, but I have this premonition that the atheling is going to fall in love with me."

"You're right. I think it's crazy."

"I dreamt last night that I was meant to re-create the House of Wessex."

"Is this anything like that dream you had where St. Wihtburh appeared to you?"

"Athelflad!" I remonstrated, "How could you think such a thing?"

"Well," she concluded, "you are going to do what you are going to do. Some things are immutable."

"Right," I agreed. Now that she was firmly in my corner it seemed like the right moment to give her her mission. There was one little practical problem I hadn't been able to solve: I needed a cart to haul my things to the palace. "Now," I said lightly, "all you have to do is come up with transportation for my things."

"Sure. All I have to do is part the Red Sea," she said. "What's the matter with the carts on your farm?"

"You're not thinking, Athelflad. What usually comes with a cart?"

"An ox."

"Besides that."

"Flies?" she asked.

"Guess again."

"Ox plop?"

"A driver, you sputtering candle."

"Oh."

"And they, unlike oxen, can talk."

"You've made your point. Why can't you drive it yourself?"

I heaved a sigh of exasperation. What a grand entrance I would make, holding the reins of a transport cart. "It's a question of protocol," I said. "But I'm not worried. You'll find one. It won't be that difficult, Athelflad. A person who can read and write can certainly figure out how to commandeer a supply wagon."

"Good-bye," she said. "It's time for Vespers."


I had crucial work that needed to be done in private to get ready for an extended visit to the palace. No doubt because I had spent so much time praying recently, Waldberg got a message later that week that her needlework supplier had just received some new materials. She made plans to go to Winchester the next day, accompanied by the step-spinsters.

Early the next morning, as soon as they were out of the way, I got to work. I had to lift several floor boards out of the bower before I could extricate the elmwood chest protecting my mother's gowns and jewels. I borrowed a rig from the barn and with great difficulty loaded the heavy container and drove to the abbey, struggling into the guest hall with my hoard. When I opened it, my hands shook as if I were unearthing a dragon's forbidden treasure.

I spread the jewels on the linen chest—how they twinkled and gleamed. Mysteriously lit from within, they were undimmed by years of darkness. Then I lifted out gowns, mantles, veils. Fluffed and arranged on the bed, they looked like a profusion of glittering flowers. I placed jeweled belts and gold headbands over a bench; on the floor in front of them, shoes embroidered with confronted birds. I looked at these wonders for a long time. I could have looked longer still, but I needed to get the cart back before it was missed.

"Look, Athelflad," I said, back at the abbey the next day, showing her the elmwood box, "I just wanted you to get some idea how big the transport wagon has to be. And it would be nice if it weren't too tatty. After all, I am supposed to be an impressive lady from a neighboring kingdom."

"Don't worry about it," she said. "It's all arranged."

"It is?" I said.

"Yes," she said.

"The wagon?"

"Isn't that what we were talking about?"

"What about the driver?"

"A good-looking deaf-mute."

"You're a miracle."

"I thought you'd like that," she said. She allowed herself a small smile.

"How did you do it?" I asked.

"Unlike you, I tried honesty."

"Honestly?"

"Was that supposed to be funny?"

"Sorry."

"Why don't you try it yourself sometime?"

"I don't know," I said. "It hardly ever seems appropriate. Anyway, what exactly did you do?"

"I told the prioress that you needed a wagon to transport some of your mother's precious things and a driver who could be trusted not to reveal their whereabouts."

"Oh," I said. I wished I'd thought of that.

"And she said that considering the great debt we owe your mother, that was the most insignificant of favors. She insisted I give you the best wagon we have, recommended the driver, and said to be sure I told you both were at your service whenever you need them."

I got an inspiration from Athelflad's handling of the prioress. I had dinner with her the next afternoon and asked if anyone was available to help restore some of my mother's gowns. She was only too happy to give me her six best seamstresses. In return I gave her two silver brooches embellished with niello.

I worked with the nuns every day until the gowns were in perfect condition. My mother was not as tall as I am and was a little wider in the girth. These clever women rearranged trims and adjusted seams like magicians until the dresses looked as if they had been made for me. They added notches to the belts and sewed straps on the shoes. Meanwhile I polished jewels and practiced draping veils and pinning headbands.

As I had expected, Waldberg was very agreeable when I said I must return for a stint at the abbey, and Wulfwaru made no secret of her happiness at my imminent departure. Hilda posed an unexpected problem: she wanted to come with me. I told her she wasn't ready yet and gave her a daunting set of spiritual exercises, trusting them to squelch her interest.

Taking leave of my family I set off for the convent. There I spent several days rehearsing my manners and drilling myself in what I could remember of the court dances. In between I worked on my appearance. I steamed impurities from my face with yarrow, renewed my skin with comfrey, softened my hands with marsh mallow. I lightened my hair with dried mullein and burnished my teeth with sage. (Athelflad accused me of running down the abbey's herbal repository. I accused her of hyperbole.) Before leaving home I hadn't neglected to swipe a little of the red glop Wulfwaru had hidden under her mattress. Even if she noticed, she wouldn't dare say anything to Waldberg. I practiced applying small amounts to my cheeks and lips, checking the effect carefully in Mother's little mirror.

The night before I left the abbey I set aside the clothing and jewels I would wear on the trip and packed the rest, pressing lavender between the gowns. In the morning I brushed my hair until it shone and dressed in a fine light tan wool gown, suitable for travel. This I accessorized with a small necklace, simple in design, of barrel-shaped gold beads and gold-trimmed garnet pendants. I pinned on my cream silk veil, wrapped myself in a marten-lined dark blue mantle, and was ready to face the world.

I rode grandly to the palace, accompanied by my cart and driver. It was a sunny St. Bride's Day, the first of February. Something in the air told the birds that spring was coming. I saw a lapwing plunge through the sky as if demented, showing off to attract a mate.

In the courtyard I tried to avoid the scuffling warriors, who were celebrating the bright day with ferocious mock fights. There was no attendant near the hall door this morning. I signaled my driver to wait where he was and took my horse to the stable myself. Walking back I could see that most of the warriors, no longer fighting, had grouped around two guys who were slamming away at each other for all they were worth. As I neared the steps so did the fighters—Helmstan jumped straight up onto the stone banister. Egbert leapt after him. Egbert had not quite touched down when Helmstan bashed him on the head with the side of his sword. Egbert, trying to regain his balance, cartwheeled through the air and collapsed at my feet.

His fall had been so comical I couldn't help smiling. He appeared to be unconscious. I covered him with my cloak and knelt down to see what was wrong with him. I was still smiling when he opened his eyes and looked up at me dreamily.

"Have I died," he asked, "and gone to heaven?"

"Yes," I said solemnly, "I'm afraid there's been a dreadful mistake."

Helmstan appeared with a bucket of water and said, "Step aside, Lady, I'll take care of him."

I quickly got out of the way. Just as he was about to pour the water over the flattened warrior's head Egbert grabbed Helmstan around the knees and toppled him. Water spewed up like a geyser. Helmstan was drenched. Egbert was on his feet. The fight resumed. Athelstan, who must have heard of my arrival, came hurrying out of the hall to greet me.

"I'm so glad you've come," he was saying. He looked it. He quickly made arrangements for my things to be taken to a bower. "Let's get out of here," he said, looking distastefully at the fighters.

Athelstan showed me around the palace explaining in detail his renovation plans, then we passed the afternoon re-anchoring gold threads that had come loose on an old tapestry that Athelstan planned to hang behind Beorhtric's throne. It was pleasant, companionable work—for the first time in my life I was glad that Waldberg had bludgeoned me into needlework when I was younger.

"Fabulous!" praised Athelstan, looking at what I had done.

Later at the evening feast I sat next to Athelstan, at the head table. Walking past on the way to his seat Egbert stopped and smiled.

"How have you been?" he said.

"I beg your pardon?" I said frostily.

"Oh, sorry," he said pleasantly. "I thought I knew you." He winked at me and went on.

"I'll have to speak to Haedde about the way this table is laid. It's too awful," said Athelstan, returning to me after a short chat with Odburh, on his right. I followed his lead and tried to talk to Yurmin, on my left. "Have you been very involved in the re-decorating?" I asked.

"No," he said. "That's Athelstan's project."

I tried again. "Will there be dancing tonight?" I asked.

"I hope not," he said.

As it turned out, there was. I managed to fake most of the dances. On the difficult ones I feigned fatigue and, trying to watch from the sidelines, promised myself I'd slip away the next day and practice before Athelstan noticed this gap in my education. Between dances we returned to our seats, and a woman—the same glamorous woman I'd noticed with Egbert the night of St. Fursey's—sang, and very well. She had amazing concentration, the tones seemed to jump around, coming each time from a different part of her anatomy: one time her head, another her throat, sometimes her chest. She radiated a kind of heat, and after a while I noticed the heat directed toward one particular spot in the room, the one where Egbert was sitting.

I wasn't the only one who noticed. Every now and then Odburh looked at the singer and then glanced at Egbert. He seemed, as usual, quite oblivious. She's wasting her time going after that one, I thought. Meanwhile, I had more important things to think about. For one thing, I needed to win over Odburh, if possible. I could tell Athelstan was trying to help.

"Odburh's an amazingly talented herbalist," he was saying.

"Not at all," said Odburh, in a way that gave me the impression she didn't want to pursue this particular topic. Athelstan got the message.

"Doesn't she look beautiful tonight?" he asked me.

"Like a goddess," I said, gushing for all I was worth. "Your clothes," I added, "are so spectacular."

This was a blunder. I didn't like the way she looked at my outfit when she answered. "I used to consider myself the best-dressed woman at court."

"Cynethrith's clothes are lovely, aren't they?" Athelstan said to her. "But no one, of course, can touch your sense of style, Odburh. In fact, I saw some cloth in town yesterday that you really must have made up. Will you excuse us, Cynethrith, if we dance?"

"Please do," I said. "It will be so lovely to watch you."

They left, and after a while Odburh was smiling on the dance floor as Athelstan whirled her around. They really were lovely, I thought, so graceful and elegant.

*SCENE* 28 CYNETHRITH PRACTICES DANCING

The weather wasn't too bad the next day, so, true to the promise I had made myself, I went to a clearing in a nearby wood to practice the court dances. The basic step, a point-step-step, was easy enough. It was the turns and the elaborate combinations that left me at times unsure. I danced around, offering my hands to invisible partners, turning in and out, dipping under raised arms.

"Not bad," someone said. I froze in mid-action, and Egbert emerged from behind a tree. "It's just that you're leaving out the middle section."

I suppressed an urge to turn and run. He took my hands and began leading me through the patterns of the complicated dance. "The trick is, always start with your right hand, and walk to your next partner on the outside."

He whistled the tune, and after a while I understood the formations. "You're fun to dance with," he said. "Do you know the one where the men lift the women over their heads?"

"Not very well," I said. Actually, I'd never seen anything like it. He put his arms around me. After a few turns around the clearing he said, "Now this is the lift part. Ready?" Holding me over his head, horizontal to the ground, we rotated in a circle. Then he straightened me out and flung me straight up like a skylark. When he caught me he swooped me through the air as perilously as a kite. Whether it was surprise, or nervousness, or just the fun of being tossed about like a two-year old, I don't know, but for some reason I was helpless with laughter. Dizzy when he set me down, I grabbed onto him to keep from falling. The way he was looking at me—I thought he was going to kiss me, but I knew I must be mistaken. After all, the curse had squelched his interest in young women.

I heard horses in the distance. "Have to go," he said, "Just when it was getting interesting." He signaled his horse, who appeared out of nowhere. "By the way," he said as he mounted, "ladies never start eating before the queen."

I never have seen that dance done at court.

*Scene* 29 An Afternoon with Elfwinne and Yurmin

A few nights later in the hall Egbert stopped to talk to Odburh. I had to smile at how jittery he made her. I guess every time she was near him she thought about how close she'd come to turning into a hag. It didn't seem to bother any of the other women, but then maybe they didn't know about it. Court gossip travels faster than a falling star, but I'd never heard anyone mention it.

Egbert turned to me. "How are you finding life at court this time?" he asked.

He really annoyed me sometimes. "What do you mean *this time*?" I asked.

"Surely you've been to court before?" he asked.

"She likes it very much," said Athelstan, "Don't you Thrith?"

"It's wonderful," I said to the atheling. "Why don't we dance?"

"I'd love to," said Egbert, extending a hand. I could hardly say no. It would have looked funny.

On our way to the dance floor I heard Odburh say to Athelstan, "I didn't know he could dance."

A few pleasant weeks passed. Athelstan and I became very close, and we were always together. "You look exactly like my mother," he said to me. Or he would catch me in a movement and say, "My mother turned just that way." She had died when he was 12. The two of us were motherless children. Odburh was his stepmother. "We could be brother and sister," he said. It was true: we had the same dark blond hair, the same wide smile, the same warm-toned fair skin.

One morning Athelstan instructed Elfwinne and me and several of the other ladies, most of whom had brought a slave along, on how to paint the capitals on the new pillars. We all got busy with our brushes, and Athelstan sat down next to me.

"Thrith," he said, "You need a slave."

"Yes," I said. "I've been meaning to buy one. One of mine got sick on the way, so she had to go home, and of course I had to send the other to look after her." In fact, I'd been hoping to buy Tecla. I was waiting until I felt sure of Athelstan's friendship before I asked for her. I saw her pinched little face across the room and decided to give it a try. "That girl over there, do you think I could buy her?"

"You want a hall drudge?" he asked.

"She looks better than that," I said. "I think I could turn her into something."

Athelstan studied Tecla. Years of servitude had not erased her innate refinement. "You, know, I think you're right. You're such a little genius." Then he changed the subject.

Later that afternoon Athelstan left, saying he had some business in town. I was surprised, and pleased in a way, when Elfwinne and Yurmin invited me to go for a walk, but as we strolled next to the stream near the palace I struggled to understand why they had asked me along. They talked exclusively to each other, giggling over muttered jokes I was unable to hear. In fact, they were enjoying their little tête à tête so much that Elfwinne failed to notice Mildred kneeling near the path.

"Damn," said Elfwinne, tripping over the woman.

"Mildred," I exclaimed, "what are you doing here?"

"You know this woman?" asked Yurmin disparagingly.

"She works in the hall," I said. Poor Mildred, who had lost her balance when Elfwinne toppled over her, lay on her side in the dirt looking terrified.

"I'm sorry, lady, very sorry lady," she said. Elfwinne raised her foot to kick the woman. Pretending not to notice, I scooted between the two of them and helped Mildred to her feet.

"What the hell do you mean sprawling all over the path and tripping people?" fumed Yurmin.

Mildred looked at me when she answered. "I never meant to cause trouble—I never saw her, lady." The old woman pointed to some hemlock seeds that had stubbornly clung to their dried umbels throughout the winter. "I was gathering these for Her Royal Highness."

I did my best to sound nonchalant. Hemlock is one of the strongest poisons around. "Did she tell you what they're for?"

"It's for her pet birds, lady."

It was an odd treat, but not impossible. I'd heard that quail, for example, ate hemlock seeds. It didn't seem to affect them at all. I made a mental note to ask Edith the next time I saw her if a bird that ate hemlock seed could poison the person who ate it. In the meantime I was glad to discover the queen was a bird fancier. At last I would have a safe topic to try at mealtime.

"Can we go on?" Yurmin said, not bothering to hide his impatience.

By the time we got back to the hall I was feeling very uncomfortable, and it wasn't because of the chilly weather. I sat with Elfwinne and

Yurmin, who didn't seem to like my company but stopped my every attempt to escape. I was actually relieved when Egbert came over.

"I've torn a button off my shirt," he said to me. "Do you think you could sew it on for me?"

Ordinarily I would have suggested he do it himself, but before I could formulate that proposition, Elfwinne piped up with, "I will."

Egbert, ignoring her, stripped off his shirt and handed it to me. I didn't know where to look. He fumbled in his bag for the button.

"Why don't you go get a needle and thread?" he said to Elfwinne.

She smiled sweetly. "Of course, Egbert," she said. That left Yurmin, so I looked at him. He seemed more flustered than I was. He squirmed in his seat and blinked his eyes for a while, finally saying to Egbert, "Heard any new riddles?"

"What has one arm, two legs, ten tails, eleven mouths, and 21 eyes?"

"I don't know, but I'd like to meet him," said Yurmin.

"A half-made bench occupied by 11 people. Ten of them hold a kite and one is embroidering?" I ventured.

Egbert chuckled. "That's better than the answer, except that you'll end up with 23 eyes."

"You're so clever, Egbert," said Yurmin. I'd never noticed his lisp before. "I can't think of a thing."

"I'll give you a hint," he said, "it's got hair and 60 fins."

"Fish." I said, "a man and . . . some fish."

"That's it," said Egbert. "A one-eyed, one-armed trout seller."

Elfwinne came back with the needle and thread and handed them coyly to Egbert. "Here you are, sweetie," she said. I almost hoped he'd plank her so she'd turn into a hag.

I sewed on the button, glad to have something to do. Egbert thanked me and left just a few moments before Athelstan returned, smiling broadly from across the hall, accompanied by a simply but smartly dressed woman. They were almost on top of me before I realized the woman was Tecla.

## SCENE 30 ATHELSTAN'S GIFT

"This lady, Lady Cynethrith, will be your new mistress," Athelstan was saying to Tecla, who looked so dignified and beautiful I almost couldn't believe it was her. I wanted to hug my old comrade in adversity, but constrained myself to smiling with the proper degree of aloofness.

"Lady," said Tecla softly, looking at the floor and curtsying.

"Athelstan," I said, "What have you done?"

"It was nothing," he said. He looked very pleased.

"Oh, Athelstan," whined Elfwinne, "don't tell me we're going to have to find room for her in the bower. It's so crowded in there already."

"Don't worry," said the atheling. "I'm moving them. Come with me," he said to me.

"Come along," I said to Tecla, taking her hand.

He led us outside to a bower close to the royal apartments. "I just finished it yesterday," he said. "I was going to show it to you this morning, but when you pointed out Tecla, I thought she would be the perfect finishing touch." He showed us a beautifully appointed room, with a curtained bed for me and a simpler one for Tecla. "Do you like it?" he asked.

I was speechless. He'd thought of everything, even unpacked my trunk and arranged my things around the room, showing off each article to its best advantage. I hugged and kissed him and danced around the room like a child.

"Were you suspicious when I had Elfwinne and Yurmin keep you busy this afternoon?"

"I have to admit I wondered why they asked me to go with them."

"I didn't want you to see me moving your things."

After everything was looked at and admired several times, individually and as a whole, Athelstan said he was going to dress for the evening and he'd see us in the hall later. As soon as he was gone, I turned to Tecla.

"How have you been?" I asked.

She looked uncomfortable with this friendly question. "I'm quite well, lady," she said, curtsying.

"Let me try that again," I said. I slumped into my servant's posture and used my raspy voice, "How have you been?"

"It's not possible!" she said.

"It is."

"No, I don't believe it."

"Believe it," I said.

"Could it be?" She fell on her knees. "Thank God."

I pulled her up, hugging her. We laughed; we cried.

"I've been so worried about you," she said.

"I'm okay," I said, "I'm fine."

"I can see you are."

"I've been worried about you, too. Why didn't Helmstan do something for you now that he's a warrior?"

She stiffened and looked upset. "I don't want anything from him," she said.

"Oh?" I said, "Success has gone to his head, has it? Thinks he can do better now, does he?" What a bastard, I thought.

"It's not that," she said.

"Then what is it?" I asked.

"You won't understand."

"I certainly won't if you don't tell me."

She was quiet for a moment. "He might as well be dead," she finally said. "The old Helmstan doesn't exist. This guy's just like the rest: a brute. Can't you see it, Cynethrith? He's everything I hate. I see him now—all I can think of is that day the raiders came, the things they did . . . it's too awful to think about."

"Well, never mind," I said, not wanting her to dwell on that terrible memory. "At least you're out of Wermhere's clutches, one way or the other."

"I must be dreaming," she said. "You're hardly recognizable. You were old, ugly, poor. Now you're young, beautiful, rich. Do you have a fairy godmother or what?"

"I'll tell you the whole story," I said. "But of course you're not to breathe a word of this."

"Are you kidding?"

I told her my story as she helped me dress for the evening. We left for the hall together. As my personal slave she would have a place in the hall, sitting with other well-born slaves who like her had been victims of raids or on the losing side of a battle. I watched Tecla settle into her new role, eating and chatting in her shy way with the others.

"You were right, as usual," Athelstan said, noticing me watching her. "She's perfect for a lady's slave."

"She is, isn't she?" I agreed. "I can't thank you enough, Athelstan. It was too generous of you."

Athelstan didn't answer. He was looking across the room at an elegantly dressed servant, carrying a plate of partridges in our direction.

"Food, at last," he said. "I'm starving." The servant offered the dish first to the king, of course, who refused it.

"Beorhtric doesn't particularly care for fowl," said Athelstan. Warr, on the other side of him, took three.

"His friend," I said, "eats it for both of them."

"Among other things," Athelstan said. We giggled. Warr was more obese than ever, if possible. As Odburh helped herself to one of the birds, I thought of what I'd learned that afternoon and leaned across Athelstan to attempt a conversation.

"I understand Your Royal Highness is a bird fancier," I said, smiling.

"Certainly not," she said.

"Oh, but—" I started. Then I thought better of it.

"Oh, but what?" she said, in that chilling tone that was hers alone.

"How stupid of me," I said, "I was thinking about the queen in the last palace I visited. I'm such a dunce."

"Yes," said Odburh.

"Odburh," said Athelstan, "The fellow that sculpted the pillars has worked out really well. Perhaps we should commission him to make you a new bed." Odburh looked at Beorhtric, in stitches over some remark of Warr's.

"Why bother?" she said.

Athelstan lowered his voice. "Maybe we could think of some job abroad for Warr."

"Getting rid of him might improve things," she said. She looked around the room abstractedly, and her gaze fell on Helmstan. Helmstan, looking as pathetic as a puppy-dog begging for a tidbit, was staring across at Tecla. The queen sighed and looked at Egbert, sitting next to him, who caught her glance and smiled. She shook her head.

"I have to pour wine now," she said to Athelstan.

When she was out of earshot I said to Athelstan. "She's awfully lonely, isn't she?"

"Yes," he said. He looked at his father, flushed, slurring his words, leaving the hall leaning on Warr. "And it's not all her fault." The fact that Athelstan was not a fan of his father was a feather in his cap from my point of view. Life in Wessex would improve when he was king.

*Scene* 31 Egbert and Saxburg

Later that evening we had the same singer as the other night, and she again sent quite a few flares in Egbert's direction.

"She's terrific, isn't she?" whispered Athelstan.

"Riveting," I said, snuggling a little closer to him on the bench. He put his arm around me.

"Do you think she might have an interest in a certain warrior?" I asked him.

"Which one?" he asked.

"Never mind," I said.

After she sang I watched to see if the singer and Egbert got together, but they never came near each other. Later that evening, however, I heard Athelwulf telling Ercenwald that he had a message for Egbert. Ercenwald said he hadn't seen him for a while, and something made me look around the room for the singer. She was also gone. When I saw Egbert a little later, I mentioned that Athelwulf was looking for him, and as he turned to leave, I noticed some cleavers stuck to the back of his clothing. Some perverse curiosity made me look for the singer. She, too, was in the hall now. I walked up behind her to get a closer look but saw none of the sticky little plants on her dress.

After we danced and watched jugglers for another hour or so, Athelstan surprised me by saying, "It's awfully stuffy in here. Why don't we go for a walk?"

It was a dry night, and the winter mild, but nevertheless I wouldn't have picked a February night for a stroll. Then it hit me: he wanted to be alone with me. I was elated, but nervous, of course.

"Sure," I said, letting all the love I felt for him shine out of my eyes. He surprised me again: "We can walk Saxburg home."

"Who's Saxburg?" I asked.

"That wonderful singer," he said.

He waved to Saxburg, and the three of us walked to the door and put on our mantles. The back of hers was covered in cleavers. I was so upset my insides shook. I studied her face for signs of deterioration. Not seeing any, I thought perhaps she had gotten away with it this time—or, who knows, maybe it didn't happen until the next day. But let's say she had been lucky: if she kept sleeping with Egbert it would only be a matter of time. Thinking about it I felt sick inside. This divine creature, needlessly ruined by that man's self-indulgent lust. It was horrible.

"You're quiet tonight," said Athelstan. I squeezed his arm and smiled, reminding myself there was no curse attached to my beautiful Athelstan.

We walked Saxburg to a nearby inn, then sat at one of the small tables drinking beer with her. Athelstan and I sat together, thighs touching under the table. It was fun. I'd never felt so accepted, so loved. Athelstan's speech was peppered with "Cynethrith and I are . . . and when we . . . and we hope to . . . ."

Finally we left the inn, holding hands. Standing outside near the inn's torch, I turned toward Athelstan. It may have been February, but the heat emanating from my body could have kept me warm without a cloak. I smiled up at him and put my arms around his neck.

I wanted to kiss him, or rather, I wanted him to kiss me. I felt shy about making the first move, so I only kissed him on the cheek to get things started. He hugged me tight, and we stood like that for a few moments. Finally I broke away. He was smiling broadly at me, his eyes sparkling. Then he said, "Let's go home."

How romantic the simplest phrase can seem when you're in love. I squeezed his hand, and we walked toward the palace.

He walked me to the door of my beautiful new bower. My heart was banging in my chest. Oh, dear, I thought, Tecla must be in there. But perhaps that's not a total impediment—I remembered all the amorous trysts in the hall. Privacy didn't seem to be an essential requirement. Anyway, she's probably asleep, and we can sneak into my curtained bed. The curtained bed—I smiled to myself in silent admiration at Athelstan's planning. As usual, he'd thought of everything, that tricky boy.

He hugged and kissed me. "Do you have the key?" he said. I handed it to him with a shaking hand. He unlocked the door and kissed me again, saying, "If we finish the capitals tomorrow, we can start on the interlace." Then he left.

Tecla heard me come in and awakened, asking if I needed help getting ready for bed. She was taking her position as my slave seriously, too seriously as far as I was concerned. "Don't be silly," I said. "I'm sorry I awakened you. Go back to sleep."

I lay in bed, unable to sleep. In my unsettled state my mind floated back to Egbert's transgression and stuck on it like an ant on honey. Should I warn Saxburg about him, I wondered, or should I have it out with Egbert? That seemed the better course—talking to her would only save one woman, and she might get the ridiculous idea that I was making it up out of jealousy. Once I'd made my decision I spent the rest of the night rehearsing the invective I planned to hurl at him. I could hardly wait for the next day. Near dawn I finally fell asleep. When I awakened it was only because I heard a strange sound. I threw back the curtains around my bed and saw Tecla, bent over one of the beautiful silver basins Athelstan had put in the room, gagging and retching. I jumped out of bed and ran to her.

"Good lord, Tecla, what's the matter?" I asked, putting my arms around her.

"I'm sorry," she gasped, tears in her eyes. She hadn't actually vomited. "I think I'm all right now. I've had this miserable flux for the last couple of months, mostly in the morning. I thought I was getting over it."

"You poor thing," I said.

"I'm all right now," she said. "Sorry to trouble you."

"It's no trouble, Tecla. We're friends, remember."

She appeared to feel better. As we were dressing I told her what I had figured out about Saxburg and Egbert. "I'm giving that man a piece of my mind," I said.

"Miserable bastard," she said. "Typical, just typical. You see what I mean now? But be careful. God knows what he might do."

"Just let him try something," I said.

## Scene 32 Cynethrith Confronts Egbert

Egbert made the confrontation easy by waylaying me the moment Tecla and I emerged from the bower.

"I'd like to talk to you," he said.

I glared at him, but he paid no attention.

"Alone," he said, looking at Tecla. That suited my purposes. "Go on to the hall, Tecla," I said. "I'll meet you there later."

"Let's walk by the river," he said. It was surprisingly balmy, one of those false spring days that sometimes teases us in February. A cross-current whipped my skirt in front of me.

"You're not your perky little self today," Egbert noted. He felt my forehead for fever. I threw off his hand.

As soon as Tecla was out of earshot he got to the point. "Do you think you can find out why Tecla won't have anything to do with Helmstan?" he asked.

"I know why."

He waited for me to elaborate. I didn't.

"Would you mind telling me?" he asked.

"Because he's a rotten son-of-a-bitch like the rest of you," I said.

He looked a little taken aback, but only said, "There was a time when she loved him. Am I right?"

"He was different then."

"How so?"

"He wasn't a rotten son-of-a-bitch."

"Let's take this from the top. There was a time when Tecla loved Helmstan, now she no longer cares for him. Do I have it so far?"

"Brilliant," I said.

"What changed?"

"He turned into a rotten son-of-a-bitch like the rest of you," I said.

He fell to his knees, raising his clasped hands to heaven. "Dear God," he prayed, "help me to understand women."

I looked at him like he was an idiot.

"Surely it's not because he stopped letting himself be used for target practice?" he tried.

I didn't say anything. He stood up. "Is that your final word on the subject?" he asked.

"Yes, but there's another subject I haven't even started," I said. The words smoldered out of my mouth.

"Go on," he said.

"There's something I want to know," I said. "How could you?"

"How could I what?" asked Egbert.

"Don't play dumb with me," I snapped.

"Is it okay to play stupid?" he asked.

I thought the sparks from my eyes might ignite the dried reeds on the riverbank. "You slept with that singer last night."

"I didn't know you cared." He looked pleased. That really got me.

"I *don't* care!" I exploded. He dropped to his knees again.

"Dear God," he prayed, "help me to understand women."

"Will you stop doing that?" I yelled.

He stood up. "Let me try to understand this," he said, "I made love to Saxburg last night, and you don't care. Am I right?"

"Right."

He stared at me.

"I mean, I don't care for my sake."

There was a pause. "I see," he said. He fell on his knees again. "Dear God—"

"I'll kill you if you do that again," I raged. "Do I have to spell it out for you? Think about that woman—because of you and your filthy appetite, she's going to wake up and look at herself—good God, she'd be better off dead!"

"Cynethrith," he said calmly, putting his hands on my arms, "I think you're overreacting. Really, she was fine with it."

"Egbert," I said, stepping back, "I know about the curse."

"The curse?"

Now I stared at him. It took a second or two to sink in, but, confronted with the enormity of his sin, I was gratified to see he was shaken. He put his hand to his mouth and started choking. I regarded him calmly, clothed in righteousness.

"The ethical depravity of some people," I said, "defies belief."

He took a few deep breaths in an obvious effort to regain his self-control. Then, wiping tears from his eyes, he asked, "How is it you know about the curse?"

"Odburh warned me," I said, thinking fast.

"Oh, that's it. Yes, I've noticed the two of you are great friends."

"We're not here to discuss my relationship with the queen."

Then he stunned me by saying, "You're awfully pretty, even when you're a prig."

I must have turned pale, like the surface of a log right before it explodes in the fire. "It's not possible. I didn't hear that. Will you stop at nothing?"

"I'll do whatever it takes," he said, a sexy look in his eye. I would have been terrified if I hadn't been so angry. As it was, I'd crossed some sort of a boundary, and, to be honest, there was something enjoyable about it. "You amaze me—"

"I think you're wonderful, too."

"Shut up!" I was ablaze. "How many have there been? Since you can't seem to control yourself, I suggest you do the manly thing and fall on your sword. How can you go on behaving like this knowing that the women you have sex with are going to be turned into miserable old crones?"

"Now wait a minute, Cynethrith—"

"Don't try to deny it."

"All right," he said. "I won't deny it. Unfortunately, most of the women I make love to will turn into hags. If they live long enough."

It took me a moment to process what he had just said. "But why would you make the queen think . . ." I was exasperated, a reaction I often had to Egbert. Then it hit me. "You didn't want to . . . And you couldn't say no to Odburh . . . ."

"Yep," he said. He paused. "But there was another reason I picked that particular story." He hesitated again before going on. "This is so crazy, I don't know if you can understand it. Have you ever wanted someone that you didn't want to want? Someone that was wrong in every way—the wrong time, the wrong place, the wrong person? Someone that could screw up everything you're working for? And the more you didn't want to think about them, the more you did? And the more you didn't want to want them, the more—you had to have them?"

Where was he going with this? "Some of us have more self-control than that," I sniffed.

"Lucky you. Since you have, you'll never understand this. But I'll try to explain." He sighed. "There was this adorable little old lady who used to work in the hall. I saw her one day, on her hands and knees scrubbing the floor, and it just hit me. I had such a crush on her I couldn't think straight. And that particular night—it was a crazy night, anyway—All Hallow's Eve, she somehow got stationed behind the queen. So while I told Odburh that story and acted like I found her irresistible, I was pretending to myself that the queen was my old lady."

I looked at him in astonishment. "You put on a performance for . .

. for . . . a little old lady?"

"Yeah, I was kind of hoping to turn her on a little, or at least get her to think about the possibility of the two of us together—"

I thought my brains might erupt right out of my skull.

"And did it work?" I wanted to see what he would say.

"No. I think I scared her off. She left the palace that very night. Even though I thought I'd made it clear that no harm would come to someone who was already old."

"Well," I said, "it hasn't taken you long to get over her, and now you've got another old lady to take her place. I hope you'll be very happy."

Egbert said, "Now why are you getting mad? I think you better run around the palace a few times until you get this out of your system. I'll talk to you when you feel better."

With that, he left. After a while I made my way back to my bower, wondering if I should slink away from the palace and never return. I thought it might be worth giving up Athelstan and a future as queen of Wessex as long as it meant I would never have to see that man again.

## Scene 33 Cynethrith has No Luck with Athelstan

Exhausted, I stole into bed and pulled the curtains around myself. I was soon asleep. The next thing I knew, it was late in the afternoon. The curtains had been drawn aside, and Tecla, Yurmin, and Athelstan were standing over me.

"She's ill," said Athelstan.

"What's the matter?" Tecla was asking me.

"I'm sorry, sweetheart, I didn't realize. I should have come sooner." Athelstan was kneeling next to the bed, holding my hand. "What do you think is wrong with her?" he asked Yurmin.

"I don't know. Maybe it's some female problem."

"She feels hot," said Tecla, laying her gentle hand on my forehead.

"She looks terrible," said Yurmin.

"What is it for fever? Pennyroyal? Rose hips?" said Tecla.

"I don't know," said Athelstan. "Perhaps we'd better get some help."

"Who's good at this sort of thing?" said Yurmin. "Oh, I know, get Egbert."

"No!" I said, sitting up. They all stared at me.

"Why not?" said Yurmin. "Just looking at him makes me feel better."

"I'm all right," I said. "Really. It was just a passing attack of, uh, green-sickness."

"What's that?" asked Athelstan.

I wasn't sure. I'd once heard Tidburg telling Waldberg that one of the village women suffered from it. "It's a kind of oppression of the humors," I said.

"Are your humors oppressed? This sounds serious," said Athelstan.

"Not at all," I said. "A little rest clears it right up."

"You're so brave," said Athelstan. "Would you like anything, darling? Tecla, get her something to drink, and I'll read to her while she rests."

Athelstan kept me company for several days, not allowing me to get out of bed. He read to me. He brought me fresh flowers everyday and arranged them in a vase on the bedside table. He had the kitchen prepare special dishes to strengthen my blood. When he tired of reading he worked on his drawing, decorating previously scripted manuscript pages with his stylish interlace patterns. He asked me if I wanted to learn how to read, and I whiled away the hours practicing.

There was something about lying in bed day after day, with so little to do, that stoked my desire. Often I'd stop writing and gaze at Athelstan, his beautiful blond head bent in concentration. Each time he looked up, I gave him my sexiest stare, and each time he smiled lovingly. He was too much the gentleman to take advantage of the situation.

When he finally decided it was safe for me to get out of bed, my limbs were so unused to activity I stumbled. He caught me as I fell, and, seeing an opportunity, I pulled him down on top of me on the floor.

"Oohhh," I moaned into his ear, holding him. I thought it sounded pretty good for a beginner.

"Darling," he said, scrambling off of me, "are you in pain?" He sat back on his heels and looked at me.

"No," I said. He held out his hands to help me up. I asked him to send in Tecla to help me dress for dinner.

Tecla helped me accessorize my gown and did my hair. She arranged my veil—she had quite a knack for it. I looked good. By this time my embarrassment over Egbert had lessened. As much as I had been dreading seeing the man again, I was so glad to be out of the bower that I almost didn't care. When I'm Queen of Wessex, I thought, I'll have Athelstan send Egbert to the Baltic. In the meantime I decided to ignore him, and I felt confident he would ignore me. I was wrong.

As soon as I entered the hall, he left the men he was talking to and hurried over.

"Are you better?" Egbert said.

"I'm fine," I said icily.

To my surprise he looked disconcerted. "Look, Cynethrith, I'm sorry about the other day," he said.

I didn't know how to take that, so I just looked at him.

"It was stupid of me to wind you up the way I did—"

"You were winding me up?" I interrupted, feeling the top of my head beginning to rise.

"Well, sort of. Anyway, I'm sorry. I should have realized you were getting sick."

"Yes, yes, I've been told I was ranting about the most inconsequential things. The fever, you know. Did we have a conversation? I don't remember."

He squeezed my hand. "You look wonderful," he said.

It was a perfect evening. Beorhtric himself, who had never spoken to me before, beamed in my direction with all the drunken bonhomie at his command, saying he was delighted that Athelstan's lady friend was now well. He clapped his son on the back, saying, "And don't think I don't know where you've spent the past three days."

Odburh also addressed me for the first time, "Why did Egbert stop you as you came in?" she asked.

"Oh him," I said. "He was very rude to me the other day, Your Royal Highness, and he wanted to apologize." This seemed to satisfy her curiosity.

## SCENE 34 WATCHING THE WARRIORS

By the first week of March the festivities begun with such enthusiasm on St. Fursey's Day had lost their momentum and wound to a close. Practically all the foreign visitors had departed for their own kingdoms. Having learned my lesson from my last stay at the palace, I sneaked away whenever I could to check in with Athelflad. She told me that my stepmother kept in touch weekly, but wasn't causing any trouble. Being Athelflad, of course, what she actually said was that Waldberg "didn't seem too concerned." In any event, there was no reason to return home, and one very good reason not to.

Although Athelstan had not yet proposed, it seemed understood by all that we were to marry. He showered me with attention and all sorts of exquisite gifts—gold earrings, cushions embroidered in pearl, and an illuminated prayer book to name a few. He praised my beauty, admired my intelligence, extolled my goodness, and was determined to believe I shared his talent. We worked together, danced together, picnicked together, did everything together—except for one thing. I discussed this with Tecla and we decided that he loved and respected me too much to compromise my virtue. Here was a prince, indeed.

Beorhtric continued to beam on me, and while Odburh remained frosty, as far as I could tell she didn't oppose the match. As for Egbert, I avoided being alone with him. Even though he had apologized for his merciless teasing, and I forgave him, I still found he made me uncomfortable. But over time that changed. At times I was bored with Athelstan' relentless redecorating projects and longed for the days when I used to play war games with the village boys. So on balmy springlike days I took my embroidery frame outside and watched the warriors practice.

There were two teams. One group was composed of Beorhtric's original champions: Erpwald, Thingfrith, Werwulf and a few youngsters they were training. They often showed up late and their training lacked focus. The rest of the court worked out with Egbert. These were seasoned warriors like Ercenwald and Athelwulf—Helmstan of course—and most of the boys, who looked at Egbert as if he were God. It soon became apparent to me that Egbert had figured out each man's weakness and attacked it until the guy improved. I entertained myself by trying to spot their flaws as well.

After morning practice one day Egbert caught up with me as I was heading back inside.

"What did you think?" he said.

"Athelwulf moves well overall, but his pivots are sloppy," I said.

"Yep," said Egbert.

"Ercenwald occasionally forgets to step into the cut."

"True."

"Most of the boys use the false edge of the sword too often."

After that morning, he sought me out whenever I had watched the practice, and he seemed to enjoy hearing my critiques. Knowing he would ask I watched carefully, which slowed down my progress on the embroidery considerably. I would have left the damn frame inside, but if Athelstan came looking for me I thought he would be displeased to think I had any interest in warfare. One morning he proved I was right. Just as practice was about to end Athelstan found me outside and sat next to me watching the drills.

"How can you watch this stuff," he said. "They're disgusting."

"I suppose so," I said, "but it's the world we live in. We have them to thank that we aren't slaves."

"When I'm king," said Athelstan, "we will have peace."

Egbert was in earshot for that remark, and he came over. "A very commendable idea, Your Highness. How will you accomplish that?"

"I will offer the olive branch. I will let it be known that my kingdom is peaceable. That we are good Christians who love mankind and want to live more like angels than demons."

"There might be those who will say," countered Egbert, "that you won't be able to get the Welsh, the Mercians and the other Saxon kingdoms—not to mention the Danes and the Frisians—to agree to that unless your warriors are strong enough to impose it."

"Mercia is an ally." Athelstan replied tartly. He turned to me. "Let's go inside." It turned my stomach to hear Mercia described as an ally. I shot a quick glance at Egbert to let him know I agreed with him. As much as I loved Athelstan, I hated Mercia, Offa, and Odburh. Beorhtric was useless. I was sure, once I was queen, that I could talk some sense on the topic to Athelstan. He was too good.

*Scene* 35 The Kiss

I still came out to watch practice when I could, even though it gave me the uncomfortable feeling that I was sneaking around on Athelstan. Egbert and I debated the comparative merits of waist locks, hip throws, head locks, double leg shots, and when it was best to use the pommel instead of the blade. I enjoyed watching Egbert teach the boys. He drilled them over and over in the basic principle: Every attack is a defense, every defense an attack. He trained the more seasoned warriors in the tricky relationship of timing and distance. Today he was drilling them on how to resolve the crossed sword bind—when to use leverage and when to yield quickly to unbalance your opponent.

When he came over after practice I said, "Helmstan's really coming along. I thought he was going to take both Athelwulf and Ercenwald when they jumped him."

Egbert looked pleased. "Yeah, he's getting good. We're having a match against Thingfrith's group tomorrow. Will you come?"

I said I would if I could, and luckily for me, Athelstan had business in Southampton the next morning. He was expecting a shipment of tapestry frames from the continent and wanted to inspect them before accepting delivery.

The morning was stormy, the match brutal. Thingfrith's team didn't care how dirty they fought—and while that's expected in battle, it's frowned upon in practice matches with your own side. It tends to create hard feelings. Egbert was everywhere, deflecting the opponents' groin kicks, eye gouges and biting. He rallied his guys, shouted suggestions, and threw most of the enemy at least once. His team's training paid off. After a while the opposition was exhausted.

When Egbert saw me walking along the hedge after the match I could see that he was pleased with himself. "Well," he said, "what did you think?"

"I thought Erpwald was going to take you for a moment there," I said.

There was a pause. "Has anyone ever told you that you're awfully hard to impress?"

Some devil made me flirt with him. I smiled. "It's the only thing that keeps you interested."

His expression changed. "It's not the only thing," he said. And he kissed me.

I was so surprised—and to be honest, the kiss was so good—that I let it go on a little longer than I should have. But then I pulled myself together and said, "What do you think you're doing?"

"I think I'm kissing you," he said. "And I think you're kissing me back."

"No!" I said. *Had I?* "Well, you'd better stop!"

"All right," he said. "I'll stop. But it's okay with me if you don't."

We looked at each other. The moment felt—how can I describe it? Dangerous. I was a little breathless. And the kiss—how could I describe that? It was the sort of kiss that would have left any girl weak in the knees. It was the sort of kiss that might have caused Athelflad to renounce her calling. But I wasn't going to renounce mine. I was going to marry Athelstan. I loved him. I was going to be queen of Wessex and help Athelstan return the kingdom to its former glory. And nothing as trifling as a kiss was going to change any of that.

"I have to go," I said. I turned away and walked back to the hall with as much hauteur as I could muster.

## SCENE 36 THE COURT PLAYS TELL-A-TALE

It would have been awkward to go on watching the battle drills, for a couple of reasons. One was Athelstan, and the other was Egbert. I filled the gap by seeking out the retired warriors and learning more about court tradition. A number of the councilors were interesting men, and they weren't shy about expressing their displeasure at what the court and the kingdom had become under Beorhtric. I was pretty sure they liked me, and yet I got the feeling they knew things they weren't telling me.

I stayed away from Egbert; nevertheless, I was often tempted to see what he was up to. The warriors that appeared to be part of his circle had increased, whittling down the ones left to Thingfrith. In some odd way Egbert seemed to be taking over the court. Was he still carrying on with Saxburg? If he was, I couldn't tell. Some nights I sensed him looking at me. If I glanced back, the look in his eyes brought back the memory of that damn kiss.

Outside strong winds howled. It was spring, but winter would not accede the succession. The king sat in a corner rolling dice with Warr, Thingfrith and his cup filler. None of the rest of us wanted to trek through the gale to the bowers, so after Saxburg ended the evening's entertainment with the hymn *Didn't it Rain?* we looked for a game to play.

Someone suggested Tell-A-Tale: it was popular in those days. In case you don't know the game, the object is to be the one who finishes the story. There are a few rules that make this more difficult than it sounds, and I'll point them out as we come to them. Athelstan was chosen to moderate. We drew for the four who would play, and Odburh, Helmstan, Elfwinne and Egbert won. A bench was placed on the dais in front of the head table, and the players sat down, facing the rest of the hall. It was Athelstan's job to choose who would speak, calling randomly on each to continue the story. Athelstan picked Odburh to start.

*Odburh:*

Once there was a very beautiful princess, Olga by name, beloved daughter of powerful King Dim of Wix. This elegant princess, who wore the grandest gowns in all the world, was as virtuous as she was lovely, and every man who looked upon her fell in love. Then one day a sassy young upstart, a social climber obsessed with ambition, arrived at court. With devilish sorcery she bewitched all around her. Before long, this nobody, whose name was Cwenn, tricked the atheling, the princess' own brother, into thinking that she was everything wonderful and desirable. [Athelstan, too taken aback to stop her, let her continue.]

Olga, realizing that for her brother's sake she must free the court from this audacious creature's spell, consulted her father's magician. He studied his books and said he thought the best solution would be to turn Cwenn into a revolting old hag, thus revealing her true nature to all the court. The princess, knowing at once this would be most appropriate, said she would be willing to pay a great sum to anyone who could accomplish this.

*[Odburh looked long and hard at Egbert. Athelstan, collecting himself, called on him to continue the story.]*

Egbert:

'I can do this, Your Royal Highness,' the magician said, 'but as you know, it is not possible even for a magician of my powers to create a curse without a qualifier.'

*[On his first turn a player is allowed to introduce new characters and/or a new plot element. Athelstan, however, stopped Egbert before he had a chance to do either. This was entirely proper: the moderator, like fate, is supposed to do the unexpected. Athelstan chose Elfwinne.]*

Elfwinne:

And the princess said, 'Very well, then. Let her be an old hag until the day that I, renowned throughout the kingdom for my virtue, make love to my father's most bitter enemy.'

*[Then Athelstan called on Odburh, who heaped still more trouble onto the unfortunate Cwenn.]*

Odburh:

'But wait,' said the princess. 'We all know how schooled in treachery is this Cwenn. For my dear brother's sake I must be sure it is impossible for her to escape this charm. Therefore, let this vile creature, expropriator of affection, remain a hag not only until the inconceivable day when I renounce my virtue but also until the day a king, mighty in battle, falls in love with her, hag that she is. And even that will not free her until this same king offers to cut out his heart if she will not have him. And, in addition—'

*[Helmstan's hand went up. Since it was not Odburh's first turn, she could be*

*challenged if she mentioned a character that had not been previously intro-
duced.]*

*Athelstan:*

Challenge from Helmstan.

*Helmstan:*

Who is this king, Your Royal Highness?

*Odburh:*

The bitter enemy that Elfwinne mentioned.

*Athelstan:*

Challenge overcome. Helmstan has two challenges remaining.
Play resumes with Helmstan.

*[Helmstan used his option as a first-time speaker to take the story in a com-
pletely different direction.]*

*Helmstan:*

Meanwhile, in a far-off land there was a warrior named Henry,
hearth-companion to a powerful thane named Eric. Henry was in love
with a woman who didn't care for him, so he went to a sorceress for a
charm, and she gave him a magic elixir.

*Elfwinne:*

Handing him the charm, the sorceress said, 'Give this to the girl,
but be careful. Whoever drinks it will fall in love with the first person
seen afterwards.' Before Henry could give his love the potion, he was
called away to battle.

*Helmstan:*

Henry, dedicating his every action to his love, marched with his
companion Eric through the forest, killing giants, trolls, dragons and
griffins. Then the men swam across the sea, under water, fully armed, to
fight the foreign warlord on his own ground—

*Athelstan:*

Challenge from Odburh.

*Odburh:*

Who are all these giants, trolls, etc?

*Athelstan:*

I'm afraid that's not a valid challenge, Odburh. Non-human creatures, as long as they don't speak, can be introduced at any time. Challenge overcome. Odburh has two challenges remaining. Challenge from Elfwinne.

*Elfwinne:*
Who is the foreign warlord?

*Helmstan:*
Princess Olga's father, King Dim of Wix.

*Athelstan:*
Challenge overcome. Elfwinne has two challenges remaining. Play resumes with Helmstan.

*Helmstan:*
Although Henry and Eric fought like the true champions they were, each killing five hundred of King Dim's battle-hardened troops in the space of an hour, they were so outnumbered that the fight was indecisive. Nevertheless, the enemy retreated, and the two men decided to camp overnight and resume the battle the next morning.

*Elfwinne:*
The men camped in a clearing, and Henry went in search of firewood. Eric, the handsome and charming thane, was thirsty. He upended his drinking pouch and found it empty. Noticing one of Henry's lying on the ground, he drained it, not realizing that this pouch contained not water, but the love potion, which Henry had brought with him for safe keeping. After drinking the potion, Eric decided to reconnoiter the area and headed in the direction of the palace.

*Egbert:*
Along the road to the palace an old lady was gathering hazelnuts. Eric heard a rustle and looked to see what it was. To his astonishment, he saw a decrepit old hag trying to hide behind a tree. To his further astonishment, he fell in love with her.

*Athelstan:*
Second challenge from Elfwinne.

*Elfwinne:*
Who is the old lady?

*Egbert:*
Cwenn, the sassy upstart.

*Athelstan:*

Challenge overcome. Elfwinne has one challenge remaining.

*Egbert:*

Eric didn't let on that he had seen the old woman, who, obviously frightened by the fierce warrior, ran away. Enchanted, Eric followed her and discovered she worked as a char in the king's palace. Eric sued for a place at court.

*Odburh:*

Dim, a brilliant king, was suspicious of the powerful-looking warrior and decided to trick him, saying, 'Three days from now you will be tested. If you can defeat in turn, with one hand tied behind you, my twelve strongest men, I will grant you a place at my table. In the meantime, consider yourself my guest.' Then the king went off to consult with his magician.

*Elfwinne:*

Eric may have looked strong, but he was now as weak as a baby: the love potion had a side effect. He suffered from frequent stomach aches, and, convinced he could never survive such a match, thought he'd better slink away during the night.

*Helmstan:*

Although Eric's reason told him slinking away in the night was the sensible thing to do, he was too valiant a warrior to run away. He decided to stay and face the twelve champions.

*Odburh:*

It was too bad for Eric that he didn't leave while he still could. For even had he been as strong as usual, by the next morning the magician discovered something that made it impossible for Eric to win an encounter: an enchantment that made a sword incapable of defeat.

*Elfwinne:*

When the magician told King Dim about it he was overjoyed, and, rubbing his hands together with glee, saw his chance to humiliate, as well as eviscerate, the hated interloper. So, telling no one his plan, he chose his eleven fiercest warriors, and one puny runt, named Albert, to whom he gave the magic sword.

*[Egbert raised his hand to challenge Elfwinne.]*

*Athelstan:*

Challenge from Egbert.

*Egbert:*

Who is Albert?

*[Elfwinne hesitated. The queen, looking none too pleased, whispered something to her. Elfwinne mumbled her answer.]*

*Elfwinne:*

Olga's brother, the atheling.

*Athelstan:*

Challenge overcome. Egbert has two challenges remaining. Resume with Helmstan.

*Helmstan:*

The chosen warriors spent the next two days honing their skills for the coming fight.

*Egbert:*

Eric, hopelessly in love, spent the next two days gazing at his old lady, watching her every move as she went about her chores. She found his attention somewhat irritating. 'Have you nothing better to do?' she asked him.[To my embarrassment, Egbert did a passable imitation of the voice I had used in my servant guise.]

'She spoke to me,' thought Eric, so overcome he sat on the bench staring stupidly into space.

*Helmstan:*

Dim's chosen champions were too busy bragging and tussling to notice their opponent was preoccupied. The morning of the fight arrived. The court assembled in the yard. The 12 chosen warriors, armed and ready, circled the area set aside for the contest.

*Elfwinne:*

Unlucky Eric, ruined by his ill-starred attachment, took up his sword. His only consolation would be to see his hideous love as he died.

*Helmstan:*

The first champion faced him, swinging his sword so close to Eric's ear that he heard it slice the air.

*Egbert:*

Then Eric heard her voice, the voice of his beloved, near the edge of the ring—

*Odburh:*

Never mind that she was saying, 'I hope it doesn't take too long to kill him. I have a lot to do this afternoon.' The sound of that voice made his palms sweat.

*Helmstan:*

Inspired by love he swung his sword like a madman—

*Elfwinne:*

—and it slipped from his damp grip, embedding itself in a tree. Soon Eric would join his ancestors.

*Egbert:*

But not so soon. The warrior standing next to Albert didn't want to see the fight end before he had his crack at the newcomer, so he grabbed the puny atheling's sword and threw it to Eric.

*Helmstan:*

As soon as Eric caught the enchanted sword his opponent fell dead at his feet. And so it went for the next ten opponents. Albert begged off, saying as anyone could see he didn't have a sword. Eric, now feared by all, was given a place at the king's table.

*Odburh:*

The king was most displeased. The noble Olga, noticing her father was not himself, asked, 'What troubles you, dearest father?'

'Dearest daughter, what think you of that handsome warrior who defeated so many of my men?'

'Not much,' she answered.

*Helmstan:*

'But he did defeat our strongest warriors,' said the king.

*Elfwinne:*

'He must have used witchcraft,' said Olga.

*Odburh:*

'Yes,' said the king. 'I happen to know that he used a magic sword that he's hidden somewhere. One day I'll get my hands on it, and then we can use Eric to test poisoned darts.'

*Elfwinne:*
The noble Olga, her tender heart laden with her father's cares, pondered what to do. Repellent as she found the warrior, she resolved to make the useless fellow fall in love with her—no man could resist her charms—and then to cajole from him the location of the hidden sword.

*Helmstan:*
It is true that no man could resist her charms—under normal circumstances.

*Odburh:*
Olga was clever enough to realize that these circumstances were not normal. Knowing the man was besotted by a hideous old serving woman, she went to her father's magician for the charm of oblivion. The seer gave her a powder to put into Eric's dinner, which she did that very evening.

*Elfwinne:*
Later that night, beautiful as carved gold, Olga arrived unexpectedly at the warrior's bower.

*Egbert:*
The warrior's eyes lit up when he saw the princess, for she was as lovely as rock crystal.

*Helmstan:*
'Why have you come here?' the warrior asked.

*Elfwinne:*
Olga smiled at him, and his blood began to heat.

*Egbert:*
Eric took her in his arms and kissed her. She kissed him back, rubbing her body against him like a cat against a post—

*Odburh:*
'Wait, my handsome lord,' she said, breaking away. 'As much as I want you,' (though, in reality, nothing on earth would have induced her to acquiesce to the man's desires), 'I can give myself only to a very special man—the man who can show me the enchanted sword that knows not defeat.'

*Helmstan:*
'Then you'd better go now,' said Eric, 'for never will I reveal the

whereabouts of that sword.'

*Egbert:*

Confident she could change his mind, the provocative princess placed Eric's hands on her breasts—

*Elfwinne:*

'I can't wait to make love to you,' Olga said. 'Quickly, quickly, show me the sword.'

*Helmstan:*

'Never,' said Eric.

*Egbert:*

'This is no time for haggling, princess,' Eric continued. 'Let's make love now, and speak of boons tomorrow.'

*Odburh:*

Alas, my handsome warrior,' said Olga, knowing full well the warrior burned with passion, 'irresistible as you are, I cannot give myself until I see that sword.'

*Elfwinne:*

Inflamed with desire, Eric agreed to lead the princess to the sword's hiding place.

*Odburh:*

As much as the princess loathed Eric, she enjoyed seeing how helpless she made him. Pretending gratitude, she kissed him, saying, 'Soon I'll be yours.'

*Egbert:*

This was too much for the fiery Eric, who completely lost his self-control, and, not realizing from her behavior that she was a virgin, threw Olga onto his mattress and had her.

*[Odburh looked stunned. Before she could formulate a thought, Elfwinne's hand shot up.]*

*Athelstan:*

Final challenge from Elfwinne.

*Elfwinne:*

I'd like you to explain why Eric was so ready and willing to make love to Olga when he was supposed to be in love with the old hag?

*Egbert:*

His true love gave him no reason to hope. There wasn't any point in resisting temptation.

*Odburh [interrupting]:*

You pack of idiots. You've forgotten the powder of oblivion: Eric wouldn't even remember the old lady, much less still be in love with her.

*Athelstan:*

Egbert, you may answer the challenge.

*Egbert:*

We know that Olga put the charm in Eric's food, Your Royal Highness, but we don't know that he ate it. Actually, the seer's powder was consumed by someone else. Every night since coming to the palace, Eric had saved a portion of his dinner and taken it to Henry, his companion, who was still in the forest encampment waiting for the battle to resume. On the night Olga put the charm into his food, Eric had one of his frequent stomach aches and couldn't eat a thing. So he took his entire dinner to Henry, who ate it and forgot all about the woman he'd been in love with.

*[Instead of ruling on his own Athelstan decided to appeal to the court for a verdict. Most of the hall voted in Egbert's favor.]*

*Athelstan:*

Challenge overcome. Odburh has one challenge remaining. Elfwinne has used up her three challenges and is out. Well played, Elfwinne. Resume play with Helmstan.

*[The audience stirred. Ercenwald stood. Addressing Athelstan, he pointed out that Odburh had interrupted a proceeding and, in addition, had neglected to raise her hand before challenging Egbert.]*

Correction from the floor. Odburh, for not following protocol, is also eliminated. Well played, Odburh. Resume with Helmstan.

*Helmstan:*

Henry, no longer distracted by thoughts of love, prevailed upon his friend to resume battle. 'I'm awfully tired of lolling about camp,' he said.

*Egbert:*

Eric, thinking that if he won Dim's throne his love would smile on him, agreed to fight.

*Helmstan:*

The men decided to rendezvous outside the palace grounds at dawn, then surprise the court. This they did, and those who didn't fall before Eric's magic sword or Henry's might quickly surrendered.

*Egbert:*

Eric, revealing his true identity as the only remaining son of the royal House of Winka, was proclaimed king.

*Athelstan:*

Second challenge from Helmstan.

*Helmstan:*

Where does the House of Winka come from?

*Egbert:*

They're Dim's dynastic rivals, which explains why Eric is Dim's most bitter enemy.

*Athelstan, after conferring with others:*

Challenge overcome. Helmstan has one challenge remaining. Resume with Egbert.

*Egbert:*

Dim the Usurper, when he realized he had been vanquished by his most ancient and bitter enemy, collapsed and had to be carried from the hall. The new king, his longing for the old lady undiminished, sought her out and fell at her feet, 'Be my lover,' he said to her. 'Be my queen, or I shall surely die.'

*Helmstan:*

Henry, seeing for the first time the wretched object of his friend's desires, was sickened. He was glad that the old lady, having nothing else admirable about her, still had her pride. 'You mock me, sir,' she answered Eric. 'Surely you can't want me, hunch-backed and hideous as I am.'

*Egbert:*

'Madam,' said King Eric, 'I'll take you any way I get you.'

*Helmstan:*

Henry, blaming himself for this sad state of affairs, suggested a remedy. 'Wait, Eric. I'll go back to the sorceress who gave me the potion. She must know an antidote.'

*Egbert:*

'No, never,' said Eric. 'A life without love is not worth living.' He dropped to his knees, placing the tip of his sword against his breast. 'If this woman won't have me, I'll cut out my own heart.'

*Helmstan:*

Before his overwrought friend could harm himself, Henry sneaked up behind him and pinned his arms, forcing King Eric to drop the sword.

*Egbert:*

At the same moment, the hag turned into none other than the beautiful Cwenn, lovelier than a goddess. Admitting she'd loved him from the moment he'd become king, she rushed to embrace the joyful Eric. It would have been impossible for him to love her more than he had, but he certainly loved her no less. They were married and ruled both Wixna and Winka wisely and well for many years.

*Athelstan:*

"Well played, Helmstan. Game to Egbert."

SCENE 37 CYNETHRITH AND EGBERT HELP TECLA

A month elapsed. April was upon us, some of her days brilliant, others tempestuous. Responding to her mysterious command, daffodils, violets, and celandines forced their way into the courtyard, only to be trampled by warriors practicing more earnestly than ever: soon the battles would resume. On the days when the weather was fine Athelstan and I worked outside to take advantage of the light. Athelstan was drawing a cartoon for an extensive new embroidery large enough to ring the hall to commemorate the anticipated final subjugation of the Jutes.

One sunny afternoon he was called away to attend to Odburh, leaving me to color part of the drawing. I was concentrating so intently on my work that it took a moment or two to notice a group of warriors hesitating nearby, as if waiting for someone. I looked up and saw Helmstan take a step in my direction. Then Ercenwald grabbed his arm and pulled him toward the hall with the rest. Only then did I feel someone leaning over my shoulder.

"Beautiful," he whispered, his lips touching my ear. I jumped. It was Egbert.

Collecting myself, I asked, "Do you think so? I think it needs more green over here."

"Oh," he said, lifting my veil and kissing the back of my neck. "The picture. That's nice, too."

I dropped the brush, smearing the bottom of the page. "What do you want, Egbert?"

"Haven't you figured that out yet? I thought it was obvious."

"Has it escaped your notice," I said, "that I'm practically engaged to Athelstan?" I stood up and started to leave. He grabbed my hand.

"Don't go. I'm sorry. I got distracted. It's Tecla I wanted to talk about. Is she pregnant?"

"What?"

"She hasn't told you," he said.

"You don't mean to say she's told you?"

"Well, no, but I do notice things. I mean, except for you and Athelstan. I missed that somehow. Are you sure he's the man for you?"

I put my hands to my face. "This is awful."

"Don't worry, he'll get over it."

"I mean about Tecla."

"It doesn't have to be," he said. "Helmstan would marry her in a minute."

"She hates Helmstan."

"There is that problem. I've got an idea. Maybe if she thought you liked me a little, she'd lighten up on Helmstan. You know how people are."

"Nice try, Egbert."

"I can't help myself."

"This is the worst news I've had in a long time," I said.

"You'll enjoy it, once you get used to it," he said.

"Will you cut it out? Do you think Odburh will make her leave?"

"Oh, probably," he said. "She takes a hard line on impropriety unless it's hers."

"Who knows about this besides you?"

"Just you."

"What about Helmstan?"

"That's another problem. He'll go nuts when he finds out."

"There's a convent I know about," I said. "Maybe I can take her there."

"You'd better talk to her," he said.


I did, and she denied it at first. We both looked at her swelling abdomen. She burst into tears. "Any child of his will only spread destruction," she said. "I'll kill it the moment it's born—just see if I don't."

"It's your baby, too," I said.

She didn't say anything. "Think of it this way," I said, grasping for a straw, "this baby was created with the old Helmstan, the gentle, lovable Helmstan, not the new one. It has nothing to do with the new Helmstan. You loved the old Helmstan, remember?"

"It seems so long ago."

"I remember how much you loved him. You used to sneak over to his bone house whenever Wermhere wasn't looking. You worried yourself sick over him."

"He was a different person then."

"That's just my point. This is a way of keeping that Helmstan alive." It was a long shot, but it worked.

"I never thought of it that way," she said, brightening a little.

"When it's closer to the time," I suggested, "I know a place you can go. Meantime, not a word to anybody."

In the hall that night Egbert took me aside. "Have you talked to her?" he asked.

"Yes."

"Do you think she might soften up on Helmstan?"

"Let's put it this way: I managed to talk her out of strangling the baby."

"Maybe you can get her into the convent before Helmstan figures out what's happening. If you need any help, let me know."

## SCENE 38 WARRIORS PUNISH DELINQUENT TRIBES

The next day the warriors went on a foray—not to fight the Jutes, but to punish the people of Andover for reneging on their food rents. Beorhtric led the raid, and he and Erpwald, Thingfrith, and Werwulf, among others, returned that night in the highest of spirits. Egbert, I noticed, looked grim and sat quietly with Athelwulf and Oswulf, drinking—I'd never seen him drink before. As Beorhtric lead the revelry and handed round prizes he announced the next attack, this time further afield in Bedwyn. This town, one of the last hold-outs in the old dynastic wars, was a thorn in Beorhtric's side. Egbert stood up and volunteered to lead the raid.

Beorhtric looked pleased—relieved, almost. "I noticed you didn't do too much fighting today," he said. Werwulf and his cronies laughed. "Who needs him?" Erpwald said.

"If you're looking to redeem yourself," said Beorhtric, "it's okay with me. You can lead it."

"It won't take all of us," said Egbert.

"It took all of us today," said Thingfrith, "but then, not everybody was fighting."

"I'll put a team together, and we'll leave in the morning," he said.

They came back a few days later, loaded with booty. None of the men had been wounded, or even scratched, and they were calm, not like men who have just returned from the fray. I did some serious eavesdropping, but all I could find out was that Egbert had gone in alone to talk to the leaders of Bedwyn and had come out with the equivalent in treasure of twice the back rents. Not a drop of blood, apparently, had been shed on either side.

Now that winter was over Athelstan was planning to go to Gaul. He wanted to hire some glaziers to make colored windows for the chapel. The morning of his departure we clung to each other outside the palace gates.

"I wish you could come with me," he said.

"I wish I could, too," I said. "I could if we were—if things were different."

"I'll miss you terribly," he said.

"You'll have Yurmin," I said.

"I'll write every day," he said.

I felt lost without Athelstan. There seemed little reason to remain at the palace. By the afternoon of the next day I had thought things over and decided it would be a good time to visit the abbey—I needed to lay the groundwork for Tecla's confinement. I dressed in some traveling clothes and headed off, telling Tecla not to expect to see me for a few days.

I felt better once I rode out of town. The day was warm. I noticed the soft, damp scent of spring. The sun was dazzling. I left the trail and dismounted. I laid my cloak on the ground and stretched out next to the river. Above my head the season's first brimstones and tortoiseshells fluttered from bush to bush. A gray wagtail hovered over the river, dancing after its prey. I enjoyed the sun's heat on my skin, the smell of the warm grass. Before I knew it, I had dozed off.

It was almost dusk when I awakened to the sound of hoof beats. Doing the prudent thing, I drove off my horse and hid behind a bush. Soon three men approached: Thingfrith, Werwulf, and Erpwald, who held up a hand to slow the others.

"This looks like a good place," he said.

"One of us can jump him from the tree," said Werwulf, "while the other two rush him from the bushes." He and Erpwald dismounted.

"There's a better spot further down," said Thingfrith, staying on his horse.

"What's better about it?" asked Werwulf.

"Tree's bigger. Two of us could jump him."

"You mean the ash?" asked Erpwald. Thingfrith nodded.

"I don't like it," said Werwulf.

"Let's stay here," Erpwald said. "Who wants to jump him?"

Silence.

After a while, Thingfrith said, "I'm sure we all do. Why don't we draw straws? I'll get some."

"No, I'll get them," said Werwulf. He picked up a twig, examined it, discarded it. He tried again. He wandered away from the group, getting closer than I liked to my hiding place.

"Hurry up, for Christ's sake," yelled Erpwald.

"Be right there," Werwulf yelled back. I could see him arrange the three twigs he'd chosen before he went back to the others.

"Give me those," said Thingfrith, grabbing for the twigs. The two started scuffling. I heard hoof beats again.

Using my foot I pushed some loose stones into a pile. "He's coming, you assholes," yelled Erpwald, shimmying up the tree. I pushed further into my bush, afraid he might be able to see me once he got up there. Both Thingfrith and Werwulf jumped for cover on my side of the road.

"Get on the other side, you idiot," said Werwulf.

"Get on it yourself," answered Thingfrith.

Neither man budged. I had an unobstructed view of the backs of their heads. Moving as little as possible I selected a few pieces of flint from the pile and waited for the rider to approach. When he was about ten feet away from the tree I yelled, "In the tree!" and simultaneously launched the stones. I got Thingfrith on the back of the skull. He fell forward. Werwulf moved—just enough—to spoil my aim. He turned around to see where the shots were coming from, and as he did, I sent one off that got him right between the eyes. "Explain how you got that to Wulfwaru," I hollered. He turned and ran, and I threw a few more rocks after him. Totally gratuitous violence, I suppose, but it sure was fun.

Meanwhile the rider had stopped his horse short the instant he heard my warning, and Erpwald, unable to check his jump, had fallen out of the tree and lay sprawled on the ground a couple of inches from the animal's hooves—not a particularly strong tactical position. As Egbert, arms akimbo, sat looking down at him, Erpwald scrambled to his feet and ran for it.

"Well," said Egbert, "that was easy."

The sweat was dripping down my face. "Easy for you," I said.

He got off his horse and took a look at Thingfrith. "He should be quiet for a while," he said. "Remind me to treat you with more respect."

"Don't tell me you'll need reminding," I said.

"Count on it," he said.

"Why did they want to kill you, by the way?" I asked. "Not that I haven't felt like it myself from time to time."

"I couldn't say," he said. "It's getting dark. We'd better ride together."

"We're not going in the same direction," I said, whistling for my horse.

"Bandits, spirits, trolls: they all come out at night, you know."

"Grow up," I said.

He held up a hand for silence. "Did you hear that?" All I heard was the congested song of a bird's mating call.

"I can take care of myself, thank you," I said, standing next to my horse and adjusting my saddle.

He spun around and looked up. "I saw something in that tree."

I looked up—a blackbird cock strutted across a limb, plumping his feathers. Bowing and turning he advanced on a female. The two were deciding whether to fight or mate. "It was just a bird, for Pete's sake," I said. "I'm not worried. I guess you've forgotten who drove off three attackers not too long ago?"

"You were magnificent," he said, mounting his horse. "Why do you think I want to ride with you? Somebody else might try to jump me." I got on my horse.

"Which way are we going?" he asked.

"Good-bye, Egbert," I said. I spurred the animal and rode off like a fury. I knew these paths like the native I was. It would be an easy job to lose Egbert. In fact, it was so easy I was a little disappointed. By the time I'd made the second turn, he was nowhere to be seen. I listened for a while, then headed back for the main path.

"Thought you got rid of me, didn't you?" grinned Egbert, suddenly next to me, his hand on my horse's bridle.

"I'm going to a convent, Egbert. They won't let you anywhere near the place."

"I'll wait for you by the gate," he said.

"I'm staying for weeks," I said.

"And I'll be waiting, cold and lonely—"

"Don't forget hungry," I said.

"Cold, lonely, hungry—"

"You are pathetic."

Athelflad was near the gate with her orphans when we arrived, picking daffodils. She dropped everything and ran over.

I jumped off my horse and embraced her.

"I'll take the horses to the stable," said Egbert.

"Wait—" I said. He went on.

Athelflad and I went to the guest cottage. Her eyes sparkled as I told her all about Athelstan and how I was sure to be the next queen of Wessex.

"He's gone to Gaul for a few weeks," I said. "That's why I could get away to come here."

"You mean he's not—"

"Not?" I asked.

"Not the man with you today?"

"Good God, no. Excuse me."

"Then who is he?"

"Him? Oh. He's my body guard. The king didn't want me riding through the forest alone," I said.

I searched for a way to broach the subject of Tecla's pregnancy. "Athelflad, there's something very serious I need to discuss with you."

"Well?"

"Do you remember that party in January for all the royals and nobles in England?"

"Sure."

"Princesses from other lands came as well, you know?"

"Yes?"

"I got to know one of them, and she's in serious trouble."

"What is it?"

"On her way to the feast, her party was set upon and robbed. Her attendants were killed."

"Disgusting."

"Yes, and that's not the worst of it."

"What could be worse?" she wanted to know.

"The princess, as innocent a virgin as ever lived, was raped, and of course it wasn't her fault, but she doesn't dare tell her family for fear they will disown her."

"I can understand why she wouldn't tell them."

"But if she goes home, they'll figure it out whether she tells them or not."

"How?"

"Sometimes things like rape leave incontrovertible evidence."

"You don't mean—"

"I'm afraid so. She's avoided the problem by extending her stay at the palace, but she can't stay there any longer because it's becoming obvious she's pregnant." I suddenly realized that if the baby had been conceived in January, it shouldn't be due until three months after the date I was planning to bring Tecla to the convent. "Babies spawned by rape grow one and a half times as fast as normal babies, you know."

"I wasn't aware of that."

"No reason you would be."

"I don't know if we can afford to take another child," Athelflad said.

"Don't worry about the money," I said. "She's terrifically rich." I could always sell some of my mother's things.

"Yes, well. I'm sure we can do something. I'll talk to the prioress."

"You're a saint."

"We're late for supper."

Although the dishes had been cleared when we got to the refectory, plates of food had been left for Athelflad and me. The nuns were celebrating St. Waudru's day. The prioress had set a place for me on her left with Athelflad on my other side. To the prioress' right sat Egbert, recounting to all the story of St. Waudru's sister St. Aldegund, who, with eleven other nuns, crossed the perilous sea in a hurricane, out-maneuvering both devils and heathen warriors, to miraculously nurse to health foreign orphans attacked by plague. You could have heard a pin drop.

"A bit over the top, don't you think?" I whispered to Athelflad.

"Shhhh," she said. After the story I heard Egbert and the prioress talking, but couldn't make out what they were saying. She didn't look in my direction until it was time to retire.

"Cynethrith," she said. "I'm so sorry. I hope you don't mind terribly if we put you in the dormitory tonight."

"The dormitory?" I said, at a loss. This was a come down.

"Yes. I am sorry. I'm afraid the guest hall is the only place we have that's suitable for Egbert."

"Oh, but he can't possibly stay," I said. "He really must get back to the palace."

"When you're ready," said Egbert.

"I'm ready," I said, "for you to leave."

"Unthinkable," he said. "I couldn't leave you to return through that dangerous forest on your own—"

"I've done it hundreds of times," I said.

"But, Cynethrith," interjected Athelflad, "didn't you tell me the king appointed him your body guard?"

"Did I say that?"

"How good of the king," said the prioress, "to take an interest in our young benefactress." She turned to Egbert, "She's practically a saint, you know."

"An angel," agreed Egbert, smiling at me. "Of course, I'll leave if you want me to," he said. "The king might not hang me when he finds out I abandoned my charge—"

"Go ahead," I said. "Take a chance."

"Cruel!" hissed Athelflad.

"This isn't a bit like Cynethrith," apologized the prioress. She put a hand to my forehead. "Perhaps she's not well. Athelflad, see that she sleeps next to you in case she needs anything."

That night, lying in the dormitory, awakened at intervals by the call to mass, I thought about sneaking to the guest hall and heaving rocks through the window. Then I got a better idea. When I'm queen, I thought, I'll make him marry Hilda.

Under the circumstances there was no point in prolonging the visit. We left after breakfast the next morning. When Egbert finally stopped waving to the nuns, all of whom had trooped to the gate to see us off, I said, "I trust you were comfortable."

"Best sleep I've had in months," he said. "There's something so peaceful about a convent." All at once he looked serious and reined up abruptly.

"Be quiet. Get off your horse," he said.

"You aren't going to try anything funny, are you?" I asked.

"Someday," he said. "But not right now." He drove off the horses and, just as he pulled me behind a bush, the king, Warr, and a few others went riding past, determined looks on their faces. As soon as they were out of sight, Egbert whistled for his horse and jumped on.

"See you later," he said.

"Now you're leaving?" I asked.

"You'll be all right."

"I've been telling you that for days," I said.

"Before I forget, I squared everything with the prioress."

"What are you talking about?"

"I told her about Tecla."

"You told her about Tecla? What exactly did you tell her?"

"The whole story. Well, most of it. No problem," and off he rode at a gallop.

### SCENE 39 CYNETHRITH IS ENGAGED

Later in the bower I told Tecla that everything was set for her to go to the convent. We decided to take her there in a few weeks before people started catching on. I went over the raped-princess story with her and told her to stick to it no matter what anybody said. Tecla started to tell me something, but was interrupted by a knock at the door. When she answered it, I heard an unfamiliar voice ask, "Is your mistress back yet?"

"Yes, my lord," said Tecla.

"May I see her at once?" he asked.

"Yes, my lord." It was the butler.

"Madam," he said, bowing.

"My lord," I said, with a curtsy.

"His Majesty, and the entire court, have been worried to distraction by your absence."

I hardly knew what to say. "I'm sorry, my lord. I didn't realize . . . ."

"His Majesty thinks of you as a member of the family. In fact, it is his very firm desire that you shall shortly be a member of the family. Have you any objection to this?"

Not the romantic proposal I'd been longing for, but a proposal, none the less. "It's a dream come true, my lord," I said. The butler seemed to relax a little.

"Good. That's fine. Well, then, good day, Lady Cynethrith."

I knew my engagement was public knowledge that evening when all the women rushed to surround me as I entered the hall. Elfwinne was the first to embrace me. "Oh, Cynethrith," she said. "I can't tell you how worried I've been. I was sure you'd been eaten by wolves. I could just hear you crying out in agony as their teeth pulverized your face—this is such a relief."

"The king was beside himself," said Athelwulf's girlfriend. "He sent out one search party after another."

"What if her throat had been slashed by an aurochs," queried Elfwinne, "and all her blood had gushed out like water from a spring?"

"Were you terribly frightened, all alone in the woods?" asked one of the queen's ladies. I was always surprised by the amount of protection they required.

"What if she'd been abducted by pirates and sold into slavery?" inquired Elfwinne. "Wouldn't that have been awful? She might have had to perform unspeakable sex acts with northern barbarians—"

The king and his party entered the room, and everyone waited for me to be the first to go before his chair and curtsy. Beorhtric glowed. "Sit next to Odburh, my dear," he said. "She'll make sure you don't disappear again, won't you my love?" After dinner, when Odburh rose to pour wine, Beorhtric leaned over her empty chair and told me how pleased he was that his son was getting married. "Women have always adored him, of course. And he's always had girl friends—had to fight them off with a stick. But I can see it's different with you." He winked at me. As I smiled I wondered how long it would be before Athelstan and I could take over the kingdom.

"We're two sides of a coin," I said.

"Exactly," said Beorhtric. "I thought so."

"Congratulations on your engagement," Egbert said later that night as I rested between dances.

I couldn't help gloating a little. "Thank you." I gave him a patronizing smile.

"Does Athelstan know about it?" he asked.

I worried over the answer to that question until Athelstan and his three glaziers returned in May, on St. Dympna's day. Yurmin was not with him. A slight cloud passed over my beloved's face. "He decided to stay in Gaul for a while." Later that evening, at the feast, we held hands under the table while the Bishop prattled on about the inevitable outcome of perverted passion, which he defined as any passion not centered on the love of God.

"But it's fun while it lasts, isn't it?" I whispered. Athelstan blushed like a bride. He was more beautiful than ever.

*SCENE* 40 AT THE CONVENT WITH TECLA AND ATHELSTAN

A peaceful time ensued. The warriors were gone, bashing the Jutes on the Isle of Wight. I let Athelstan in on the secret about Tecla. While it was obvious he found the whole thing distasteful, he agreed to accompany us to the convent later in May. While the prioress showed Athelstan around, and a nun took Tecla to her new quarters, Athelflad pulled me aside.

"Isn't he a dream?" I asked.

"I suppose so," she said. "How's Egbert?"

"Still alive, I'm afraid," I answered. She gave me one of her all too common reproving looks.

"And this young lady," she said, lowering her voice, "Is she the princess/slave, rich/indigent, raped/victim-of-momentary-weakness we were expecting?"

"She's the princess I told you about."

"Is someone else coming as well?"

"Not that I know of," I said. Athelflad's persistent stare didn't faze my guileless expression.

"I'm confused," I said. "Did you hear some other version of the story?"

"You might call it another version," said Athelflad, "except that it agreed with yours on no particulars whatsoever."

"Let me think: someone obviously made up a spurious story. Did you say it was about some pathetic slave girl tempted into sin? Why would anybody do that?" I shook my head. "Perhaps it's some misplaced gallantry, some feeble attempt to protect the maiden's true identity. Do you think that's it?"

"I give up," said Athelflad.

"I don't understand it, either," I said.


Athelstan and I rode back alone, through the forest, beneath the still bare oak canopy. We passed a grove of coppiced hazel beginning to leaf. Ash buds sprouted their hairy flowers. Along the sides of the path comfrey and burdock were up but not blooming, and beyond the path the woodland floor was covered with bluebells. I stopped to admire their intense color in the filtered light.

"Let's stay here a while," I said to Athelstan. We got off our horses. He spread a blanket on the ground, and we sat down. I watched a robin plunk herself down nearby and begin to feed. I edged close to Athelstan. He looked serious.

"We have to talk about your wedding gown," he said. A cock robin appeared, puffing up his red breast to chase off the female, but she paid no attention. "I think you'd look great in light blue. I'd like it cut tight from the bust to the hips to show off your body—somebody could sew you into it for the ceremony."

"Who's going to sew me out of it?" I said, flashing my sexiest smile. He blushed and looked uncomfortable. The cock robin gave up trying to intimidate the female and flew back to his perch, watching her and singing his heart out.

"The stole could be dark purple lined in red," he went on, "so the color flashes a little when you move. What do you think?"

"Sounds wonderful," I said. The female robin moved farther into the male's territory, trilling her song. The cock started toward her, then backed off, eying her suspiciously.

"Then for the veil—white, I think. Or gold? No, white—sheer enough to see all your braids underneath—with a solid gold circlet to hold it on." He stood up and put out a hand to hoist me to my feet. "Let's go," he said. "We've got to get started." Our sudden movement must have startled the female robin. She flew off to another part of the forest.

*SCENE* 41 THE BET

When Athelstan and I returned to the palace the warriors were back. The campaign, thanks to Egbert and Helmstan, had been a complete success. The subjugation of the Isle of Wight was complete much sooner than expected.

"Oh, my God," said Athelstan. "I've got to get that embroidery finished." He was talking about the commemorative hanging he'd started before his trip to Gaul. It celebrated the anticipated victory that had just prematurely occurred. Five embroiderers were working on it at present, but it had a long way to go. Thoughts of the wedding gown temporarily shunted aside, he told me to start stitching while he rushed into town to find some extra hands.

"We're going to have to embroider day and night," he said when he returned. "Otherwise it'll be stale by the time anybody sees it."

"Not that gorgeous design," I said.

"Unfortunately, there's only one person I didn't already know about. They say there's a woman in Easton, really good, fast as well, and reasonable."

I got a sinking feeling. "Easton?" I said. "They're all hicks over there. Famous for it. I seriously doubt anybody from Easton could possibly meet your standards."

"You may be right," he said, "but I'm a desperate man. I've sent a messenger to tell her to come to the palace tonight so we can see what she can do. We don't have to take her on if her samples don't look good."

"What's her name?" I asked, grasping for a straw. Maybe there was some other lady from Easton who embroidered, and I'd never heard of her. Maybe God would strike Athelstan deaf before my stepmother told him I was a sham.

"Who? The new woman? Wald—thingy. I don't know; Wald-something."

"I just remembered," I said, "I meant to break my back this afternoon."

"What?"

"I meant to braid my plaits," I said. "Got to go." I ran to the stable and jumped on my horse. I didn't have time to think it out, but I knew I had to do it while there were witnesses in the courtyard. I spurred my horse and started screaming.

"Watch out, watch out, he's out of control."

"Hang on," I heard someone yell. It was Egbert, riding toward me at a full gallop.

"Oh, shit," I thought. I had planned to "fall" out of sight behind a stable, after stopping the horse. Now I was going to have to go for it right here and now, in front of everybody. Egbert was next to me, his arm out, reaching for the reins. I crouched down low, and, keeping my body close to the animal and my arms and legs tucked, I rolled off the horse and onto the ground.

"What did you do that for?" I heard Egbert yell. "You could have got yourself killed for Christ's sake."

Luckily, I didn't. I could have struck my head on a rock or gotten kicked by the horse, but neither happened. Suppressing a smile of relief, I lay back and pretended to be unconscious.

Before long, Athelstan was standing over me, demanding to know what had happened. Egbert must have left. I didn't hear him say a word. Athelstan cradled me in his arms.

"Poor, poor darling," he said. "So beautiful, so frail. Is this the end of our exquisite, tragic love?"

*Not quite yet, Athelstan. I'm still breathing.*

He put his ear to my nose. "She's breathing, but just barely. Don't move her until I get a stretcher." Soon he came back and I was lifted onto some sort of silk contraption, by the feel of it. I was transported to my bower.

"Put her on the bed," said Athelstan. I was deposited with great ceremony. After the others left I could feel Athelstan arranging my clothes. I bet I look great, I thought. He left for a while, and when he came back I smelled honey-suckle. Later when I peeked I saw the room was bedecked with that and other flowers. He'd even placed some on top of me. He sat with me for a while, then said, "I have to go, my love, but I'll send someone over to look after you."

Once he was gone I got up and stretched a little. There was a knock. I jumped on the bed, shutting my eyes and going limp just as the door opened. I heard the bolt sliding into the catch. When he spoke, his voice came from the foot of the bed. It was Egbert.

"You can open your eyes now. I saw your fall—it was almost convincing."

Keeping my eyes firmly closed I writhed on the bed and cried out. Egbert walked to the side of the bed and sat down. "Cynethrith, I know there's nothing wrong with you," he said. "Why did you pull this ridiculous stunt?"

Why don't you mind your own business?

"This one was dangerous. You could have been badly hurt."

But I wasn't, was I? I can take care of myself, thank you very much.

"Why was it so important that you not show your face at court tonight?"

He couldn't stand it if he didn't know every last thing that was going on. He was getting close to the truth, and I didn't like it. I contorted my face and groaned. I probably overdid it. He began checking for broken bones. First he felt my head all over. Then, slipping his hands under my body, felt the back of my neck, my shoulder blades, my spine. I soon learned to be quiet when probed—the noise only prolonged the examination.

"Nothing so far," he said, lifting each arm in turn and bending it at the elbow and wrist. I could hear music coming from the hall. The dancing must have started. Egbert moved on to my legs, feeling each thigh, kneecap, and calf. I concentrated on keeping my muscles relaxed. "There's nothing wrong with you, not a thing," he said, lifting one of my feet to rotate an ankle. "You're perfect." He replaced my foot with a little pat. "So—what are you up to?"

Of course I didn't answer.

"Could it have anything to do with a woman from Easton coming to see Athelstan early this evening?"

He thinks he's so damn smart. He's got everybody and everything figured out. Well, I'm tired of it. Sick to death of it—and if he thinks I'm going to bare my bosom or reveal one little thing to him, he can think again.

"Oh well, all right—I'll make a bet with you," he said, "I'll bet you regain consciousness before the musicians finish their third song."

So—he wants to make a contest out of it. That's Egbert. Everything is a competition with him. Game on, and I bet I'll lie here comatose until noon tomorrow, or dawn, anyway. I might get hungry.

The second song began. It was a maudlin ballad about the pitfalls of lust. I wondered what he'd try. I steeled myself for some minor brutality like a pinprick or the hot flame of a candle. Maybe he'd bite me or something. I wasn't worried. I knew that the thing to think about when you're being tortured is your tormentor's technique. I was pretty sure I could withstand anything he intended to inflict for the duration of two songs.

He stretched out next to me on the bed. I felt his eyes on me. I hoped my lids weren't fluttering. He was quiet and still, and that made me nervous. Anticipation is often worse than the event. It's hard to defend against something that hasn't happened. Is he planning to give me a really hard pinch? Or tickle me? Jab me with something? He touched my face with his fingertips. When he spoke again his voice was completely different.

"You're so beautiful," he said slowly. I didn't expect that, but leave it to Egbert to come up with a creative tactic. Even though I knew it was a trick, I had to admire the way he said it. He whispered in my ear, "I want you." That surprised me: so direct. His hand moved across the skin just above the neckline of my dress. "I've wanted you since the first time I saw you, your legs wrapped around that tree. I wanted you to wrap them around me like that."

*Just jump right in, Egbert. No need for subtlety.*

He kissed my neck, where the pulse beats. "I wanted to rip those rags off your body and lick off that brown goop you'd smeared all over yourself." I felt an odd tingle at the back of my throat.

"I almost hoped you'd try to jump me. I would have taken your knife and then taken you."

I had learned something from watching Egbert in action over the course of several months—what you could believe about what he said was that not a word of it was true. And anyway, what sort of bastard takes advantage of an unconscious lady, even if she is faking?

He was kissing me. After a moment I felt his tongue gliding against my lower lip, on the inside.

Now what? I thought. Would an unconscious person's jaw be slack or rigid?

He solved the problem for me by running a fingertip across my upper lip, then between my front teeth. I had to open my mouth.

If he thinks a few kisses and some dirty talk are going to scare me into conceding he can think again.

"After I slammed you against the wall that night I couldn't get the feel of your body pressing against mine out of my head." He put one of his legs between mine, pressing his thigh up against me. I felt as if a large fish did a flip in my abdomen. He made an impressive groan. "I want to have you every way a man can have a woman."

Okay, so I knew this was his typical seductive bullshit, maybe a little more extreme than usual—at least my mind knew—but my body was getting fooled, and I had to focus on precisely modulating my breathing. Meanwhile, his breathing got heavier, and he moaned a little more, pressing his face against my shoulder. He kissed the soft flesh on the inside of my upper arm. "Oh, God, Cynethrith," he murmured, with credible intensity. "When I saw you in Easton that day I wanted to pull you onto my horse and take you into the forest and make you come until you couldn't remember your name."

*Whew! Is this the way he talks to his lovers? Of course I don't give a damn what he says to them, or what he does to them for that matter.*

I felt his hand against my skin, under the neckline of my tunic.

*This is getting hard to ignore.* He was kissing me again. I listened to the music. The second song was over. *Just one more*, I told myself, *I can hold out for one more song.* Saxburg was singing *In the Upper Room with Jesus.* I tried to reconstruct the last sermon I'd heard.

He caressed my breasts, massaged my left nipple. Then I remembered what the sermon had been about: Quintianus' passion for St. Agatha. I decided instead to think about the last fight I'd had with my stepmother. That cooled me off a little, but then between kisses he said, "Let's make a baby."

*Good God! What did he just say!*

Egbert's other hand was lifting my skirt. He investigated the contours of my calf muscle, then pushed on to my inner thigh, lingering before continuing the search. This time he wasn't looking for my knife. "Cynethrith," he said, "I don't think I can stop myself."

I opened my eyes. "Stop! Where am I?" I did my best to keep my voice flat and even. Egbert looked at me, his eyes all smoky with desire.

As I held his gaze my hand searched for something to brain him with. When I lifted the pitcher from the bed table I discovered that nothing interfered with his warrior's instincts. His hand shot out to grab my wrist. The pitcher clattered to the floor. I tried to sock him with my free hand and found my arms pinned over my head. I heard applause from the hall. The third song had just ended.

He released my wrists. His fingertips caressed mine.

"Oh, good, you're awake," he said. "Now you can kiss me back."

Of course I had no intention of doing that. And yet—I did. I threw my arms around his neck and kissed him. I started to shake, and I made sounds I can't describe. It was as if some alien spirit had taken over. I was too far gone to care how it would end, and he had no reason to stop.

But he did. He sprang to his feet and straightened my dress. He whispered, "When you think of me tonight, I'll be thinking of you." Then he was across the room. I heard a sharp rap at the door. As he opened the door I resumed my unconscious pose.

"Why was the door bolted?" It was Athelstan, sounding annoyed.

"I'm sorry, Your Highness," said Egbert. "A warrior's reflex." That seemed to satisfy the atheling.

"How is she? Good heavens, she's red." He placed his hand on my forehead. "She's awfully warm. Covered in sweat. She must have a fever."

"It will be short-lived," said Egbert. "She has a temporary excess of yellow bile."

"Has she said anything?"

"No. She did moan from time to time."

"Yes, I heard some of that when I tried the door. Well thank God she isn't moaning now. It would be so distressing to listen to."

"It was unsettling," said Egbert.

"When do you expect her to get better?" asked Athelstan.

"She'll cool down before the hall is cleared."

"Have you done all you can?"

"For the time being. There's something feverish in her brain. Sometimes the body has a mind of its own."

## SCENE 42 BACK TO EASTON

Egbert got that one right: there was something feverish in my brain. I could believe I had an excess of yellow bile. I wished Athelstan would go away, so I could think. But he didn't. I could hear him moving around. He picked up the clothes I'd been leaving where they dropped ever since Tecla had gone to the Abbey. When they started clearing the hall he came over to me, felt my forehead, and said, "You aren't a bit feverish anymore."

I took some deep breaths and risked opening my eyes. "I feel ever so much better," I said. He took my hands in his. I had decided that I had to get away for a while, to a place without distractions where I could sort myself out.

I said, "There is something very serious I need to tell you." He looked concerned. "My head was very troubled this afternoon. I think that's why I fell off my horse. I've had bad news."

"What is it my darling?"

"My mother is very ill. I must go to her at once."

"I will come with you."

I was ready for that one. "I love you too much to let you. I know how important the embroidery is to you and to the palace, and you must be here to supervise its completion. I could never forgive myself if it didn't come out perfectly, and you know that it won't if you aren't here."

I could tell he agreed with my argument but didn't want to appear too hasty. "And besides," I added, "I don't know what she has. It would be a disaster for Wessex if you were to get the plague or something."

"But what about you? I can't let you expose yourself to that."

I had gone too far. "Well, nobody has said that's what it is, and I'm sure they would have told me if it was. You can see how feverish in the brain I've become to even think of something like that."

"I will send someone with you."

"There is no need, sir. Tecla's child was born last week. She can leave her at the abbey and accompany me." I hoped Athelstan had not been paying too much attention to the length of time Tecla had been gone.

"Where does your mother live?" he asked.

"Far away," I said, "in an enchanted land in the North. It's inaccessible to all but blood relatives—and their slaves, of course."

Athelstan yawned. "Well, my love, I'd better let you get some sleep.

232

You've had a hard day, and there's a long journey ahead of you tomorrow. I'll miss you terribly." He kissed me on the cheek and left.

I spent a restless, almost sleepless night. I kept hearing Egbert say, "When you think of me, I'll be thinking of you." When I did sleep my dreams were vivid. In one I looked into the linen closet and spotted a lizard with the head of a man, a foreigner from his features. There was a very beautiful pattern etched upon his skin. A red cloisonné flower near his center was set off by a dark green ground. He headed for the bedroom. My family was there, uncomfortable so near a lizard. I kept saying, "but he is so beautiful." He climbed up the wall near a small window. I looked out the window and the back fence was gone. It wasn't as if it had fallen. It was more like it had been removed.

I left for Easton before dawn. I wanted to avoid seeing the king, who might have given me more trouble about leaving than Athelstan had. I knew I wanted to think, but what exactly was it that I wanted to think about? I was drowning, or maybe wallowing is more honest, in an abyss. Once I got home I sat around the house, staring into space. Maybe it wasn't the best place to have gone. I'd been seeking peace and quiet, but being there seemed to intensify my fugue state. I wasn't sleeping, and I couldn't eat. I'd begin to do something and then forget what I had started. Even Waldberg noticed and asked me if I were well. Hilda said, "Maybe she's in love." I felt a spasm right below my rib cage.

"Don't be silly," said Wulfwaru, "who could she have possibly met at the abbey?"

"There's definitely something wrong with her," said Hilda, "no snappy answers, no schemes, no insults."

"Well," said Wulfwaru, "at least she's still as useless as ever. She hasn't changed that much."

It was easy to screen out the noise of the family's chatter. I kept rerunning that night with Egbert in my mind. I could feel his touch and hear his voice. What would it be like, I wondered, to come until I couldn't remember my name? I wanted to know. I'd never given a thought to having a child—they were tiresome little creatures as far as I was concerned—but when I remembered hearing "let's make a baby," I got weak with desire. Would he really have taken me on the forest floor if I'd jumped him that first day? That one really got to me because as much as I had always understood that I'm indomitable, as much as I would resist the attempt, and as disgusting as I found the idea, I wanted him to do it. It was all I could think about. That was the part of me I was grappling with. And I remembered another thing he had said a while ago—about wanting someone you didn't want to want. And the more you didn't want to want them, the more you did. Yes, that about summed it up.

It went on this way for several days. My stepsisters started asking Waldberg if I was going to die. If I hadn't known them better, I would have said they sounded concerned. My stepmother consulted the nearest healer so none of the villagers could say I had been neglected. He pronounced me possessed. I wondered why that hadn't occurred to me. He prescribed the heart of a vulture wrapped in wolf-skin. It didn't help. He must have harvested the organ incorrectly or misspoken the incantation.

After a few more days I felt I had to move, so I pretended that the vulture cure was working. The family didn't object when I said I wanted to go to the abbey. Maybe they thought I was going there for last rites. I went over to see Tecla, and she took me on a tour of the babies in the nursery.

"What is it?" she asked, "You seem subdued. Kind of like you're not all here."

I would have liked to talk to her to see what she would think about what had happened, but knowing how she felt about Egbert and Helmstan I knew what she would say. Before I left she said, "You aren't in love, are you?"

"I've been in love with Athelstan for a long time, " I said, a little glumly.

"Hmm. This is different."

*SCENE* 43 CYNETHRITH'S NEW PLAN

Yes, it was different, I had to admit. Not to her of course. Loving Athelstan was fun. We joked and laughed. He dressed me in beautiful clothes and thought I was clever. This felt more like a whack in the head with an anvil: unpleasant and disconcerting, with no guarantee of recovery. I hugged Tecla and left the abbey.

I spent another week mooning about, sighing, but I added long walks through the countryside to my inactivity list, and they began to clarify my mind. I began to understand the difference between the feelings I had for the two men, and the germ of a plan was born.

I loved Athelstan, absolutely. He was beautiful, kind, artistic and elegant, a delight to be with. As I had told the King, we were two sides of a coin. On the other hand, what I felt for Egbert was an exhausting state of stomach churn, shortness of breath, and a collection of strange and bewildering sensations. That was the difference. I'd heard about lust during church sermons, and more descriptively from eavesdropping on the village women at the well. I never thought I would fall victim to something so despicable, but I forced myself to face it. Putting a name to my condition was a start. Now I could figure out a way to conquer it.

It was clear to me that it would be wrong to marry Athelstan while in a state of lust for someone else. I certainly didn't want to end up like Odburh, having affairs with any available warrior. I knew what came of lust was never good, in any case. On the other hand, everyone said that lust is a short term kind of thing, and that meant there had to be a way to get over it. I thought some more and remembered what the women used to say: "He'll have his way with her and then leave her. He's only after one thing." Invariably, it seemed, once the act has taken place, the sinner never wants to do it again. And there would be no dire penalty: the priest fathers made sure we knew that whatever the transgression, if you confessed and repented you would be forgiven, and it would be as if it had never happened.

This line of thought lead to a perfectly logical solution, beautiful in its simplicity. If I had sex with Egbert I could put this madness behind me. From what I had heard, the one who initiated sex lost interest first, and from my point of view that was a plus. Even if Egbert had started it earlier, at this point the initiator would be me. Of course there was a good possibility that Egbert would lose interest afterwards as well. That would be good for his soul, so it would be something I could be proud of. And more practically, he'd stop trying to trick me at every turn. I gave out a great sigh and smiled to myself. This was as perfect as the music of the spheres. At last I had a way forward, and I would soon be a free woman. Time to seek out Egbert and get it over with.

This was easier said than done. As I mulled over how to bring my plan to fruition, I had to face how embarrassing it would be to admit to someone else, especially Egbert, that I'd succumbed to this weakness. He'd probably see it as some sort of victory. I had to come to grips with the fact that my plan might involve some awkwardness, and I spent a few days thinking very hard about how to go about it. How would I put it? Where would we do it? Were there things I hadn't thought about, details that needed attention? I wasn't sure. I didn't doubt that Egbert would cooperate, even if I had to put up with some gloating, but I still needed to steel my courage to start the process. Of course it shouldn't be difficult: if I offered myself for a one-time dalliance, nothing more, Egbert would jump at the chance. I decided that the best course was to be straightforward—no point in beating around the bush. And when my opportunity came, landed on my doorstep so to speak, I seized it. "She who hesitates is lost," I told myself. "The battle goes to the brave."

The next day I began to hear rumors gleaned from the chat around the well that the king was very put out that the atheling's betrothed had left the court, and he was sending search parties across the country to find her. They were going so far as to search houses. The king let it be known he was concerned that I had been kidnapped by one of his enemies. I figured that if I could only hide out long enough to get Egbert out of my system, I could go back to court and happily marry my beloved Athelstan. For the moment all I could do was try to get a message to Egbert. I kept my rags handy so I could don a disguise if a search party showed up. I also practiced rolling under my bed and into the little cellar beneath it.

A day later word came that the search party was headed in our direction. As a precaution, I dressed in my servant garb. Just before noon there was a rap at the door. The king's men had arrived and were starting to search my house. I jumped into the cellar, then heard an all-too familiar voice ask my stepmother where I was. She led him to the bower door and would have come in, except that he said, "Please leave us, madam."

My heart leaped. It was as if he had been delivered to me on a silver platter. It might be risky to do it here in the house, but I was sure Egbert could solve that problem: he was so resourceful.

I scrambled out from under the bed.

Egbert looked at me. "Aren't you a sight?" he said. "You know the king is looking for you?"

"Yes," I said.

"How do you feel about going back to court and marrying Athelstan?"

A perfect opening! "I can do that, and I want to do that," I said, "but there is something I have to do first."

"Well?"

I forged bravely on. "I have to have sex with you." A pause that went on too long. "You're surprised."

"Yes. Not that you want to, of course, but that you would be so—blunt."

"It's very simple," I said. I had planned what to say in case I needed to spell it out for him. "I need to get over these feelings for you that are simply lust, and the best way to do that is to have sex with you."

"I don't think so," he said.

"Kind of like scratching an itch," I said.

"What if it's more like eating? If you feast tonight does that mean you won't want dinner tomorrow?"

I'd expected success to come quickly. This dithering rattled me. And I was irritated. "I guess there's only one way to find out whose analogy is more apt."

Egbert got quiet again. Finally he said, a little grimly, "This is the most romantic proposition I've ever had." Another pause that went on too long.

Oh God, this really isn't going well.

"So," he finally said, "—basically you're saying you want to use me for sex."

I was floored. "Aren't you the little outraged virgin!"

"You thought all this was about sex?" he said.

"Forgive me! My mistake. I thought you were the man who had his hand up my skirt the other night."

He was outrageous enough to say, "That was for your own good."

"Thank you! How kind." Definitely not going according to plan.

"I thought you should know what you'd be giving up with Athelstan."

"And you know this how? Oh, wait, because you notice things."

"How's it working for you so far?" he asked. "Are you going to be happy painting floral borders and making embroideries for the rest of your life?"

"You can't possibility predict my sex life with Athelstan," I said. "Just because he's a gentleman and refuses to take advantage of me."

He didn't say anything.

"So," I said, "you aren't going to do it?"

He looked as if he were thinking about it. "Well, I will, of course."

"Well?" I was waiting for him to do something.

"As soon as we're married."

"Good God!" I said. "I never saw that stopping you."

"You are a virgin," he said.

"Are you asking me or telling me? Oh, never mind." How could he have noticed *that*? "What's that got to do with anything!"

"No man of honor would deflower a virgin."

What was I to make of this new, sanctimonious Egbert? "Just tell me one thing," I said. "The truth this time—why did you do it?"

"You could have stopped me at any time, Cynethrith."

"You're forgetting that I was unconscious."

"You were not unconscious," he said.

I maintained what I hoped looked like a self-righteous silence.

"Your eyes were closed, but mine were open. When I said I wanted you, your eyelids fluttered. Every time I touched you your breathing changed. Your heart was racing when I kissed you. Nipples don't respond when a person is unconscious. And people who are unconscious from an injury are cold, not hot." Then he sounded annoyed: "How could you think I'm the sort of jerk who would take advantage of an unconscious woman? You know you could have stopped me: why didn't you?"

"The wager—" I said. My voice trailed off. It sounded lame, even to me.

"You would let any man maul you so you could win a bet?"

"Of course not!" I said. "It wasn't just anybody, it—" I realized there was no good way to answer that one, so I started to cry.

"I tried to tell you in so many ways," he said.

Tell me what? What was he talking about? "Except," I said, "actually telling me."

"I had to use the one thing I had that Athelstan didn't have—I mean besides the ability to fight and lead men. The one thing you might care about—"

I glanced at him and saw something I had never seen before. He was at a loss. He was vulnerable. The way he was looking at me—as if I'd rendered him defenseless. Was it possible? If he was weakening maybe I still had a chance. Maybe I could still make him do it.

So I kissed him, gently and sweetly. He let me, but he didn't respond. He just stood there, but soon I noticed his breathing had changed. Why not try some of his tactics? "I haven't been able to stop thinking about you. You made me so hot that my dress had scorch marks." I pressed up against him and moaned. "All you have to do is look at me, and I turn into wet daub."

When he moaned a little, I cranked it up a few notches. "It's like I've turned into oozing slime or something." I pushed him back onto the bed. He didn't resist. "I have to have you. How about now, before I decompose altogether?" I was pretty sure this was working. The thrill of victory made me giddy. What an amazing turn around, just when I'd given up hope. I was so happy to be winning that I smiled as I kissed him. It hadn't been easy but I'd done it! I anticipated smooth sailing going forward, and I abandoned myself to the fun of it. My upper arms were tingling, and I could feel my heart pound—but I didn't mind any of it this time: soon I'd be cured.

He pulled away for a moment and said, "I love you."

I hadn't planned for this maneuverer, and I didn't have a defense. All of a sudden I was no longer in control. My womb raced about my body: into my neck, then my shoulders, my thighs, my toes. My spleen went into spasm, and vibrated so fiercely I began to shake. No woman can resist seeing she's vanquished the strongest man she knows. There I was, an over-fermented flagon of mead, exploding in every direction.

He was kissing me now as if all the passion of all the lovers on earth had been compressed into his longing. "Say you'll marry me," he said. At that moment I would have said any damn fool thing requested—that it was impossible to fall off the ends of the earth, or that the sun didn't sink into the sea: I was bereft of reason.

"I'll marry you," I gasped.

"Swear it," he said.

"I swear it."

## SCENE 44 THE TRUTH ABOUT WALDBERG

The ravishment I was expecting, and indeed felt I had earned, did not take place. Before I knew what was happening I was outside the house, where Egbert had carried me. There were six guards with spears near the entrance, and the entire gawking village assembled in the front garden with Tidburg the gossip front and center. Waldberg, Wulfwaru and Hilda were in hysterics.

"I have an announcement to make," said Egbert.

But he couldn't make it, because Waldberg had thrown herself at his feet and was begging him to release me. To my astonishment she was so upset that she was practically incoherent. "My lord," she implored, "have mercy on this foolish, foolish girl. Whatever her offense, let me pay the price. I beg you not to torture her or sell her into slavery to be used and abused by cruel and perverted men. Her mother was my best friend, and I swore to her as she left for her last battle at King Wulf's side that I would love and protect her daughter. I owe my friend this oath. I love the child more than life itself, and I will willingly suffer or die in her stead."

You can imagine the shock—and shame—I felt hearing these words.

Egbert put me down so he could lift Waldberg to her feet. "Calm yourself, madam. I mean the girl no harm." I thought this might be a propitious moment for me to slink away. I made a slight move to get behind Egbert. He grabbed my hand and held it—tight.

The villagers were restless. I wondered if they would try to rescue me. I don't think they knew what to do. The leaders knew Egbert well and liked him, but of course my family had lived in Easton for generations. They watched and waited.

"No one knows better than I do," said Waldberg through her tears, "how rash she can be. Her father died four years ago, and I've failed miserably in controlling her. She means no ill, but she's impulsive and—and—"

"Headstrong?" suggested Egbert.

"Yes! Headstrong. At times she lacks self-control—"

"I've noticed," said Egbert.

"I know she's deplorably sassy. Of course it's disrespectful, but she doesn't mean it. She is at that stage of life when she knows everything, and makes judgments that are—"

"—wide of the mark."

"Wider than a church door, my lord. Girls her age are besotted with romantic notions. I should know, I have three of them."

"My sympathy, madam."

Waldberg, probably from the strain of all she feared was going on in the bedroom a little earlier, had lost all sense of propriety. She was babbling. Under normal circumstances she would not have aired our dirty laundry in public, and certainly not to a member of the court. Oblivious to her surroundings, she allowed herself to enjoy a sympathetic listener. She had been terrified of Egbert a minute ago. Now here she was, having a cozy little chat with him. The villagers who had been thinking about attacking him were beginning to enjoy the show. *How does he do it?* I wondered.

I hoped Waldberg and Egbert might go on about Wulfwaru and Hilda a little, but Waldberg quickly returned me center stage. "Cynethrith is too imaginative. She loses sight of reality and rarely knows—"

"What's going on."

But let's pull away from their friendly exchange for a moment and take a look at it from my point of view. There I was, dirty, dressed in rags. The entire village, no longer restive but fascinated, listened raptly to this recital. Tidburg was as close to heaven as she's ever likely to get. Of course I was annoyed, but at the same time I was so stricken by the way I had misjudged Waldberg that I looked upon this humiliation as a penitence I owed. I stood erect but not proud, determined to bear this trial with dignity. That was just as well, because my mother wasn't done yet.

"She comes up with these ridiculous schemes that she calls 'plans'—"

"Her last one sure was a doozy," said Egbert.

I could feel myself turn pale, and I prayed that a merciful God would open the earth to swallow me.

"Don't tell me," said Waldberg.

"I won't."

"You seem to know her well, my lord."

"And yet, madam, and yet—"

"Yes?"

"I want to marry her."

For the first time, Waldberg looked at me. "My God, Cynethrith," she said. "What are you wearing?"

What she said hardly registered. At that moment I was so overcome by the way I had abused her that dignity abandoned me. I ran to her sobbing. I embraced her. "Mother, Mother, forgive me! Forgive me."

"Oh for heaven's sake, Cynethrith, you look frightful, but it isn't the worst thing you've ever done."

As I embraced Waldberg my sisters joined in and embraced us both, and we all stood together, a family, holding one another and crying. If I had been detached I might have been pleased to notice that Egbert didn't know what to do. He let us bawl for a while, and then he said, "Ladies, please, can we get back to my proposal?"

Waldberg's arms shot out wide, and she pushed me behind her, the picture of protective motherhood. My sisters put me between them, holding me close, and glared at Egbert as if he were threatening to take away their most sacred treasure.

"My lord," began Waldberg, "Nothing would make me happier than for Cynethrith to marry a fierce warrior and an upstanding member of the court like you. But I beg you not to force the girl. For many months she's been living at the abbey, praying and fasting." Nothing was going right today. I risked a panicked glance at Egbert. Thank God he merely looked interested. She went on, "It was a great surprise to me at first, but I've come to believe it's likely she has a calling. She must be allowed to make her choice."

"Her Christian virtue," said Egbert, "is one of the things about her that I most admire. When she swears an oath she keeps it. What's it to be, Cynethrith, me or the convent?"

Childish as it was—whether or not I wanted to marry Egbert wasn't what I was thinking about. I was thinking that I didn't want him to win. More important, there was my engagement to Athelstan, which Egbert insisted on ignoring, and I was in no position to bring up. If I wasn't going to marry Athelstan the only way I might be able to get out of it short of being executed was to choose the convent. But then there was the lust issue. Even though I wasn't feeling it at the moment, I figured I was most likely still in its grip. If the last week had taught me anything, it was that I was unsuitable for the religious life. I was stuck. I didn't know what to do.

Like a deus ex machina, a distraction appeared on the horizon. In the distance I saw the tips of spears clearing the top of the downs to the west, and I knew a large contingent of the king's men was about to arrive. This liaison with Egbert had become public enough that I had as good a chance to burn as to wed Athelstan. And even though men are rarely blamed for indiscretions, there was a chance that if the king— or more likely the queen—got wind of Egbert's shenanigans he wouldn't survive either. There was no point in both of us dying, so I decided to do the decent thing and warn him. I looked at him and was trying to say, "You know the king's men are cresting the hill?" I got as far as the "You—" when Egbert cut me off.

"The lady has chosen me," he said.

The villagers cheered loudly. My sisters and mother embraced me in happiness. The six guardsmen were smiling. I was the only one who seemed to realize that this happiness would be short-lived.

The approaching warriors were accompanied by a herald, two trumpeters and the entire Witan. I'd never seen anything like it. As the group pulled up the herald dismounted and made a proclamation. "Hear ye! Hear ye! The King is Dead! Long live the King!" So—I thought, Athelstan is now king. For a moment that was exciting, but then the unwelcome thought sprang to mind that he might not be the best man for the job. He was far from a warrior. Who would protect us? Affairs of state interested him not at all. I'd known all this while living at the palace, but I hadn't seen it as insurmountable. I had been sure that once we were married I'd have time to train him before he was called upon to perform—but now I realized our kingdom was in jeopardy. The crowd had gone quiet and solemn. The entire village must have felt the same. I saw myself queen of a giant disaster.

"Whereas the queen has poisoned the king and fled in the night to her father King Offa of Mercia, enemy of Wessex, for protection—"

"And whereas his son Athelstan has left for Gaul—"

Athelstan was gone!

"Whereas the Witan has learned that the young atheling taken to Charlemagne's court for safe keeping at the time of Beorhtric's usurpation of our throne has returned—

"Whereas this atheling, now a man, has proved himself a worthy warrior, a skillful negotiator and a leader of men—

"The Witan proclaims Egbert King of Wessex!"

This was greeted with cheers and jubilation. All knelt to their new king, and I felt Waldberg's hands pressing my shoulders to remind me to do the same. This was going to take some getting used to. This wasn't Egbert anymore. This was the king.

Egbert spoke. "Friends—please rise. As Wessex will rise." The village leaders were elated. They had met with Egbert on and off for months. The men wouldn't talk so I never could find out why, but I knew the friendship dated from the time of the dragon escapade. I later learned that Egbert had met the leaders of most villages in Wessex. He made a very pretty speech that was enthusiastically received about how the enemies of our kingdom from the Welsh in the West to the Mercians to the North, and all the kingdoms from Cornwall to Kent— all would succumb to our will. And blah, blah, blah, the usual sort of bragging hyperbole that kings feel they must say, and the people feel they must hear. Most of this came to pass, but that doesn't take away from the fact that it was not very likely at the time. He talked about lower taxes and more grain sales abroad and building cathedrals to the glory of God. The people ate it up, and Egbert was cheered again and again. My mind wandered.

For the sake of Wessex and the sacrifice my mother had made for our kingdom, I was glad Egbert was king. He was the best warrior we had, and he had an undeniable knack for getting his way. Whether I had agreed to marry him or not was irrelevant now. As strategic as I knew him to be, it only made sense that he would choose a foreign princess. I comforted myself with the thought that marriages based on political alliances are joyless. I knew my behavior had been scandalous, and I could never again show my face at court. I imagined a life of penitence. *I would fast and pray, and wander the forest, a waif—beautiful and sad, so very beautiful, so very sad. Egbert would spot me there one day and be enchanted by my mystical otherworldliness. He would regret my peripatetic life of exile and realize it was his fault: the predictable result of his thoughtless seductive teasing. He would be able to tell that I had become pure and conquered lust, but even so he would be struck with a longing he couldn't deny, the sort of longing you can only have for someone that you know will never be yours.*

This pleasantly dismal reverie vanished when I noticed the king by my side. I put all my energy into breathing and projecting an expression of serene dignity. I'd been humiliated enough for one day. "Today, people of Wessex," he was saying, "you have a new king. And I would like to introduce you to your new queen. This gentle lady, as true a model of Christian virtue as any woman who breathes on earth, has agreed to be my wife." He took my hand. The villagers were once again ecstatic. It's no small thing to know the queen.

Prodded in the back by my mother, I had the presence of mind to curtsy before him and say, "Your Majesty." I did an impressive rendition of feminine virtue and womanly dignity. He was king now. I'd have to behave. Nevertheless, I couldn't resist shooting him the tiniest glance that said: *I submit. Or do I?*

He raised me to my feet, and I thought I might collapse, but before I could my mother and sisters were around me, weeping again, but this time from happiness. I couldn't stop smiling. The rest of the villagers surrounded us. There was joy all around.

You're probably wondering whether Egbert overcame his moral fastidiousness about sleeping with a virgin before marriage. It's none of your business, of course, but I will tell you his moral probity lasted until moon rise. That was how long it took him to go to Winchester, organize the government and get back to Easton. We had a premature 7 pound 9 ounce baby seven months after we wed. No one raised an eyebrow. They expected Egbert's child would be precocious.

The weeks after his proposal were busy ones, as my family and I prepared for the move to the palace. I flew around, packing, organizing, and sorting out what we should take and what we should give to the poor. I made sure the servants had suitable clothes for court and trained them in palace protocol. I worked at the palace supervising the building of new accommodations for my family. That's when I missed Athelstan the most. He was so good at that sort of thing.

My mother and sisters worked harder than I did on the wedding festivities. One day Wulfwaru looked at me and said, "You aren't going to be all sweet and helpful and appreciative for the rest of your life are you? I'm not sure I can live with it."

"The transformative power of love," said Hilda.

I laughed and hugged them both.

On our wedding night, after we escaped the feasting and the revelry, Egbert poured ox blood from a small vial onto a sheet and threw it out the window to quiet down the raucous villagers. The beer had been free. They had drunk too much, and they had a prurient interest in the consummation of our marriage. When they finally disbursed we stretched out on the bed and smiled at one another.

"There's something I've been wondering," said Egbert. "Do you love me a little, or is it still only lust?"

"Lust, my lord," I said.

"Scratching hasn't cured the itch?"

"Oh," I sighed, "it helps for a while, not very long. Then the condition roars back worse than ever."

"I'm so sorry. Must be awful." he said.

"It is," I said. "You won't stop trying to cure me, will you?"

"You know I love a challenge."

"And there's something I've been wondering," I said.

"Hmm?"

"I wonder what cook is planning for dinner?"

"Oh," he said, "I think you'll like what's on the menu."

*Epilogue*

By now you've probably figured out how wrong that story you've heard is: the one in which I'm portrayed as a pathetic victim who lives in the fireplace, wears rags, and does everyone's bidding without complaint, all the time being abused by a stepmother and two ugly stepsisters. And you might even have a good idea who started these rumors. Tidburg's stories about seeing me washing rags, scrubbing the floor, or being left at home while the rest of the family went to the ball got little traction in Easton. They knew all of us too well—and if they thought I had been left at home they would have figured I had it coming. However, Tidburg's tales stuck when she took them to the Buttercross in Winchester, and she did—every week when she sold eggs there. People who didn't know us enjoyed retelling this claptrap.

Of course it's upsetting. Every time I hear this spurious fable I'm ashamed of having complained so bitterly and so publicly about Waldberg. I'm embarrassed by how determinedly wrong-headed I was. Besides that, the story encourages girls to believe that if they sit passively by the fire and take orders life will give them everything they long for. Nothing could be farther from the truth. It is far better to be as rash and foolish as I was and take a few risks.

Do you want to know why the queen murdered Beorhtric? That was a mistake. She kept a bevy of quail that she fed hemlock. When the birds had eaten enough to make their flesh poisonous, she planned to dispatch Warr. While fowl was one of the man's favorite foods, the king never ate it. That night, however, the king had started drinking earlier than usual, and with the bonhomie of the drunkard became curious to know why his friend loved this dish so much. He laughingly plucked a bird off his friend's plate, and the rest is history.

How did the other characters in our tale fare? As you know, my family came to live with me, and with the changing seasons we made the rounds of the kingdom's palaces as was proper. It was a great comfort to have them with me during the long stretches each summer when the king was at war. My sisters became my best friends, and we laughed at the memory of our childish fights. Well, to be honest a few of them still rankled, but very few. They hung on my every word when I filled them in—after they swore never to tell mother—on the adventures I'd had when I pretended to be sequestered in the abbey. "What a tangled tale!" Hilda said.

Egbert allowed Hilda to marry Wermhere, who was a changed

person compared to the petty tyrant he had been when he bossed the scullery servants around. The couple wrote poetry together, and pretty soon the king appointed them our court poets. This worked out well for Egbert, because they wrote and performed epics that glorified his adventures to such an extent that his fame spread throughout England and across the sea.

Wulfwaru couldn't be allowed to marry a man as vile as Werwulf, but of course it would have made her want him more to forbid it. So Werwulf was sent to Cornwall on a mission and never returned. In the meantime, a handsome warrior, a friend of Egbert's from their days at Aachen, arrived to join our court. He paid a lot of attention to Wulfwaru, and when the news arrived that Werwulf was dead she allowed him to console her.

Egbert summoned Tecla back to court, and told her to bring her baby. He asked me to free her and to see to it that she could afford to dress as a proper lady. I saw him talking to her on occasion after dinner, and after a while he started to bring Helmstan along. I was almost afraid to ask, but one morning when Tecla and I were alone together I steered the conversation around to her feelings for the man she had once loved. "I am ashamed of the way I treated Helmie," she surprised me by saying. "I now know that the only reason Helmstan agreed to become a warrior was so that he could protect me. He never again wanted me to face the horrors I had seen." They were wed. Our children grew up together, and she was my closest friend after my sisters and Athelflad.

I tried to persuade Athelflad to leave the convent and come to court. She would have none of it. She was promoted to prioress at the death of the old one. Years later when I retired to the Abbey, as queens do if they don't remarry when their husbands die, it was a great comfort to have her there.

And what did I do? What were the duties of the queen? I was the keeper of the keys. My job was to run the castle, mind the storehouses, see the fields were worked, and care for the people. When Egbert was away I settled complaints and judged the petitions that came before the court. It was expected that I set an example of Christian charity by helping the poor and sick. And I took on one extra task. Having seen first hand the cruelties visited upon the servants, I insisted on reform. I put Tecla in charge of supervising the kitchen and the hall to make sure there was no brutality. We built separate sleeping quarters for the women. Tecla felt we shouldn't insist they use them, but now they had a choice. We saw to it that food was prepared for the workers so they didn't have to eat those disgusting leftovers, which went to the pigs. If a slave or servant showed promise they were promoted, and now slaves could earn their freedom. These measures worked out as well for the court as for the staff. We had the most dedicated servants and slaves in Europe.

Egbert surprised me by asking if I would like Athelstan to return to court. The king offered to make him chief designer and head architect if I wished. "Yes," I said. "I'd love to have him here." Knowing that Egbert would be away for months at a time, I was surprised he would suggest such a thing. He knew I had once been in love with Athelstan. "You are okay with that?" I asked.

"I trust him completely," he said.

So Athelstan returned, and it was delightful to have him with us. He was very sweet with the children, who loved him dearly. I was the best dressed queen imaginable, and the court ladies benefited from his eye for style as well. Even Hilda started looking good. In time I noticed that Athelstan loved Waldberg at least as much—maybe more—than he loved me. They spent days on end together, running around the palace looking at the things they had created or commissioned and saying nonsensical things like "it's not speaking to me," or "it doesn't read well in that spot," or "do you think this color is too assertive?" They were overwrought when something disappointed them. There was no question, however, that they made the palace very elegant and heightened the splendor of the place. Before long all Europe knew we had a court to rival the ancient palaces of Byzantium.

Over time Egbert accomplished all that he had outlined in his first speech as king. When autumn came and the warriors had finished fighting for the year, he returned to court to dispense justice in the daytime and hospitality over the long winter nights. Early in the evening, before the members of the court assembled, he devoted to the children—and later the grandchildren. He saw this as part of their education. He would start with a fable or a tale, followed by a lesson in how to succeed in  royal office or in combat. One afternoon a minstrel had been entertaining the children with songs of love, and when we met with them they wanted to know our story.

"Grandpa, when did you fall in love with Grandma?"

"The very first day that I saw her."

"Tell us!"

"Well, as you know I had come back to Wessex from Charlemagne's court, with the intention of dethroning that impostor and enemy of Wessex Beorhtric. I had set up camp deep in the woods. When you're doing something dangerous, like planning a coup, it's important to be hyper-vigilant. So I was. My hearing was super acute. I heard barking in the distance and getting closer, and someone calling the name of a Mercian king. Naturally that put me on edge.

"I left my tent to see if I could see anything, and caught sight of a woman up a large tree not far away. She had white hair sticking out under her veil, was dressed like a servant, and her teeth were black. Her skin was mottled and brown."

"Who was it, Grandpa?"

"Your grandmother."

The children gasped. "She's not mottled now," one said.

"I stared at her for a moment, and I could see she was scared—that was prudent—but when she pulled a knife out from under her skirt I got the idea that she was thinking about jumping me. I was nowhere near her, and even if I had been that would have been a very bad move, but I had to admire her courage. I made my face as blank as possible, and pretended I hadn't seen her before she did something stupid like fall out of the tree and get herself killed."

"Was that because you were in love?"

"Maybe a little. But more to the point, if someone from a local village was found dead it could have created a lot of trouble for my mission.

"So you weren't in love yet?"

"Not quite."

"But then you did fall in love—with a toothless old white-haired servant who later turned into Grandma?"

"It was Grandma all along. She wasn't old, and I knew it," said Egbert.

"How could you know?"

"She couldn't have gotten so far up the tree if she was old. She had to be young and athletic. Her teeth may have looked black, but her jaw was firm so I knew she wasn't toothless. Her chin didn't stick out and her nose wasn't long. Her eyes didn't sink into her face. And I got a pretty good look at her legs because it took her three tries to get her knife out of the holster."

"But she was a servant? Grandma was a servant?"

"Her hands weren't red and cracked like a servant's. With all those clues, I figured she had probably used a herb to turn her skin brown, like maybe gipsywort. I'd seen some growing by the river. She hadn't ground it enough, through, so her skin looked mottled and blotchy, not like naturally brown skin. I knew there was chalk everywhere around here, so that was probably how she had made her hair white. And she must have gotten those humble clothes from one of her own servants.

"So—there was this girl, clinging to a tree, disguised as an old woman and scared, yet thinking about jumping a seasoned warrior. It was the most outlandish thing I'd ever seen a girl do, and I went back in my tent and laughed so hard I cried."

"So that's when you fell in love?"

"No, that came later. I think I would have forgotten about her except that I couldn't figure out what she was up to, and I wasn't in a position to dismiss someone spying on my encampment. I had one of my men follow her. She went to a convent, left her dog there, and headed for Winchester. That's where I was going, so I had to keep thinking about her. I asked myself, had she been spying? What sort of fool would bring an untrained dog on a spy mission? Who put her up to it? Was it the plan all along for her to jump me—if I hadn't seen her she would have had the advantage of surprise. But who would send a young girl out on a mission like that? And if she was supposed to kill me, wouldn't she have been smoother getting her knife out? Was it possible she was only looking for the dog I had heard barking? But if she were only looking for her dog, why was she dressed in that ridiculous outfit? None of it made any sense, so I couldn't get her out of my head. When you can't stop thinking about someone, you start to think you're in love."

Then Egbert apparently remembered he was trying to teach the children about kingly responsibility. "But what really cinched it was when I got to know her and realized that she was a terrific administrator, the kind of person who could run the kingdom in my absence. Kings can't marry only for love, you know."

"What about Grandma? When did she fall in love with you?"

"Oh that's easy. She fell in love with me the first moment she saw me."

"When she was up in that tree?"

"Yep. She was smitten all right, but it took me a long time to trick her into realizing it."

"How did you trick her, grandpa?"

"That's a story for another day. Would you like me to tell you the warrior's three basic rules of conquest?"

They were all ears.

"Your first job when you want to vanquish someone is to figure out their weakness. Next, you exploit that weakness every chance you get . . . . I see your nurses heading over: it must be your supper time."

"You said there were three! Tell us the third!"

"Never let your guard down, especially when you think you're winning."

## CHARACTERS

*Names in the text have been simplified for the contemporary reader. Suggestions for the pronunciation of the name, if needed, are followed by its Old English form.*

AGATHA: A determinedly virginal saint who would not succumb to Quintianus' carnal passion. Her torture included having her breasts cut off with pincers

ALBERT: The atheling in Tell-A-Tale

ARKIL: A smart Easton farmer

ATHELFLAD (ATHEL FLED: Aethelflaed): A nun, Cynethrith's girlhood friend and later prioress of St. Wihtburh's Abbey

ATHELSTAN (ATHEL STAN: Aethelstan): Beorhtric's son, an atheling (prince). In our story (but not historically) the heir apparent of the Wessex crown

ATHELWULF (ATHEL WOLF: Aethelwulf): A warrior, one of the decent ones

BADANOTH (BAD A NOTH): A warrior who dies unexpectedly in the night

BEORHTRIC (BEE OR TRICK): King of Wessex, 786–802. A close ally of the Mercian king Offa. Married to Offa's daughter Odburh

BRANWALADER: A saint, a British monk

CERDIC: An early king; the villagers name their dragon after him

COLE: A smart Easton farmer

CUTHRED: An early king

CWENN (K-WHEN [*WHEN WITH A K SOUND IN FRONT*]: Cwoenflaed): A character in the game of Tell-A-Tale

CYNEBURGA: A saint who was married to a Northumbrian prince and later ruled a convent. Feast day March 6

CYNETHRITH (KIN A THRITH): A young woman living in the village of Easton

Cynric: (KIN rick): A contender for the Wessex throne against King Wulf.

Daniel: The village priest

Denis: A saint, the martyred first bishop of Paris

Dim (Dimmred) of Wixna: The King in the game of Tell-A-Tale. Olga's father, and the enemy of Eric's tribe

Dympna: A saint whose father desired her and killed her when she resisted him. Her feast day is May 15

Edgefrith (EDGE frith: Ecgfrith): An early king of Mercia. In a show of disrespect, Cynethrith has named one of her dogs after him

Edith: (Eadgyth): The village herbalist

Edwulf: A servant who is nominated for King of All Hallows

Egbert: A warrior; King of Wessex, 802–839

Elfwinne (ELF win: Aelfwynn): A court lady, a friend of Odburh's

Ercenwald (ER cen wald: Eorcenwald): A warrior, one of the good ones

Eric: (Eadric): A character in the game of Tell-A-Tale

Erpwald ( ERP wald: Eorpwald): One of Beorhtric's warriors

Etheldreda (ETHEL dray da): A saint who wed two kings and managed to maintain her virginity throughout, even though her second husband put up a fight

Fenrir: A character in Norse mythology, a wolf.

Frida: (Ecgfrida): Queen of All Hallows. Wermhere is her King.

Fursey: A saint who helped to get Christianity started in England. He reported seeing visions of the afterlife

Haedde (Had): Dish thane, the person in charge of the king's dishes and cutlery

Helmstan: The man that the warriors pelted with bones after dinner

HENRY: A character in the game of Tell-A-Tale. Eric's fellow warrior and friend

HILDA: One of Cynethrith's stepsisters

HWICCE: A tribal kingdom in Anglo-Saxon England

MAUGHOLD: The magician in the game of Tell-A-Tale

MILDRED: (Mildrith): A low ranking hall servant

ODBURH (ODD BURR: Eadburh): The Queen of Wessex—daughter of King Offa and wife of King Beorhtric

OFFA: King of Mercia, enemy of Wessex. In a show of disrespect, Cynethrith has named one of her dogs after him

OLGA: The princess in the game of Tell-a-Tale

OSBERT: The bishop's reeve; a leader of Easton village

OSWULF: A warrior, one of the decent ones

PENDA OF MERCIA: The seventh century king of Mercia, who ruled at a time when the kingdom may still have been pagan

QUINTIANUS: a low-born Roman who rose to magistrate. His unreturned passion for St. Agatha left him resentful of her having dedicated her virginity to God. When his efforts to change her mind failed he persecuted her for her Christian faith

RED, RETCH: (Osred): The village storyteller

RUMWOLD: A saint, an infant prodigy granted the gift of speech

SAMSON: A saint who worked with St. Branwalader in Cornwall and the Channel Islands. One of the seven founder saints of Brittany

SAXBURG (SEAXBURG): A talented singer and sexy lady

SIGEBERT: An early king

TECLA: A low-ranking hall worker who had been high-born, but sold into slavery when her homeland was invaded. She loves Helmstan

TEILO: A saint, a British monk, bishop, and abbot of monasteries and churches in Wales

Thingfrith (THING frith): One of King Beorhtric's warriors

Tidburg (TID berg): The village gossip

Tyr: A character from Norse mythology

Unferth (UN firth): One of Beorhtric's warriors

Waldberg (WALLED berg): Cynethrith's stepmother

Warr: A heavy drinking warrior and close friend of Beorhtric

Waudru: A saint. Her feast day is the 9th of April. Sainthood, it appears, was the family business: her parents, sister, husband and 4 children were all venerated as saints.

Wermhere (WORM here: Wyrmhere): He supervises the lowest rank of hall servants

Werwulf (WERE wolf): One of Beorhtric's warriors. He bites off his lover's nose in spite, and later takes up with Cynethrith's stepsister Wulfwaru

Wihtburh (WIT burr): the abbey Cynethrith's mother endowed is named after this saint who built a convent in Norfolk and fed her workers on doe's milk provided by the Virgin Mary

Wulf (WOLF: Cynewulf): A disgruntled atheling who wrested the Wessex crown from the previous monarch. He became an effective king, and Cynethrith's mother was an archer in his artillery. Cynric rebelled against him.

Wulfwaru (WOLF wah roo): One of Cynethrith's stepsisters

## *GLOSSARY*

ATHELING: A man of the royal blood, eligible to be king. This group included the king's sons, his brothers, and his brother's sons. More like contemporary Saudi Arabia than contemporary England

AGUE: Fever

AUROCHS: An extinct species of large wild cattle that inhabited Europe, Asia, and North Africa

BLACKTHORN WINTER: A cold snap in spring

BLOOD PRICE: Wergild. The price that a murderer is required to pay the murdered man's family in compensation. Price is determined by rank

BORAGE: Leafy herb with a delicate cucumber flavor

BUCKTHORN: Medicinal herb used as a laxative

BURDOCK: Edible herb

BURH: Fortification, a castle

CANTLE: Raised part at the back of a saddle

CHARLOCK: Wild mustard

CELLARER: In charge of provisions in a monastery

COMPLINE: Evening prayer in a monastery

CULVERHOUSE: Dovecote, a house for pigeons

CYNWIT: Fort in Somerset

DAUB: A cement used to build fences in medieval times: wattle (straw) and daub

DITTANDER: Edible herb in the mustard and cabbage family

EALDORMAN: Governor of a shire

ELFTHONE (ELF THONE: Aelfthone): Nightshade, believed to protect against elves

EWER: Wide-mouthed pitcher

Ewery: Hand-washing station

Freeman: A ceorl. The lowest ranking free man. At the time of the novel, the word hadn't devolved into the contemporary meaning of "churl"

Frontal: A cloth that covers the front of a church altar

Garth: An open area outside; for example, the central open area in a cloister

Gipsywort: Herb that grows in wet areas, used for darkening the skin

Goosegrass: Also known as *cleavers*, the plant is edible and has been used to make a tea. It clings to clothing and skin.

Groundsel: Medicinal herb that was mashed into a poultice to relieve discomfort or infection

Hail (Haegl): The rune that predicts disruption, literally means "hail"

Knapweed root: A herb used to treat wounds

Marcus: Gold coin in early medieval Europe

Mangelwurzel: This edible plant's roots were once used for food or making beverages. Athelstan carves them into ghoulish faces for All Hallow's eve

Mead: Fermented (alcoholic) drink made with water and honey

Minster: A large, usually important, church such as a cathedral

Nobleman: An eorl. Warrior, leader

Nones: Early afternoon prayer in a monastery

Pellitory: Plant in the nettle family that grows on walls

Pennyroyal: A mint flavored herb

Poultice: Mashed herbs applied to wounds to relieve discomfort

Prime: Morning prayer in a monastery

Rebec: A bowed string instrument

Roundel: A decorative circle or medallion

Rowan: A small tree once believed to protect against witchcraft and enchantment.

Runes: Characters carved on stone, bark or bone that were used for fortune telling. The character that the crone reveals when Egbert encounters her is "H", *haegl* in Old English, translated "hail." Egbert refers to its literal meaning, ignoring that the rune predicts disruption

Silverweed: Edible herb, the root has a nutty flavor

Scabious: A plant with purplish pin-cushion shaped flower

Scramasax: A dagger used by Anglo-Saxon warriors. They were called Saxons because of it

Scriptorum: Room in a monastery used for the production of manuscripts

Sloe: Blue-black fruit of the blackthorn bush

Sneezewort: Medicinal herb believed to relieve toothache

Teasel: Tall plant with elongated prickly flower heads

Tormentil : Herbal remedy for inflammation and gastrointestinal disorders

Trencher: A slice of thick stale bread used instead of a plate

Underwood: The small trees and shrubs in a forest

Verjuice: Sour juice from unripe fruit or crab apples

Vespers: Late afternoon prayer in a monastery

Witan: A council made up of the highest ranking noblemen who advise the king and select the next one from among eligible athelings

Woodward: Caretaker of a woodland

Wormwood: Medicinal herb used to treat fever and stomach problems. Also used in the Middle Ages to induce abortion, menstruation, and labor

Woundwort: Herb used to treat wounds

Yarrow: Medicinal herb used in decoctions to treat wounds or rashes

CPSIA information can be obtained
at www.ICGtesting.com
Printed in the USA
FSHW011249200319
56528FS

9 780983 323686